GENA SHOWALTER

JEANIENE FROST

FORBIDDEN CRAVING

HQN™

ISBN-13: 978-0-373-80191-6

Recycling programs for this product may not exist in your area.

Forbidden Craving

CONTENTS

THE NYMPH KING

Gena Showalter

To Jeaniene Frost—what an honor and dream come true
to be in a duology with you!

CHAPTER ONE

Atlantis

VALERIAN, KING OF THE NYMPHS, lover extraordinaire and greatest leader of the greatest army in the history of Atlantis, untangled from the naked, slumbering woman beside him...only to discover his legs were entwined with two other naked, slumbering women.

He truly thought to leave this paradise?

With a sleep-rough chuckle, he abandoned all efforts to escape and relaxed against the softness of the bed. Satisfaction hummed inside him.

The females curled closer to him, soft tendrils of hair—a delightful mix of black, brown and red—cascading across the muscle and sinew he worked hard to maintain.

Did life get any better than this?

Had he known what awaited him in this massive palace, he would have fought the dragon shape-shifter army for rights to it years ago rather than mere weeks.

Nymphs, once touted eternal wanderers, had desired a permanent home almost as desperately as they desired sex.

Sex was like air to nymphs. Without it, they suffered, and they died.

They'd won the palace with only minor losses, expecting to charm and seduce the female dragon shape-shifters still in residence. Within minutes of victory, however, the entire enclosure had emptied, leaving no one to wine, dine and recline.

Until yesterday.

Beneath the palace were catacombs. There, Valerian discovered a strange, upright pool—or rather, a portal leading into another world. The *human* world. Earth, it was called.

All his life he'd heard rumors about the portal and the topside world. Everyone inside Atlantis had heard, considering there were humans scattered among them. But Valerian had never dreamed *he* would become the gatekeeper.

He'd watched, dumbfounded, as the trio of femininity currently occupying his bed stumbled through the pool. A sleek black beauty, a plump redhead and brown-skinned goddess.

At first, they'd looked at him and panicked.

"Where are we? Who are you?"

"What happened?"

"I can't... I want to go..."

"Oh, wow. You're hot. Take off your clothes."

The pheromone Valerian exuded every day...hour... minute was the most powerful in the world and considered a potent aphrodisiac. Pair that aphrodisiac with his angelic face, and who could resist him?

In the back of his mind, he heard other immortals calling him conceited, narcissistic and boastful. He considered himself honest.

Besides, he'd never really cared about the reasons why women preferred him over other men. He'd simply enjoyed the end results. Again and again.

The trio of beauties had basically attacked him, kissing every inch of him while ripping at his clothes. He'd barely gotten the females into his bedroom with his nonexistent virtue in tact.

Between rounds one and five, he'd finally managed to question his lovers. One moment they'd been swimming in the ocean, the next they'd been sucked through a swirling black hole...the next they were inside the catacombs of the fortress.

Welcome to Atlantis. Home to creatures you've only ever considered myth.

Vampires, Minotaurs, griffins, Amazons, trolls, centaurs, winged horses, mermaids and more. The Greek gods had trapped the different immortal races in a dome under the sea. Less competition for human adoration, Valerian supposed.

Peering up at the ceiling, he braced his nape with one hand. The dome had been created with naturally grown crystals and had always protected the fortress from the elements. Now, light uncoiled from the sparkling minerals to caress the chamber he'd claimed as his own.

The master's suite. An enormous space with luxuries beyond imagining. A unicorn pelt had been turned into a rug and draped in front of a marble hearth.

Valerian would rather the unicorn still lived, wild and free.

Never-ending fires crackled from bejeweled torches that hung along golden brick walls. A dresser forged from a massive diamond pressed against a vanity that had been cut from one of the last trees to grow in the Forest of Wisdom Eternal.

The bed occupied the center of an island cutout, with three separate bridges leading to and from the rest of the room. In the spaces between each bridge, a dark abyss loomed. One wrong step...

The perfect precaution against attack.

"Valerian." The bronzed goddess stretched her arms above her head and arched her back, her expression soft from slumber. "You weren't just a dream."

"No. I'm very real." He caught her hand and lifted her knuckles to his lips, licked. "And I'm very appreciative of your sweet sweetness."

Warm breath fanned his pectorals as she chuckled. "I've never slept with a man after a two-second introduction, but I find I can't regret my actions."

"Regrets never do anyone any good," he told her.

She giggled. "While multiple orgasms do a *whole lot* of good."

She had no idea.

Need arose, and he considered going for round six. Problem was, good sex required half an hour, at the very least, and his men awaited him in the training arena. He could spare another five minutes, perhaps, but no more.

The surviving dragon shape-shifters would return and attack; they would be willing to do anything to regain ownership of the fortress.

He sighed. "I must go."

Moans of disappointed erupted.

"Are you sure?" The black beauty wrapped her fingers around the base of his erection. "Because your body says *I want to stay.*"

Three sets of hands and breasts were suddenly all over him. Hot, greedy mouths sucked at him. Wet, needy female cores rubbed against him. The scent of desire enveloped him, and he gnashed his teeth, wanting, needing, to please.

The blessing and curse of a nymph.

"Ladies—" he began.

"Just being near you makes me desperate to come."

The plump redhead with her deliciously ample curves purred at him.

"I can't get enough of you."

"I'm addicted to you and pretty sure I'll die without you."

He ignored the fiery heat that ignited in his blood. At times, when the need overwhelmed him, he was reduced to an animalistic state, taking his lovers with a savage intensity better suited for the battlefield.

Valerian leaped from the bed and swept up his leathers. The women pouted as he dressed and strapped on his weapons.

"There are other warriors here," he said. "Men just like me. You're welcome to seduce anyone who catches your eye."

He'd never had a problem sharing, and doubted he ever would.

"Dibs!" one said.

"On whom?" another asked.

The brown-skinned goddess fluffed her hair. "All of them."

The black beauty punched the pillow. "Greed will be the death of you—because I'll kill you dead!"

The nymph pheromone usually erased inhibitions to reveal true desire, but these humans struck him as particularly susceptible. Willing to kill for pleasure?

The perfect females.

"There are hundreds of warriors here," he said. "More than enough to sate each of you for months. Years."

If they heard him, they gave no notice. They continued arguing among themselves...until the heat of anger morphed into the heat of desire. Lips kissed and hands wandered.

Well. I'd say my job here is done.

CLANG. WHOOSH. CLANG.

Sweat trickled down Valerian's bare chest and back as he swung his sword. The heavy metal slammed into his opponent's upraised weapon.

Broderick toppled, crash-landing, dirt flinging in every direction. Some of the grains sprinkled over Valerian's freshly polished boots.

He waited for his friend to stand, but Broderick remained prone. "Get up, man."

"Can't," was the panted reply. "Also, I don't want to."

Valerian frowned. Four times he'd put the fierce Broderick on the ground. In only one hour.

And Broderick wasn't even the worst case!

If his men grew any weaker, the fortress would be lost the first time they were challenged. They needed sex. Today.

The humans would probably love a go at his nymphs, but they would have to choose one warrior, only one. The more nymphs they bedded, the more addicted to the pheromone they would become, until they lived and breathed for their next nymph lover. And yet, the second the females made their selection, fights would break out among his army.

"I hate this," Broderick muttered, his voice strained. He sat up, head bent and anchored in place by his upraised hands, his golden hair shielding his eyes. "Weakness is for women, babies and the elderly."

Nods throughout the room.

Valerian slashed his sword's tip into the sand. A tip that had been shaped and honed into the image of a skull—a tip that inflicted irreparable damage to his opponents.

His gaze traveled the ranks of his army. Some of the men were sitting on a bench, sharpening their blades, while others leaned against a stone wall, their expressions lost, faraway. Only Theophilus appeared ready for anything more than a nap.

Well, that wasn't quite true. Though Joachim was hunched over, his elbows resting on his knees, his head was tilted to the side as he gazed up at Valerian with undeniable sparks of fury.

What was his cousin angry about now?

"Line up," Valerian commanded the entire group. "Now." The sharpness of his voice finally snagged everyone's attention.

The men stumbled into a clumsy zigzag formation. What he saw? Skin stretched tight with strain, shaky grips and unsteady legs. At this rate, Valerian would be the only one to offer any sort of resistance if the dragons attacked. And the dragons *would* attack. Darius the Heartless, their exalted king, wasn't known for his forgiving nature.

"I need you ready for action." His hands fisted at his sides. Defeat wasn't something he allowed. Ever.

A warrior won. Always. Without exception.

Broderick sighed and scrubbed a hand down his grim features. "We need sex, Valerian, and we need it now."

"I know." He considered his options. There were few.

Possibility number one: he could send a handful of soldiers into the Outer City a few miles away. Sirens—women who seduced with their voices—lived there, and they could be convinced to move into the fortress.

First problem: sirens sided with dragons, and they could strike the nymphs while they were weak.

Second problem: sirens usually killed those they bedded, an impulse as fierce as a nymph's need for sex.

Third problem: since the march to the fortress, the

females of Atlantis had avoided nymphs as if they came with a side of plague.

Word had spread. Give yourself to a nymph, and you lose yourself to his dark, sexual hunger.

Possibility number two: rethink possibility number one.

"You've been with humans," Dorian said. "I can smell them on you, and it's *destroying* my ability to concentrate." With his obsidian hair, godlike features and mischievous sense of humor, women of every race usually flocked to him. There was nothing mischievous about him right now; he radiated jealousy and resentment. "I almost—*almost*—want to have my wicked way with *you*."

Guilt consumed Valerian. He'd taken care of his needs while neglecting those of his men. He had to make this right.

There *was* a third possibility: entering uncharted territory. Why the previous owner of the palace hadn't thought of it, Valerian wasn't sure and didn't care.

No risk, no reward.

He studied his men. They were a range of heights and colors, from the palest ivory to the darkest onyx. Some were cut with muscle while others were *stacked*.

"I found the portal into the human world," he said, bracing his hands behind his back. "A small group of us can venture there and convince whatever females we find to return to Atlantis with us."

A chorus of "Yes" immediately erupted. Smiles abounded.

"Thank you, great king." A beaming Shivawn patted the shoulder of the man beside him.

"We can't stay long." Not with dragons foaming-at-the-mouth eager to reclaim the fortress.

"Perhaps I'll find my mate," someone called.

Everyone cheered.

Valerian nodded in agreement. When a nymph mated, he mated for life, no matter his age or circumstances. His body would never crave another; his heart would beat only for one. *The* one.

The very idea should have been terrifying to him. But just like the other warriors, Valerian wanted his mate more than he wanted...anything.

His twin brother had died years ago, leaving a hollow ache in his chest. An ache he prayed his mate would fill. He'd searched for her. For centuries. No stone in Atlantis had been left unturned. Eventually he'd begun to despair. *What if I don't have a mate?*

I do. I must.

He wouldn't give up hope.

His father had told him a nymph would know his "one" the moment he scented her, and she would, in turn, recognize him, choosing him above all others.

"I'll lead five of you to the surface." Valerian wondered what kind of world waited on the other side of the portal. Dangerous, no doubt. "We'll go in, find as many women as possible as fast as possible and return with those who wish to follow us."

Joachim's dark brows knit. "Why don't we simply take the women we want? Why must we give them a choice?"

"We aren't dragons." In other words, they weren't barbarians.

"Well. My ravishment of you can be postponed, it seems." The dryness of Dorian's tone failed to mask his excitement.

Broderick frowned. "What if human females want nothing to do with us?"

Laughter erupted.

Grinning, Valerian patted him on the shoulder. "Good one."

Broderick's frown melted, revealing a smile. He snickered. "I thought so."

"How will we decide who beds whom?" Shivawn asked.

"My elite will go first, from the highest ranked to the lowest." The elite had fought in more wars, were stronger, faster and needed sex more than an average solider. "I have no need to choose, of course."

Broderick rubbed his hands together. "How soon can we leave?"

There was no reason to wait and every reason to hurry. "We leave now."

CHAPTER TWO

A BAREFOOT BAY destination wedding. Complete with a wide expanse of glistening beach, crashing cerulean waves, a magical pink-gold sunset and a warm, sultry breeze. White rose petals formed a line along the fine-grained sand; as the wind blew, a few of those petals danced and twirled away. The couple even now pledging their undying love stared deeply into each other's eyes, their hands clutched tightly, their lips parted in expectation of the coming kiss.

They presented a beautiful sight—but Shaye Holling only wanted to gag.

However, she maintained her smile, brittle though it was, and fought the urge to adjust her ill-fitting seashell bikini top. The grass skirt itched her calves.

The more horrid-looking the bridesmaids, the more exquisite the bride, eh?

Thanks, Mom.

Yep. Her mother was the bride.

Shaye shifted uncomfortably, her shoulders burning. She'd been standing in the sunlight for only half an hour, but her ultrapale skin had already turned a lovely shade of lobster red.

In fact, the richly dressed crowd of onlookers no longer eyed the bride and groom. Instead, they stared at *Shaye*.

And why not? Red skin. White hair. Brown eyes. Blue seashells. Green skirt. *I'm a freaking rainbow.*

She shifted again and dang it, her seashells dipped, forcing her to adjust.

Silver lining: a new idea for her business, Anti-Cards, popped into her mind.

Thank you from the bottom of my heart. Because of you, I found religion. I finally believe in hell.

She sighed. Her mother's long silvery-white hair—so like Shaye's own—waved down her back, a perfect mimic of the creamy satin slip dress billowing at her ankles. Nowhere was there a woman more gorgeous than Tamara soon-to-be Waddell. No one more surgically enhanced. No one else who went through men like sexual Kleenex.

Okay. There was probably someone else who went through men like sexual Kleenex. But come on! This was her mom's sixth marriage.

Tamara looked over at her and frowned. *Back straight, Shaye*, she mouthed. *Smile.*

A straight back displays your breasts to their best advantage, Shaye.

A smile is honey and men are flies, Shaye.

Do you want to die alone, Shaye?

Shaye straightened her shoulders to make her mother happy and pretended to focus on the minister.

"'To love, honor and cherish…'" His smooth baritone created a perfect harmony with the gentle lap of waves.

Mostly, she heard *love, blah, blah, blah.*

Love. How she despised the word. People used love as an excuse to do ridiculous things.

He cheated on me, but I'm going to stay with him because I love him.

He hit me, but I'm going to stay with him because I love him.

He stole every penny from my savings, but I'm not going to press charges because I love him.

Her mother had said each of those things at one time or another.

And how many times had Tamara's boyfriends groped Shaye herself, claiming they'd fallen in love with *her*?

Her, a mere child.

Shaye's father was another prime example of the "love is all that matters" idiocy.

I can't live with you and your mom, Shaye. I don't love her anymore. I love Glenda.

His secretary. Of course, after Glenda had lost her sparkle, he'd fallen for Charlene, then Kasey, then Morgan.

When Morgan divorced him to be with another man, Shaye sent him an *I'm so sorry* card. What she'd really wanted to send was a *Finally getting what you deserve sucks big-time, doesn't it?* card, but none had been available—the very reason she'd started making her own.

Over the years, her Anti-Card business had only grown. There were a lot of people out there who wanted to tell someone to screw off—in a fun way.

She worked close to eighty hours a week, but she loved every second. A love that would never come back to bite her.

Thanks to popular cards like *I'm so miserable without you, it's almost like you're here* and *You can do more with a kind word and a gun than with just a kind word*, she provided jobs for twenty-three like-minded men and women and made more money than she'd ever dreamed possible.

Life, for the weird-looking little girl who'd only ever

disappointed her parents, was finally...not good, not really, but good enough.

She sighed.

"You may now kiss the bride," the minister said.

Amid joyous applause, the brow-lifted, cheek-implanted groom laid a wet one on Tamara, who returned the kiss with vigor.

How long would this marriage last?

Not my problem. Soon Shaye would be on a plane, returning to Cincinnati and her quiet little apartment. No family. Few friends. Absolutely zero romance.

Life would be worth living again.

The glowing couple turned and strolled down the aisle, hand in hand. The lyrical thrums of a harp echoed behind them.

Daughter duty done at last. As everyone else filed toward the reception tent, Shaye inched closer to the sandy shore, moving away from the masses, escape within her grasp.

"Where are you going, silly?" A bridesmaid latched on to her arm with a surprisingly intense grip. "Remember, we're supposed to take pictures and serve the guests."

She swallowed a groan. Basically, the torture had only just begun.

AFTER AN HOUR of posing for a photographer who finally gave up trying to make the antisocial daughter of the bride smile, Shaye served cake to a line of champagne-guzzling guests. As expected. Most of those guests ignored her, merely grabbing a plate and ambling away. A few tried to talk to her, but quickly retreated when she snapped a cranky reply.

When the line stopped progressing, she glanced up, her eyes narrowed. A man—one of the groomsmen—

had claimed his dessert but hadn't stepped out of the way. Instead, he grinned at her.

"No, thank you," she said, being preemptive in case that grin meant *Let's get our flirt on.*

He balanced the cake in one hand and swirled his champagne flute with the other. His green eyes twinkled with merriment. "I'll take a little slice of you if you're serving it."

Wow. Talk about inappropriate.

Should she throat punch him now or later?

Being nice is a choice, her therapist once told her. *You don't have to be cruel to others, physically or emotionally, to get your point across. All you need to do is communicate your desires in a firm but polite manner.*

"I'm not serving myself to anyone." *Choose your attitude. Communicate your desires.* "I'm not interesting in flirting, either." Good? Good.

Groomsman's grin only broadened. "How about a dance? I'll do all the flirting, and you can simply enjoy the fruits of my labors."

"No, thank you," she repeated. She turned to the man standing behind him and handed over a plate. "Sorry for your wait, sir."

Groomsman's grin slipped a little. He drained his glass and set the empty on the table, exactly where it didn't belong. "I get the feeling your mother…exaggerated about the best way to approach you. I should probably—"

"Shaye, darling," her mother called airily. The scent of her expensive perfume wafted as she floated to Shaye's side, blending with the aroma of sugar and spice. "Wonderful. You've already met your new stepbrother, Preston."

Stepbrother? Well, that showed exactly how much

contact Shaye had had with her mom these past few years. She hadn't known groom number six had children. Actually, she hadn't even met her newest daddy until an hour before the wedding.

Shaye glanced at Preston. "Nice to meet you."

"A true pleasure," he said, a little unsure.

He was a very handsome man, but he wasn't even close to her type: absent.

She gathered two plates to pass to the couple behind him. *Communicate desire.* "If you'll excuse me, I really must finish serving the guests before there's a revolt." A few ladies at the back of the line looked ready to claw out her eyes just to eat the jelly inside.

Tamara uttered a strained laugh. "There's no reason to be rude, Shaye. You can do your duties while getting to know your new brother."

"No, thank you." He wouldn't be her brother for long. No reason to forge a relationship already doomed to fail.

Her mother hissed, "I hate when you speak those three little words."

"Why? They're polite."

"You," her mother said, pointing to one of the other horrendously clad bridesmaids. "Take over the cake. Shaye, you will come with me."

Strong fingers curled around Shaye's wrist. A second later she was being dragged out of the reception tent to the edge of the beach.

Sand squished between her sandaled toes as a warm, salty breeze wrapped itself around her, swishing her grass skirt over her knees. Sunlight had faded completely. Now slivers of ethereal moonlight illuminated their path. Waves sang a gentle, soothing song.

Her mom's velvety-brown eyes—eyes exactly like her own—narrowed slightly. She dropped Shaye's hand as if contact could cause premature wrinkles. "Do you want to kill my hopes and dreams? Because that's what you're doing."

Shaye wrapped her arms around her middle. "Your hopes and dreams...for me?"

"Of course for you! At the rate you're going, you're going to die alone, not just unloved but despised. I'll never have a grandbaby."

"There's nothing wrong with dying alone. I imagine it's quite peaceful."

"Would it kill you to be nice?" Tamara smoothed a wisp of hair from her face. "To pretend you have a heart for just a few hours?"

That stung. Badly. "I'll worry about me, and you worry about you, okay? This kind of upset could cause you to shrivel up like a raisin."

Horrified, Tamara patted the skin around her eyes. "I just had Botox. I shouldn't have a single line or wrinkle. Do you see a wrinkle? Tell me!"

A new card flashed through her mind.

There's only one person worthy of dating you—YOU!

"Mother, you inspire me," Shaye replied honestly.

Somehow mollified, Tamara brushed her fingertips over the side of her face. "Yes, well. I try."

"So...are we done here?"

"No! Not even close." Her mom stomped a high-heeled foot. "Tell me why you spurn *everyone*. Tell me why you never date."

She *used* to date. She'd quickly discovered men never called when they said they would. Most hadn't been interested in getting to know her as a person; they'd wanted to get her out of her clothing. Some guys had admired other women while they were out with her.

Some had lied straight up. One had used her for her money. Another had cheated on her.

Relationships were too much trouble for too little reward.

Shaye twirled a strand of the grass skirt around her finger. Instead of explaining her reasons to her mother, she said, "I love you, and I'll call you when you return from your honeymoon. Now I'm going home."

"You're not going anywhere, young lady. Not until you've apologized to Preston." Tamara shoved a finger in her face. "You treated him shabbily, and I won't have it."

Had she treated him shabbily?

Shaye valued and prized honesty, and that's what she'd given him. Shouldn't he thank her?

Would she ever understand the complexity of human interactions?

"Mother. Nannies raised me." A gentle reminder. "Your orders hold no sway with me."

The color drained from Tamara's cheeks. "But... I'm your mother."

"And I'm the Ice Princess of Bitterslovakia, the Grand Duchess of Rancorstonia and the Queen of Hostileland." The many names Tamera had called her over the years.

Waves splashed in the distance as her mother snapped, "All I've ever wanted was a nice, normal daughter. Instead I'm stuck with you." Tears welled in her eyes. "You won't be happy until you've ruined my wedding."

Fighting the newest sting, Shaye allowed a familiar icy numbness to encompass her. The same numbness she'd relied on during her childhood. A sweet relief against depression and desolation.

Tamara stared past her. "Conner tried to tell me.

You're jealous of me. Admit it! I should have disowned you long ago. Conner says negativity must be purged to allow positivity to flourish."

Wow. Of all the things her mother had said over the years, that little gem might have cut the deepest.

She thinks I'm *the problem.*

Wow. Just...wow!

As a little girl, Shaye had craved her mother's attention, approval and adoration more than breath. But nothing she'd tried had worked. Not gifts or fits or pretending to be the woman's shadow. Once, Shaye had even run away.

The police had found her, and the nanny had come to pick her up.

"Why don't you do us both a favor and take responsibility for your own life," Shaye said, her voice as cold as her internal armor.

The tears began to pour down Tamara's cheeks. "Conner and I wanted so badly for this day to be perf—" Her eyes widened and glazed with lust. "Perfect," she finished on a dreamy sigh. "Hmm. So perfect."

Her voice had dropped to a husky purr.

"Mother?"

"Man." Tamara stretched out her arms. "My man."

"I don't understand." Shaye dragged her gaze to the ocean—her mouth fell open in shock.

There, rising from the water like primitive sea gods, were six gloriously tall, muscled barbarians. The moon glowed behind them reverently, providing each male with a golden halo.

The warriors were shirtless, revealing washboard abs and skin so tanned it made her think liquid gold had been poured over steel. They looked like supermodels. Only better. Yes, so much better.

Unbelievable…surreal…magnificent.

As the six warriors focused on Shaye, molten air snagged in her lungs, melting her precious ice armor.

The urge to strip and splay herself atop a table to offer her body as the dinner buffet bombarded her. She would be an all-you-can-eat buffet. No charge.

She moistened her lips. Her mouth watered, her skin tingling, and her stomach clenched.

I'm…turned on? By strangers?

What's wrong with me?

The men continued to prowl toward her. They were so close she could see the silvery water droplets sliding down their chests and gathering in their navels.

Other droplets slid lower…

Her gaze snagged on the man in the middle, and she forgot how to blink.

Dangerous, her most feminine instincts whispered. *Lethal.*

He was taller than the rest of the group, his dark blond hair hanging in a wet tangle around features that had been chiseled by a master. His eyes… Oh, glory hallelujah, his eyes. They were blue-green, neither color blending with the other but standing alone, so wickedly mesmerizing she felt the pull of them all the way to her bones.

Her nipples hardened, and an ache suddenly throbbed between her legs.

There was something wild about him. Something untamed and savage. His confident swagger, perhaps. The deceptively calm glint in his expression that said he did what he pleased, when he pleased.

As she stared at him, he stared at her. He studied her face, searing arousal flickering in those magnificent eyes, the blue-green deepening and mixing at last, becoming smoldering turquoise.

Raw, masculine perfection.

"Mine," her mom said on a wispy catch of breath. "All mine."

A previously missed detail hit her awareness. The warriors carried swords.

They're armed for war.

She gulped. The one in the middle cocked his finger, beckoning her to join him.

Shivering, drowning in the flood of his maleness, she struggled to shake her head no.

Go to him, her stupid whoremones beseeched.

She shook her head, violently this time.

He frowned at her. "Come here." His husky voice drifted across the small distance, almost as intoxicating and heady as a caress.

In seconds, a sensual fog wove through her mind. Her knees quaked, and another shiver traipsed the length of her spine.

What would happen if he actually touched her?

What would happen if he trailed those luscious pink lips along her every curve and hollow?

Images flashed through her mind. The man's mouth on her breasts, his fingers slipping deep inside her, her legs parting to give him better access...

He's seducing me without even trying.

Either that, or she was seducing herself!

"Come here," he repeated.

"Yes," Tamara said, already stepping toward him. The dreamy glaze in her eyes had darkened with eagerness. "I need to touch you, or I'll die. *Please* let me touch you."

The part of Shaye that recognized how dangerous

these men were also realized there was something wrong with the entire situation—she still couldn't bring herself to care.

Must fight this!

Scowling, she reached out to latch on to her mom's arm and jerk Tamara to a halt. "Don't go near them."

"Let me go." She struggled against Shaye's hold. "I've never been so in love. I need to be with my man."

"We're going back to the tent." Dragging her flailing mother behind her, Shaye raced toward the outside reception area, where laughing voices, soft music and unsuspecting guests greeted her.

She dared a glance behind her. The warriors hadn't slowed or changed direction. They'd followed her, lust in their eyes.

"Help us," she shouted, flinging sand with every step. She swept the curtain aside and entered the tent. "Someone call 911!"

No one paid her any heed. They were too busy dancing and drinking themselves into oblivion, thanks to the open bar.

"Let me go," her mom continued to shout. When that failed to gain her release, she sank her teeth into Shaye's arm.

"Ow!" Not knowing what else to do, Shaye hooked her foot behind her mom's ankle and pushed, inadvertently sending the bride hurling into the dessert table. Platters of food crashed to the ground.

Several people glanced at Shaye before concentrating on the fallen bride with confusion and horror.

"There are men—" Shaye pointed "—out there. Dangerous men with swords. Does anyone have a gun? Did someone call 911?"

Tamara jolted to her feet, unconcerned by the red-

and-white frosting now streaking her ten-thousand-dollar dress. She elbowed her way past the guests. "Where he is? My love! My heart!"

"Tamara?" Conner, her new husband, rushed to his bride to lock her in his arms, his expression both concerned and incredulous as she struggled to break free. "What's wrong with you, kitten?"

"I need...*him.*" The last word was uttered on a relieved, happy sigh.

The six sea gods had just stepped into the tent; they consumed every inch of breathable space and blocked the only viable exit.

The music suddenly stopped. The male guests cowered, as if death had just arrived, and the females gasped in bliss, already moving toward the warriors, reaching out, eager to touch the exquisite display of masculinity.

This couldn't be happening.

The one in the middle scanned the crowd, as if drinking in every detail...but also searching...searching... and finally locking on Shaye. Satisfaction glowed in his eyes.

She trembled as dizzying warmth speared her. More images rushed through her mind. This man naked and sweaty, pressed against her, licking her...

No, no, no. She forced her mind to blank.

Who were these men?

And how did the tall one make her forget who and what she was, and simply enjoy the pleasures she somehow knew he alone could give her?

He alone? What madness!

She grabbed the cake knife from the floor, icing coating her fingers, holding the weapon in front of her. Her heart thumped erratically in her chest.

After multiple physical altercations with different

stepsiblings—and sometimes having to fend off a new stepfather—Shaye had considered self-defense classes prudent. The problem? She'd never had to put the lessons into action.

Wait. There was an even bigger problem. None of her instructors had ever prepared her for a sword-wielding giant.

The warrior in the middle—what was his name?—narrowed his eyes and motioned her over. His kissable, lickable lips lifted in a slow, wicked smile. In the candlelight, he exuded a far more potent sensuality...

A silver hoop winked at his nipple.

Her mouth watered all over again.

"Come," he said, the single word weighted, as if it had more than one meaning.

She shivered, everything inside her screaming to obey him, to come...to suck that hoop into her mouth while she ground herself against his erection—

Crap! She hadn't meant to look between his legs, but now she couldn't pull her gaze away.

Black leather pants molded to his thighs, displaying every muscle...every inch of hardness...every bit of perfection.

Talk about instant inspiration! A new card took shape—a ridiculous card.

A good wine will make you feel sexy, brave and ready for anything. Oh, wait. I meant a sea god.

He took a step toward her. She took a step back, even though she wanted to rush forward.

A laugh burst from her, zero humor, all hysteria. *I'm seriously screwed, aren't I?*

CHAPTER THREE

MY MATE, VALERIAN THOUGHT, filled with joy, pride and even anger. After centuries of searching, he'd finally found his mate.

The moment he'd spotted her, the world around him had faded, ceasing to exist. Then he'd caught scent of her. Ice and wildflowers.

As legend claimed, he'd known who she was to him in an instant. Known beyond any doubt. His every cell had awakened for her.

I am hers, and she is mine.

There was no woman more beautiful, in this human world or in Atlantis. Her face…utterly angelic, with a luscious little chin, radiant cheeks and a daintily sloped nose. Her eyes were big and brown, a rich brown, almost gold, filled with dark secrets and undeniable determination, offset stunningly by pale, gloriously long lashes.

He'd never seen skin more fair or luminous. Not even on a vampire. Like the very moon he'd spied shining in the heavens, she was soft, dazzling and ethereal.

Moon. Yes. That's what she was.

His hands itched to reach out, to caress her, to linger and savor, to learn her, to anchor her against him, ensuring she wouldn't disappear when the sun rose, as unattainable as a dream.

His moonbeam was his wildest dream made flesh.

She was tall, her slenderness making her appear almost fragile. Definitely vulnerable. And yet, she also had delicious curves. Her breasts were more than a handful, and her hips flared. Her legs…oh, those legs. Deliciously lithe, leading straight to the new center of his world.

Possessive hunger consumed him. Already his blood boiled with a seemingly unquenchable fire, his skin tightening over muscle and bone.

Never again would he be able to enjoy another woman.

Enjoy? he thought and nearly laughed. Had he ever truly enjoyed a woman until now?

In seconds, the little moonbeam had become essential to his well-being. But for the first time in his existence— and that's what he'd been doing until just this moment, existing without really living—he suspected a woman would reject him.

This one had disobeyed him, run from him and now pointed a weapon in his direction. She radiated an icy veneer his warrior instincts longed to melt.

A moan of pleasure sounded a few feet away. He didn't have to look to know a female had just offered herself to a warrior, and that warrior had eagerly accepted.

"Sheathe the beast." There were too many unknowns around them. Dropping their guard—or their pants— would be foolish. "Gather the unmated females." He spoke in his native tongue, never taking his gaze from the object of his fascination. "Only those who wish to accompany us."

His moonbeam would have to be convinced.

She retreated a step. When she realized what she'd done, she stilled. She straightened her shoulders and raised the blade higher.

My woman has courage. I couldn't be more proud of her.

His shoulders straightened.

"Why are you here?" she demanded. "What do you want with us?"

Her pink-as-roses lips moved sensuously, entrancing him.

Going to taste those lips every day for the rest of my life...

"Hello, handsome." An unfamiliar female voice sounded beside him.

He tore his gaze from the moonbeam at last—surely one of the most difficult things he'd ever done—and glanced down. Three females now surrounded him, purring as they caressed him and rubbed against him.

"Only the unmated ones?" Broderick asked, his eyes closing in surrender as a pretty brunette licked his collarbone. "You're sure? This one really wants to come with us."

"Only the unmated ones," he confirmed. He'd never—wittingly—taken a married woman from another man, and he wouldn't start now.

If the little moonbeam is mated?

He stiffened. *She's mine! Only mine!*

Needing no other encouragement, his men leaped into action, beckoning unmated females to wait outside the tent. Broderick had to pull the trio off Valerian. They protested, only to glom on to the other warrior.

Smiles abounded from his army and the chosen alike.

Mated females cried in distress before attempting to shove their way out of the tent.

One of the human males decided to object. He pointed a small, black handheld device in Valerian's direction. A gun, he thought the weapon was called.

Before a shot could be fired, Dorian sneaked up behind him. A sword hilt slammed into his temple, and he collapsed.

Excellent. Valerian returned his attention to the moonbeam. She remained in place. Slowly he approached her, her dark eyes widening.

The closer he got, the more her delectable fragrance drew him like an invisible chain. Except...

One of his warriors reached her first, his strong arms wrapping around her from behind. Shivawn disarmed her and swooped her up into his embrace. She screamed and kicked, fighting like an enraged vampire out for blood.

A feral growl rose in Valerian's throat, and he bit back a wave of fury. Fury over his woman's torment; fury over his intense surge of possessiveness. *Mine! She belongs to me!* He'd never experienced a moment's jealousy in his life, and yet the sight of another man holding his little moonbeam pushed him into madness.

"Mine," he barked. Even though he wanted to rip the warrior's arms away from her, he remained still. "She's mine."

Shivawn paused, the beads in his hair clanging together. The moonbeam continued to fight, pounding her fists into his face, making him grimace and bleed.

"She isn't willing to go with you," Valerian said, doing his best to remain calm. *She only wants* my *touch.*

Frowning, Shivawn released her to clasp another woman against him. A dark-haired beauty who also looked less than pleased by the happenings around her.

Hmm. Very odd. Another unhappy one. What was wrong with these surface females?

His moonbeam quieted and stilled at last.

"Do you know who I am?" Valerian asked, using her

language, his tone gentle. *Recognize me.* He sheathed his sword.

"What do you want with us?" she demanded a second time, ignoring his question.

"I want nothing to do with the others," he replied honestly. "My soldiers have issued invitations to the single females to come and live with us. Invitations that are being accepted, as you can see."

She gaped at him. "Only because you've somehow drugged them."

"The only thing we've done...is breathe."

"And what do you mean, live with you?" she continued. "Live with you where?"

"Under the sea."

"The sea," she echoed. She licked her bottom lip, the sight of her tongue nearly unmanning him. "You're lying."

"I will *never* lie to you."

Now confusion knitted her brows. "You sound so sure, so determined."

"I am."

"You don't even know me, and I certainly don't want to know you. After I pick you out of a police lineup, I hope to never see you again."

She had no desire to accompany him. The realization dumbfounded him.

My mate would rather live her life without me.

No. No! His sudden appearance had shocked her. She just needed time. With him. With his pheromone.

Time she would one day thank him for giving her.

"You're not going to like what happens next," Valerian told her. "I apologize for that." He gently lifted her in his arms. The side of her body pressed against his chest, and everywhere their skin touched, he burned.

Unable to resist, he burrowed his nose in the hollow of her neck, breathing in her delectable fragrance while relishing the softness of her pale skin.

"Are you *sniffing* me?" she demanded.

"Yes. Would you like to sniff me in turn?"

"No!"

His shoulders slumped with disappointment.

"If you don't put me down," she said, each word sounding as if it were being forced from her throat, "I'm going to claw out your eyes and eat them in front of you."

He chuckled, his disappointment forgotten. She had a sweet face and a bloodthirsty disposition. What a delicious contradiction.

"Why are you laughing? I'm not teasing, and I'm most certainly not accepting your invitation and going with you."

He did stop laughing. "You alone have no choice. You are coming with me no matter what."

A muscle ticked in her jaw.

When their gazes met, blue against golden brown, he inhaled sharply. Awareness sizzled inside him, stronger than before. Such beauty. His nostrils flared, and he knew his pupils dilated. His body hardened painfully.

She gulped, her already pale skin becoming pallid.

"You're going to kidnap me?"

"Have you changed your mind about coming with me?"

"No!"

"Then yes. Yes, I am going to kidnap you."

CHAPTER FOUR

"Yes, I am going to kidnap you."

To Shaye, the quiet determination in the warrior's voice proved more frightening than a bellow because he wasn't overcome by emotion, and he knew his mind wouldn't be swayed.

She should be screaming for help. Instead, she only wanted to snuggle against her captor. Her freaking captor!

A delicious heat had woven through her blood. A heat that begged her to stop resisting and enjoy every stolen touch, every caress of the man's warm, clean breath on her skin.

"This is wrong," she grated. "This is not okay. This mantitlement will not stand!"

"Mantitlement?" He chuckled. "I vow to you here and now, I'll never harm you. I will protect you with my life. I will cherish and pamper you. You'll see."

"Said every captor to every victim." Her stomach roiled. "Why do you want us to live with you?" Maid service? Sex slaves?

Her stomach roiled *harder*.

Never mind that other women were petting the warriors as if they were innocent house cats.

He ignored Shaye's question...kind of. "My name is Valerian, and I'm king of the nymphs. I intend to make you my queen."

Wait, wait, wait. His queen? Was he talking *marriage*? After a two second introduction?

Can't process...

In an effort to remain calm, she concentrated on the more trivial details. "Valerian, like the flower? And do you mean you're king of the *nymphos*?"

The women were definitely meant to be sex slaves.

"No. We're nymphs. The word rhymes with lymph." A pause. "You humans have a flower named Valerian?"

Humans? "Yes, we humans do, and its root is lauded for helping people fall sleep."

He laughed. "So this strong, mighty root gets women into bed? How appropriate. Your flower must have been named after me."

Part of her wanted to laugh with him. The other part just wanted to whimper. Had there ever been a more sexual sound?

Her ovaries might have just exploded.

Give in to his desires. They match your own...

What? No! Panicked by her weakening will, Shaye launched into action, slamming her palm into Valerian's nose.

His head whipped backward, and blood trickled onto his lip.

A shocked pause ensued.

Then, "Why did you do that?" he demanded.

"You're as dumb as a box of rocks if you can't figure out the answer on your own." As she spoke, she bowed her back and kicked her legs. "Let me go!"

His grip on her loosened...as if he feared hurting her? She managed to squirm free and—

Thud. She crash-landed, only to jump to her feet and race away. *Go! Go!*

No, not without her mom. She switched direction,

dragging her gaze over the masses. Her breath emerged in shallow, ragged pants.

Preston lay unconscious on the floor. When he'd aimed a gun at Valerian, another warrior had knocked him out. There was Conner, her new stepdad, frantically crawling away from a redheaded warrior. But there was no sign of Tamara.

Where was she? They might have a rocky relationship, but Shaye couldn't—wouldn't—abandon her to... this.

Arms seized her from behind, the grip gentle but firm. Valerian! He'd only touched her once, but she would have recognized the feel of him anytime, anywhere. A white-hot brand.

Her blood ran from blistering to frigid as different emotions flooded her. Relief, lust, anger, confusion and fear.

Choose your attitude. She focused on the anger, turned and kneed Valerian in the balls.

He released a strained wheeze as he hunched over. He might have said, "My precious!"

"Not so eager for me now, are you?"

"That...hurt," he rasped.

"Of course it did, and there's more where that came from if you grab me again." Once again she darted away, still searching...searching...

There!

Conner hadn't been trying to leave, she realized. He'd been on the lookout for his bride. He now had Tamara trapped in his arms as she struggled to accost a warrior.

Shaye jumped over fallen chairs and skirted around overturned tables, slipping and sliding along a river of red punch. Someone else snaked an arm around her waist and hauled her against a stone wall of a chest.

His scent wasn't quite as exotic as Valerian's. Even his skin felt different, cooler, smoother. While his arms had a thick veil of dark hair, Valerian's possessed only a dusting of honey-blond.

She slammed the back of her head into his chin, her entire body vibrating with the force of the blow.

He growled a word she'd never heard, no doubt a curse. His arms fell away from her; she whirled on him, ready to fight to the death. His!

She never should have come here. Nothing good ever happened at her mom's weddings.

The he-man regarded her through narrowed blue eyes. "I only meant to kiss you," he said, in English this time, his voice so heavily accented she had trouble deciphering the words.

When her frantic mind deduced his meaning, she slapped him.

"Ow!" He rubbed his cheek.

"Kissing a woman without permission is not okay," she shouted.

He…pouted?

Shaye leaped around him and closed in on her mom. "Let's go! We have to get out of here." Before Valerian noticed.

Tamara continued fighting her husband. "If you don't release me, I'll stab you while you're sleeping!"

Lines of strain bracketed the groom's too-thin lips while concern and fear gleamed in his eyes. "What should I do?" he asked, looking to Shaye.

Urgency beat her with brass knuckles. "Just throw her over your shoulder fireman-style and run. I'll—"

"Be staying with me," she heard behind her.

The familiar, husky voice made her shiver. Made her muscles clench, desperate for sublime satisfaction.

He slid a hand around her bare stomach; his fingers were long and thick, tanned and hard against her pale softness. Goose bumps broke out all over her body. His other hand glided across her collarbone to stop beneath her seashell-covered breast. He tugged her backward, locking her against a muscled chest.

She melted into him. No, no. She forced herself to stiffen. He smelled like dark magic. Sultry. Heady. Powerful.

She should protest. At the very least, she should scold him for such daring.

The words refused to leave her mouth.

Whatever madness had overcome the other women, well, it had obviously affected her, too.

Valerian's warm breath stroked the hollow of her ear, shooting dangerous sparks of pleasure across her nerve endings. "My nose still hurts. As does my co—manhood. Kiss me and make me better?"

A strange weakness invaded her limbs. "No, thank you?"

A question? Really?

She'd always thought herself immune to lust. None of the men she'd dated had ever made it past first base. Kisses goodbye had been more of an obligation than a desire.

Cold fish, one man had even lobbed at her.

She'd had to agree with him. Cold equaled safe.

But she wasn't cold right now. She *burned*.

She burned because of a stranger intent on kidnapping her!

He rubbed his cheek against hers. "I was born to please you, moonbeam. You are my paradise, and I will be yours. Imagine it. You're naked. I'm naked. We grind together, reaching heights we never before thought possible."

A moan bubbled up, but she swallowed it back. He'd launched a full assault on her senses. Touch, sound, scent, sight…each giving her a taste of the delights she could find in his arms.

His soft lips brushed the shell of her ear; his tongue darted inside, only to retreat and leave her shaking, hungry for more. "Let me take you to my home. Let me give you untold pleasure."

Fight this! Fight him! "I—no, thank you." A statement this time.

"Shall we bargain, then? My kingdom for your heart."

He expected her to hand over rights to her heart after meeting him only five minutes ago? No way. Just no way. *Fight!*

"You don't want me or my black heart. Trust me. But I *will* give you trouble, and a lot of it. I'm mean and cranky, and most people can't stand to be around me."

"I want everything you have to give. In return, I'll give you everything right back."

Tamara ripped free of Conner's clasp to curl around Valerian's ankles and kiss his feet. "Take my heart! It's yours!"

Valerian didn't seem to notice he had a woman slobbering on his boots.

"Get up, Mom," Shaye demanded. Seeing her newly wed mother humble herself in such a way snapped her out of whatever spell Valerian had cast. "Run. Escape!"

"She is your mother? Fear not. No harm will come to her and her husband, I swear it." Without releasing Shaye, Valerian gently lifted Tamara to her feet and urged her toward Conner.

"Only if I cooperate with you, right?" Shaye asked with bite.

"No. No harm will come to the pair regardless of your actions."

A lie, surely.

"What's your name?" he asked her, having to speak over Tamara's pleas.

Mutinous, Shaye pressed her lips in a thin line. *Defy him at every turn. Ignore the heady, seductive tingle in my veins.* Maybe then he would tire of her.

"You surprise me," he said, his honeyed timbre rich with confusion. "I expected my mate—"

A string of foreign words suddenly cut him off.

His mate?

Stiffening, Valerian faced the speaker. Shaye did the same. The man had black hair and eyes as blue as a cloudless sky. Like the others, he wore only pants and boots, his bronzed chest on display. He said something else.

Valerian responded in the same, clipped language.

What were they saying to each other?

The dark-haired man motioned to Shaye with a tilt of his chin.

Whatever Valerian's reply, it wasn't nice. His tone hardened, becoming unbending and dripping with command.

The warrior paused only a moment, shrugged and strode away.

"What was that about?" Trying not to panic again, she angled her head to stare up at her captor.

Mistake! Their gazes locked, and a wave of sexual energy sparked between them, stronger than before, undeniable and irresistible.

Need coiled between her legs, hot and wet, before spiraling through her stomach, her nipples.

Look away. Look away!

"What was that about?" she repeated.

"I'm breaking my own rules." He bent to nuzzle her cheek with his own, an action seemingly as natural to him as breathing. "The fact isn't…appreciated. What Joachim failed to understand is that you are not a rule, you are an exception."

"I don't understand."

"I'll explain. Later." Without another word, he spun her and hefted her onto his shoulder as if she weighed nothing more than a bag of feathers.

"Put me down!" She fought and kicked with all her might, and her knee slammed into his stomach. "Valerian!"

"I love the sound of my name on your rose-petal lips," he said, striding out of the tent, past the line of waiting—eager—women. "Would you like to hear your name on mine?"

"Never!"

He sighed, heading for the ocean he'd risen from. At least her mom wouldn't be forced to endure…whatever these men were going to make her and the others endure.

The warriors fell into place behind him, and the young, single women happily, blithely followed suit. Those singles were a mix of every race, size and age, though no one looked to be under twenty or over fifty; the prettiest of the bunch even had a prosthetic leg. To the warriors' credit, they peered at each woman as if she were the ultimate prize, despite the flaws modern-day trolls would have most likely issued.

Wait. Was she praising douche bags just because they found everyone equally attractive?

I need more therapy. Shaye *didn't* need praise from

someone—anyone—else. She liked herself just the way
she was.

Feminine sobs echoed from within the tent.

"Take me with you," someone called. "Please. I'm
begging."

At the shoreline, Valerian stopped to whisper, "Beautiful. So very beautiful. A sky without a dome." He
spoke in English—for her benefit?

"The heavens seem to go on forever," another said,
clearly awed. He, too, spoke in English.

"I'd dreamed of this land, but never imagined such
majesty."

"Are you sure we can't stay here?" one of the warriors asked. "We could bring the rest of the army
through the portal and—"

Valerian shook his head, silky tendrils of his hair
brushing her bare back.

Portal?

"I'm sure," he said. "Layel was very clear. To remain
on the surface is to die on the surface. Let us tarry no
longer." He walked into the water.

He was going for a nighttime swim? Or did he plan
something more nefarious? Like a mass drowning?

Fear sprouted. "Valerian." She slapped his butt
with all her might. "This is illegal. You're going to get
caught. Criminals always get caught. At your trial I'll
request the death penalty." *If I'm still alive.*

"As long as you're in my arms, I can die a happy man."

She beat her fists into his back, watching water
splash at his feet. The echo of churning waves filled
her ears. "Don't do this. Please, don't do this."

"I told you I would never hurt you. This is the only
way to my home. Once there, I'll beg for your forgive-

ness for any hardships you endure. I'll gift you with more jewels and gold than you can imagine. I'll—"

"I don't want jewels and gold, you brute! I want my freedom."

Waves lapped at his knees...his thighs...his midsection. Cool, salty droplets sprayed over her face and burned her eyes. Though he slowed his pace, he continued on, sinking deeper and deeper into the water.

She swallowed a mouthful of the stuff—and choked. He stopped, patting her butt in a vain effort to help her catch her breath. Then he resumed his slow, torturous journey. The other women still followed merrily, each wearing a giddy smile, as if frolicking to their deaths was perfectly acceptable. Even fun.

Wait. No, not every woman followed merrily. The one with dark curls, a petite beauty, looked ready to vomit.

Shaye's heart pounded in her chest, an erratic drumbeat. A war beat. "Don't do this. You're going to kill us all, you—umph."

Butt smack. "Hold your breath, moonbeam."

The next thing she knew, she was completely submerged. The salt stung her eyes. Her throat constricted. Hair floated around her face like strands of ivory ribbon.

The idiot man kept his strong arms locked around her, one at the bend of her knees, one at the small of her back. His palms were hot, so hot, a startling contrast against the chilly liquid.

Colorful fish swam past her. She wanted to scream, but every time she opened her mouth, she swallowed more water.

He tilted forward and began using his powerful legs to swim even deeper....deeper still. Her lungs shrieked for air. She desperately needed to breathe. Now. Now!

Can't...

Terror devoured her.

I'm going to die, she realized. *My life will be over before I ever truly lived.*

A thousand regrets surfaced, along with all the lies she'd told herself. She *didn't* like herself. She *wasn't* happy. She should have forgiven those who'd wronged her. Clinging to hurt instead of embracing love seemed so silly now. Like wasted time. Every moment counted, and hurt only ever, well, hurt. Love healed, always. She should have written a book instead of simply talking about it. Her characters could have had the happy ending she'd secretly craved for herself.

She should have gotten a second tattoo. A rose in full bloom, or a cross, or a butterfly. Basically the opposite of the skull and crossbones she had on her lower back— an image she'd gotten to make her parents notice her.

Her mom had definitely noticed and still mailed her articles about new methods of tattoo-removal every few weeks.

Her mind suddenly blanked, becoming as dark as the water, wiping her thoughts clean.

Have to breathe, she mentally shouted.

Between one heartbeat and the next, the murky water cleared, so glassy she could see as perfectly as if she were on land. Even the salt dissipated, soothing her irritated eyes.

Valerian tugged her forward so that they were eye to eye. She tried to push away from him—her tormentor—but he held tight.

Breathe, she mouthed. *Please.*

With a hand on her nape, he drew her close and pressed his mouth to hers; he used his tongue to open her lips…and then he exhaled, gifting her with the last breath he'd taken.

The burn inside her cooled, the vise-grip easing from her throat and lungs.

Lifting his head, he motioned with a tilt of his chin, and she squelched her panic long enough to turn and look. Her eyes widened when she spotted the swirling, gelatinous whirlpool that loomed ahead.

What was *that*? And why was Valerian swimming straight for it?

She fought to paddle in the opposition direction, but an undeniable suction pulled her closer…until she shot through the whirlpool and into dark nothingness.

She began to spin, faster and faster, left and right, tumbling toward the unknown. Nausea churned in her stomach, and needles jabbed at her pores, the pain nearly too much to bear.

She didn't understand what was happening; she only knew the water had disappeared, leaving the spiraling black abyss that seemed to stretch for eternity.

Zipping lights whizzed past her, firefly flickers extinguished all too soon. A bevy of screams assaulted her ears, and a sharp ache began to hammer at her temples. Her blood flash-froze in her veins even as sweat beaded over her skin.

As a little girl, her favorite fairy tale had been *Alice in Wonderland*. Alice had fallen down a rabbit hole, and Shaye had envied her. A whole new world! Adventure!

Suddenly she *pitied* Alice.

Brighter streams of light appeared. Gusts of wind erupted, blustering around her.

Where was Valerian? She shouted his name.

Dizziness invaded her mind as she continued to twirl, twirl, twirl, alone, frightened…finally crash-landing inside a new world, just like Alice.

CHAPTER FIVE

"I'VE GOT YOU, MOON."

Strong arms lifted Shaye, and she gratefully buried her face in the hollow of Valerian's neck. In that moment, she no longer cared what the warrior was doing to her; she was just happy he was with her. She even wound her legs around his hips to prevent any kind of separation.

I'm safe?

"Don't you dare let me go," she cried.

His hold tightened. "I will *never* let you go."

The vehement tone should have frightened her, but oddly enough she felt comforted instead.

Maybe because he clung to her as if she were a treasure. As if she were someone special. As if he'd waited his whole life to meet her and now couldn't imagine living without her.

A deception, she knew. But that was okay. For now, that was okay.

"Take a moment to breathe." He petted his fingers down her spine. "Breathe for me. I don't feel your chest moving."

Right. In, out. Air filled and exited her lungs. In, out. Surprisingly, she *did* calm. The scent of salt and Valerian's particular brand of black magic teased her nostrils. His heart beat against hers. His hard strength welcomed her soft femininity.

Valerian set her on her feet and framed her jaw with his big, callused hands. "You are pale," he said, a hint of concern in his voice.

"I'm always pale," she muttered.

She forced her gaze to abandon the stunning beauty of his chiseled features in favor of studying her new surroundings.

They'd somehow entered a cave. The walls were rough and rocky, silver stones painted with streaks of crimson. Blood?

She swallowed the barbed lump growing in her throat. A metallic tang layered the cold, cold air, and that cold, cold air continued to stroke her nearly bare body, chasing away Valerian's delicious warmth, making her shiver.

A shuffle of footsteps sounded behind her.

Gasping, she looked over her shoulder. Tendrils of mist curled toward a domed ceiling as, one by one, warriors walked from a clear, jellylike whirlpool identical to the one she'd seen under water. The women still followed, but they were no longer smiling.

"Where are we?" she asked Valerian.

A pause. "Look at me, Moon. Please."

The nickname made no sense to her, and yet it somehow delighted her—the only reason she obeyed him.

The rest of the world vanished as her gaze traveled from his booted feet to his muscled legs, skipping over the ridge between his legs to stop on his chest—where rope after rope of bronzed masculinity awaited. Droplets of water trickled over perfect male nipples—even through the silver piercing—and pooled in his navel.

How could one person be so…delicious?

He had perfect sandy brows, perfect crystalline eyes

framed with spiky black lashes and a perfect nose. His lips were plump and pink—and perfect.

Confidence clung to him like a second skin, making him the most sensually erotic creature she'd ever seen. Even better—or worse!—he radiated primal ferocity.

"We are home." Gently, so gently, he traced his fingertips over her face to wipe away the water.

She stood completely still, not encouraging him but not rebuking him, either. His touch reverberated through her like a live wire, hot and scorching.

"This isn't my home," she said. "I live in Cincinnati."

"You *used* to live in Cincinnati. Now you live with me in Atlantis, the capital of the gods' finest creations. Home to nymphs, vampires, Amazons and many other races."

Wait. Wait, wait, wait. She blinked rapidly as her mind attempted to make sense of his words. Atlantis...the city buried under the ocean? Like the ocean she'd just exited? Her mouth went dry. No way. Just no way.

"Home of nymphos and vampires? You're lying," she grated. "Why are you lying?"

He frowned at her. "I told you. I'll never lie to you. And I'm a nymph. Nymph."

"Well, guess what? You're my abductor, so I'll *never* believe you."

His frown deepened. "Do you have another explanation for entering the sea and appearing here?"

"Yes. I drowned," she told him. "You killed me. But someone—a *human*—found my body and restarted my heart. Only, I'm in a coma and my brain is short-circuiting."

The corners of his beautiful mouth twitched. "If that's true, I'm nothing but a dream. A midnight fantasy. You can enjoy me without fear of the consequences."

Dang him. He had an excellent point. "You're right. I can murder you and avoid jail time."

His smile bloomed full force, causing a precious gasp of breath to snag in her lungs. "You and you alone have cart blanche with my body. If you'll receive pleasure from my pain, then you may hurt me any way you'd like. You can always kiss me better…"

Did nothing faze him?

Choose your attitude. "No, thank you," she muttered. "To everything."

"Men," he called, his penetrating stare never veering from her face. "Escort the women to the dining hall. The ceremony will soon begin."

"Ceremony?" she asked.

With an air of eager anticipation, the warriors leaped into action. One of them tried to grab her arm, but Valerian stopped him with a feral, "I'll escort this one," even as she slapped at the offender's hand.

"As you wish, my king."

King? King!

Footsteps echoed through the cavern.

Once again, the women were all smiles, happily trailing their captors.

"Who do you desire?" one warrior asked another.

"The redhead. Her breasts are…"

Their chatter faded.

A single man remained behind. Or perhaps he'd been waiting in the cave. He wasn't drenched like everyone else, his white shirt and tight black pants completely dry.

Valerian released her from his stare to face the remaining warrior. "How are the prisoners?" he asked.

Prisoners? Her eyes widened, and she clutched at her throat, the barbed lump back in place.

The man gave a brusque answer in that odd language Valerian had used earlier, but he—the freaking king—shook his head. "Speak in the human tongue."

"Alive," the man responded with a frown.

Human tongue.

That wasn't the first time he'd referred to her as a human, implying he himself was something else entirely. Like the creature of myth he claimed to be...

"Have they given you any trouble?" Valerian asked.

"None at all, my king."

"Very good. Continue to see to their needs." He waved in dismissal, scowled, then called the man back. "Has there been any word about our females?"

"None."

"Very well." He rubbed the back of his neck. "On with you."

The man nodded and clomped off, leaving her alone with her abductor.

"What prisoners?" Shaye asked on a trembling breath. Would *she* end up in a prison cell?

"Dragon shape-shifters. Killers."

Dragon shape-shifters. *Valerian is insane, plain and simple.*

He traced his knuckles along her cheekbone, and she shivered. The water in his hair had dried somewhat, lightening the locks to a rich, honey gold. Several strands fell over his forehead. Part of her longed to reach up and smooth those strands away.

Part of *her* was clearly insane.

"Do not fear," he added, "for the dragons won't be allowed near you. Some are to be gifts for my friend Layel, and some are to be used as bargaining chips."

His delusions were more than her fragile mind could

deal with right now. "The ceremony," she repeated. "Tell me."

In an instant, he radiated possessive intensity without a hint of amusement.

"The men," he said, "will chose their lovers."

She'd been right. Sex slaves. "And if the women protest?" she croaked.

"They won't."

Too cocky! "But if they do?"

His frown returned. "They'll never be forced."

Truth or lie? "What if they're too scared to protest?"

He thought for a moment. "If you'd like to speak with every woman before she joins her warrior, to ascertain her desires for yourself, you may."

The offer surprised her.

He flattened his hands on the boulder behind her, caging her in. Electric shocks skittered through her.

Icy rock at her back, pure heat in front.

"What are you doing?" She hated the breathless quality in her voice.

"Right this moment? Wishing you were kissing me. In a few seconds from now, showing you our world."

He twisted his wrists, and the huge rock wall slid backward. She would have stumbled, but Valerian caught her by the waist and turned her, his chest pressing against her spine.

The contact delighted her body while irritating her mind.

She watched, flabbergasted, as the wall descended, a smooth, glassy crystal suddenly exposed. Her jaw dropped as water flowed behind the enclosure, and sand swirled at the sea's bottom. Pink coral and multicolored fish danced a lazy waltz around emerald plants.

"Breathtaking, isn't it?" Warmth fanned the back of her neck.

As she peered out, trying to come to grips with the bounty before her, a gorgeous woman swam up to the crystal. No, not a woman. Shaye gasped. A mermaid. A bare-chested, tail-wagging mermaid.

Her knees shook. The creature frowned...until her gaze latched on to Valerian. She smiled and waved, pleasure gleaming in her eyes.

"You know her?" Shaye managed to say.

He nodded but didn't elaborate.

The woman—mermaid—had the face of an angel, innocent, lovelier than a long-awaited sunrise. Long black hair curled around delicate shoulders and lush breasts. Her tail glimmered like spun glass, different shades of violet, yellow, green and pink creating a kaleidoscope of color on every scale.

"Do you believe me now?" Valerian asked.

How could she not?

"I...do." The admission left her on a ragged breath.

She had been transported to a mythical world. The man behind her wasn't human but a nympho—oops, a nymph.

"What's the difference between a nymph and a nympho?" The words trembled as they left her.

"Nymphs are—everything! Everything is different."

Basically, they were the same. A sexual being, both seductive and irresistible. Obsessed with sex. Or rather, *addicted* to sex. Probably willing to sleep with anything that moved. Perhaps able to give pleasure to others with only a glance...or a whispered word. Definitely beauty personified.

Valerian fit the description completely, and that

frightened her so much more than if he'd said he was a soul-sucking demon from the deepest depths of hell.

Welcome to Wonderland, Alice.

Another mermaid joined the brunette, this one a symphony of curves. She pressed herself against the crystal and offered a wanton smile to Valerian, passion glazing her amethyst eyes.

Bet the lovelies were thinking *Score! Three-way.*

"Take me home, Valerian." Please. Tremors rocked her. Where had her numbness gone? "I don't belong here."

"You do." The rocky wall returned to its place, gradually hiding the mermaids, who were banging on the crystal. "We belong together."

"No." Shaye angled her head to give him the dreaded side-eye. "We don't even know each other."

"A fact I look forward to changing." His husky tone beguiled, promising endless nights of passion and days of wild abandon.

Resist. Flee. She squared her shoulders and raised her chin. "No, thank you."

"Give me a chance. One chance. Please."

Had a man ever begged for her attention before?

Stay strong. "I did," she said. "I gave you the chance to leave me behind and respect my wishes. Had you, I might have agreed to a date. But you didn't. Now I want nothing to do with you."

He rested his forehead against her shoulder.

A position of defeat? A pang cut through her chest. Why? Why should his pain affect her?

Act! Act now!

Shaye wrenched from his embrace and sprinted toward the whirlpool. Her sandals dug into rocks and twigs. Breath caught in her throat, burning. Almost there…just one more step…

Valerian grabbed her by the arm, stopping her.

"No!" She kicked his shin.

"If you enter the portal without me, you'll die." The words held an unmistakable edge of fury, his grip tightening on her. "You'll never be able to swim to the surface alone. Do you understand? You'll die out there, your body nothing more than fish food."

She stilled, panting, the blood in her veins chilling. The water…how could she have forgotten the water?

"Is death preferable to my pursuit?" he asked.

"If I'm to be a captive, yes!" She'd fought hard for her independence and would relinquish it to no one.

A heavy pause stretched between them. Valerian radiated both sadness and anger.

Sadness? The pang returned to her chest, and she sputtered with indignation.

"I can't live aboveground," he said, "and I don't want to live without you."

"That's ridiculous. You're ridiculous. I… I…" Had no idea how to respond. "How many human girls have heard those words from your lips?"

Don't know how to respond, so you go with jealousy? You are ridiculous!

"One. Only one. And I haven't yet learned her name."

"Up yours," she said. He couldn't mean the things he was saying to her. He just couldn't. "That's what you can call me."

He sighed. He secured her against him, his body an impenetrable force. "Come then, Up Yours, and I'll show you the palace."

As he ushered her up a crudely built staircase, she

offered no more protests. She needed time to consider her options.

Try to find another way home?

Was there another way?

Make nice with Valerian and enjoy his pampering while it lasted?

Save the dark-haired girl who'd looked as upset by the circumstances as Shaye?

Ding, ding, ding. We have a winner!

Shaye studied the markings on the wall to help her find her way back—just in case. The higher up she traveled, the less jagged the rocks became...until the walls appeared to be dusted with glitter. She brushed her fingertip over the smooth surface, leaving a mark behind. Her own personal bread crumb.

Valerian stopped abruptly, causing her to bump into his back. Fiery, full-body contact. She gasped as he backed her into the wall, his frown fierce, his crystal-line eyes gleaming with purpose.

"You wouldn't happen to be planning your escape, would you?"

She arched a brow. "What do you think?"

"I think your determination matches mine."

"Is that a compliment or an insult?"

"What do you think?" he asked, mocking her. He brushed the tip of his nose against hers.

An innocent action and yet her bones liquefied.

Dang it! Where's my armor?

"What if I promise not to try to escape?" she asked. She didn't plan to try; she planned to succeed.

Another brush of his nose against hers. "I would want to believe you, but still I would doubt you. Trust between us will take time, but it *will* come. I know this."

Even as deluded as he was, considering he thought a

happily-ever-after—or happily ever until-the-new-wears off—was possible between a captor and his captive, he still understood trust had to be earned.

Ugh. Was she hoping to give herself permission to like him?

Probably. Because, with every second that passed, some of her animosity faded.

I'm a fool!

All right. It was clearly time to do what her therapist had told her never to do: use a snotty attitude to create distance with the people around her.

Cruel to be kind...to myself.

She lifted her chin. "What happens if I want to hook up with one of your men?"

His brow furrowed. "Hook up?"

"You know, get my groove on. Offer myself up on a silver platter. Do the dirty bump and grind."

Rage exploded inside his eyes. "You will not *hook up* with one of my men. Ever."

"Wrong! My body. My choice."

His nostrils flared as he fought for control and oh, wow, the sight actually...turned her on. He wanted to keep her all to himself.

"You're mine," he grated.

"Actually, I'm *mine*."

"Fine. I'm willing to share you with you and only you."

She almost—almost—laughed. "How kind of you," she muttered.

"Yes. I'm *very* kind." He stepped back and offered his hand. "Shall we?"

The distance...displeased her, the most feminine parts of her body actually pouting.

She peered at his blunt-tipped fingers...at the calluses and scars slashed across his palm, a contrast to his otherwise flawless beauty. As strong as he was, he could have killed her at any moment. He could have crushed her and yet he'd been nothing but gentle with her.

Oh, yes. I'm a fool.

She willingly twined her fingers with his—and gasped. A blast of heat slammed into her. Tingles raced over her.

She tried to tug away from him, to sever the connection, but he held tight. He even lifted her knuckles to his lips and kissed.

The heat—a thousand degrees worse.

The tingles—a thousand times stronger.

"You are precious to me," he said. "The one I've been searching for all the days of my life."

She bit the inside of her cheek, battling the pleasure his declaration had wrought. "Are you saying you... love me?"

"No. Not yet. But I have no doubt love for you will come."

"How?" No one had *ever* loved her. "How can you believe that?"

"Every nymph has a fated mate, and you are mine."

"I don't understand," she rasped. "I don't understand *at all.*"

"You will. In time."

The words—a warning? a promise?—rang in her head as he led her up the rest of the stairs. At the top, two gleaming crystal doors slid open.

They traveled down a series of long, winding hallways. *Luxurious* hallways. Gold brick walls had been draped with strands of emeralds that wound this way and that to resemble ivy. Alabaster columns were decorated with fist-size diamonds that had been carved to look like roses in full bloom. From the ceiling hung multiple chandeliers, each in the shape of a dragon's head, crimson-colored crystals dripping from fangs that might have been fashioned from pearls.

The magnificence overwhelmed her.

"Do you like your…the palace?" he asked. "We'll be replacing the chandeliers with a less hideous design."

"It's beautiful. It's all beautiful."

They turned a corner, vivid wall murals coming into view. Each scene showcased a man, doing something kind for a woman. Feeding her grapes. Undressing her. Bathing her.

"I had to paint over dragon portraits," he said, noticing where her attention was fixed.

"*You* painted these?"

"Yes."

"Your talent is…" Compliment her captor? No! "Decent."

He squeezed her hand. "Perhaps you'll pose for me one day."

Her heart rate increased. Had nothing to do with Valerian, of course. She'd obviously developed an early-onset heart arrhythmia.

"Why did you take the palace from the dragons?" she asked, desperately returning to the previous topic of conversation. The safer topic.

"Nymphs have always been natural wanderers. For centuries, we flittered from one location to the other in search of our next sexual conquest, but I grew weary of such an existence. I wanted more for myself and more for my people."

"Why? What changed?" According to her therapist, transformation required a catalyst.

"A sense of restlessness plagued me for months. I

knew if I wanted a better life, I had to do something different. This is my different."

Basically, he'd changed his mind. Just as he would change his mind about Shaye.

"Usually nymphs attack only when provoked," he added, "keeping our bestial natures under strict control, but dragons are an enemy to the vampires, our only ally."

"Do the other races not like the nymphos?" *Bet I can guess all the reasons why.*

"They don't like our power over women. Layel, the vampire king, finds it amusing."

She shuddered, praying she never came face-to-face with a blood drinker. "Do you regret the decision to steal?"

"Not in the slightest," Valerian replied easily. "Once I entered the palace, my restlessness was replaced by rightness. Now, having met you, I understand why."

She scowled at him. "Stop saying things like that."

"Why?"

"Because—just because!"

They turned another corner. Valerian stiffened.

So did she. They'd entered what was clearly the dining hall...where the ceremony was set to begin.

CHAPTER SIX

For years, Valerian had imagined his perfect future. He would lead the strongest army in Atlantis. His queen would rule at his side, happy to belong to him. She would adore him. Of course she would adore him. He would treasure her. Their days would be hot, but their nights would be hotter.

Finally he'd found her—only to lose her?

What if another warrior selected her during the ceremony?

Someone would. Surely. What man could resist the fire burning beneath her cool facade, begging for release?

Rage detonated inside him. He'd said he wouldn't choose a woman, but he regretted the vow with every fiber of his being.

He couldn't go back on his word, but he couldn't allow his Moon to end up with anyone else, either.

What was he going to do? Not all of his men loved him. A few would choose her simply to strike at him.

His cousin might even attempt to trade her for his crown.

He'd also vowed he would never relinquish his reign. But what good was his crown without his queen?

He wanted—nay, he *needed*—her. To kiss her. To know the taste of her tongue and her skin. He'd come close to kissing her in the cave. Would she have fought him…or melted for him?

Like you really have to wonder.

She would have fought him. For some reason, she wanted to get to know him before she allowed herself to enjoy him. A novel concept. One he actually…appreciated?

He'd never before cared about the reasons a woman desired him. The pheromone. His pretty face. His strength. His exalted position. Whatever! But for the first time, he wanted someone to desire him for…dare he think it?…his personality—the man he'd become.

Doubts surfaced. *You kidnapped her, putting your needs above her wants. Your personality is lacking.*

Pain tore through the center of his chest. Could he win her affections despite his crime?

Perhaps. But he would have to win her the same way he'd won the dragon palace. With cunning, precision and an absolute lack of mercy.

Slowly his lips lifted in a grin. Oh, yes. She would soon find herself on the receiving end of a full-scale attack.

"Take me back to the beach," she said, tugging against his hold. Her heartbeat drummed erratically against his back, and he could feel the shallow exhalations of her breath against his skin. "Right now. I'm through playing nice. Do you hear me?"

"Everyone hears you, Moon." He wrapped his arms around her, hugging her body to his. "The answer is no."

Their bare stomachs pressed together, and she sucked in a breath. His muscles jumped in excited reaction.

She might deny it, but she was aware of him in a very sexual way. A wonderful start!

"You are frightened," he said, "and I'm sorry for it."

"Frightened? Ha! I'm so angry I could spit."

"Spitting is a sign of your anger? Noted."

For some reason, his response caused her to screech.

At her outburst, several of his men flinched. A few regarded her with weary reluctance.

Hope bloomed. Had he just found the answer to his dilemma?

"Whatever you do," he said, "do *not* attack my men as they make their selection."

Her head lifted, and her eyes glared amber fire at him. "You can't stop me."

Do not smile, he thought. *Get this over with.*

Anticipation thickened the air. A contingent of warriors lined one side of the room while a sweet-smelling cluster of females lined the other.

"I'm not placing myself on the menu of this—this smorgasbord." She slammed her elbow into his stomach, almost knocking the air from his lungs.

His men watched them with varying expressions of horror. For their benefit, he said, "Be still, woman."

"Sure. If you'll do me a favor and die."

The horror intensified, just as he'd hoped. If he, the most desired of nymphs, failed to entice this woman, his men were destined to fail with her, too. No one wanted to risk failure. Or even a lengthy wooing. Not while sex could be easily had with another.

Valerian forced a frown, feigning disappointment, and tapped her on the backside. Once again, she reacted as he'd hoped.

"Did you just spank me?" she bellowed. Her eyes were dark velvet, rich and warm, absolutely riveting in her pale face. "Tell me you didn't just spank me, Valerian."

Ah, he loved hearing his name spill from her soft,

pink lips. The rest of the world faded away, as it always seemed to do when he looked at her.

"I told you I would never lie to you," he said.

"You also told me you wouldn't hurt me."

"Did my love tap hurt you?"

Her perfect white teeth flashed in a scowl. "Pain isn't always physical."

True. "Did I hurt you mentally? Emotionally?" The idea hurt *him*, physically, mentally and emotionally.

How many others had hurt her throughout her young life?

She crossed her arms over her chest. "I plead the fifth."

"Fifth. Five. Is that the number of ways you hope I'll take you?" he asked softly.

Another bellow. "Stop acting as if you adore me," she grated. "It's creepy."

"But I do adore you."

"You can't! How many times do I have to tell you? You. Don't. Know. Me."

"I know you have a temper."

"And so do millions of other people."

"I know you like to be touched, whether you admit it or not." Many times she'd leaned into him before coming to her senses and stiffening. "I know you like when I compliment you." Her gaze always softened.

She huffed and puffed. "You're wrong."

"Would you rather I say mean things to you?"

"Yes!"

He also knew she meant that and blinked with confusion. "Why?"

"Why don't *you* tell *me*?" she challenged.

Only one reason made any sense, and he thrilled. "When I'm kind, your defenses threaten to crumble."

She gave an adamant shake of her head.

He only thrilled *harder*!

"My king," Broderick prompted. "We're ready. We have instructed the women to remain in place until they've been chosen."

Valerian blanked his expression. He picked up his woman and carried her to the end of the line. A quick count revealed more men than women.

Many warriors would be going to bed alone tonight. What if someone decided having a chance to woo Moon would be better than having no chance at all?

"Stay quiet," he told her, suspecting she would do the opposite. "Everyone will want a good look at you without any distractions."

She lifted her chin. "This T and A pageant sucks balls. I won't passively stand here—and neither should you," she shouted at the other women. "We are human beings, and we have rights. Men do not choose us, we choose our men. We say *no* to these nymphos and their demeaning ceremony. We demand to be returned home. Who's with me?"

Silence.

"Who's with *me*?" Broderick asked.

One female jumped up, her arm extended in the air. "Pick me! Pick me!"

"No. Me!"

Shaye's shoulders brushed his chest as they rolled in, and several strands of silken hair snagged in his nipple ring.

"If I help you remain unchosen," he whispered, "will you tell me your name?"

"I—maybe." Her eyelids slitted, the length of her lashes casting spiky shadows over her cheeks. "Why would you help me?"

Why indeed. The answer should have been obvious

to her. "I intend to keep you for myself." He stated the words as baldly as possible. He needed an extreme re-action from her—something to appall his men further.

"I'm not a piece of meat, and this isn't a buffet. You should be ashamed of yourself." Her gaze blazed over his men. "All of you should be ashamed."

Valerian heaved a mighty sigh. "If you won't remain in line," he called loudly, "I'll be obligated to hold you in place."

"Keep your hands to yourself! I don't want to be touched. I'll *never* want to be touched."

Nymphs recoiled in horror.

A wave of triumph swept through him. "Broder-ick," he called.

"Yes, my king." The warrior stepped forward, ex-citement radiating from him.

"As second in command and leader of the elite, you are granted first choice." Valerian loosened his hold on his captive so that her movements were more obvious.

She squirmed, her murmured curses and grunts fill-ing the air.

Broderick grinned and approached the females, start-ing at the far end. Feminine twitters and purrs echoed throughout the spacious enclosure.

A new chorus erupted. "Pick me, pick me!"

"What have you done to them?" Shaye demanded.

Full disclosure. "We produce a potent pheromone all…well, *most* women find pleasing."

She stiffened. "By *pheromone*, do you mean *drug*?"

"The word drug implies wrongdoing on our part. Just as humans have no control over the way they perspire, we have no control over the way we pheromone. And it doesn't drug. It frees hidden desires."

Broderick slowly edged his way down the line, stop-

ping here and there to study a woman more closely—
even to touch. But he didn't ask questions, getting to
know the women better, and it clearly irritated Shaye,
who mumbled under her breath.

By the time he reached her, the warrior had yet to
make his selection.

He reached out to touch *her*.

Valerian had to swallow a harsh rebuke.

She reared back, calling, "Shaye Octavia Holling.
That's my name."

Shaye. Valerian rolled the name over his tongue, savoring its delicacy. "I like your name."

"Thank you," she snapped. "I got it for my birthday."

Funny girl. "Kick him." He breathed the command
straight into her ear. "As hard as you can."

Without hesitation, she slammed her knee between
Broderick's legs. The stunned warrior hunched over,
gasping for breath; the rest of the army burst into gales
of laughter.

"I'm not your chattel," Shaye grated. "You disgust
me. I hope your testicles have to be surgical removed
from you intestines."

Valerian bit back a grin. His second in command
quickly selected the curviest woman in line. The pair
rushed from the dining hall without a backward glance.

One down...

"Dorian." Valerian nodded to the man often referred
to as the sexiest male in Atlantis. "You're next."

To Shaye—would he ever get enough of her name?—
he whispered, "When he approaches you, ignore him.
Don't even look at him."

"You're sure?" she whispered back.

Valerian had expected the process of elimination to

infuriate him. Instead, he and Shaye were working together, and he loved it.

"I'm sure."

SHAYE COULDN'T BELIEVE she stood in a line of singles, being ogled by nymphos while relying on Valerian to ensure her safety. He'd gotten her into this mess in the first place! But she could think of no other alternative. Letting one of these barbarians "claim" her and drag her away to do who knew what to her held zero appeal.

"Won't ignoring him bring out all his caveman instincts?" she asked softly.

"Anyone else? Yes. Not him." Valerian sounded amused. "His pride will demand immediate soothing— from someone else."

Well. Consider him ignored.

The one named Dorian had onyx hair and irises so pure and blue they rivaled the ocean. His mouthwatering beauty was something out of a fairy tale, his features somehow even more perfect than Valerian's.... but he didn't make her ache.

He didn't fill her mind with X-rated images of naked, straining bodies.

As Dorian followed Broderick's example and considered every woman in line, Shaye's hands curled into fists.

How would these men like it if the tables were turned? If *they* were the ones being looked over and judged?

Who was she kidding? They would love every second of it.

There had to be a way to override the nympho pheromone and convince these women they did *not* sexually desire their captors.

When Dorian reached Shaye, he made sure to remain out of striking distance. He studied her, his intense gaze lingering on her every curve.

Just as before, Valerian stiffened.

She peered down at her cuticles as if she hadn't a care.

"You intrigue me, female," Dorian told her.

She faked a yawn. His intrigue? Probably nothing more than the pride Valerian had mentioned. Winning the one others had failed to win would come with a side of bragging rights.

"Female?"

Another yawn.

The warrior expelled a frustrated breath.

Maybe she had a cruel streak, because she *liked* upsetting him.

"Look at me," Dorian commanded, reminding her of a petulant child.

She brushed an invisible piece of lint from her arm.

He tangled a hand through his hair and eyed his boss. "Valerian. A little help, if you please."

Valerian lifted his shoulders in a shrug. "I can't force her eyes on you unless I remove them."

"But—"

"Is she the one you want or not?" The words lashed from him, abrupt and harsh. Filled with impatience. "Others await their turn."

A scowl darkened Dorian's features before he spun from Shaye and stalked to an Asian sweetie with a lily in her hair. "I choose you."

Lily actually cheered.

"If you guys are going to select women based on their appearance," Shaye muttered, "you should first make sure you're Chris or Liam Hemsworth."

A growl rose from him. "Who are these men to you?"

"Only my lovers." In her dreams.

Just because a real man had never really tempted her, and just because she'd encased her heart in icy armor, well, that didn't mean her mind had never fantasized and her body had never ached. She'd ached. Oh, she'd ached.

"No longer," Valerian grated. "You're mine."

A new card took shape. *I love watching you sleep... through the crack in your bedroom curtains.*

"Are you familiar with the term stalker?" she asked.

"Stalk. Noun. The stem of a herbaceous plant. To stalk. Verb. To pursue or approach stealthily. Therefore stalker must be...one who pursues stealthily."

Smart man. "One who pursues someone who doesn't want to be pursued."

A sharp inhalation. "I'm not stalking you."

"Whatever you have to tell yourself, buddy."

The ceremony continued for another half hour. Only one other woman appeared upset by the proceedings— the same one who'd been unwilling to blithely walk into the water.

She was a tiny thing and very pretty, with dark, curly hair, wide, dark eyes and a button nose. Of Spanish heritage, maybe. Despite her innocent, schoolgirl features, she radiated a wild sensuality that had intrigued many of the nymphos. They'd passed her over, however, because she'd trembled with fear rather than eagerness.

But pickings were becoming slim, and a tall warrior with beads in his sandy-colored hair eventually selected her. One of the men still waiting for his turn slammed his fist into the wall, the force of the blow reverberating through the entire room.

"Choose another. I want that one," he bellowed.

"Too bad for you, Joachim," was the smug reply. "She's mine now." Beaded Hair clasped the girl's hand and tugged her from the line.

Her tremors worsened, and she dragged her heels, but she never uttered a word in protest.

Obviously puzzled by her lack of enthusiasm, her would-be lover glanced over his shoulder and frowned. "Do not be afraid, little one. I won't hurt you."

She chewed on her bottom lip, tears in her eyes.

"Valerian," Shaye said, "you told me no one would be harmed. Well, she's being harmed. Stop him."

"Shivawn isn't striking her, and he won't. He'll feed and care for her. He'll—"

"Listen to me. She doesn't want food, and she certainly doesn't want to be alone with him." Unwilling to wait for Valerian's response, Shaye shouted, "Let her go! Now! You might have picked her, but she doesn't pick you."

Shivawn's frown deepened. "But... I'll be good to you."

Her frightened, watery gaze landed on Shaye, and she chewed on her bottom lip. Still she didn't speak a word.

"Valerian." Shaye latched on to his wrist and squeezed. "You have to do something about this. Please."

Seconds passed in absolute silence, everyone in the room waiting for the king's decree.

Shaye wrenched away from him to rush to the girl— who she then freed from Shivawn's grip. She stepped between the pair, her gaze searching for...she wasn't sure.

"I know you want to go home," she said. "I'll find a way, I swear it." *Will never give up.* "But until then, how do you want to handle this situation?"

Silence. The Spanish girl even looked away from her, as if she couldn't bear to be the object of anyone's scrutiny.

"Obviously she doesn't want anything to do with *you*, either." Shivawn clasped Shaye's wrist, clearly intending to move her out of the way.

Her self-defense training kicked in, and she pivoted, grabbing hold of *his* wrist and dropping to the floor, her weight and momentum dragging him down with her. Upon impact, she thrust out her legs, nailing him in the chest and causing him to flip over her head.

He remained on his back, staring up at the crystal ceiling. Held immobile by shock?

Other warriors gaped.

Valerian raced to her side to pull her to her feet. He focused on the other woman. "Do you wish to be chosen by another warrior? Do you wish to be given a room of your own? I'll ensure you are undisturbed."

Her eyes roved over the remaining, eager men. She shrank back, gulped, then slowly shook her head.

No to Shivawn? Or no to the room? Or both?

"You may take her to your chamber, Shivawn, but you are not to touch her tonight. If one of the humans I...met...yesterday is interested in...meeting you, you may...meet her in a guest room."

Why the hesitation? Did *met, meeting* and *meet* actually mean *screwed, screwing* and *screw*?

"Why don't you take her home instead?" Shaye asked as Shivawn stood.

"Do you wish to go home?" Valerian asked the other woman.

Again, the girl shrank back and shook her head no.

Shaye didn't understand. "Do you want to go with Shivawn?"

A nearly imperceptible nod, but a nod all the same.

She glared at Valerian. "Can Shivawn be trusted to obey your command?"

"All my men can be trusted to obey me. More than that, they aren't rapists." There was a good amount of affront in his tone. "Go," he told the couple.

Shivawn and the girl hurried out of the room.

The man who'd hit the wall punched the guy next to him.

"Happy?" Valerian asked as he escorted Shaye back to the line.

"No!"

Of course, the "selection" continued.

This time, none of the soldiers approached her. Perhaps because she'd proved too much trouble for zero reward.

The line dwindled significantly.

"It's almost over," Valerian whispered. His breath fanned her ear, and he trailed a fingertip along the bumps of her spine. A caress to arouse…or a gesture of comfort?

Did it matter? Either way, she almost slumped into a boneless heap. So good! Only the sudden, unexpected feeling of being watched strengthened her resolve to appear unaffected. Her eyes darted across the remaining men—and collided with hate.

Every fiber of her being recoiled.

"Lean on me if your feet hurt," Valerian said, mistaking her reaction.

"No, thank you." Leaning on another—relying on another—would never appeal to her. Even though the idea of being enveloped by his heat and strength actually did appeal to her.

In her experience, the moment she softened and allowed someone in, that someone would leave her, disappoint her or betray her.

"Joachim," Valerian called. "Your turn has arrived."

"That one." Joachim, as it turned out, was the man with hate in his eyes. "The pale one in your arms."

Valerian cursed, and Shaye gasped. She'd been so sure she'd scared everyone away. Now ice chilled every inch of her.

"What did you say?" Valerian wrapped his arms around her waist, holding her tightly, his fingers digging into her skin, probably bruising.

The shocking thing? She didn't want him to let go.

Joachim braced his legs apart, his expression stern and smug. He wasn't a man besotted or even consumed by lust. No, he looked ready for a fight. "Give her to me. She is mine."

CHAPTER SEVEN

"Valerian," Shaye said, her voice shaky. As shaky as her limbs. "I'm unwilling. I don't want him. If he tries to lead me away—"

"He won't. I'll take care of him. Worry not." All at once, Valerian was infuriated that someone would dare try to take Shaye from him, overjoyed that she felt safest with him and frightened that he might actually lose her.

And to his cousin, no less. The man would break her beautiful spirit.

He and Joachim had never enjoyed an easy camaraderie. Through no fault of his own. Over the years, Joachim's thirst for power had transformed him into a rebellious fool. He'd become far too wild to control.

How Valerian would change his mind, he didn't yet know.

The only question that mattered, he supposed, was how far was he willing to go.

Easy. To the death.

"There are two other females in line. They want you. This one doesn't."

Joachim never once glanced at the others. "Don't care. I've already chosen the pale one."

"Well, I haven't chosen *you*." Shaye pressed her soft body more firmly against Valerian. Her frosty scent enveloped him, fueling his determination.

"Challenge me." Valerian pinned his cousin with a hard stare. "I'll accept."

"And turn me into a prize?" she gasped. "No. Absolutely not."

Valerian ignored her. He had to. He knew the way of the nymphs; she didn't.

Joachim had issued challenges in the past. He longed to prove his strength. Valerian had always turned him down. Not because he'd feared losing. On the contrary. He'd known beyond any doubt that he would win, and his cousin would die.

Despite their acrimony, he had no desire to kill the male.

For a moment, an all-too-short flash of time, Joachim considered the offer. He even began to nod. Then he stopped himself. "Unacceptable. You had sex yesterday. You're strong. I've been neglected for weeks. We aren't on equal ground."

A muscle jumped in Valerian's jaw. Did his cousin hope for a night with Shaye, *then* a fight with the king? "I'll bargain with you as I bargained with Shivawn. If one of the humans in my chamber desires you, you may spend the night with her and rebuild your strength. On the morrow, we will fight for Shaye."

Shaye...who uttered another round of protests.

Joachim's black brows arched, and something—an unreadable emotion—brightened his blue eyes. "You said you wouldn't claim another surface woman, yet there you stand, attempting to do just that."

"Do you accept my offer or not?"

Lips curling in a cold smile, Joachim pointed to Shaye. "I do not. I want that one. As is my right."

"You have *zero* right to me." Shaye shook a fist in his direction. "Cart me away. Go ahead. I dare you.

While you sleep, I'll cut off your balls and use them for earrings."

Inventive. At least she'd only wanted to cut out Valerian's *eyes*.

"Females are precious to us, necessary for our survival," he told his cousin. "We do them no harm. Ever. You would have to hurt her to have her."

Joachim swallowed. "I'll woo her."

So confident—for no reason!

Am I this foolish, thinking I can win the moonbeam?

"Joachim—" he began.

"No!" the male shouted. "I'll take what's owed to me."

"So you'll accept your ball-less life, then?" Shaye asked, her tone casual. "Because *that* is all you're owed from me."

Valerian admired her spirit even as frustration and fury flooded him. His cousin wouldn't relent, and Valerian wouldn't go back on his word.

Would he? For Shaye...

He'd taken over the army as a young lad, after his father had died in battle. Over and over again, he'd had to prove himself worthy of the honor.

Esteem your men, and they'll esteem you. His father's dying words.

If Valerian took Shaye, no one would naysay him—but no one would respect him, either.

And how could he expect her to fall in love with such a dishonorable man?

"I said I wouldn't claim the female, and I won't." The announcement pained him. "Yet."

Shaye closed her hands over his arms—arms still wrapped around her—and dug her fingernails into his skin to hold him in place or punish him, he wasn't sure.

He switched to his native tongue and added, "Not without reaching amicable terms. Allow me to buy her from you."

Once more, Joachim shook his head. "No."

"What can I do, cousin? The woman—" he stopped, pressed his lips together "—she is my mate."

Joachim's grin returned, colder than before. "She doesn't agree. She clearly hasn't accepted you as such."

"She will." Believing otherwise would destroy him. "If you take her, she'll hate you." They both knew the ways of nymphs and their mates. The bond was inescapable. "You might seduce her, but you'll never win her. She'll wish she were with me. Can your pride withstand such a horror?"

His cousin clenched and unclenched his fists.

"What did you say to him?" Shaye looked between them. "Tell me."

Joachim's gaze remained narrowed on Valerian. "I must think on what you've said. Let us both stay away from her this night and discuss her ownership in the morning."

Since he'd spoken in the surface language, Shaye understood. "Ownership?" she said between gritted teeth.

Stay away from her for an entire night? Valerian's body recoiled in horror. *Need her in my arms, now and always!*

No other way. "I'm in...agreement."

"Well, I'm *not* in agreement." Shaye stomped her foot, determined to be acknowledged. "Let me save you both a lot of trouble. I don't want either of you. Now, I'm a reasonable—"

Valerian snorted.

"—woman," she finished, glaring at him over her shoulder. "And I'm willing to forget this entire episode of *The Male Whores of Atlantis* ever happened. All you have to do is take me home."

Ignoring her, Joachim crossed his arms over his chest. "Where will she stay tonight?"

Where she will stay every night. "My chamber," he answered in their language. "We'll both guard the door."

His cousin paused for a moment, running the idea through his mind. Finally he nodded. "Very well."

Valerian released Shaye from his embrace and instantly mourned the loss of her softness and heat. She must have felt the same sense of loss, whether she would admit it or not, because she laced her arms over her middle and shivered.

"I love being disregarded, I really do." She drummed her fingers against her sides. "So who's taking me home?"

"I am," Valerian answered before Joachim could respond. "When the ceremony concludes, I'm taking you home."

With a startled gasp, she faced him. "Really? Seriously? Today's ceremony, not some ceremony a few years from now?"

He drank her in, struck anew by the beauty of her. How could one woman make him ache so intensely? Make him forget everyone who'd come before her until only she existed?

"Yes." Reaching out, he offered her a callused hand.

Suspicion suddenly darkened her features, but not even that detracted from her beauty. "Is this a trick?"

He knew she'd misunderstood his intentions; *this* was her new home. But he said nothing. Not yet.

"What makes you think I have a sense of humor?" he asked.

A smile bloomed, stealing the breath from his lungs.

Want to see that smile everyday—every hour!

"Thank you." Tentative, she placed her palm against his.

Joachim offered *his* hand to her.

Seconds ticked by, every muscle in Valerian's body knotting. If she took Joachim's hand, simply to punish Valerian, she would encourage his cousin's attentions and disprove the validity of Valerian's declaration.

One heartbeat passed. Then another.

She kept her free hand at her side.

Triumph flared deep in his chest.

Valerian called to one of the remaining men. "You're next."

That man selected his prize quickly, leaving a single female in line.

Valerian called another name. The nymph cheered, taking the hand of the remaining female, while the other nymphs hissed with disappointment.

"Aeson," Valerian said to one of the disappointed. "Prepare my chamber for Shaye." Hopefully the loyal man would know what he truly desired—the removal of all traces of the human women he'd pleasured last eve.

The warrior nodded and rushed to obey.

"The rest of you are dismissed for the night," he said. "Sneak into town, if you wish, but stay aware. Trust no one at your back."

Off they went.

"This way." He led Shaye out of the dining hall.

A few of the warriors, he noticed, hadn't made it to their rooms. Couples were having sex right there in the hallways, leaning against the walls.

Moans, purrs and groans of delight echoed.

"My eyes," Shaye gasped out. "My poor eyes."

In a nymph household, such a sight was common. But he kept that fact to himself.

With her close on his heels, and Joachim close on hers, he ushered her past the kitchens, the training arena and the warriors' barracks—where more moans and purrs abounded.

"Do they ever stop?" She'd probably hoped to sound exasperated. Instead she'd sounded breathless.

Primal excitement brewed within him. If she were his, he would have explored the reasons for her reaction. Namely—did she want Valerian to take *her* against a wall?

Soon, he vowed. Very soon.

His personal suite occupied the opposite end of the palace. An area he'd chosen for the large bathing pool and panoramic wall of windows that offered a breathtaking view of the Outer City below.

What would Shaye think of the luxuries?

Did she like antiques or modern furnishings? Bright colors or pastels? Did she prefer warmth to cold?

She was right; he didn't know her well. But he wanted so badly to learn.

"Thank you for agreeing to take me back," Shaye said. "I know you don't want to, and I'm truly grateful."

He'd never heard such a gentle, tender tone from her. She even wore an expression of gratitude, the sweetness of it softening her features and gifting her with bright radiance.

He couldn't allow her to entertain the false assumption any longer. "I'm not taking you back to your world, Moon. I'm taking you to your new home."

She jolted, her nails digging into his flesh. "You knew what I thought but didn't correct me."

"I did correct you. Now."

"Yes, you're practically a Boy Scout. If this is how you think to win my affections, well, good luck," she spit at him. "You and Joachim should consider dating. You're perfect for each other."

"Does she always speak this way?" Joachim asked, expressing his first doubt about his selection.

"Always," Valerian and Shaye snapped in unison.

"By the way. I'm not staying anywhere near your room," she informed Valerian. "I'd rather return to the sea and drown."

"That isn't an option for you." He had to drag her—gently, of course—the rest of the way.

Joachim watched the interaction with an unreadable countenance.

Finally they reached the outskirts of Valerian's suite.

Aeson exited the main doorway, his face flushed with pleasure.

Having caught his scent, the three humans chased after him. Soon, they trapped him in a circle.

"Be with me."

"No, me."

"I *neeeed* you."

Then, "Valerian! You came back for me."

All three swung around to beckon him over.

Mated nymphs didn't usually attract females with the same potency and fervor as unmated ones. Still. He pulled Shaye in front of him, using her as a shield.

"Take one and go, Aeson."

"You're taking me." The black beauty stepped forward and clasped Aeson's hand.

He gazed at her with adoration as he led her from the room.

The other two females pouted.

Shaye *humphed*. "So. You're a pimp as well as king."

He ignored her and waved in his cousin's direction. "Joachim is in need of a lover. Any interest?"

Both women sashayed to him without question.

"You're so big," the darker skin woman cooed.

"And strong," added the delightfully plump redhead.

Joachim backed away, determined to resist. "I've already made my choice?" he said, the words a question rather than a statement. "The...the pale one is to be mine, and I must guard her door this night. For that reason, you...cannot...touch...me. *Touch me*." The last was an unrestrained moan of helpless capitulation.

They'd reached him, their hands already stroking him.

Valerian almost grinned. "Shaye won't mind if you forgo standing guard at her door this night. A man has needs, and she understands." Or rather, he *prayed* she understood.

"Needs," the lost-in-a-passion-haze warrior repeated.

"I need your naked skin sliding against mine," the redhead said, breathless.

"I need you, hot in my mouth."

Joachim audibly swallowed. "Valerian," he began, a tremor in his tone.

Shouldn't smile. "Go. I'll see you in the morning."

"The pale one—"

"Will remain untouched." Tonight. Only tonight. "I've given you my word, and I'll keep it." Even if Shaye begged him for more.

The thought caused him to harden painfully. *He wanted her to beg*.

The redhead shoved her friend and jumped into Joachim's arms. "I'll make you forget her."

"I trust you, cousin." Joachim strode away then, and the woman clung to him.

"Wait," Valerian called. "Take the other to Shivawn. If you'd like a man of your own?" he asked her.

She brightened. "Yes, please."

Joachim held out his hand, and the other woman eagerly rushed over to claim it.

The trio disappeared beyond the corner.

Valerian allowed his grin to peek through. He had Shaye to himself, Joachim otherwise occupied.

"Unbelievable," Shaye muttered.

He gripped her shoulders to twist her around. "Just what do you find so unbelievable?"

"The amount of communal sex to be had, of course. Haven't you people heard of STDs?" Her pique painted her cheeks a soft shade of rose. As if the moon would soon vanish in place of the sun.

Lust *boiled* in his blood. He'd touched the softness of her skin today, but he had yet to taste her. He'd held her, but he had yet to make love to her. He wanted to strip her. To sink deep inside her. To pound, hard and fast, pleasuring her with long, demanding strokes.

She looked at him, as if she herself had just realized they were finally alone, and her nostrils flared. With desire?

He fisted his hands at his sides to keep himself from reaching out again.

"Listen to me very closely." The words were nothing more than a growl of barely restrained need. "I want you, but I can't have you. If you don't lock yourself inside the suite right now, I'm going to forget my vow to leave you untouched and use every weapon in my sensual arsenal to tempt you."

Her eyes widened, the rich velvet-brown flicking with sparks of arousal. Her breath caught, and she inched away from him.

"If you exit the suite," he added, "I'll view it as an invitation to begin your seduction."

She spun on her heel and sprinted past the door. *Click.*

For a long while, Valerian stood in place, desperate to follow her, willing the door to open.

When his blood cooled, he scrubbed his face with a shaky hand. Having a mate was going to be murder on his body, it seemed, for he foresaw a long, painful night ahead—with no real end in sight.

CHAPTER EIGHT

SHAYE'S HEART THUNDERED in her chest, pounding so hard she feared her ribs would crack; her ears rang loudly, and she covered them with her hands to block out the awful sound. She sank onto the edge of a decadent made-for-sex bed with red silk sheets and a velvet comforter.

Not daring to breathe, she stared at the door.

She remained in that exact position for over an hour, *anticipatory*. Part of her wanted Valerian to storm inside the room to begin seducing her.

Begin. As if he hadn't already.

Before she'd left him, his gaze had scorched her. If she'd remained with him, that heat would have burned her alive.

A new card idea had taken root. *We should probably have sex before we rush into dating.*

She gulped. If any man could tempt her...

No! She wouldn't be a fool for lust or love or whatever the heck he wanted to call...whatever the heck was going on between them, accepting whatever crap he happened to dish.

She rested her head against the bedpost, which was intricately carved with—what else?—naked females.

So far Valerian had proved to be a man of his word—which meant he would remain guard just outside the door all freaking night.

He would *always* tell her the truth, huh?

"This is your personal love shack, right? And those three women, you bagged and tagged them?" she called.

A pause. She expected the silence to continue.

Then he said, "Yes."

Well, well. The truth, even when it hurt. A rarity. A trait she admired greatly and had always hoped to find in someone else.

Maybe I should stay with him? Just for a little while.

Okay, wow. Part of her had to be looking for *any* reason to stay. Which was the very reason she had to escape *tonight*. No way she should stick around until morning, when he and the other warrior, Joachim, would fight for ownership of her, as if she were property.

"I'm not a trophy," she muttered. "I'm not a prize for Valerian and his sex squad to battle to the death over."

"Yes, Moon, you are."

The huskiness of his voice gave her a jolt of pure pleasure, making her heart skip a beat and heat coast over her skin.

Trembling now, she jumped to her feet and traversed one of the bridges, careful to avoid the pits. She paced. A large, sunken tub had been filled with bubbling water. Or the water never drained. Tendrils of steam curled to the vaulted crystal ceiling, which showcased the now turbulent ocean above. Waves churned and swirled, leaving wisps of foam behind, no horny mermaids in sight.

Maybe...maybe a night with Valerian could go on her bucket list?

What! *What are you doing? Stop! Escape!*

Right. She traced a fingertip over the vanity. The rings in the wood actually warmed to her touch, a slight vibration rising up her arm.

An eerie voice suddenly whispered through her mind. *Love heals; it doesn't hurt. Love is the answer, not the problem...*

With a gasp, she yanked her arm away, severing contact. What. The. Heck?

"You mentioned...*lovers*." Valerian spoke up again, his tone dripping with irritation. "Are they the reason you want to return home?"

Ugh. She'd yelled at him for misleading her, but she'd done the same to him. "I have a business. I have dreams."

"What's your business?"

Genuine interest? "I sell anti-cards." Did Atlanteans celebrate holidays?

"Or, more accurately, I sell sarcasm to people who have stopped romanticizing life."

A pause, as if he needed a moment to store every bit of info about her. "Give me an example of an anti-card."

She thought for a moment. "Congratulations on your new job. Before you go, would you mind taking the knife out of my back? You'll probably need it again."

He chuckled, surprising her, delighting her—arousing her. Which was so freaking frustrating!

"Now tell me about your dreams," he said.

A safe topic. One she embraced. "Well, while I was busy drowning, I admitted I'd like to write a book."

A soft growl. "You were never in danger of drowning. And you can write a book here."

"I have a feeling *just do it here* will be your answer to everything," she told him dryly.

"Yes, I'm very wise."

She had to cut off a laugh.

Twice, she realized. Twice he'd amused her—the moody, broody cold fish—in a way no one else ever had.

"I notice you mention nothing of your family," he said, his tone now careful. "Not your mother and her new husband. Not your father."

"We've never been close," she admitted.

Love heals; it doesn't hurt.

Argh! Those words!

"Their loss," he said.

Love is the answer, not the problem.

"I…thank you?"

Another pause stretched between them. "I'll be your family," he said, and she could picture him banging his chest with his fists. "It will be my honor and my privilege."

She rolled her eyes. "See! Told you *just do it here* would be your answer to everything."

Let's say she agreed to date Valerian. Would she ever be able to trust him? Was he capable of being faithful?

Shaye despised sharing. She'd shared her parents with their ever-changing lovers. She'd shared her childhood and her toys with stepsisters and stepbrothers.

If ever she gave herself to someone, it would be to a man who wanted her and only her. A man willing to give up his life just to make her happy. And she, in turn, would do the same for him.

Was she asking and offering too much? Maybe. But it was what she wanted, and she wouldn't settle for less—even though she knew it was an impossibility. Perhaps that was why she wanted it in the first place. If she couldn't really have it, she never had to worry about heartbreak.

Valerian talked a good talk, and granted, he could probably walk a delectable, mind-shattering walk all over her body, but how long would his affections last?

"As my queen," he said, "you'll be wealthy beyond imagining."

"So. You think you can buy me?"

"I *wish* I could buy you," he grumbled.

She wanted to laugh again. *What is* wrong *with me?*

She valued her independence and being with a nymph—*the* nymph, actually—would strip that independence away layer by precious layer. How many times had she seen her father's girlfriends change their personality to fit him? Countless! Shaye refused, absolutely refused, to allow the same fate to befall her.

And yet, she told Valerian, "As long as I'm a prisoner, you won't be a viable date for me." As if there could ever be hope for more.

"No. I refuse to believe that. One day you'll forgive me. And our children will love the story of our meeting."

She nearly choked on her tongue. Children?

"Tell me a secret," he said. To distract her?

Her shock must have loosened her tongue, because she admitted, "I like the color pink. Which is borderline humiliating! Pink equals girlie. A frilly princess."

"And you don't want to be a girlie princess because…"

"I'm tough, as hard as nails?" A question? Really? She hurried to remove the focus from her. "What about you? Tell me a secret."

"One moment, Shaye," he said, then muttered something she couldn't discern.

Her brow furrowed with confusion until a male replied, "Yes, Majesty." Footsteps rang out.

"All right. We're alone again," he told her.

Her first thought? *Good! He's mine, all mine.*

I need help.

"As a boy," he said, "I liked to nap in fields of lavender."

"Because being so beautiful was exhausting?"

"You think I'm beautiful?" How happy he sounded.

"You know you are."

"More beautiful than Joachim?"

Not going to travel that road. "Good night, Valerian."

He sighed. "Sleep well, Shaye. I'll protect you."

In that, she believed him. An odd but undeniable fact.

She searched the rest of the room but found no other doorway. Disheartened—yes, that had to be it—she dug through the closet. A few feminine garments were mixed in with the array of masculine shirts and leathers. From past lovers?

Probably. Not that she cared.

Really!

Almost defiantly, Shaye selected a black T-shirt and a pair of pants she had to roll at the ankles. More comfortable, she moved to the window and parted the violet curtains.

Her eyes widened. Oh, wow. Thick, dew-kissed trees—some as bright as emeralds, others as white as snow—circled the landscape. Clear waterfalls spilled into pristine rivers while rainbow-colored birds soared overhead.

Absolutely magnificent.

In the heart of it all was a crowded city pulsing with life. Buildings of stone and wood created a maze of winding streets. Fading streaks of light emanated from the dome above, twilight giving way to night.

The crystal dome also acted as the sun, she realized.

She would have loved to visit the city, to stand in the midst of such spectacular beauty and bask.

"This has to be close to heaven," she breathed.

"We call it the Outer City," Valerian replied.

"A boring name for a specular paradise." Her gaze swept over the cliffs; she spotted bull-faced men with horns sprouting from their heads, beautiful women with horse bodies—centaurs?—and lions with wings.

"There was no need to travel to my world, Valerian," she said. "Your perfect mate was here all along."

"Only you would do, Moon."

Her stomach tightened. "Annnd that's the end of our conversation." Shaky legs returned her to the bed, where she eased onto the mattress.

"I'd like to bargain with you," Valerian said. "Let's negotiate."

Her brand-new heart arrhythmia acted up again. "What are you offering, exactly?"

"I'll be silent for the rest of the night…if you give me a compliment. A real one."

Dangerous territory. She would have to consider all the wonderful things about him and most assuredly, she'd begin to melt. Diabolical man.

If she were home, she would be alone right now. *And lonely*, her mind piped up.

Lonely was safe. Lonely was familiar.

A hot ache squeezed at her chest.

"Why are you doing this to me, Valerian? You could have any of the other women. Someone who would eagerly come to you…who would do anything you asked of them."

"They aren't you."

A simple sentence, yes, but it rocked her to the core. "What's so special about me? I defy you to name one thing."

Silence stretched between them, and it both elated and defeated her.

How stupid could I be? She'd actually craved praise from him. "You seriously need this much time to think about it?"

"You asked for *one thing*. I'm having trouble deciding which one to mention."

Her anger deflated. This man...oh, this man.

"How about I tell you three things?" he asked.

"Sure," she managed to croak.

"Your scent is so incredibly sweet, I could pick you out of a crowd of thousands, even if I were blindfolded. You remind me of a rose—there are thorns, but beneath them, your soul is as soft as silk. You fascinate me. You are brave, but vulnerable. Kind but selective. Jaded yet hopeful."

She reeled. No one—not her mother, father, stepbrothers or stepsisters, or an endless string of nannies—had ever made her feel so important, so *necessary*, with only a few softly spoken words.

She barely knew Valerian. In their short time together, she'd railed at him, desired him, cursed him and attacked him. Now she wanted to storm out of the bedroom and throw herself into his arms. To be the brave girl he considered her to be, to destroy every wall she'd ever built and melt every piece of ice surrounding her heart.

This. This was the danger of the nymph, she realized. Not the beauty or the physical strength. Not even the pheromone Valerian had mentioned.

This. The belief that you were special. That you would be different from every other woman seduced and discarded. That a happily-ever-after wasn't just possible but imminent.

How was she supposed to resist him?

CHAPTER NINE

VALERIAN SPENT THE entire night posted in front of Shaye's door, hyperaware of every move and sound she made. Only a few minutes ago, she'd drifted to sleep with a heavy sigh. A quick peek inside the room had confirmed his suspicions, her lithe form sprawled across the bed, her hair spilling around her like a snowy curtain sprinkled with starlight.

She was a winter goddess. A snow nymph. His greatest satisfaction and most decadent pleasure.

Ripe for the taking...

Her eyelashes were light, only a shade darker than her hair. Her lips, those soft, lush, all-your-dreams-come-true lips were parted, begging to be kissed.

He wanted so badly to touch her.

"I'll have you yet," he told her. "Say nothing if you agree with me."

Silence greeted him, and he grinned.

"Dream of me, Moon. I'll dream of you, I have no doubt." If he slept at all.

The pink tip of her tongue swept over her lips. A wave of desire swept through him as he imagined meeting her tongue with his own. The two twining, dueling, tasting.

Devouring.

His stomach clenched, and every muscle in his body turned to stone. He needed to leave...at the very least, to look away from her. Already he clung precariously to a sense of honor he wasn't sure he possessed anymore. The longer he stood there, the worse it would be for him.

How he longed for the night she would breathe her sighs in his ears, or across his chest—or lower still. And how dare Joachim attempt to lay claim to her!

Valerian scowled. Shaye was meant for him, and only him, and those who thought otherwise deserved a painful death.

He'd never wanted anything as much as he wanted her, and not being able to have her immediately was... hard. Very, very hard.

I have to win her. I cannot let another have her.

Perhaps his cousin would become so enamored of his current lover he would forgot all about Shaye. If not... well, Valerian would just have to think of something Joachim would find irresistible. Something he would place above the importance of a bedmate.

Joachim was a good man—at times—and a strong warrior with a—slightly—loyal heart. What were the man's weaknesses? Women? Beyond a doubt. Women were the weakness of all nymphs. Power? Definitely. Weapons? Most surely. Joachim collected them, taking them from every warrior he'd ever killed or bested and hanging them on his bedchamber wall.

Valerian considered his own blade, resting against his back. The Skull. Large, sharp and lethal. One of the finest swords ever made. No, *the* finest ever made. Crafted by Hephaesteus himself, the blacksmith of the Greeks. The weapon had slayed many of his enemies, rending them with injuries that could not be mended. The sword was the only one of its kind, with a twisted frame and elongated skull tip that were envied by every soldier who spied it.

He would hate to give it up, but his mate held so

much more importance to him. Even a mate who wanted nothing to do with him.

Would Joachim accept the Skull?

Valerian released a sigh of his own, the answer remaining a mystery—as much a mystery as the best way to win Shaye's well-guarded heart.

She'd scoffed at money and jewels. She'd shown no interest in his crown.

Did she have enemies in need of slaying? If so, he would gladly gift her with their severed heads.

He pushed a hand through his hair. Uncertainty was foreign to him. And horrible and challenging but also exciting.

Winning her—appeasing Joachim and overcoming Shaye's own resistance—had awakened his deepest warrior instincts.

"You will be mine," he told her. "Somehow."

"Majesty?"

He closed the door with a quiet *snick* and focused on the warrior who'd returned at last, bearing the supplies Valerian had requested. A canvas, an easel and three colors of paint. Black, white and red.

He dismissed the warrior and carefully placed the canvas on the easel. He spent hours painting, losing himself in the joy of creating. The subject of his art had never appealed to him more. Had never *mattered* to him more.

When he finished, he stood back to study the image and ensure he'd gotten every detail right. His chest swelled with pride. He had. Oh, he had.

Let Shaye try to resist him now…

THREADS OF LIGHT flowed from the crystal dome above, gradually brightening the bedroom. Different-colored shards shot in every direction, a lovely rainbow spray of blue, pink, purple and green.

Shaye eased up, surprisingly relaxed. She yawned and rubbed the sleep from her eyes before scanning the room, hoping an exit would reveal itself in the bright light of day. The bathing pool still steamed and bubbled with hot water. Violet cloth still draped the windows. Columns still rose to the ceiling, majestic and—

She gasped. A painting had been hung on the wall, beside the vanity. A painting that hadn't been there last night.

It was a painting of *her*. A close-up of her face. In black and white, with only spots of color. Twin pink circles highlighted her cheeks while her lips were dark red.

Her eyes somehow sparkled with mischief, her eyelids at half-mast, heavy and slumberous; she looked ready and eager for a man. But not just any man...

Her lips were slightly kiss-swollen, a smile threatening to break free.

Valerian must have spent the entire night working on it.

Is this how he sees me?

Her mind rebelled. She wasn't mischievous, and she rarely smiled. He must have painted his desires—the way he wanted her to be.

Disappointment delivered a one-two punch to her midsection.

Can't you be nice for once, Shaye?

Why can't you be more like your stepsister, Shaye?

What will it take to get rid of your perma-scowl, Shaye?

Mumbling under her breath, she lumbered from the bed and crossed the bridge, avoiding the surrounding pits. Why did Valerian have those death traps in here, anyway?

Wait. The palace—fortress, whatever—used to belong to the dragons, he'd said. They must have used those pits to fly in and out of the room.

And how scary that she had begun to think like an Atlantean, considering the different races as part of everyday life.

Anyway. Maybe she could climb down? Or scale down with a sheet, since she didn't have a ladder.

Yeah, and she could also fall to her death.

So. No scaling.

Shaye used the surprisingly modern bathroom to brush her teeth and wash up, hoping the water would also wash away her darker emotions. A pipe dream.

She wanted to go home, and she wanted to go home now. Nothing and no one confused her there. Nothing and no one made her wish for more, for better.

Her employees were probably missing her. Or had they not yet noticed her absence? She was always the first one there and the last to leave, her time spent locked inside her office.

Whatever. If she wanted to leave, she'd have to walk out the front door. And what better time? Valerian could be sleeping.

Unbidden, his image rose front and center in her mind. He was so strong, so proud. So danged sexual. A hedonist to the extreme, with skin that looked like dark, lickable cream, hair as radiant as spun gold, and eyes...oh, his eyes. Those turquoise irises beckoned. They teased. They *promised.* His long, dark lashes acted as the perfect frame, the perfect contrast.

Stalling?

As quietly as possible, she tiptoed toward the door. The closer she was, the stronger Valerian's masculine scent became, a heady mixture of aroused man and determined warrior. Her skin prickled with heat. She tried to hold her nose, to fight the scent's allure and the weakening effect it had on her.

Her heart drummed a staccato rhythm—*da-dum da-dum dadada-dum*—as she clasped the knob and twisted. Would Valerian be out there, awake and waiting?

"Good morning, Shaye."

His husky voice jolted her, and as she flattened a hand over her throat, she belted out, "Crap!"

He stood just in front of her, his muscled arms crossed over his massive chest, his legs braced apart. Their gazes clashed, her treacherous heart losing track of its rhythm and skipping a beat.

He looked even more unbelievably mouthwatering than before.

Golden hair tumbled onto his forehead and shoulders. He was still shirtless, his body roped with the tightest abs she'd ever seen. A leather band wrapped around him, holding a sword against his back.

Trembling now, she licked her lips. "What are you doing here?"

His gaze raked over her, and she suspected he had just peeled away her clothing. "Waiting for you, of course. You are gorgeous."

She shifted from one foot to the other. His voice had dipped as he'd uttered the compliment. A take-no-prisoners timbre. Pure temptation and utter decadence.

He's a lecherous abductor. Dangerous in every way.

Right. She mentally reinforced the icy walls around her heart.

"Did you like your painting?" he asked.

A shiver tripped along her spine. "Yes. No."

He arched a sandy brow. "No?"

"Honestly? I both love and hate it. You painted an almost-smile on my face."

"A look you tried to hide from me but couldn't."

He *had* amused her on several occasions. But...

He was *that* aware of her?

Dang him. He was seducing her again, and he wasn't even trying!

It wasn't fair. He had experience. She didn't. But just as he was learning about her, she was learning about him. He wasn't needlessly cruel or even merciless. He clearly loved and respected his men and wanted the very best for them.

"Be honest," she said. "If we got married and had a daughter—" *ovaries threatening to exploded again* "—what would you do if some man came along and kidnapped her?"

Tension radiated from him. He raised his chin. "I would kill the bastard."

A pang of envy—all for a make-believe daughter! Her own father would be too afraid of someone like Valerian to act against him.

"You would kill someone for doing exactly as you've done," she said softly.

A muscle ticked beneath his eye. "I will die without you, Shaye. You would sentence *me* to death?"

He didn't mean he would literally die. No way, no how. "You're describing love at first sight. Which I don't believe is possible."

"No, I'm describing mate at first sight."

"What's the difference?"

"Everything and nothing," he replied cryptically. He waved a hand through the air, a regal command to move on to the next topic. "Did you dream of me?"

She allowed the subject change because she'd made her point and given him something to consider.

"Yes," she admitted grudgingly. She had. She'd dreamed of his hands on her body, caressing her...of his mouth doing delicious things.

His lush lips inched into a surprised but pleased smile. "Tell me. Every detail."

"You were naked," she told him.

His grin spread, and his eyes gleamed with satisfaction.

"And you were tied up…"

He appeared *intrigued.* "I had no idea bondage would excite you."

"Oh, I adore the idea of tying you up." She paused dramatically, and just like the Shaye in the painting, she fought a grin of her own. Maybe he knew her better than she'd given him credit for, after all. "You were secured to an anthill, being eaten alive."

He barked out a charming laugh. "Such a cruel woman, my Shaye."

His Shaye. Tremors nearly toppled her, her good humor vanishing in an instant…replaced by stunning desire.

He propped his shoulder against the side wall, a pose of carnal relaxation. *Fall into my arms,* his posture proclaimed. *I'll catch you.*

"I dreamed of you, too," he said.

Shivers cascaded through her. "Do tell."

"You were naked, as well."

Suddenly light-headed, she backed up a step. "Is it too much to hope I was tied to an anthill?"

"Yes." He stepped toward her, intent and intense. "You were splayed on my dinner table, ready to quench my hunger." His eyes were heavy-lidded, deliciously wicked. "I *devoured* you."

Breathe; she had to breathe. The oxygen she did manage to draw in burned her throat, singed her lungs. As he'd spoken, his words had painted a picture in her mind. A terribly beautiful picture as vivid as the one he'd painted on the canvas.

His tongue...on her...*in* her...

"Come," he said, extending his hand. "I'll feed *your* hunger."

Yes, oh, yes. *I want him.*

No! She batted at his wrist. "I'd rather starve than feast on your body."

"I wasn't planning to feed you from my body...yet."

Oh. Disappointment—

Did not bloom. Nope. Not even a tiny spark.

"What about the warrior?" she asked. "Joachim?"

The muscle began to jump under his eye again. "I'll deal with him when he awakens. Until then, you need sustenance if you're to keep up your strength."

Well. Maybe if she starved herself, he'd take her home? "No, thank you. I'm good."

His eyes narrowed. "We could bargain," he cajoled.

What was with the man and his bargaining? "I eat and you'll...what?"

"Kiss you anywhere you'd like."

Save me.

She had to force her mind to blank. "Um, you really need to work on your bargaining skills. They suck." Had her voice shaken?

"I understand." His eyes twinkled down at her. "You would rather I offer you an orgasm."

"What!" Her cheeks fused with heat, and a tremor stole over her. "No!"

"You're sure?"

"Yes?" Her cheeks burned hotter. "Yes. Very."

"Too bad." Valerian took another step toward her, his masculine scent wafting to her, filling her nostrils.

Strong and spicy—so arousing her tee abraded her nipples and an ache throbbed between her legs.

She'd never been a sexual creature, and these new sensations rocked her to the core. How long could she fight them? How long could she resist this man?

"What thoughts are rolling through your head, hmm?" he asked, his voice huskier than before.

Did he know she was aroused? No, no. He couldn't. *Please!*

"I was—" What? She wouldn't admit the truth, but she wouldn't lie, either. "You're right. I'm hungry."

For several seconds he remained quiet. She used the time to cool her molten desires, reciting math equations in her mind.

Men = Heartbreak × Wasted Time.

Of course: Heartbreak = Wasted Time.

So: Men = Heartbreak × (Heartbreak) = Relationship.

Therefore: Relationship = Pain + Suffering.

Conclusion? Men = Pain + Suffering.

"Come, Moon." Once again, he extended his hand. "I will feed you."

"Food?" she asked, just to be certain.

"Food."

Very well. She placed her hand in his. Such heat! Such strength! His calluses *delighted* her.

Contact had been a mistake. A big—really big—mistake. But she didn't pull away. He brought her knuckles to his mouth to kiss…to lick and taste, and she shivered.

"Valerian."

"Shaye." He smiled at her, a slice of heaven in a life that had been hell.

To distract herself, she drafted a new card. *Roses are red, Valerian is sex. This poem makes no sense. Trouble.*

CHAPTER TEN

JOACHIM LAY IN HIS BED, his arms propped under his head. He stared up at the glistening ceiling, wishing he could take comfort in something, anything. Or someone. Would he even recognize comfort nowadays?

Night had long since passed, and morning had arrived. He shifted and eyed the wall of weapons he'd acquired over the years. A weapon for every man, woman or creature he'd slain. Their numbers were so vast, he'd stopped keeping count.

He wasn't ashamed of his violent past. Far from it. He reveled in his victories. The bloodier the better.

He was a man without honor, compassion, or mercy. *A mistake*, his mother had once said. *The true nymph king*, his father had then retorted.

So. Joachim's behavior with the redhead had *shredded* his pride.

After leaving his cousin and the pale-haired female, Joachim had brought the lushly rounded redhead to his chamber. He'd been poised to enter her—ready to burst. She'd been writhing in passion, opening herself wider, pleading for more.

So of course he'd stopped. Just stopped! Like a trembling lad about to claim his first female, afraid of blowing his load before he was able to sheathe himself completely.

As he had peered down at her, the sense of all-consuming need had abandoned him, there one moment, gone the next. An image of the dark-headed witch he'd wanted so badly at the selection ceremony had flashed through his mind.

He yearned to tangle his fingers in her curls, to put his mouth on her ripe little body—to roll *her* body under his. Hers, and only hers.

Craving a specific female was new to him.

Next he'd pictured the little witch in Shivawn's arms, moaning, mindless with pleasure, and a terrible rage had blackened his mood.

Your mood is always *black.*

True. But never to such a terrible degree.

Joachim's bed partner had tried her best to reignite his passions, but she'd failed miserably. He should have given her an orgasm anyway. He might have strengthened, at least a little bit.

Instead, he'd sent her away to find another lover.

Fool! He was as weak as before. But at least Valerian, too, was weakened this day, having gone without a woman's touch—his mate's touch. *If* his claims were to be believed.

Mate. How Joachim longed to find his own mate; that one woman who would love him above all others.

He sighed. He didn't want to take the pale woman from Valerian. She didn't excite him. Not like the dark-headed witch, with her lush curves.

What was her name? She hadn't said. Hadn't spoken at all. He wondered what her voice would be like. Low and husky? Sweet and soft?

If he'd had the opportunity to choose her, the night would have ended differently. Now Shivawn would pay for taking her, forcing Joachim to push Valerian into issuing a challenge before the appointed time.

Do nothing until you're ready, his father had told him. *Until you're absolutely certain you'll win.*

Joachim liked and admired his cousin, but he liked and admired power more.

He'd never enjoyed being told what to do. He preferred to give the orders, forcing others to do *his* bidding. Even his women. He was master. He was commander.

Never bend, never break.

His cousin ruled with an iron fist, expecting total and complete obedience, even from family.

Perhaps the appointed time had arrived. Joachim had an opportunity to take the crown at long last.

Valerian had offered to fight him, true, but Joachim wouldn't become king if—when—he won. And he *would* win. His cousin's honor would prevent him from doing the dirty deeds, the things that needed to be done. Like kicking a man while he was down.

My specialty.

No, Valerian had to willingly *agree* to surrender his throne. Would he?

His cousin had spent an entire night considering his limited options. Surely he'd realized there was only one way to keep the pale woman.

"I will be king," Joachim snarled.

Some men were meant for greatness. Some were not. Valerian had made many foolish mistakes lately.

The first: he'd left the nymph females behind to lay siege to this palace, citing their safety mattered more than the strength of the army.

Nothing mattered more than the strength of an army!

The women were now lost, probably captured, with no trace of them in either the Inner or Outer City.

Yes, Valerian had a contingent of men searching. But

that wasn't enough. The women wouldn't need finding if the king had brought them along.

The second mistake: Valerian had slept with the three humans who'd exited the portal, thinking of his own needs rather than the needs of his men.

I would have thought of the men.

A lie.

A lie he embraced, using it to fuel his ire.

Everything fueled his ire this day.

The pale woman was a means to an end. He'd seen the way Valerian hovered over her, protecting her, silently willing the other warriors away from her. The only reason Joachim had chosen her—he'd hoped his cousin would do *anything* to keep her.

He would find out if his hope had paid off.

And perhaps, when he became sovereign, he would simply take the dark-haired witch from Shivawn.

He grinned at the thought.

Oh, yes, he was going to like being king.

VALERIAN'S CONFIDENCE SOARED. Shaye had willingly placed her hand in his. The contact had set his every nerve ending on fire.

Would she always affect him this way?

As he led her down the hall, he smiled at her over his shoulder. His breath caught. The dome cast rainbow flecks over her rosy cheeks. Those roses...the only source of color in her skin. She could have been a dream, a ghost or a phantom come to torment him.

Like a siren, she lured and tempted him.

Her pale hair tumbled down her back. Some of the ends curled while some fell straight. What he would give to sift his fingers through the thick mass. His home? His crown? His life?

Yes, each of those things.

He would willingly go to his death for this woman.

She scowled at him, her rich, brown eyes crackling with a fire of their own. "Why are you smiling?"

"I'm with you." However long it took, he would chip at her resistance, and he wouldn't stop until she'd caved. *I'll have you begging for me, Moon.* "Why *wouldn't* I smile?"

"Um, I don't know. Maybe because I'm being a cranky witch? And FYI, I shouldn't have to explain something so simple to you."

"FYI?"

"An acronym. Usually it means 'For Your Information.' In your case it means 'Fact, You're Idiotic.'"

He chuckled, his confidence only intensifying. He knew the ins and outs of warfare better than most and knew this woman was brandishing her crankiness like a weapon.

The only viable conclusion: she was at war with her own desires.

He couldn't have been happier.

No, not true. He would've been *a lot* happier if they were both naked and in bed.

"Why don't I kiss you out of your crankiness, hmm?" he asked, practically purring the words.

She sucked in a breath. "Tell me. Will one kiss lead to one touch?"

"Only if I'm lucky."

"You're not."

"Believe me, I know. Otherwise I'd be the main course at breakfast." As he spoke, he pressed his fingers against the pulse in her lower palm. It raced.

Oh, yes. She'll be mine. And soon...

While her mind hadn't yet accepted him as her mate, her body already recognized him as such.

What she would learn: when the body desired someone, the mind would create excuses to seize the opportunity to take. Anything to assuage the ache.

Her awareness of him would ultimately become her downfall.

"Do you ever wear a shirt?" she grumbled.

"Once upon a time, yes. Then I noticed the way your gaze caressed my chest, and I decided it was in my best interest to forgo shirts for the rest of my days."

"Caressed?" she sputtered. "My gaze did no such thing."

He tsk-tsked. "You lie to me, and you lie to yourself. I expected better of you."

"Well, too bad." She attempted to yank her hand from his, but he tightened his grip. "Get used to disappointment, because that's all your supposed mate will ever offer you."

"Another lie." He tugged her in front of him before pressing her against the wall. "Let's bargain. From now on, if you lie to me—or to yourself—I get to spank you."

Her eyes narrowed on him. An action that expressed anger. And yet, she couldn't quite catch her breath. An action that expressed arousal. "And if you lie to me?"

"*You* get to spank *me*."

Her pulse raced faster. "Why would I ever agree to such a *bargain*?"

"Because you're desperate for any excuse to put your hands on me without admitting you want me."

Her lips pursed. "Fine," she said.

What! She'd just accepted? If so, he would lie to her right here, right now—which would mean he would have also lied to her about never lying to her, so he would actually need *two* spankings.

"You're gorgeous," she added, and his excitement plummeted. "Your muscles are exceptional, and I could stare at them all day. But I also like to look at lions, tigers and bears, oh my. Touching them would be detrimental to my health. They'd eat me!"

"So would I." Unwilling to give up, he rubbed the tip of his nose against hers. "Slowly. Thoroughly."

She shivered and softened against his. "No?"

Do not smile. "You can tell yourself it won't mean anything. A momentary pleasure, nothing more."

"Right," she said, her voice low and husky with want. "Because that's all it would be."

He nuzzled his cheek against hers. "Of course, I would then have to spank you for saying so. For *lying* to us both."

Another shiver. Her hands settled on his shoulders, her nails digging into his skin. "How could I know whether I had lied or not...until you'd actually pleasured me?"

A spark of triumph, every fiber of his being demanding he push her for more. Here. Now. She craved his mouth on hers, and he had to strike while she was receptive.

Honor be damned.

But he straightened. Only in the midst of a struggle did a man reveal his true character. Valerian would prove to Shaye she could trust him at all times, even when he had to forgo what he wanted most.

Wide brown eyes regarded him warily. She'd expected him to pounce.

How would she have reacted? Accepting at first, angry afterward?

So vulnerable, his little Moon. What kind of life had she led? Had someone hurt her? Had a man betrayed her trust?

Proving his worth wasn't just important, he realized. Proving his worth was *imperative*.

"Valerian?" His name drifted from her lips, a husky entreaty...a confused plea.

"Breakfast awaits." His harsh tone would have sent anyone else running for cover; his need for this woman was so great he wasn't sure how he'd managed to keep his hands to himself. "Come."

Her eyes narrowed, and he realized he'd used the wrong word, considering their conversation. If "wrong" now meant "right."

She bristled. "Are you secretly a tease?"

At any other time, he might have laughed at the intended insult. "No, Moon. I'm a warrior determined to win the war rather than a single battle, and *that* is hot, hard truth."

"You mean *cold* hard truth."

"No, it's definitely hot."

Her mouth opened and closed and, in her delightfully stunned state, she offered no protest as he linked their fingers to lead her through the commons, the central meeting point for the barracks.

Several couples had decided to camp there and now lay intertwined out in the open. Unlike the frantic moans that had rung out last night, silence reigned.

"You nymphos need a sexual etiquette coach."

He stopped only long enough to pierce her with a hard stare. "Nymphs. *Nymphs*."

Eyes full of innocence, she said, "Nymph... Ohs."

Frustrating female.

"So, what are we going to do about Joachim?" she

asked. "Don't tell me we'll deal with him when he wakes up. Give me an answer this time. I hate not knowing our plan."

We and *our,* she'd said. Not *I.* Not *your.* But *we* and *our.*

He liked that she considered him a partner in this. "Worry not. *We* will do whatever is necessary to remain together."

"Whatever is necessary.... Are you talking about—" she gulped "—committing cold-blooded murder?"

"Yes." He kicked a pile of clothing out of the way and turned a corner. "But I would swing the blade, and you would merely watch."

"Yeah, because that's the problem I had with the plan." She sighed. "Is cold-blooded murder not a crime here?"

"The strong govern the weak. If the weak refuse to obey, they must be pruned from the vine. In what way would it be crime?"

"And you wonder why I want to go home," she muttered.

He wished he could wipe her memory of the surface world! "You will *never* be harmed here."

"Because you plan to protect me. Yeah, yeah. But I'm sure I'm considered a weakling to the rest of your world. At least physically. So what's to stop the strong from attempting to *govern* me when you aren't around?"

"You are my queen. You govern others. They do not govern you."

A fresh, warm scent wafted to him just before the dining hall came into view, the table piled with food. The male centaurs and Minotaurs he'd hired from the Outer City had prepared a feast to welcome the new additions to the household.

Shaye's stomach growled, and he experienced a flicker of guilt. He hadn't fed her dinner.

He would have to take better care of her in the future. His woman should never go hungry.

"Usually at this time of day, my warriors surround the table," he said. Now he and Shaye were alone. Even the servants were gone. "You'll have to wait to test your power."

"One, I'm not your queen yet. Two, I don't want to order anyone around."

His pulse leaped. She'd said *yet*! "You order me around all the time."

"Supposed queen, remember?" she said and fluffed her hair. "If you don't like my rule, you can cut me loose."

He snorted.

She eased into the chair at the head of the table and eyed him. Expecting him to balk, he was sure. When he didn't, she shrugged and filled a plate with food.

As she swallowed a bite of coconut cream, her eyes closed in sweet surrender. "Oh, wow. Who prepared this? Surely not your army. They may look like beefcake, but I seriously doubt they know how to cook it."

"As if I would allow my men to cook," he said, filling a plate of his own before taking the chair beside hers. "They would inadvertently poison us."

She popped a grape into her mouth. "So…you're a chauvinist. Your men belong on the battlefield but never in the kitchen."

"Not even close. Food can mean the difference between life and death." He leaned back and bit into a strawberry. How he would have loved to trace the fruit over her lips and lick the juice away. "The kitchen is a battlefield in its own right. My men simply have no real talent for it."

"Perhaps they're too much like you. Arrogant, bossy, pigheaded, stubborn, half-witted, spoiled, demanding, self-absorbed and morally corrupt."

When she paused for breath, he grumbled, "Is that all?"

"No. Horny. Overbearing. Mean." She paused, tapped a finger against her lips before nodding. "That's all."

"'Mean'?" He frowned. "I've been the epitome of nice, catering to your every whim."

"Did you not steal me from my home? Have you not refused over and over again to return me?"

He tossed his arms up. "This again."

"This *always*."

"Perhaps I can give you something better to think about." He leaned forward and placed his hand on her thigh; she sucked in a breath.

What she didn't do? Rebuke him.

Slowly, languidly, he slid his fingers higher. He stopped only a few inches away from the center of both their worlds.

"Shall we bargain, sweet Shaye?"

The pink tip of her tongue swiped over her lips and almost proved his undoing. "I'm listening."

"Give me time." Would she find ten years objectionable? Five? Probably. He sighed. "A year. A mere blip in a lifetime. If I fail to win your affections, I'll return you to the surface."

"You're kidding, right?" She bit into a strawberry of her own. "By the end of that year, I would be considered dead. My business would fail. My home would be sold. My bank accounts would be emptied."

He tensed with incomparable need, once again over-

come by the desire to lick juice off her lips and chin...
to dribble the sweet but tart droplets into her navel...
between her legs. She would writhe as his tongue followed every path taken by the liquid. She would tunnel
her hands through his hair while her knees squeezed
his temples.

"Valerian?" She snapped her fingers in front of his
face.

He blinked. Their gazes met...heated.

She had to suspect the direction his mind had
gone—and she had to like it. Her pupils were blown,
those velvety-brown irises utterly consumed.

"How long do you propose?" he asked, his voice
more of a growl than anything.

She shifted in her seat, uncomfortable. "A week."

Risk losing her forever for a mere seven days of her
company? No! "Six months."

"You ask for far too much."

"I ask for far too little when I long to demand an
eternity."

A moment passed in heavy silence. Then she grated,
"If I'm going to consider this bargain thing, I need to
know a few things first."

"Anything."

She arched a brow. "Be honest. Do you want to wear
my skin?"

"Pardon?"

"Yes or no? I have to know how deep this stalker
slash creeper thing goes."

"No?"

"Do you want to hump my eyeballs?"

"Interesting, but no."

She drew in a deep breath, held it and released it. "A
month," she said. "I'll stay a month."

A month. A mere four weeks. Or thirty days. Or 720 hours. Or 43,200 minutes. Or 2,592,000 seconds.

Not. Long. Enough.

Could he win her in the allotted time frame? With anyone else, he would have said yes. With Shaye...

"Well?" she prompted.

Two of his warriors strode into the room, saving him from having to reply.

Both men sported wide, toothy smiles. Unlike the day before, each sported a relaxed posture. Strength radiated from them, so strong it was nearly tangible.

"Shaye, meet Broderick and Dorian."

Broderick had an arm slung around Dorian's shoulders. They smiled at Shaye.

They wore gilded breastplates, black pants and jewel-studded armbands, ready to train.

"Good morning, great king." Broderick patted him on the back. "This promises to be a pleasurable day."

"Highly pleasurable," Dorian agreed.

The males whistled as they circled the table and heaped their plates with food. They must have worked up hearty appetites.

Valerian glared at them, actually...envious? Yes. Yes, he was. A first for him. Another blow to his pride.

Shivawn entered the room. He wasn't smiling or relaxed but stiff; he glowered at everyone. He slammed himself onto the bench beside Valerian, the beads in his hair rattling, and silently filled his plate.

"Problems?" Valerian asked him.

"Maybe one or two. My woman vomited when we reached my room," Shivawn muttered.

"Did you touch her?" Shaye asked, inserting herself into the conversation. "Fair warning. Your next words dictate my next actions."

"No," Shivawn snapped. "I obeyed orders."

"Well, you just saved yourself a painful forking." She set the fork in question beside her plate. "Let's discuss the fact that you've decided to act like a child and pout." She shook her fists in front of her face. "Boo hoo. Poor you. Now you'll actually have to work at a relationship before having sex. Oh, the travesty!"

"Women love me," the warrior grated.

"Wrong. They love your pheromone." Her gaze slid to the others. "There's a big difference, guys. Huge. Without that magic drug—and it's a drug, I don't care what your king says—I wonder if *anyone* would *ever* want any of you. You've got A-plus looks, sure, but after last night's ceremony? You've got solid F-minus personalities."

Having been on the receiving end of her sharp tongue more than once, Valerian sat back and enjoyed the show—enjoyed her.

She was born to be a queen.

And really, her words made him think. He'd never before taken the time to discuss his life—past, present or future—with any of his bedmates. He hadn't cared to discuss his secrets, and they hadn't cared to ask.

He wanted Shaye to know him. All of him. The good, the bad and the ugly. He wanted to tell her about himself and gauge her reaction, hear her thoughts.

He wanted to know *her*. All of her. No detail was too small. He wanted to know what had given her joy, what had pained her. He wanted to know about the men she'd dated.

Had she favored scholars? Warriors? How had the men treated her?

Had she ever been in love?

Valerian's hands clenched on the arms of the chair,

nearly snapping the wood. A need to maim, destroy and kill any man who'd once held this woman's affections consumed him, hotter than a dragon's fire. Her passion—his. Her affections—his.

Her heart—his!

He yearned to brand his very essence into her. She would know no scent but his. Would feel no touch but his. Would crave him, only him, as he craved her, only her.

He wanted her to feel the same way about any woman who'd come before her. He wanted *her* to brand *him*.

"My personality is as delightful as the rest of me," Dorian said, cutting into his thoughts.

Broderick nodded. "As is mine. I've never gotten a single complaint."

"What do you think I've been doing?" she asked. "Complaining."

Both males looked to Valerian. He hiked his shoulders in a shrug, all *what can I do?*

"Get to know the women," Shaye said. "You might be surprised by what you learn. Like, maybe they're right for you but maybe they aren't. And give *them* a chance to get to know *you*, to *like* you without any kind of chemical interference. Hey, here's a thought. Maybe even go a step further and gift them with something special—prove *they* are special to you. And I'm not talking about the supposed gift between your legs."

Mumbling under his breath, Shivawn swiped up his plate and stalked from the room.

Everyone watched him leave, each with a different reaction. Broderick laughed. Dorian frowned, confused, and Shaye heaved a sigh.

"When you are queen," Valerian said, hoping to tempt her, "you can make as many decrees as your heart desires. You can command the men to do whatever you wish."

"What!" Broderick shouted.

Dorian banged his head against the tabletop.

Shaye crossed her arms over her chest, causing the neckline of her shirt to gape, revealing a deep plunge of cleavage. His need for her intensified—not because of her cleavage, though he loved the sight, but because the corners of her mouth twitched, as if she were fighting a grin.

Gorgeous girl.

"Well. I see my chosen has quenched one hunger," a male voice suddenly said from the doorway. "Why don't I quench another?"

Valerian stiffened. Because of the implication, and the reaction the words elicited in Shaye. The mischievous glint faded from her eyes, and the color drained from her cheeks. The corners of her mouth no longer twitched.

Gnashing his teeth, Valerian twisted in his seat to meet his cousin's narrowed gaze.

Joachim stood in the doorway. He appeared no more relaxed than yesterday. In fact, he appeared ready for war, weapons strapped over armor.

Joachim wanted to war, so they would war.

It was past time he showed his power-hungry cousin the error of his ways—beginning now.

CHAPTER ELEVEN

TENSION AND TESTOSTERONE heated the air, burning Shaye's lungs every time she inhaled. Fury sizzled and snapped between Valerian and Joachim, making everything worse; a raging inferno, barely banked, threatened to destroy, well, everyone.

As a child, she'd lived with emotional people. How many tirades and fits of jealous rage had her mother thrown over the years? Countless. If a husband ever came home late, china was thrown at his head—right along with accusations of infidelity. If a birthday or anniversary was forgotten, tires were slashed.

How many times had her different stepmothers raged?

How often had her father and stepdads experienced mansteria for some silly reason or another?

Shaye had usually hidden in her bedroom.

But none of those people had ever looked as scary as Valerian. The need to kill had darkened his expression. His lips were thinned and pulled back from his teeth—an animalistic scowl.

Until this point, he'd shown her desire, amusement and patience.

"I have a bargain for you, Joachim." His voice lashed like a barbed whip.

Joachim gave no outward reaction. Although his eyes *did* bear the same trace of dissatisfaction as Valerian and Shivawn.

"I'm listening."

"I'll give you my sword," Valerian said. "You may have it with my blessing, but you must renounce all claim to the girl."

Traded for a sword? *Be still my heart.*

"Unacceptable." Black brows winged into Joachim's hairline in a display of arrogance. "If you want the girl, you'll have to renounce your role as king."

Dorian and Broderick snarled like animals.

Okay. Enough. Valerian had faults—a lot of faults—but judging by the things she'd seen so far, he was a good king. Most certainly, this black-haired man would be a merciless dictator.

"No," she said. "As acting queen, I refuse on Valerian's behalf."

"You don't have a voice in this," Joachim snapped at her.

"And you won't speak to her in such a manner," Valerian snapped right back at him.

Shaye blew Mr. Dictator a kiss using her middle finger.

Valerian rubbed the back of his neck. "I cannot simply make you king. You know that. My men would never follow someone who hadn't proved himself worthy."

"That's true," Joachim agreed. "Which is why I'm willing to prove myself worthy."

Valerian hands flexed, as if he imagined holding a sword. "And just how do you plan to do that?"

"Yeah," Shaye said. "How do you?"

"Yesterday you were willing to fight me." Joachim lifted his chin. "Are you still?"

A nod without hesitation. "Yes."

"Are you willing to relinquish your crown when I best you, thereby proving myself worthy?"

A predatory stillness came over Valerian. He muttered, "I knew it."

She'd never seen him fight. She'd never seen *either* of them fight. Joachim possessed the same confidence as Valerian, and yet he also struck her as bloodthirsty.

Could Valerian win?

And what if he were injured?

The thought…displeased her. Because she needed him to remain in charge so that he could escort her home. Not for any other reason. Really.

"What about a game of chess?" she suggested. "Hey. Not that it matters, but are either of you good at chess?"

Valerian's eyes narrowed on her—and churned with more fury.

"What did I do?" As many insults as she'd tossed at him, he'd only ever smiled at her. But a mention of chess pushed him over the edge?

"You doubt my skill with a sword," he barked. Then he looked away from her, as if he couldn't stand her, and that was somehow far worse.

"Such a thing has never been done," he said to Joachim, his tone careful, even guarded.

Joachim wrapped his fingers around his sword hilt. "Yet such a thing has often *needed* to be done."

Well. Shaye had thought tensions were already high. Wrong! The room pulsed with danger.

If she didn't do something, and quick, the two males would come to blows right here, right now. But what could she do?

Flash her breasts? No, thanks.

Dance a jig, hoping everyone would laugh at her? Bad idea. She had a feeling *any* dance would be considered a *mating* dance. No, thanks.

Food fight?

Not great, but not terrible, either. A girl had to make do.

Shaye scooped a handful of the coconut-cream pudding and tossed it at Joachim. Success! The pudding splattered over his cheeks.

As he blinked in surprise—and before she could talk herself out of it—she launched a handful at Valerian.

His gaze returned to her, hot so very hot. And so much better than the fury.

No, no. So much worse!

He gathered as much cream as he could on his finger and licked it away. Her insides *quivered*.

The reactions this man roused in her...

A grinning Broderick and Dorian leaned toward her...hoping to get nailed, as well?

She might never understand these nymphos. But. Mission accomplished, tensions reduced.

"Why did you do that?" As Joachim straightened, his armor clinked ominously. "Never mind. The answer doesn't matter. What say you, Valerian? Shall we fight, the winner awarded the woman and crowned king with all the rights the title entails?"

She had to swallow a shout of denial.

At first, Valerian offered him no response. He took her hand and brought her fingers to his mouth. Out came his tongue, licking the pudding on *her* skin.

Oh, my stars, what have I done?

Delicious heat flowed from the top of her head to the soles of her feet, melting her bones.

Earlier she'd thought she could handle a month with this man. Obviously she couldn't handle five minutes!

"He declines," she said with a tremor in her voice. "*The woman* will choose her own man."

Valerian leaned into her. "If you think I would risk losing you, you don't know me at all."

Was he serious? "Um, like I've tried to tell you a thousand times, I *don't* know you. We literally just met."

Frustration and disappointment flashed in his beautiful eyes, and she kind of wished she could take back her words. Even though they were true!

"Valerian?" Joachim prompted.

Without looking away from her, Valerian stood and said, "No."

His cousin hissed with surprise.

"We'll fight for *the crown*, only the crown, and not the girl," Valerian finished. "She's mine, no matter what."

Shaye gaped at him. She meant more than his kingdom?

"Agreed," Joachim replied.

Valerian splayed his arms, encompassing the room and everyone inside. "What is your weapon of choice?"

"Swords, of course. The weapon of a true warrior."

"To the death, then."

"No," she said, horrified.

"I don't want to kill you," Joachim said. "I don't hate you and never have. We were friends once, as children, but I should have been crowned after my father."

"And yet Poseidon chose *my* father."

"I was too young. Now I'm older. And how long since Poseidon has deigned to visit us? Decades."

For a long while the two males engaged in a staring contest. Finally Joachim cursed and blinked.

Valerian lifted his chin. "Go to the arena, cousin. I'll be there shortly."

"That's the last command you'll ever give me." Scowling, Joachim pivoted on his heel and strode away.

Shaye had to put a stop to this.

"Dorian," Valerian said, not giving her a chance to speak. "Gather the rest of the men. They'll bear witness to the battle—they'll see what happens to those who think to usurp my rule. Broderick, go and prepare my gear."

Chairs skidded backward. Footsteps pounded.

I can't believe this is happening, Shaye thought.

She'd been kidnapped from her mother's wedding—shrug. She'd been dragged underwater, through a portal and into a lost city—yawn. She'd been chosen as the king's mistress—could someone pass a nail file?

This battle…it was a nightmare.

"I'm asking you not to do this," she said to Valerian. They were alone now, no one else in sight. "He'll make a terrible king."

Valerian sat down and once again regarded her through narrowed eyes. "He will *never* be king."

Ugh. She'd insulted his skill again, which hadn't been her intention.

"So you'll win," she said. "What will happen afterward?"

He popped a grape into his mouth. "You'll admire my strength."

Probably. Not that she'd admit such a horror aloud.

With a sigh, she plopped into her chair.

They finished their breakfast as if they'd never been interrupted. As if her stomach wasn't churning with nervousness.

When they finished, he pushed to his feet and held out his hand, palm up. A silent command.

"They are awaiting us in the arena."

She studied his palm, knowing the moment she intertwined her fingers with his, warmth would rush up her arm. Such a drugging warmth. She would tingle and ache.

Her throat constricted.

She stood, keeping her arms at her sides. "Go ahead. Lead the way."

He frowned and beckoned her with a single wave of his fingers.

Stubborn, she crossed her arms over her chest.

Their gazes locked in challenge. The long length of his black lashes cast shadows over his cheeks. How did a man with honey-blond hair have such dark eyelashes?

"I need your touch, Shaye." The words dripped with determination, but drifting beneath them was a very clear challenge: *every resistance will be met and conquered until you've soared over the sweet edge of surrender.* "My victory depends upon it."

"No way."

"Nymphs are strengthened through sex," he said.

What! "I am *not* having sex with you."

Not even to save him?

Well…

No. What? *Can't believe you're even considering this.* Death was an exaggeration on his part, surely. A way to get her into bed.

"Contact—any contact—helps."

"Fine." She clasped his hand.

The warmth she'd feared speared her, spreading up and out and soon overtaking her entire body.

He closed his eyes, as if savoring her.

Once again, her insides quivered. Such an innocent touch, and yet he affected her so…wantonly.

"One day…" he said.

A promise…or a warning?

He stalked out of the dining hall, dragging her with him.

"Slow down," she said, struggling to keep up. "Please."

He could have ignored her, but he obeyed. As if her words carried weight with him.

A girl could get used to that.

Her gaze snagged on the wall, where white marble was inlaid with silver stone, crumbling in spots. There were also scratch marks, she realized, as if someone had taken a tool to every inch.

"What happened here?" she asked.

"I was told humans invaded."

Her gaze pierced his back, where hard muscle and sinew strained under his beautiful bronzed flesh. "Humans willingly visit Atlantis?"

"Some do, yes."

Wow. People actually knew about this place, yet they'd managed to keep it a secret. If they'd returned home, that was.

"How long have you lived here?"

"My army claimed the palace from the dragons only a few weeks ago."

Claimed. Aka "stolen," she was sure. "In stories, dragons spew fire and eat humans as tasty snacks."

"Stories are correct." He sounded amused.

"Won't the dragons want their palace back?"

"Oh, yes."

Her eyes widened at his nonchalance. "And that doesn't bother you? The thought of battling such fierce creatures?"

"No. Why should it?" He stopped to glare at her, his chest seeming to expand right before her eyes. The heat of his skin caressed her, and the heady scent of him filled her nose, fogging her head.

Sconces blazed from the walls, their glow flickering over the contours of his face. Shadows and light fought for dominance, playing over his cheeks, making him appear menacing.

"I'm fiercer," he said. "I'm stronger."

Hello, male arrogance. "Well, I'm sorry I don't share your confidence," she said dryly.

He frowned. "If the thought of dragons scares you—"

"Terrifies me," she interjected. In this land, you were either predator or prey. Since she wasn't a predator...

"How will you react when I introduce you to the vampires?"

A strangled gasp wheezed from her throat. "I'm *not* meeting vampires."

"They are our friends."

He talks as if we're already a couple.

"Look. I know you told me those creatures existed, but I never actually thought you'd make me interact with them. Vampires drink blood, Valerian."

"They won't drink yours, Shaye."

She sighed. There was simply no arguing with him. He had a response for everything.

"Let's bargain," she said. "You won't introduce me to vampires, and I'll..." What?

In the distance, swords clanged together. Grunts sounded, and male laughter abounded.

"I like where you are headed with this conversation," he said. "We'll revisit what you're willing to do after the fight."

"No. We finish it now." She jumped in front of him to stop him and flatten her hands on his chest—oh, how he burned. "Forget the vampires. Win the fight, and I'll kiss you."

Desire flared in his eyes. The same consuming desire she'd encountered when she'd first watched him stride from the ocean.

"Give me a preview of this kiss," he said.

Desire consumed *her*. "Or what? You'll lose? I don't think so, babe." Babe? Her cheeks heated. What an embarrassing slip of the tongue. "You'll do anything to keep your crown."

"Obviously I won't. I'm fighting my cousin, risking my crown, to keep you."

"I thought there was no real risk for you."

His eyes gleamed with calculation. "Kiss me now, and I'll end the fight as quickly as possible. I won't drag it out."

Well...

Her gaze lowered, lingering on his lips, and her breath caught in her throat. If her touch strengthened him, how much more so would her kiss? And he needed his strength, right? The future of his kingdom was at stake!

"Fine," she whispered, already rising on her tiptoes.

He needed no other prompting. He tangled his fingers in her hair and slammed his mouth onto hers. His hot tongue pushed inside, past her teeth, past any thought of resistance.

In seconds she felt burned alive. The woman who'd once eschewed dating became wild. Someone who existed only for pleasure, sex and debauchery. For *this* man.

Valerian consumed her. Dark need consumed her—and she discovered that she liked every second of it.

His taste was pure sexual heat, raw masculinity, exotic and addictive; his tongue worked hers with expert precision, her every nerve endings leaping to blissful life. Her nipples hardened, the apex of her thighs ached, and her stomach quivered.

She wound her arms around his neck, accepting him

fully, demanding more; a feral growl of satisfaction escaped him.

"I want you," he whispered fiercely and as always, the sound of his wine-rich voice excited her.

He was made for her, only her—his every action, every breath, they happened simply to please her.

The thought intoxicated her. Like the man himself.

"I want you," he repeated. "Give me everything."

"Never," she forced herself to say. Then, of course, she contradicted herself by running his bottom lip between her teeth.

His callused hands slid down the ridges of her spine to settle softly on the curve of her hips.

"I need your breasts in my hands. Please, Shaye."

Yes! Oh, yes. Her nipples hardened more, and they hurt. They actually hurt, desperate for contact.

He tunneled his hands under her shirt, his fingers tickling her skin. She gasped in wonder when his thumbs grazed each aching crest.

"I wish I could stand you in front of a mirror and slowly remove your top, baring your flesh inch by precious inch," he said. "I would cup your breasts in my hands, framing your nipples with my fingers as they pearled for me."

Her knees trembled. "I should hate the thought," she told him, breathless. She brought *her* hands to *his* chest, brushing *her* thumbs over *his* nipples. They were hard little points she wanted to lick and suck. And, as her fingertip curled in the steel loop anchored in the right one, she wanted to lick and suck that, too. "Should absolutely, positively hate it."

He groaned. "If this is the way you hate…"

"The pheromone. Only the pheromone."

"No." He grated the negation.

Angry with her now?

She licked the seam of his lips, and his anger returned to passion. Their breaths had mingled. Now their gazes locked, a sultry clash of turquoise against brown, passion against passion.

"Hate me some more," he told her.

She rose on her tiptoes—her body seemed to have a mind of its own—placing her lips just in front of his.

He kissed her harder than before, his hands returning to her waist and tightening, his grip needy, firm and commanding.

His message was clear: she could not escape.

Why would she want to escape?

He pulled her closer, until she nestled against the long, rigid length of his erection. A hot, raspy gasp left her, spears of pleasure arcing through her, spawning other bursts of sensation.

"I want to hate you, too," he told her in that same soft tone. "I want to hate you hard and fast the first time, slow and tender the second."

Behind them, someone cleared his throat. "My king?"

Shaye heard the voice distantly and despised the interruption. *More kisses.* She wanted more of Valerian's kisses. And he very clearly wanted to give them to her. Wicked intent gleamed in his eyes.

"I'm so sorry, my king," the voice said. "The fight…"

Valerian's fingers clenched on her hips. "I don't want to stop hating you," he said softly, the words nothing but a growl.

Saying "You must" almost killed her.

He brushed his nose against hers. "Must hate you?"

"Must stop." *Never stop!*

He ran his tongue over his teeth. Then his nostrils

flared, as if her taste lingered there. "For now," he stated. "I will."

She gulped. She'd never been kissed with such passion or fervor. As if the man claiming her lips truly savored her and would be utterly destroyed without her.

He's dangerous, her mind whispered. He made her hope, even though there was only one way the relationship would end. Painfully.

All relationships ended. Period.

But going from the beginning to the end will be worth the heartbreak later on, her body responded.

She tugged from his embrace, suddenly cold and empty. Hollow, as she'd been through her entire childhood.

His eyelids compressed to tiny slits, his thick lashes nearly intertwining top with bottom. "You melted for me. That isn't reason to withdraw from me, Moon. That's reason to rejoice."

"Valerian," yet another man called. Joachim, this time. She recognized the deep baritone, now filled with impatience. "Have you decided against fighting me? Do you concede the victory to me?"

Shaye drew her arms over her middle, tamping down a tremor of dread. "No," she said. "He doesn't."

Valerian cupped her cheeks. His gaze searched hers. He had to wonder why she'd protested the fight before but supported it now.

The answer—whatever he'd decided it was—didn't please him. He scowled.

Did he think she wanted him to lose now that they'd kissed? Now that fear held her in an obvious choke hold?

"I will never concede," Valerian said, the words more lethal than the sword strapped to his back. His eyes never left her face. "Never."

CHAPTER TWELVE

VALERIAN REELED, HARD, as he peered at the exquisite Shaye. Her eyes were wide and haunting—haunted—her lips puffed and red, and a pulse hammering at the base of her neck as she struggled to catch her breath. If he hadn't already known she belonged to him, he would have known the moment, the very second, he tasted her sweetness. Nothing and no one had ever affected him more profoundly.

I'm owned. She owns me.

Joachim—the man who had interrupted Valerian's first kiss with his one and only mate—awaited him.

Wrong phrasing. What he and Shaye had done had been more than a kiss. Joachim had interrupted Valerian's first *consuming* with his one and only mate.

Yes. Better. They'd consumed each other.

He wanted to *consume* her again.

My cousin's death warrant has been signed, sealed and soon, delivered.

Looking away from a female had never been difficult, but fury seethed and bubbled in his veins, a rushing river of acid, giving him the strength he needed to glare at Joachim.

"You will pay for this," he snapped.

"Only if you beat me," Joachim replied, smug expectation coloring his face.

The man truly thought to win and become king.

"I've changed my mind about the fight," Shaye muttered. "He deserves a royal spanking pronto."

Valerian reached back, palm extended, waiting for her to willingly place her hand in his. To his delight, she laced her fingers with his without a moment's hesitation. Her hand was soft and delicate, the bones fine, the skin smooth. Her perfectly rounded nails were painted the color of coral shells.

One day, he would suck them into his mouth.

She tightened her grip, and his delight only magnified. Was she offering him...comfort?

Was she coming to care for him?

Perhaps, perhaps not, but he *had* made progress with her. Never had a woman reacted so passionately to him, erupting from ice-cold to white-hot in seconds.

I'll have that—her—again, he vowed. *Soon.*

"I'm waiting," Joachim said, tapping a booted foot.

"So ready to die," Valerian snapped.

His cousin ignored the threat. "Unless you've decided to challenge me to a staring contest?"

Valerian lifted his chin. "Come," he said to Shaye. As he ushered her down the rest of the hallway, determination fueled his steps.

He barreled past Joachim, shouldering the foolish man out of the way. Such disrespect would only ever be met with pain—more than the warrior had ever before experienced.

By the time their private war ended, any other male who'd ever harbored thoughts of taking the crown would apologize.

A thought occurred to him. Should he have Shaye escorted to his chamber rather than take her with him, allowing her to watch the fight? If she bore witness to his most vicious side, the animal inside him...an animal that maimed and conquered...

She might grow to fear him.

The thought of her cowering from him...

It was more than he could bear.

But already she doubted his ability to win. Let her see the true depths of his strengths and know beyond any doubt he could take care of her at all times, in all ways.

"Um, I feel silly saying this, but it's got to be pointed out," Shaye said. "He's wearing armor. You're still shirtless."

"I know. He is such a fool," Valerian replied.

"He's protecting vulnerable organs, and he's the fool?"

"Have you ever been in a sword fight?"

"Metal, plastic or lightsaber?"

There were other kinds of swords in the surface world? Might be worth another trip topside to gather supplies. The lightsaber, especially, piqued his interest.

"Metal," he finally said.

"Then no. No, I haven't been in a sword fight."

"I'm unencumbered. He's weighted down."

"Quick reflexes over blocking. Got it."

Wait. He stopped to gape down at her. "Are you taking notes, actually *planning* to engage in a sword fight of your own?"

She lifted her chin in a mimic of him. "Perhaps I'm planning to challenge you."

He couldn't stop his smile. "I look forward to the day you do."

A blush stained her cheeks.

Joachim stalked past him, his boots flinging sand in every direction, and a chorus of "boo" rang out.

Valerian resumed his journey and the chorus turned

to cheers. The arena overflowed with men and women brimming with anticipation and eagerness.

The females were draped in traditional nymph robes—scarves that had been woven together with golden thread. Fine, metal links cinched the material at the waist, showcasing the shapely curves of some and the lean delicacy of others.

He would love to see Shaye draped in one of those robes.

Valerian stopped in front of Broderick. "Is all ready?"

"I've taken care of every detail." Broderick grinned and wound his arm around the curvy beauty at his side. "Women and war in one day. Would only be better if I could watch the battle while having sex and eating grapes fed to me by a bevy of beauties."

"Our definition of *better* differs," Shaye muttered. "Hey! New card idea. Barbarian Mentality 101 for women stuck with a Neanderthal. It could say something simple like, 'Got Razors' or even 'Ugh'?"

Valerian sometimes had no idea how to decipher her words, but this he understood. He grinned. "Broderick, my friend, you're going to watch this little morsel for me." He gently thrust Shaye in the warrior's path.

She *humphed*.

"Guard her well and allow no one to touch her." He paused, considered Broderick's past liaisons and current desires, and added, "Not even yourself."

Broderick lost all traces of amusement. "What do I do if she tries to run away?"

"She won't." He turned his gaze on Shaye and met her rebellious stare. "Will you?"

She buffed her fingernails. "We never agreed on a time frame."

He expelled a hot breath. "Promise me you'll stay

here while I fight. If I'm worried about you, I won't be able to concentrate on the sword being swung at me."

She paled, a lovely ice queen. "So. The only thing I get out of this newest bargain is the life of my captor?"

"Contain your excitement. This isn't a dream," he said dryly. "Just…promise me."

Her expression softened ever so slightly. "Fine. I promise. But after the fight…"

Satisfied, he looked to Broderick. "When I return, I want her in the same condition I've left her."

"What about him?" Shaye hiked her thumb in Broderick's direction. "Do you want him in the same condition?"

Valerian fought a grin. "Yes. Please."

The woman at the warrior's side pointed an accusing finger at Shaye. "You're standing too close to my Broderick."

Shaye rolled her eyes. "Sue me."

Broderick puffed up his chest. "Martina is possessive of me, what can I say?"

Valerian crossed his arms over his chest. "Just make sure your Martina keeps her hands off Shaye, as well."

"You mean I won't get to catfight over a man I have no interest in?" Shaye twisted her fists under her eyes. "Tears. Sadness."

"Fine," he said in a mimic of her. "You can catfight her if you desire, but if you break her, I'll owe Broderick another woman."

Broderick nodded. "He would."

Martina hissed at the warrior. "You would let someone hurt me? You wouldn't protect me with your life?"

"Yes?" he said, looking to Valerian for help.

Shaye held up her hands, palms out. "All right. I can

admit when I'm wrong, and I was wrong about the pheromone. It *can't* overcome a bad personality."

Valerian wanted to laugh. He wanted to kiss his woman again. Wanted to luxuriate in her heat and wetness as he tasted her sweetness.

She licked her lips, as if she read his thoughts. "Stop looking at me like that."

"I can't." More important, he didn't want to.

"You must. Get your head out of my pants and into the game."

"Valerian!" A female squeal echoed behind his mate. "You're here!"

His muscles turned to stone. Heading straight toward him? The redhead Joachim had slept with last night. On a mission, she shoved her way through the crowd.

"I came to wish you well." She even shouldered Shaye out of the way, her focus solely on Valerian. "I just heard about the fight and wanted to cheer for you."

He scowled at her, ready to issue a stinging rebuke. Without asking permission, she caressed his bare chest and cupped his backside. He reared back.

She chuckled. "You're even sexier than I remembered. How about a quickie?"

He shook his head. "Our association is now and forever at an end." He used a gentle tone, determined not to inflict unnecessary hurt. "I have a mate now."

Her pink lips dipped into a pout. "So? I want you."

"And I want a pony," Shaye snapped. "We don't always get what we want, do we?"

His first thought: What kind of pony? He would buy her an entire stable full.

She loved pink, and he remembered seeing a pink pony on his last trip through the Outer City.

His second thought: Was she jealous? He wanted her

to be jealous. To long to keep him all to herself the way he longed to keep her.

"Valerian?" the redhead said. "I'm fine with you having a mate. She can join us."

First things first. "I'll never be willing to share my mate. With anyone."

"Supposed mate," Shaye interjected, her expression softening.

He frowned at her before continuing. "She's all I want, all I need."

Color flooded her cheeks, and she looked away from him.

The redhead's shoulders drooped, and guilt pricked at him. He should have explained his intensions before he'd bedded the human. Should have made sure they wanted the same thing: momentary pleasure.

"Valerian." Joachim's voice rang out. "I've waited long enough."

Everyone in the arena stopped speaking.

"Then by all means," Valerian replied. Time to push Shaye from his thoughts. "Let's hurry your execution along."

He faced his opponent. Joachim stood in the center of the sandy arena, swinging a spear overhead to loosen his muscles. The metal whistled and zinged, like a war cry. In his other hand, he held a silver shield, two wings embossed on each side. A sword was sheathed in the center.

Joachim slid his helmet in place, his armor glinting in the light.

Valerian held his hand out, and Broderick slapped a spear into his grip. He felt its familiar weight and nodded.

Next Broderick handed him a shield of his own.

In the center rested the Skull. With it, Joachim would die, guaranteed. What Valerian had thought he wanted only seconds ago. Faced with such an inevitable outcome, his fury wrestled with uncertainty.

He returned the shield. "Replace the Skull with one of my training blades."

"My lord." Broderick gaped at him. "You've never—"

"Do it." Joachim could be killed any day. But if he died today, Valerian could never bring him back.

As his cousin had pronounced earlier, they *had* been friends as children. The best of friends. Only when Poseidon had given Valerian's father the crown had Joachim's resentment sprouted.

Under normal circumstances, Joachim would have been the chosen, continuing the line. Eldest son to eldest son. As young as he'd been—as sickly as he'd once been—Valerian's father had been the better choice.

Joachim believed Valerian had stolen his legacy, and he wasn't wrong. But now, looking back, Valerian wondered if the sea god had known what he hadn't. Joachim would have destroyed the nymphs.

If Poseidon had even visited once since the coronation, perhaps this could have been avoided. But the male had forgotten them.

"Any sword will do," he added.

A pause before the shield was taken out of his hand. Footsteps rang out. A few seconds later, the cool press of the shield's handle weighed in his grip. A sharp-tipped blade now rested in the center. He nodded in approval.

"Your helmet, my king," Broderick said.

"No." He kept his gaze on Joachim. "Not this time."

Broderick frowned. "What of your other armor?"

"No."

Valerian hefted his spear in one hand, his shield in the other, and stepped into the arena.

"Shall we begin?"

"We shall."

Determined, he circled Joachim. "You will forever be an example of what happens to those who challenge my rule."

"Is this the part where I taunt you back?" Joachim continued to swing his spear.

"I'd hoped it would be the part where you listened to reason. You are too war-happy to be king."

Eyes narrowing, his cousin said, "Such a quality should be lauded."

"Lauded? When the hunger will never be appeased? In the end, you might conquer all of Atlantis, but you will also destroy the entire city."

"Better to rule a decimated land than no land at all."

"That. That is why you are unfit. You don't see the foolishness of your words."

"I'm no fool!" With a roar, Joachim leaped at him. Valerian met him halfway. He'd told Shaye he would handle this quickly, and he would.

Their spears clashed together midair. Immediately Valerian countered, ducking low, pivoting and slashing. He missed as Joachim sliced to the side. *Clang.* Their spears met again. In the next instant, Joachim raised his lance and Valerian rammed it high. He spun, aiming for his cousin's neck.

Joachim darted out of the way with a grin. "Getting slow, Valerian." He removed his helmet and tossed it aside.

Valerian stabbed forward, his spike and shield swinging simultaneously. Joachim quickly lost his smile as he was forced to duck. He stumbled backward. Valerian's spear nearly sank into his stomach, but Joachim blocked, swung. Thrust.

That low thrust grazed Valerian's thigh, slicing cloth rather than skin. Valerian dropped to one knee, absorbing the next blow with his shield. When he regained his footing, he lunged forward. The tip of his weapon whizzed past Joachim's side, taking a hunk of armor with it.

"Still think I'm slow?" Valerian asked.

Their fiery gazes met, blue against bluer, and Joachim scowled. He swung to the left, missed, then swung to the right. As the lance dipped toward the ground, Valerian leaped over its middle, trapping it between his legs and jamming his elbow into Joachim's nose. Blood squirted and Joachim howled as he tripped, falling away from striking distance and flinging dirt in every direction.

"Get up," Valerian commanded.

"You'll pay for that." His cousin jumped to his feet and ran straight at him, continuously stabbing forward.

Valerian circled on swift feet, his shield blocking. His muscles began to burn, and sweat began to run down his face and chest in rivulets. Already his breath emerged in shallow pants. At this rate, his strength would be rapidly depleted. Lack of sex did that to a nymph.

Looking tired himself, Joachim arched high, intending to puncture his shoulder on the downward swing, but Valerian hit Joachim's wrist and his cousin dropped the spear. At a disadvantage, Joachim dived, rolled and reached for it. His fingers closed around the middle. Maintaining a fluid pace, he spun back to his feet. But Valerian was already there, stomping on the lance and snapping it in two.

Growling low in his throat, Joachim kicked up. His foot slammed into Valerian's wrist and Valerian, too, lost his spear. Both men sprang apart, unsheathing the swords centered in their shields.

As blood continued to drip down his face, Joachim launched forward, wildly swinging. Air whistled, zinged, just like it had before the battle began. Movements slower than normal, Valerian didn't duck in time. The blade sliced his forearm. He felt the sting of it, the burn of torn flesh.

He didn't give a reaction, didn't allow it to slow him further.

He stabbed low, then up, twisting before Joachim could counter. The tip of his sword whizzed by his cousin's face, and the man paled. He raised his shield and slammed it into Valerian's other arm, the sharp wings cutting skin. Valerian used the momentum to spin and slice into Joachim's thigh.

His cousin shouted, and his knees buckled into the sand.

"Get up," Valerian snarled. "We finish this."

Gritting his teeth, Joachim lumbered to his feet. He still clutched his weapon and shield. His eyes were dark with rage, his irises bright with his thirst for power; he dropped his shield and slid a second dagger from his side.

Valerian hurled his shield aside, as well. He held out his free hand, and Broderick tossed him a second dagger. He easily caught the hilt. Two blades against two blades.

Instantly he and Joachim leaped for each other. One blade clashed, then the other, a lethal dance of dodge and slash. Valerian spun as he worked his blades, lunged and stabbed.

"I should have killed your father. I should have been king," Joachim panted as he ducked.

"But you didn't. You aren't." Stab. Turn. Stab.

"I was created to rule."

"How can you rule an army when you cannot rule your own emotions?" The first blade finally slammed home, sinking into Joachim's side.

His cousin screamed and dropped to his knees. Valerian's momentum kept him from drawing back his other weapon. He wasn't sure he would have, though, even if he could. But he did angle his arm, his second blade embedding in Joachim's shoulder, close to his heart without damaging the organ. The silver glided smoothly through the links of armor. Joachim gasped for air as a trickle of blood ran from his mouth.

Total silence filled the arena.

Valerian straightened, panting.

Blood gurgled from Joachim's mouth. "Should have... killed...me."

"You will live, and you will regret," Valerian said, unemotional and loud enough that everyone could hear. "If you ever again challenge my leadership, I *will* kill you. Without a thought, hesitation, or mercy. No matter that we are family. No matter that we were once friends."

Joachim's chin fell to his chest as his eyes closed. Dark shadows spread over his blood-coated face just before he tumbled into the dirt, unconscious. Grains of sand sprayed onto Valerian's boots.

He slammed the tip of his dagger beside his cousin's body and eyed the crowd of warriors who watched him in openmouthed shock. Perhaps they had expected him to kill his cousin. Perhaps they had expected him to deflect the final blow completely.

His gaze connected with Shaye's. *Mine*, his mind shouted. *Mine now.* No one could say otherwise.

Like his men, her face projected her shock. And horror? He knew he must look a sight, blood and sand covering him from head to toe, strands of sweat-soaked hair clinging to his temples.

He couldn't regret what had been done. She belonged to him, would live here with him now and always, so it was best for her to learn his way of life.

Tearing his gaze from her, he looked at each of his men. "Is there anyone else who wishes to challenge my authority?"

The echo of his voice settled. Silence reigned.

He paced through the arena. "Now is the time to issue such a challenge. You won't be given another chance."

No one came forward.

He stilled, hands clenched at his sides. "Then I hereby claim Shaye Octavia Holling as my mate. Your queen. Any protests will be met by my sword."

"Now hold on just a moment," Shaye called. "We haven't agreed—"

"Except hers," he interjected. Her protests would never be met by his sword.

"Valerian," she said.

He ignored her and moved in front of Broderick.

Broderick kneeled, bowed his head. "What should we do about Joachim, my king? Say our goodbyes?"

Valerian still didn't want Joachim to die, and banishment would get him killed in a hurry.

He searched for the females among the crowd. "Is there a healer among you?"

After a pause, Shivawn's silent, black-haired wench stepped forward. Tears glistened in her eyes as she raised a tentative hand.

Excellent. "Take Joachim and the healer to the sick room," he told Broderick. "She's to bandage him up and nothing more. Make sure she doesn't touch him sexually." If she did, Joachim would heal speedily, his injuries forgotten far too soon.

Broderick nodded and stood.

Now. Time to see to his woman.

Without another word, Valerian clasped her hand and tugged her from the arena.

They were meant to be together—and now he would prove it.

CHAPTER THIRTEEN

POSEIDON WAS BORED.

He was god of the sea, ruler of fish, merpeople and ocean waves, and nothing excited him anymore. Not even the storms and destruction he'd recently caused. People had screamed, people had died, yada yada yada.

Perched on a boulder beneath a cliff, he traced his fingers through the dappled liquid surrounding him. There had to be something to combat this constant sense of ennui.

Create another hurricane or tsunami? No. The last few had been yawners.

Start a war? No. Too much effort for too little reward.

Abandon the water and enter Olympus? No again. The other gods were selfish and greedy, and he had no desire to deal with them, his temper too sharp.

What could he do, what could he do? Once he would have visited Atlantis—

Atlantis, he thought, straightening. Oh, oh, oh. Was that…yes, yes, it was. For the first time in an eternity, he experienced a flash of excitement.

He hadn't considered Atlantis and its people—his subjects—in years. Many had called for him, but he'd ignored their pleas for help. The last time he'd offered aid, he'd received no thanks, only complaints.

Perhaps the people—or rather, the *abominations*,

as his brothers often called them—had learned to be appreciative.

There was only one way to find out.

Poseidon grinned.

SHAYE'S ATTENTION REMAINED on Valerian's back as he led her through the palace, following the same path they'd taken earlier. She offered no protests. Muscles strained and bunched in his bare shoulders. Blood blended with sand, both splattered all over him, forming lines and circles on his skin.

He'd very nearly killed a man without hesitation or remorse. His own cousin, no less. But the biggest surprise? She'd watched him do it, and she hadn't flinched.

She'd been too relieved. He'd won, as promised. He would live and keep his crown.

The fight had unfolded like something out of a movie. Valerian had moved with grace and fluidity, each intricate step as beautiful as it was dangerous. Her heart had drummed erratically in her chest, only to stop altogether when Valerian received his first injury. She'd been unprepared for the blast of anger she'd felt toward Joachim.

More than that, she'd been unprepared for the fright she'd felt on Valerian's behalf.

She could have run—should have run. What better time to escape? Like a girl besotted, she'd stayed. Not because she'd promised Valerian—a promise made under duress wasn't really a promise, to her way of thinking—but because she'd had to know the outcome of the battle.

In the end, he'd shocked her. He'd purposely missed his cousin's heart, allowing the man to live to fight another day.

He cared about his people. Even those who defied him. How many other kings could say the same?

And then, what he'd said...

I hereby claim Shaye Octavia Holling as my mate. Your queen.

Again and again the words had whispered through her mind, making her shiver.

I should be...outraged?

Yes, of course. Most definitely.

After all, this thing with Valerian, it wasn't a game. It was her life. Unlike him, she wasn't immortal.

Wait. Were nymphos immortal? How old was Valerian? Anyway. *She* didn't get a second chance.

"You did good out there," she said grudgingly.

"Some women abhor violence," he said. "Some are titillated by it. Which are you?"

"Neither," she said. "But I'm certain there are other ways to be, like ambivalent or confused."

"So...you don't fear me?" Fear now saturated *his* voice.

"No." Truth. He could have harmed her a million times over by now, but he'd only ever treated her gently. He'd even placed himself in harm's way in order to protect her.

"But you *do* desire me?" Hope had replaced the fear.

Rather than answer his question—the truth would get her into trouble—she said, "By the way. I'm *not* your woman."

He cast her a pitying look. "Cease your protests, Moon. They'll only embarrass you when you at last admit your love for me."

So. No more talk of lust. He'd moved on to love. She snorted.

"Are surface dwellers allowed to combat each other with swords?" he asked.

"When countries are at war, yes. When the men are caught up in a personal vendetta, no. Not without consequences."

"What of protecting yourself or those you love?"

"It's allowed, but sometimes there are still consequences."

"You are clearly far better off here."

Another snort. "I should have known you'd go there."

They turned a corner and Valerian stumbled—over nothing. His injuries must have weakened him.

Her concern for him doubled. "You need a healer, too," she said.

"I have *you*. I need no one else."

She had a sinking suspicion he meant those words in more ways than one. Despite everything that had happened—or maybe *because of* everything that had happened—she couldn't deny this man saw only the best in her.

While she administered aid, would he "accidentally" touch her? Would he purr his warm breath into her ears, over her skin, and let his white-hot gaze devour her?

Better question: Would she be able to resist him?

Already her resolve teetered on precarious ground. Perhaps playing doctor wasn't a smart move.

"Valerian, O mighty king of the nymphos. Please listen to me. I know absolutely nothing about wound care."

"I don't care. I trust you."

"Trust doesn't matter. Not in this. I could do more harm than good."

"And you want me well?" Satisfaction dripped from his tone.

"Uh, don't read too much into it, big guy. I'd want my worst enemy to get well. Because I'm nice."

"Nice?"

"All right. That's fair. I'm *sometimes* nice."

He pushed out a breath. "I meant I trust only you to be with me while I'm in such a weakened state."

How did he always manage to say the exact right thing to melt the ice around her heart? "But why? You don't know—"

"Not this again, little Moon. I know you. But, if it will make you feel better, you can tell me all about your life while you patch me."

"I can, can I?" she asked dryly. "How generous of you."

"If you're nice, you'll agree. You'll distract me from my pain."

Her concern instantly resurged. "You're in pain?" Stupid question. He'd been slashed by a sword. Of course he was in pain.

He winked at her over his shoulder, his eyes gleaming with amusement. "So. Much. Pain."

Well. She pursed her lips. "If you're talking about blue balls—"

"Blue balls?" His shoulders shook, and she heard the rumbling purr of his beautiful laughter. "Oh, but I like your wicked mouth, Moon."

Unbidden, her lips inched into a half smile. "Well, I've somehow managed to resist you for twenty-four hours. That's got to be a record, right? Your groin must be seriously neglected."

"I'm glad you understand. Kiss it and make it better?"

She snorted. "In your dreams."

"Yes, please. You've seen my life, yes? My dreams always come true." His tone was husky and rich but also honey warm, as if the thought of her ravishment was an exquisite bliss. As if, in his mind, she was already naked and he was already inside her.

She would have to remain on full alert with this man. Being with him, she suspected, would be like shooting herself full of heroin. Addictive, wild, a high beyond imagining, but also lethal and stupid. So, if she could resist taking that first, experimental taste—well, a second taste—she wouldn't have to deal with withdrawal.

Her new mantra: *Resist!* "I think I'm more of a nightmare waiting to happen."

He brought her knuckles to his lips and stroked them with his tongue. "If you have sex with me, I'll be healed by the time you're screaming my name. Win-win for both of us."

Shivers down her spine, fire in her blood. He said nothing else, letting her mind and body battle for supremacy.

Stay strong. Be cold.

If he touched her... Wait. He *was* touching her, his hand clutching hers, and it felt good.

"I'm going on record right now," she said.

Once again he looked over his shoulder. This time he silenced her. He licked his lips, as if he knew exactly what reaction he'd caused in her and planned to exploit it by whatever means necessary.

A foreign part of her—a part happy to reveal itself only around him—urged her to reach up and run her fingers through his hair...across his beautiful face. His decadent flavor was still in her mouth, the press of his lips imprinted on her memory.

The very reason she had to resist him.

"Sex isn't happening." There. Stated now, so that he had no excuse later. Because, if a nymph's pheromone could drug, what could a nymph's penis do? "If you push me, I'll resent you."

"Will you resent me the same way you hate me?"

He'd just had to remind her about that, hadn't he? Her free hand fisted, and her belly quivered. "No," she said.

He sighed. "If you insist on abstaining—"

"I do."

"Then I'll spend the rest of the day—" he grimaced "—talking with you."

Probably shouldn't laugh.

Really, he could have claimed she owed him.

Once a date had felt entitled to sex after paying for dinner. If not for her self-defense classes he might have succeeded in his endeavor to exact payment. But Valerian acted as if only her delight would spark his own.

No self-defense class in the world could protect her from his appeal.

"How altruistic of you," she finally said, forcing a dry tone.

"Tell me. Have you had a bad experience with sex?" he asked gently. "Because I would be happy to return to the surface and punish anyone who ever hurt you."

The urge to lean against him, simply enjoy being with him, bombarded her. "No." *Try* zero *experiences, buddy.* How would Valerian react to *that*?

And she wanted to lean against him? Fear raised its ugly head to screech, *Fool!*

Why begin something destined to end?

"What if Joachim challenges you again?" she asked, changing the focus of the conversation. "Or what if he just stabs you in the back without bothering to engage in a fair fight?"

"He won't."

"How can you be sure?"

"Joachim lost. Everyone knows his skill is inferior to mine. Whether he kills me in the future or not, he'll never be accepted as leader."

They turned another corner, torches lighting the hallway, revealing familiar nicked-and-scuffed walls.

At the entrance to the master suite, he opened the door with his free hand.

She released him to soar inside—and gasped.

The large bed had been made, with a new comforter. A pink comforter.

Jewelry had been scattered over the vanity. Every piece boasted pink diamonds or pink crystals. A full-size mirror hung on the wall, the frame made from pink-veined marble.

Steam curled from the bathing pool, twining around the pink flower petals that floated on the surface.

"I can't...how did you...?" *Use your words.*

An impossibility at the moment.

"I sent a man to the Outer City bright and early this morning to buy things I thought you'd like. I want you comfortable in this room. Want it to be ours, not mine."

She swallowed the lump growing in her throat.

"Thank you," she managed to say. "This might be the nicest thing anyone has ever done for me."

"This, Shaye, is only the beginning."

STANDING THERE, VALERIAN drank in the sight of his mate. Then he drank in the sight of the bed. He wanted Shaye there, splayed and open for his view. His touch.

No, no, no. Control yourself.

She'd made her desires clear. Talk. Nothing sexual.

Now his mission was clear: tempt her into begging for more.

He'd never before had to use sexual prowess to seduce a woman. Anyone he'd ever desired had desired him in return, no encouragement necessary. Shaye made him feel at a loss. While he hungered for every part of her, she continually pushed him away. And of all the women in the world, she should crave him most.

How much longer could his body withstand her rejection?

Not much, he suspected.

"I'll gather the supplies," he said. He unearthed clean rags, a basin of hot water, a jar of cleaning oil, and a vial of healing sand from the Forest of the Dragons and placed each item on a tray.

His ears were attuned to Shaye's every movement, lest she decide to bolt for the door. Surprisingly, she remained exactly where he'd left her.

Their gazes clashed as he walked toward her. How lovely she was. Her pale hair draped over her shoulders, an erotic curtain. Beneath her shirt, her nipples were hard.

He was hard. He'd been hard since he'd last taken her hand, and memories of their kiss had played through his mind.

She gasped as if she knew the path his thoughts had just traveled…as if she *liked* the path his thoughts had just traveled.

Oh, to be so lucky.

Instead of placing the tray in her outstretched hands, he leaned down slowly, giving her ample time to misunderstand his intentions. He had to know her reaction.

His lips hovered over hers, as if he meant to kiss her, her snow-sweet scent filling his nostrils. She trembled, her breath catching in her throat. What she didn't do? Rebuke him.

The stubborn woman yearned for him to kiss her,

whether she would admit it or not. But she'd already told him no, and he wasn't going to violate her trust.

He lifted his head *without* touching her in any way. "Thank you for tending to me," he told her, his voice soft.

"Yes. Well." She nibbled on her bottom lip. "I warn you. I'm not known for my gentleness."

"I'll love having your hands on me."

After he explained what she needed to do with each item, he carried the room's only chair next to Shaye and tried not to grimace.

With somewhat shaky fingers, she brushed the dark sand from his shoulder, careful to avoid his wound. He winced as sharp pain radiated throughout his body.

"Distract me," he said. "Tell me what you enjoy doing in your free time."

"Work. For years I've only really worked. I didn't just write cards, I ran a company. And I guess I spent some time intimidating people."

"Your intimidation techniques are adorable."

She rolled her eyes as she soaked one of the rags with oil. "This smells good. What is it?"

"Soap, I think your people call it."

"Our soap doesn't smell like this. Like magic."

He shrugged and returned to the previous subject. "A company is like a kingdom, yes?"

"Yes. I suppose."

"So you were already a queen."

"I...never actually thought of it that way but kind of wish I had. Bow to me!"

He chuckled.

"What about you?" she asked. "What do you do in your spare time? Paint?"

"Yes. I also—never mind."

"Let me guess. Have sex."

He gave a single nod.

"There's never been anyone special?" As soon as she asked, he knew she wished she could take back the question.

"No one. Nymphs have one mate. Only one."

"What happens if that mate dies?"

"The nymph dies with her."

"Wow." She searched the tray for the item she wanted. "How are mates chosen?"

"Chemistry. Fate. A thousand others things, I'm sure."

"So you don't really know. Got it."

A corner of his mouth curled up. "Do you have a pet?"

Longing lit her features. "No. As a child I wasn't allowed. Fur would have dirtied my mother's clothes."

"But you wanted one." A statement not a question.

"Yes." With a scowl, she slapped the cloth against his wound. "This topic is stupid. Let's discuss something else."

He was beginning to see a pattern to her bouts of anger. Only when her sense of detachment was threatened did she react with waspishness.

"You like people to think you are cold and unfeeling," he said. "You've even tried your hardest to convince me of this. Several times. Why?"

"Look, my mom made me see shrinks when I was a kid." More gently, she cleaned away every impurity. "I don't need an amateur diagnosis right now."

"Tell me," he beseeched. She might think she wanted to be cold, but he saw the moments of warmth and softness she tried so hard to hide.

"There's nothing to tell, really. Over the years, I learned that relationships—love—always lead to pain and upset."

He frowned. "That isn't even close to the truth. Love heals."

"I've never seen an example of that." She probed the edge of his wound with her fingers. "This cut is pretty deep. I think you need stitches."

He bit his lip to hide his wince. He'd never had to deal with a wound before. After a battle, he'd always gone straight to a woman and had sex, his wounds disappearing of their own accord.

"What I need is sex," he muttered.

"Are you pushing me? That sounds like pushing." She scowled, even as she tenderly dried the injury. "I'm more than willing to go get one of the other women for you."

As her words echoed between them, she pressed her lips together. A combination of rage and trepidation flitted over her expression. Did she fear he would take her up on the offer?

"Ah, little moonbeam. When will you learn? Only you will do."

She relaxed, her expression softening. "When will you accept the fact that I don't sleep around?"

He plucked the ends of her hair and sifted the silky strands through his fingers before he brought them to his nose to sniff. Ah, sweet heaven. "You smell so good."

"Yes, well, I can't say the same for you."

He took no offense. "I'm most definitely in need of a bath. Would you care to join me?"

A quiver raked her, and she tossed the bloody rag into the hearth. "No, thank you." Next she picked up a clean rag and scooped sand into a gaping pocket. "You do realize I'm about to put sand in an open sore, right?"

"Right."

"And you still want me to do it?"

"Of course."

She shook her head, incredulous. "Whatever. It's your infection." But she hesitated a moment before smearing the grains into his injury.

He didn't speak for a long while. He concentrated on her breath, gently fanning his shoulder. He concentrated on her teeth, nibbling on her lower lip. He grew painfully hard all over again.

When *wasn't* he hard lately?

After she'd wrapped the wound in a bandage, he stood. His nerve endings were sensitized, his skin pulled too tight over bone. He burned from the inside out.

Her gaze lowered, and she gasped. She jumped away from him, as if he'd morphed into a monster.

"Put that thing away," she said. She even pointed.

Feared the mighty sword between his legs, did she?

"That," he said, "is a *he*, and he is here to stay."

"Don't tell me you've named—"

"King Longstaff and his trusty knights," he interjected, teasing her more fun than he'd had in a very long time.

She seemed to choke on her tongue, and he had to swallow a laugh.

"King Longstaff insists his subjects bow before him…orally praise him."

Color high in her cheeks, she tossed the rest of the bandages at his chest. "King Longstaff is about to lose his trusty knights—and his head!"

There was no swallowing his laughter this time; loud guffaws burst free.

"Methinks the lady protests too much."

"Oh, really?" She took a menacing step toward

him, and he immediately cupped his precious. Now *she* laughed. "Methinks the king fears his lady's mighty wrath."

He stilled. He didn't even dare to breath. *His* lady, she'd said. His. Not "the" lady. She was beginning to see him in a romantic light.

Perhaps she realized the implication, as well. Her laughter died, and her smile faded. "Um. I…" She gulped.

"No," he said, before she could do her best to ruin the moment.

While at war, he'd learned to always end every battle on a positive note. So. That's what he would do here.

"Thank you for patching me up. Enjoy the rest of your day. My lady." He left her then, striding out of the room without a backward glance.

CHAPTER FOURTEEN

DR. BRENNA JOHNSTON tied her black curls on top of her head with a thin strip of cloth. As always, a few of the shorter curls escaped confinement to cascade over her temples.

How did I end up in this situation?

She studied the unconscious man draped across a bed of sapphire silk. His beautiful dark hair reached the rise of his powerful shoulders. Long eyelashes etched spiked shadows along his cheeks. His nose was slightly crooked, his lips lush.

He looked like a fallen angel.

A dying, pain-entrenched fallen angel.

Blood oozed from thick gashes on his chest and thigh. Before the fight, his skin had been deeply tanned. Now it was pale and tinted blue. He'd gone into a mild form of shock.

As a surgeon, she'd seen worse. She could fix him. Though she would have preferred to use *her* tools in *her* hospital with *her* nurses aiding her. Not the jars of oil and sand she'd been given, an unsterilized environment, and the lug head standing guard at the door.

At least there was one fact in her favor. She'd been terrified since being taken hostage by these giant, hulking beasts, but for the first time since entering this... whatever it was, she felt in control. Like herself, confident and in her element.

With a wave of her finger, Brenna summoned the guard. He approached her warily. She didn't back away, but forced herself to stand her ground as she signed what she needed.

His face scrunched with confusion, and he held up his hands, a command for her to be still. "I have no idea what it is you're doing. Can you not speak?"

She sighed inwardly. Her vocal cords had been severely damaged years ago. There weren't any scars on the outside; no, her scars were internal. She'd been attacked—a blurred, blackened, hated memory she couldn't allow herself to relive. Not if she hoped to function. But. While she could speak, her voice was... not pretty.

"Needle," she croaked. "Thread." Primitive that he was, he probably wouldn't know a scalpel from a butter knife. "Operating tools."

He cringed at the rough, broken sounds she'd made but nodded and raced off. When he returned a short while later, he handed her a lumpy black satchel. She unrolled it, finding a bronze scalpel, plus thin hooks and several needles.

"Fire," she said now. "Hot water."

He removed a blazing sconce from the wall and tossed the entire thing into the hearth. The logs inside quickly caught flame, crackling and burning.

"Bowl. Water."

He found a bowl and filled it with water before attempting to hand it to her.

She pointed to the fire.

After he'd hung the bowl over the flames, she dropped the instruments inside the water.

Once everything had been sterilized, her hands scrubbed clean, she approached her patient, ready to act. He had yet to move. Had yet to make any noise, really. His features were no longer pinched with pain; they were relaxed.

That both elated and worried her. At least he wouldn't feel the pain of her needle. But such a deep sleep...

Brenna squared her shoulders and got to work. She cut off his pants, cleaned the gaping wounds on his legs and chest, and did her best to repair the torn tissue—which was in better shape than she'd dared hope. Sounded easy, sounded quick, but she was by his side for several hours, sweat trickling from her. Toward the end, fatigue caused the muscles in her arms and lower back to quiver.

That will have to do.

She would have liked to give him a transfusion, but without blood-typing, she could do him more harm than good.

Would that be such a bad thing? If he died—if all the warriors in the palace died—she could escape.

She desperately wanted to escape.

The man who'd chosen her last night—Shivawn—had attempted to ease her distress by explaining where she was and why she'd been brought here. Of course, his explanation had only intensified her fear.

Atlantis. Nymphs. Sex for survival. At first she hadn't wanted to believe him. However, after everything she'd witnessed today, she no longer had the luxury of disbelief. Sword fights and bejeweled walls. Silk pillows lining every wall with warriors having sex atop them. Mermaids and a crystal ceiling that produced light. Women going mad, becoming sex starved.

Shivawn had been ordered not to touch Brenna, so he'd tried to talk her into touching him. He'd expected the same easy and enthusiastic response. How surprised he'd been when his efforts were met with bouts of hysterical sobbing. Finally, though, he'd left her alone. And he'd been oddly sweet about the entire situation. Also surprisingly protective.

Still. He had to regret his choice already. He *did* regret. This morning, when she'd caught glimpses of the other warriors in bed with their chosen—no one closed their doors here—Shivawn had cursed at the couples, anger steeped in envy.

He wanted that for himself. But she couldn't give it to him. Not now, not ever.

Brenna had only allowed Shivawn to pick her from the lineup so that she would be taken away from the large group of men. One warrior she could fight and disable. But all of them? No way.

Part of her had wanted to go home, but she hadn't been sure she would survive another trip through the water. The other part of her *hadn't* wanted to go home. For the first time, she didn't have to worry about her ex-husband's threats.

Leave me, Bren, and I'll kill you.

He was in prison, yes, but soon he would be up for parole.

She sighed. For the next several hours, she remained seated beside the unconscious man—Joachim—sponging a warm, wet rag over his forehead and doing everything in her power to make him comfortable and keep him from getting cold. As much blood as he'd lost, he was susceptible to hypothermia.

"Brenna." Shivawn's voice drifted from the doorway, jolting her. "Now that I know you're capable of speech, I long to talk with you. I'd love to know more about you."

"I…" She cleared her throat.

She'd been born in the US, though her family had

come from a small village in Mexico. Different sicknesses killed her parents and sibling. Probably the reason she'd decided to become a doctor. She'd moved from foster home to foster home, from bad to worse to not too bad to worse again. Probably why she'd been so eager to hook up with Ethan. At eighteen they'd married.

Gonna have a family of my own again, she'd thought.

Shivawn sighed. "All right. We'll return to my chamber. You don't have to tell me anything until you're ready."

Her heart kicked into overdrive. *Remain calm.* She twisted in her chair. He stood there, strong and sure.

The guard remained in place but pretended to study the floor.

"Brenna," Shivawn repeated, extending his hand.

He was a handsome man, with brown hair and green eyes, and a part of her wished she were a normal woman who enjoyed men and sex and...fun.

Oh, I miss having fun.

But she shook her head in negation.

His shoulders slumped, his lips compressing into a thin line. "Why do you continue to deny me even the smallest concession?"

She hoped her narrowed gaze told him everything she wished she had the courage to say: *You, caveman. Me, captive. Us, enemies.*

The fact that he and his buddies saw nothing wrong with abducting women, well, they clearly needed some sense knocked into their thick skulls.

"Have I hurt you in any way?" he asked.

She shook her head a second time. He hadn't, and it still shocked her.

He stepped forward, his features softening. "I only wish to give you pleasure."

No. No! Fact was, she didn't think she was capable of experiencing sexual pleasure. Too many bad memories would taint the experience.

Again, she shook her head. "I'm staying here."

"Joachim doesn't need you. I do."

"No."

He stopped. His lips pursed.

Would her continued refusal cause him to erupt in fury? Would he try to force her? Would he morph from nice guy to beast?

A terrible sickness churned inside her stomach.

"I will never hurt you, Brenna. I will always protect and defend you. I'll even cherish you."

Maybe he would. Maybe he wouldn't.

She'd been watching and listening and she'd picked up a few tidbits. Every nymph had a mate. Someone he obsessed over.

She wasn't Shivawn's mate. Clearly. He wanted her, but he didn't need her. Not the way the king seemed to need the white-haired girl, Shaye.

One day, Shivawn would meet his mate and happily wash his hands of Brenna. What would happen to her then?

"No," she repeated. If ever she decided to risk being with a man and battling the worst of her memories, it would be with one far less intimidating. Someone who couldn't snap her neck with a flick of his wrist.

"Brenna, please. Give me a chance."

She jabbed her finger in the direction of her patient. "He needs me."

Shivawn regarded her for a long while, different emotions playing over his face. Disappointment. Regret. Resolve. Finally he spun on his heel and stalked out of the room.

She breathed a sigh of relief and, shockingly enough, disappointment. She'd liked his company?

Forget him. She rotated back to the injured warrior and smoothed a hand over his too-cold brow. No progress.

Would he survive? He'd lost so much blood.

He was a lot bigger than Shivawn. Probably a lot stronger, too. Which meant he was more dangerous.

Actually, his *disposition* made him more dangerous. He'd challenged the king to a sword fight. But right now he was as weak as a babe and utterly helpless.

She hated to see anyone suffer. No one knew better than Brenna how it felt to lie in bed, broken, beaten and near death.

With a sigh, she leaned forward, as if pulled by a power stronger than herself, and placed a soft kiss on his forehead; she willed him to get better.

"No touching," the guard said.

The patient's eyes blinked open, as if the kiss—innocent as it had been—had given him the strength he'd needed to awaken at last. He spied her hovering over him and frowned. Confusion darkened his eyes.

She straightened with a jolt of panic.

"Did I die, then?" she heard him say.

His voice was strained. *He's feeble. He can't hurt you.* Still…she had to force herself to remain in place.

Hand shaking, she once again flattened her palm on his brow. He'd warmed, but only slightly.

He leaned into her touch. "Did I enter Olympus?"

A nymph's idea of heaven? She shook her head.

His gaze darted around the room. "Why are you here? Why am I—" His words ground to a halt. "Valerian," he grated. "The fight. I lost." He tried to sit up.

She gently pushed him down and smoothed his hair

from his face, attempting to soothe him and defuse
his anger.

If he decided to fight her, she'd...what?

Shockingly enough, he relaxed.

Drawing in a deep breath, he even reached up and
wrapped his fingers around her wrist.

Remain calm, remain calm, please, remain calm. Patients touched her all the time. She'd had to train herself
to maintain a casual expression.

When she attempted to pull away, he tightened his
grip.

"What are you doing here, Shivawn's woman?"

Her pulse hammered in her neck as she pointed to
his bandaged wounds.

He studied her more intently, his brows drawing together. "You are a healer?"

She nodded and once more tried to extract herself
from his hold, but once more he tightened his grip.

"Can you not speak?" he asked.

He wasn't the first to ask, but he was the first to
ask without any hint of pity. He looked curious, nothing more.

"Broken," she said, motioning to her neck with her
free hand.

He...didn't flinch, and amazement filled her.

He released her to trace his fingers over her neck,
where the pulse still fluttered wildly. His fingers
brushed the soft skin, as if searching for an injury.

She shivered, both appalled and...needy? What was
wrong with her? She hadn't reacted to a man in years.

"How?" he asked.

People always asked, as if they were inquiring about
the weather or about where she bought her shoes. In
the beginning, the question had thrown her, brought

back the horrible memories of being pinned down and choked by her enraged, jealous husband. She used to answer with a casual, "Car accident," but she doubted this archaic warrior would understand what that meant.

Brenna bit her lip and, tentative, wrapped one of her hands gently around his neck and shook, then pointed to her own neck with the other.

His eyes narrowed, and his hands closed over her wrists, far more gently than before. "Someone choked you?"

Nod.

"A man?" The words were so quiet she barely heard them.

Again she nodded.

"No touching," the man in the doorway suddenly barked. "The king's orders. Release her, Joachim."

She'd forgotten about the guard.

Joachim's gaze spit hate at the male. A second later, the two men engaged in a heated conversation in a language she'd never heard. During it all, Joachim retained his gentle grip on her.

She finally managed to wrench free. Relief swept through her, and she rubbed her wrist. Where he'd touched, her skin had warmed. Sensitized.

Joachim was frightening, volatile and *violent*, traits she absolutely abhorred. She shouldn't like his touch. No, she shouldn't.

"Would you like me to kill him for you?" Joachim asked, surprising her.

She blinked in confusion and pointed to the sentinel at the door.

"Good luck with that," the man in question said.

Joachim ignored him. "The one who hurt you."

She hesitated a moment. The idea appealed to her. No

denying that. Most of her problems would die with her
ex. His continued threats. Her fear of every shadow and
unexplained noise. Her inability to date another man,
certain her ex would harm him out of spite. Not that she
wanted to date. But how could she justify such an action?

Killing Ethan would be an act of hate. Would make
her as despicable as he was.

So. She forced herself to shake her head.

"Power is good," he said, his voice nothing but smoke
and gravel. "Hurting a woman is not." His eyelids drifted
closed...

He pried them open. Determined to stay awake?

She didn't know whether he believed what he'd said
or not. Either way, he struck her as someone who would
be uncontrollable in the midst of a rage. After today's
sword fight...

"What's your name?" he asked.

"Brenna."

"Brenna," he said, as if he savored the sound on his
tongue. An instant later, his mouth pulled tight in a
grim line. Fury darkened his eyes, churning like a violent sea. "Where is Shivawn?"

She found herself rising from the bed, trembling. In
the blink of an eye, he'd become angry. Why? What
had she done?

He frowned as his eyelids dipped shut once more.
"Why are you backing away from me, woman? Are you
going back to your lover?" The last was said with a sneer.

Before he could rise from the bed to grab her, she
turned and fled the room, unsure where to go. Only
knowing she had to leave this place. Had to leave *him*.

"FOLLOW HER," JOACHIM commanded. "Make sure she
arrives at her destination safely."

"You had best watch who you order about," the warrior posted at his door growled—before doing as commanded and taking off after Brenna.

He cursed. He'd never felt so powerless, and the feeling infuriated him. He didn't want her to be with Shivawn. He wanted her here. With him. Wanted her to talk to him and touch his brow again.

Had he been able, he would have vaulted from the bed and forced her to return. *He* was master here.

You are master of no one. You can't even govern yourself.

He'd let anger drive her away before he could comfort her for the horrors of her past. Before he'd thanked her properly for taking such good care of him.

She had feared his anger. He'd seen it in her eyes.

Now Shivawn would have the privilege of comforting her.

Joachim wanted to blame Valerian for this predicament, but he couldn't. He'd issued the challenge, and his cousin had beaten him fairly. As a man who valued power above all else, he respected Valerian's win.

And, at the moment, he understood his cousin's need for the pale woman…understood his willingness to do anything to keep her.

Just then, Joachim would have done *anything* to have Brenna.

CHAPTER FIFTEEN

DESIRE PLAGUED VALERIAN as he stormed into the dining hall. The worst desire of his life. And the best. Wooing was hard. Literally! But he'd made progress with Shaye. He knew it. They'd talked, gotten to know each other better—her primary objection to his courtship would soon be obliterated entirely—and even flirted with each other. She'd laughed. She'd enjoyed his company.

There at the end, she'd forgotten to keep him at a distance. She'd opened up and let him in. At least emotionally.

Soon she would trust him fully. Physically. Until then, he just had to survive. And he would. Because she would kiss him again.

Their kiss…

She'd erupted, become a living spark. She hadn't hidden her desire but had reveled in it. Her body had burned for his, desperate for him to quench her sexual thirst.

Only thing to do now was drink himself into oblivion.

He halted when he spied Shivawn at the table, a different flask in each hand. The man already possessed red, glassy eyes and wobbled in his chair.

Shivawn was young, nearing one hundred years of age. A babe, really, when compared to Valerian's six hundred three. Shivawn was a strong warrior, though, and swift on his feet. He'd never hesitated to render a

deathblow when necessary. In fact, whenever an
required torturing, Shivawn had often volunteer
the job.

Good man, that.

However, Shivawn could be impulsive, allowing his
emotions to lead him.

Emotions were unreliable. They changed often and
rarely offered a clear—or truthful—picture about circumstances.

Perhaps Shivawn preferred emotion to logic because
his father had been as cold as ice, utterly *without* emotion. Very much like Valerian's own father.

Both males had died while battling demons who'd
claimed to be allies, only to change their minds directly
after peace talks; they'd slaughtered every nymph present.

Such was the way with demons.

While nymphs strengthened through sex—pleasure—demons strengthened through death—sorrow.

Babe that Valerian had been, he'd rallied the army
and attacked the demon camp the very next day. Rivers of blood had spilled. Demon blood.

His first victory—the first of many.

Where was his victory now? He could defeat a horde
of demons, but not one small wisp of a woman.

"Females," Shivawn groused.

"Females," Valerian agreed.

He plopped beside the warrior and confiscated one
of the flasks. "As your king, I'm entitled to half of your
belongs."

"Better than the alternative, I suppose, which is all
my belongings." Shivawn gulped from the remaining
flask.

Valerian drained the contents of his own in a single gulp, but found no comfort in the ensuing burn.

"My bedmate doesn't want me," his friend said, his tone bitter. "How is that possible? I'm a nymph."

"As am I. I'm king. I rule this place. My word is law. Except with Shaye." She had a mind of her own. A trait he liked, admired...but currently despised.

He would like it again just as soon as she decided she trusted him.

"Maybe—maybe Brenna prefers other women?"

"Have you tried wooing her?"

"Woo? Who has time to woo?" Shivawn's shoulders slumped. "I don't understand her. She actually fears me. Fears *me*, as if I'm a monster out to hurt her. I've never hurt a woman, Valerian. Never. All women worship me. Desire me." He sighed heavily.

"Not all women. Clearly." Valerian appropriated the other flask and drained it. "Why are you complaining, anyway? Brenna isn't your mate. Why don't you focus on the woman who does want you? The one you slept with."

"I would, but she's currently in bed with someone else."

At least Shaye hadn't turned to another.

His grip tightened on the flask, cracking the center. He would die before he allowed another man to touch her.

Even if she *wanted* that other man?

He...didn't know.

Valerian gnashed his teeth. Her happiness mattered to him. If she couldn't be happy with him, he would have to give her up, wouldn't he?

The thought blackened his mood. He would just have to woo her *harder*.

"Why don't *you* focus on another woman?" Shivawn asked. "Just because you can't finish with someone else doesn't mean you won't *enjoy* someone else."

"I don't want another woman." He couldn't abide the thought of having anyone other than Shaye in his bed.

His arms craved Shaye, only Shaye. His legs craved her. The heart slamming against his ribs craved her. She exuded a special scent, and every part of him recognized every other woman as an imitation. An impostor.

Shaye had wrapped him in a terrible and wonderful and hated and loved cloud of lust. How could he win her?

He planned to buy her a stable of ponies. On his way to the dining hall, he'd sent a man into the Outer City to purchase the pink pony he'd seen. The first of many.

What else could he do? She missed her job. Those anti-cards. And she was toying with the idea of writing a book.

First thing in the morning, he would deliver paper and ink.

Would she react as she had when she'd spied the new decorations in their bedroom? A mix of shock, joy and delight had radiated from her.

He could only hope.

"...than they are worth," Shivawn said, cutting into his thoughts.

"I'm sorry. I was thinking about Shaye. You'll have to repeat your statement."

Frowning, Shivawn plucked a crumb from the table and tossed it aside. "I hate that we nymphs must rely on another being for our survival. Women are more trouble than they are worth."

Shaye would say men were more trouble than they were worth, he was sure. "One way or another, people rely on other people. That's a fact of life for *everyone*, Shivawn. We were never meant to exist in solitary confinement."

A moment passed in silence.

Finally Shivawn sighed. "Females," he repeated. He stood, stalked to the kitchens and returned with an armful of new flasks.

"Females," Valerian agreed. He claimed his 50 percent and quickly drained the contents, no longer experiencing any kind of burn.

"I explained to Brenna I can give her more pleasure than she's ever known. Did she care? Noooo."

Valerian frowned. His friend sounded so...cocky.

His cheeks heated as he recalled the time *he* had said similar words to Shaye; he slouched in his seat. *Perhaps I'm not so irresistible after all.*

In his defense, he would have loved hearing about *her* ability to pleasure *him*.

"Perhaps Brenna needs to hear a few testimonials from my former lovers," Shivawn continued.

The alcohol hit Valerian like a boot to the face, and he swayed. And...suddenly the warrior's idea seemed *wise*. No testimonials—*that's* where Valerian had gone wrong. And he hadn't been cocky. No, no. He'd been proactive!

Shaye had probably assumed his profession of expertise had been nothing more than pride. But she would *have* to believe the women who'd actually experienced the bliss of his touch.

"Never mind. I don't think Brenna would care about testimonials." Shivawn's voice was a little slurred. "I think she would still fear me. Females," he said, growling this time. "We don't need them."

"Don't need them." Valerian seized another flask.

"Except for Shaye. Need her always and forever." And he wasn't ashamed to admit it.

"At this rate, I'm going to become as weak as a babe," Shivawn admitted. "Earlier I tripped and fell in the hall like a clumsy dragon hatchling." He rubbed the spot just over his heart. "Theophilus's human bedmate isn't giving him any problems. Why is that, do you think? What's he doing that we aren't?"

As he leaned back, Valerian linked his fingers at his nape and cast his gaze to the ceiling. He blinked in surprise. Two shell-less mermaids pressed against the crystal, staring down at Shivawn and him with lusty smiles.

Both females waved. One even licked her lips.

He returned the greeting simply to be polite, not to encourage. But the mermaids banged against the crystal in an attempt to shatter the dome.

Once Valerian would have laughed. Now he worried about Shaye. If the mermaids succeeded, Shaye could drown. He shooed the two away.

Shivawn slapped his arm to gain his attention. "Do you not have an answer?"

"I've forgotten your question," he admitted. "My apologies."

"I wished to know why Theophilus's human bedmate has given him no trouble."

Valerian, too, would have liked to know the answer. He pictured the woman in question—a timid little bird, plain and yet she possessed a deliciously plump body made for a man's hands.

Theophilus had spotted her while passing through the Outer City. She'd put up no fight whatsoever as he lifted her into his arms to carry her away, had simply clung to him while smiling.

Next Valerian pictured Shaye. She wanted him to

believe her arctic and untouchable. No, she wanted *to be* arctic and untouchable. Poor darling would never get her wish. Too much passion burned inside her.

"Perhaps our women have secrets—sad, painful secrets—allowing them to fortify themselves against us," he said.

Actually, he *knew* Shaye had secrets. Unlocking them became an obsession. A necessity, like breathing. No, a necessity greater than breathing. Like sex.

Shivawn jerked a hand through his dark hair, the beads at the ends clanging together. "I'll try to unearth Brenna's secrets. Maybe then she'll accept me." He paused, his head canting to the side. "How do you unearth a woman's secrets?"

"Hard work?"

"Hard work," Shivawn echoed. "Where's the fun in that?"

Valerian believed he would have a *lot* of fun. Already anticipation fizzed in his veins. Learning more about Shaye? Yes, yes, a thousand times yes.

"Females," Shivawn grumbled.

"Females," Valerian agreed with a grin.

They clinked their flasks and drank deeply.

A soldier rushed into the room. "My king. A dragon army marches toward the fortress."

Valerian jumped up—and swayed. He cursed the dragons, and he cursed himself. He shouldn't have drunk so much. He should have stayed ready for action.

Well, no help for it now. He would have to fight. He would protect Shaye, whatever the cost.

A WEEK PASSED. Shaye spent a lot of time in Valerian's room, alone. For a man who'd professed his desire to be with her, he'd certainly seemed to enjoy his time away from her.

Typical!

Often she'd found herself wondering where he was, what he was doing—*who* he was doing.

Had he decided to be with another woman?

She wasn't worried. Or obsessed. She wasn't! She'd told him how silly the mates-for-life thing was; maybe he'd decided to believe her.

Her nails cut into her palms as she plopped in front of the vanity.

Love heals; it doesn't hurt. Love is the answer, not the problem.

The voice drifted through her mind, and she sat up straight, her brow knitting with confusion. She'd heard that voice before. She'd heard those *words* before.

Heart racing, she stood. One second, two. Her mind remained her own.

Her imagination? Magic?

Chewing on her bottom lip, she eased into the cushioned chair.

Love heals; it doesn't hurt. Love is the answer, not the problem.

Argh! There it was again.

This time, she stayed put. "Is someone here?" she whispered. Like, someone trapped inside the mirror, maybe? Here in Atlantis, anything was possible.

"I can't love him," she said. "I don't know him."

And she couldn't get to know him if he wouldn't freaking come around her!

Love heals; it doesn't hurt. Love is the answer, not the problem.

Enough! "Screw you," she muttered, stalking away.

All she'd done these past seven days was think about

Valerian, bathe in the pool, think about Valerian, try on the array of pink gowns he'd bought her—she wore one even now—think about Valerian, sleep, *dream* of Valerian, and spend time with Brenna and the other women. At least once a day, a guard had come to escort her to a hobby room. Oh, and she'd thought about Valerian.

She suspected she...missed him.

Why had he stayed away?

Buck up! Did the reason really matter?

She was done waiting around. Done feeling like a discarded piece of garbage. Today—through fair means or foul—she would be going home.

Major pat on the back for refusing to give herself to Valerian after his fight with Joachim, gifting him with her trust and virginity. If she had and he'd still ignored her, perhaps choosing to be with someone else, she would have regretted her actions every day for the rest of her miserable life.

She had enough regrets, thanks.

"Come, Moon."

Every muscle and cell in Shaye's body jolted in reaction to that voice. *His* voice. Her heart fell out of rhythm as her gaze found him—the man who'd tormented her with his absence.

He stood in the doorway, the very picture of masculinity and dirty sex, despite the new lines around his eyes and the hollows in his checks. He wore black pants, and miracle of miracles a black shirt covered his spectacular chest. His dark blond hair gave new meaning to sexy disarray, the locks endearingly windblown.

"Where have you been?" she snapped. Then she blushed. *Stay cool. Reveal nothing.*

He glowered. "A dragon army arrived in the Outer City. I had to send them back to their king."

So…he hadn't been with another woman. Relief washed through her because—just because! "You should have told me."

He scrubbed his free hand down his tired face. "Mates pleasure their men before sending them off to war. I refused to pressure you for such a gift."

Balloon pop. What remained of her anger deflated.

"Come," he repeated. There was no hint of emotion in his tone. He held out his hand and waved his fingers.

"Why?" She rubbed her arms. "Where are you taking me?" Home?

The thought panicked her when it should have delighted her.

He's screwing with my head!

"Today I'm your escort. It's time to visit with the other women." He again motioned with his fingers.

Why was he so unlike his usual self? Had he given up on her, as she'd suspected?

"Were you harmed during battle?" she asked, remaining in place.

"No."

"You won?"

"Of course."

Finally. Emotion. He glared at her with irritation for doubting his ability. "Yeah," she said in an attempt to assuage his masculine pride. "You probably sent those pesky dragons running home, crying for their mommies."

He blinked at her—confused?

Well. Confusion was better than the irritation. *My job here is done.* "All right. Let's go." She walked over and clasped his proffered hand.

Instant currents of electricity! Tingles raced up her

arm and heat pooled in her shoulder before zooming through the rest of her, igniting sparks of arousal.

In seconds, he'd reduced her to a puddle of heat and hormones.

He tugged her through the hallway. If contact had affected him, he gave no notice.

The jerk! "What are *you* doing today?"

"Training with my men."

He said no more.

"What's wrong with you, Valerian? You're like a pod-person right now."

"I have no idea what a pod-person is." He released a heavy sigh. "Word of our mating has spread faster than I intended. The horde of dragons came here hoping to take you away from me. To use you against me."

Her mouth dried. "And?"

"And I promised you I would protect you. I will. Aways. But I knew you would use the information to rally your cause and return home."

I should. I really should.

And she suspected he would hear her this time, and might even return her—the real crux of his fear. He didn't want to.

"How did you maintain your strength?" she asked, doing her best not to melt against him.

Oh, crap. That's right! Without sex, nymphs weakened. He needed physical intimacy to live, but the only thing she'd given him was grief.

"I took matters into my own hands," he said, every word stilted.

Oh. Ohhh. Heat burned her cheeks.

"This pleases you?" he asked, a brow lifted.

Yes! No. Maybe. "I'm going to plead the fifth," she said.

The corner of his mouth twitched. "I asked another

human what that means. You don't wish to incriminate yourself with your answer."

Her cheeks burned hotter.

Thankfully they reached the luxurious room where the lovesick, sex-crazed females from her mother's wedding were already gathered, saving her from having to think up a reply.

As usual, several men stood guard at the entrance. One guy held a bundle of paper, a feather and an inkwell.

Valerian scooped up the items and handed them to her. "I thought you would enjoy writing your anti-cards or starting your novel."

Her mouth fell open. He was giving her another gift? But…but…

"Thank you," she said softly, clutching the bundle to her chest. He could have gone the easy route and given her flowers and candy. Instead, he'd searched for something specific to her.

How am I not throwing myself at him right this very second?

"My pleasure," he said, his voice rough and raspy.

Licking her lips, she stepped toward him.

He stepped back. "I must go."

No! Stay! Their eyes met, and she had to fight the urge to rise on tiptoes, breathe in his scent and absorb his strength.

Kiss me, she silently beseeched, hating herself—hating him. *Help me figure out my next move.*

In the end, he turned and walked away, leaving her wanting more. So much more.

CHAPTER SIXTEEN

"I'VE NEVER, IN ALL my life, been pleasured like I was last night."

"Me, either."

"Uh, we know! Your screams were almost as loud as mine."

And so it began. The women had the same conversation every day.

The room hadn't changed, either. There were two couches, a thousand silk pillows, a table with snacks and bottles of wine, books and baskets containing needles and thread. This wasn't just a hobby room. This was a keep-the-women-busy-while-the-men-do-important-work room.

Already the other captives had formed groups. Or rather, dreaded cliques. Smiles and laughter abounded, and though many girls waved at her, no one asked her to join a conversation. All because she'd become known as the troublemaker.

But come on! This was a modern day harem, a concubine taken out only when her master had need of her body.

So. Decision made, no take-backs. *I'm going home today, as planned.*

No more lingering. No more hoping to learn more about Valerian...or dreaming about kissing him. She stomped her foot. No more!

"Ladies." She clapped her hands to gain everyone's attention. "I know you've had fun here. The men can be...distracting. But our vacation is over. It's time for us to return to the good ole United States of America. We have families mourning our loss."

Everyone ignored her.

Frustrated but determined, she continued. "There are enough of us to overtake the guards. We can bust free and beat feet to the portal."

So many gasps of outrage sounded, they could have been background music to a song.

"My family would want me to be happy. I'm happy here."

"I'm not leaving," someone else said. "I've waited my whole life to a meet man like Rueben."

"If you try to run, I'll scream for help. I'm not going to let you ruin this for us."

Shaye gripped the sides of her gown, nearly ripping the fabric as her frustration pummeled her determination. "That's how we settle our problems now? We tattle? Why do you want to stay here, anyway?" She said the words for *her* benefit, as well. "We're nothing but T and A to these guys. One day, they'll meet their mates and cut you loose."

"The poor girl's repressed, y'all. She's got lady blue balls, and it's made her daft. Let's offer support."

Almost everyone gathered around her, concern darkening every gaze. *I'm part of a cult. Or at the center of an intervention.*

For the next hour, she endured major TMI as the women told her their preferred sexual positions. If she tried this or that, they said, her mood would finally improve.

She countered with a speech about being worth more

than temporary pleasure. And that's all the nymphos could offer to anyone other than a mate.

In fact, *she* was the only mate here.

And yet I'm the one who wants to leave?

Eventually, the crowd grew tired of listening to her and called for the guards...summoned Valerian.

Her insides quivered. She paced. If there'd been a clock, she would have watched the hand mark the seconds. How long would Valerian make her wait for—

He strode into the room without preamble, shirtless once again, sweat and dirt smeared over his muscled chest. Her adrenaline levels spiked.

Silent, he homed in on her like a heat-seeking missile. She stood, dumbfounded, as he wrapped her in his arms and—

Made dirty, filthy love to her mouth.

The kiss had nothing to do with exploration and everything to do with persuasion. But it ended far too quickly, his tongue thrusting inside her mouth once, twice, staking a claim...just long enough to remind her of his taste, consume her senses and drive her crazy.

He lifted his head, leaving her wanting and desperate. Her lips tingled as she struggled to catch her breath.

Women had closed in on them...and they were now running their fingertips all over him.

Mine! Shaye scowled at the offenders.

What am I doing?

Control! "What was that for?" she asked, hating the tremor in her voice.

He brushed his fingers over her cheekbones. "Rather than wallowing in the fear of losing you, I'm striving to romance you."

Sweet fancy roses. If he hadn't started romancing her until now... *I'm in serious trouble.*

"Over the years I've learned that what you fear, you welcome into your life," he added. "Like a self-fulfilling prophecy."

She gulped. Was that what she had done to herself? Feared the collapse of her relationships so much, everything she said and did ensured the collapse happened?

"Be good," he told her, "and I'll take you into the Outer City when I finish training my men."

"Be good?" She bristled. "I'm not a child, and you are not my parent."

"Maybe not." He bent to run the lobe of her ear between his teeth. "But I spank."

I'm melting into him. I'm actually melting. She straightened with a jolt, snapping, "Well, I bite."

He grinned. "I look forward to having your teeth all over my body, Moon."

He left her then, while she reeled.

Disappointed sighs filled the room.

Trying to slow her erratic heartbeat and cool her heated skin, Shaye found an open corner and plopped onto a pillow.

If she managed an escape, could she really leave these women behind? No! She might have to trick them into going with her. But how?

She racked her brain but the answer eluded her. Feeling as if she were about to give herself an aneurysm, she used her new supplies to make anti-cards. Her version of therapy.

Card one, attempt one: *Benefits of dating me? You will be dating me. Enough said.*

Yes? No? Too cocky? The nympho attitude must have rubbed off on her. She ran a line of ink through the words.

Card one, attempt two: *Let me say this in a way you'll understand—I think your hot.*

Would half the population fail to recognize the grammatical error?

She crumbled the paper.

Card one, attempt three: *Roses are red, violets are blue. Nymphs.*

That one certainly fit everyone in the room, so… Done!

Card two, attempt one: *You don't always cheat, but—just kidding! You do. You always cheat.*

Or what about: *You're cheating? Good news! I am, too!*

Oookay. Two cheating cards in a matter of seconds. Had to be a record.

Card three, attempt one: *Some men aren't so bad. I guess.*

Ugh. What had Valerian done to her?

"I'm so jealous you were chosen by Valerian, king of the beefcakes." A brunette sat next to her. "Is he as good in bed as he looks?"

Silence descended over the room. Every eye focused on her.

"He even fought over you." The brunette sighed dreamily. "How romantic is that? Oh! I'm Jaclyn, by the way."

"I'm Soshanna," said an elegant black woman. "I've decided to keep Aeson. He takes orders *very* well."

"I'm Barrie," said a plain brunette.

"Martina," said the plump brunette who'd wanted to fight her for standing too close to Broderick. Not to mention the one who'd summoned the guard for attempting to plan an escape. Now she acted as if Shaye were an old friend.

Jaclyn had to be the ringleader, then. Everyone else followed her lead, introducing themselves. Though most of them had been wedding guests and friends of her mother's—or maybe the new husband's—and though they'd spent the last week together, everyone had been too blissed-out to think of anything but sex.

Maybe humans could build immunity against the nympho pheromone?

"Aren't we the luckiest girls in the world?" Jaclyn said.

Several squeals of delighted agreement erupted.

"Well, is Valerian good?" Barrie asked eagerly. "If he walks like a wet dream and talks like a wet dream…"

"I'm sure he is," Shaye muttered.

A sense of possessiveness rose up inside her, hot and angry; it was a nail-baring, teeth-snarling possessiveness that surprised her with its undeniable force. Other women shouldn't be wondering about Valerian naked. *He's taken and I will cut you!*

Excited twitters rang out.

"You mean you don't know? You haven't slept with him?"

"What! You would have had to resist him. How could you resist him?"

"Nymphs need sex. You're going to kill him. Give him to me!"

Shaye's nails dug into her knees. She should be happy someone else wanted him. She should play matchmaker. *Valerian, meet the new object of your obsession.*

A little voice inside her said, *Mine. Only mine.*

A sense of greediness held her in a vise-grip.

Barrie and the others soon got tired of awaiting her answer. Actually they forgot about Shaye entirely, planning ways to ensure Valerian "survived."

Whatever. Shaye stretched her legs and propped her feet on top of a pillow. Frustration—for so many different reasons—ate at her. Sexual frustration? Yes. Confusion? Definitely.

Sighing, she set her new cards aside. Enough business for one day. She would concentrate on having fun—like writing her novel. Yes! Excitement bloomed.

First, she had to decide what kind of book to write. A slice from her own life? *My Adventures with The Nymphos.* Or maybe a modern woman's tale about the hazards of dating and love. Of course, there wouldn't be a happy ending.

Someone had to tell the world the truth.

The heroine could be disgusted by all the lovesick fools around her—while fighting her attraction to the sexiest man on the planet.

If I go that route, I might as well name her Eyahs. Shaye spelled backward. The hero would be Nairelav—Valerian spelled backward—and he would be king of the sohpmyn. Nymphos spelled backward.

Well. Why not? Write what you know.

So, Shaye wrote: *Chapter One. Nairelav, king of the sohpmyn, who considered himself the greatest leader of the greatest army and the greatest lover ever to live, untangled his glorious body from the naked, slumbering woman beside him...only to discover his legs were entwined with two other naked, slumbering women. Because he was a manwhore with no self-control. He'd say he needed to be spanked—but he'd like it, so, punishment was a no-go.*

Well. Not bad, but it definitely needed tweaking.

As the hours passed, different warriors straggled into the room, collecting their women. They were covered in sweat and sand, even blood. Each time the door opened, she found herself tensing with dread...and anticipation.

Dang it! Where was Valerian?

Soon only Shaye and the girl with curly black hair and sad brown eyes remained. The one who'd ended up with Shivawn.

She sat on the couch, staring at nothing. For the first time, she appeared unafraid.

Shaye gathered her supplies, stood and closed the distance. "Hi. I'm, uh, Shaye." *So* awkward. Not waiting for the invite she might not receive, she sat.

Curls flicked her a nervous glance. "Hi. I'm Brenna." Her voice was deep and extremely rough. Her vocal cords must have been damaged at some point.

"I've noticed you're the only other person who isn't ecstatic to be here."

Brenna tapped her temple. "Sane."

"So how's life with Shivawn?"

The girl shrugged. "He hasn't touched me."

"Good." Shaye leaned forward and swiped a piece of bread from the snack table. She tore the piece in two and handed one to Brenna. "Are you still in charge of Joachim's care?"

A hesitant nod.

"How's he doing?"

A gleam of something...hot and dark entered her brown eyes. Oh, oh, oh. What was this? Did Brenna have a crush on her patient?

"He's well."

"You like him?" Shaye asked.

"What? No!" Brenna gave a violent shake of her head. "Scared of him," she admitted.

Shaye tensed. "Has he hurt you?"

Delicate shoulders drooped, but her lips pressed into a defiant frown. "No."

So...she wasn't scared of him physically but...emotionally?

That, Shaye understood. If she desired Valerian so intensely now, what would happen if she actually fell in love with him?

"I wonder why all the women are slaves to the mighty nympho pheromone but we aren't," she mused aloud.

"*In*sane," Brenna said, tapping her temple, and they both laughed.

The door opened, and Shivawn entered. Disappointment—

No, excitement!

Valerian entered on his heels. He stopped, his gaze finding her. A cut marred his lip, but he was still the most beautiful sight she'd ever beheld. He'd cleaned up, the sand and blood washed away. Once again he wore a shirt—Boo hiss!

He was right. She preferred him bare-chested.

A shiver of awareness swept through her. Grip tightening on the papers, she stood. Brenna stood beside her.

"You're hurt," Shaye said. Should she offer to patch him up?

"I couldn't stop thinking about our kiss," Valerian said, his tone wry. "My men took advantage of my distraction."

Guilt flared.

"I missed you," he added, and a pang lanced through her.

Tell him how much you *missed* him. He deserved the truth.

The words died in her throat, however. *Shouldn't give him hope. Shouldn't start a relationship doomed to fail.*

Disappointment glowed in his eyes, but he extended his hand. "Come. Let me show you our home."

VALERIAN ESCORTED SHAYE to the stables. Overhead, the crystal dome shone brightly and cast the perfect amount of heat. Birds whistled playfully as they flew past.

He motioned to the pink pony of her dreams. "This enchanting beauty is yours."

She gasped. "She can't be...she's... My Little Pony is real!"

"Yes. She's very real."

Rich brown eyes peered up at him. "You bought her for me?"

"I spent our money, yes." He would use the word "our" every chance he got. A reminder they belonged together. Hopefully she would cease her escape attempts.

But then, why would she want to stay? He'd treated her poorly all week, his days spent in battle, his nights plagued by nightmares of losing her.

She trembled as she combed her fingers through the pony's mane. "You have to stop buying me gifts, Valerian. You have to stop being so..." She grimaced. "Nice."

"Why?"

"Because...just because!"

Because leaving her new life would be more difficult than she'd expected?

If that were the case, he would buy her all of Atlantis.

"Okay, I have a confession." She nuzzled the pony's nose. "I don't actually know how to ride."

"I will take great pleasure in teaching you. Another day. Today you'll ride with me." Already burning with anticipation, he whistled.

His centaur trotted around the far corner.

"Shaye, this is Henry. Henry, this is Shaye. My mate. We're going to the Outer City."

Henry bowed low. He had long hair the same dark shade as his skin, strong features and an even stronger flank. "Of course, sire."

Shaye stumbled back a step. "Valerian. Your horse is a *man*."

"Yes. I know."

"And you expect me to *ride* him?"

He fought a grin. "Yes."

She gulped. Valerian set her atop the centaur and mounted behind her, loving the feel of her against him... loved the way they rubbed together as Henry descended the cliff.

The palace sat at the top, and the town began at the bottom. Took them half an hour to make the journey.

As usual, the moment he was spotted other men hid their females. By the time he and Shaye dismounted, only males—centaurs, Minotaurs and formorions— manned the tables and booths, selling their wares. Everything from food and drink to jewelry and clothing.

"This is amazing," Shaye said, glowing with awe.

He wanted so badly to kiss her, but now wasn't the time. He had to remain aware. And he did. He led her down the cobblestone streets and through the crowds, never dropping his guard.

When she expressed a desire for water, he fetched her a drink. When her stomach growled, he purchased delicious meat pies.

The first time, she asked, "Are you going to demand payment for this?"

"Payment?" he'd replied.

"You know, a kiss, since I don't have Atlantean money."

"Why would I? I want your kisses offered free of charge."

She blushed, delighting him.

Two young griffins—lion-eagle hybrids—charged past them, one chasing his tail while the other chased his friend. Shaye snickered at their antics.

Light created a halo around her, and his chest swelled with...an emotion he couldn't name. One he'd never before experienced.

"Is anyone selling oranges, do you think?" she asked him, her gaze scanning the booths.

"Surely." But though he searched high and low, he failed to find the fruit. "I'm sorry."

"Don't worry about it. Sure, I'll have to scratch purveyor of oranges from your résumé, but I'm certain you'll recover. One day."

She...teased him? "As far as first dates go, how'd I do?"

"Wait." She jumped in front of him, stopping him, her eyes wide. "This was a date?"

"Of course." Something else he'd done this past week—speak with the other human women, asking about their customs.

"The first date. Implying the first of many."

"Of course," he repeated.

"Not *of course*. Not if I don't know. You didn't even ask me out. You just said you'd reward me if I behaved. Which still irritates me," she said, glaring up at him.

"But how was the date?" he insisted.

She buffed her nails on his shirt. "Well, on a scale from one to ten, I'd give it a five. Perfectly mediocre."

He snorted. Funny girl. She teased him now; he knew it.

He whistled for Henry, who came charging over. He

helped Shaye mount and settled behind her. Going up the cliff required an extra half hour. An extra half hour he used to his advantage, holding her close. At the midway point, she stopped trying to maintain distance with him and actually leaned against him.

Progress!

Upon arrival, Shaye accepted his help down—his touch—without hesitation.

More progress!

She spent the next hour playing with her new pet, now named Strawberry Shortcake.

He stepped away to send a few of his men to search the land for oranges.

Finally he and Shaye headed to their room. "I hope you're still hungry," he said. "I had a meal prepared for us while we were gone."

"Did you request coconut-cream pudding?"

"Moon, you moaned with bliss every time you took a bite this morning. So yes. Yes, I requested coconut-cream pudding."

"Well, you shouldn't have!" She crossed her arms over her chest. "I told you. You're being too nice to me, and I don't need the extra fat grams."

He kissed her knuckles, stealing a small taste, and said, "Being nice to you gives me pleasure. I never deny myself pleasure. And the more of you there is, the more of you there is to love."

Inside the room, satin pillows now surrounded the coffee table. The dinner table. They sat across from each other.

As he filled two goblets with wine, he said, "I was going to have former lovers advise you of my wondrous skill in bed, but in the light of day that didn't seem so wise."

"Agreed," she said, nearly choking on her first sip.

"Instead, I'll tell you something about myself. Then you'll tell me something about yourself. Do we have a bargain?"

She licked her lips. "We do."

What bits of his past should he offer her? "I...had a brother," he said. Yes, as good a place as any to start, and something he rarely spoke of—though never with a woman. Shaye would be the first.

"Had?" she asked softly.

Nodding, he pinched a piece of fish between his fingers and popped it into his mouth. He chewed, swallowed. "He was my twin. He was stolen when we were children."

Her eyes widened with horror. "Who took him?"

Familiar rage filled him, but he tamped it down. "The Gorgons."

"The Gor—what?" She crossed her legs, one over the other, and leaned forward, propping her elbows on the table.

He had her full attention, her usual shields down.

"Gorgons are a race of creatures who can turn a man to stone with only a glance. Snakes slither on their heads. They are evil. Pure evil."

"Ah. Like Medusa." She motioned for him to continue. "So why did they take him?"

He slid a platter of grapes toward her. "They hoped to trade him for my father's aid—which he denied. Verryn died that very day."

"I'm so sorry."

He nodded. "He and I shared a mind connection, and when it darkened I knew he was gone. I've felt his loss every day...until you." The last emerged as little more than a whisper. "Now it's your turn. Tell me something about yourself."

WHAT SHOULD SHE TELL HIM? Shaye wondered. He'd divulged something personal and painful. She could do no less. Except...the more she shared with him, the closer she would feel to him.

Proceed with caution!

She would tell him something only *slightly* painful. "Once I had a stepsister who chopped off all my hair. I was sleeping and didn't know what she'd done until the next morning." The "trim" had been punishment for cutting the hair of her stepsister's favorite doll—a crime Shaye hadn't committed. That honor had belonged to her stepbrother.

The real pain had come when ten-year-old Shaye had cried to her mother about what had been done. Tamara accused her of butchering her own hair in an attempt to ruin her relationship with the girl's father.

Valerian's features darkened. "Seems Atlantis isn't the only land with demons. Your hair reminds me of moonlight and stars, and anyone who cuts it can only be spawned from evil."

Gratification filled her—*he* believed her. She ran her hand through the thick mass. "I...thank you."

"Living with the little demon must have been difficult."

"Thankfully, Mom was only married to her father for a year."

"You mother married your father, then this other man, then another male last week. How many mates has she had?"

"Six."

He shook his head, as if he couldn't trust what he'd just heard. "You will not share the same fate. You will have one mate. Only one." His gaze lingered on her mouth, reducing her to a trembling, aching mess.

"Tell me a happier memory now," she croaked.

He thought for a moment. "I lost my virginity to my mother's favorite servant. She carried clean clothing into my room, spotted me in the pool and decided to join me."

She struggled to catch her breath. Valerian...naked...beads of water trickling down rope after rope of muscle and—

Stop! "I would have guessed you'd lost your virginity in an orgy."

He smiled. "The orgy happened the next night."

She nearly choked on her tongue, and he laughed.

"What about you?" he asked. "Tell me about your first time."

"I, uh..." She stumbled over her words, another blush heating her cheeks. Time to admit the truth, she supposed.

Why?

Excellent question. Because...because she was an adult, and she could do what she wanted. That was why.

"I haven't had a first time," she admitted, stacking the grapes in the bowl. "Yet."

"What!" His mouth fell open. "Surely you jest."

"Hardly. Look," she said, growing defensive. "I never wanted to deal with the problems that walk hand in hand with a sexual relationship."

His brow furrowed. "What problems?"

"Well, love never lasts. Someone always gets hurt, using their feelings as an excuse to do terrible things to their partner. *Those* problems."

At first, he said nothing, only peered at her with shock.

"Well?" she prompted.

"I need a moment. I just found out my mate is a virgin. She's completely untouched. I don't think this has ever happened for a nymph. A woman—my woman—is to be mine, only mine."

Must stop shivering. "Back up, buddy. *She* hasn't agreed to be yours."

"But she will," he said, his gaze holding hers. "It's only a matter of time."

She licked her lips and whispered, "How can you be so sure?"

His eyes glittered with heat and determination. "Because, as you saw with Joachim, when I fight, I fight to win."

CHAPTER SEVENTEEN

"I'M GLAD YOU RETURNED," Joachim said.

Brenna inched toward his bed. Even though she'd visited him every day for a week, she wasn't yet 100 percent comfortable with him. Or 50 percent.

Shivawn stood in the doorway, watching and guarding her. Usually she had a panic attack if anyone took up a post behind her. That was how the attack had happened. Ethan had snuck up on her, flipped her around and—

She cut off the thought.

She'd been with Ethan for four years. At first, he'd been wonderful. The man of her dreams. But within three months of marriage, his temper had begun to grow blacker and blacker.

The first time he'd hit her, she filed for divorce. He'd apologized on his knees and begged for her to take him back. Said he'd made a mistake, he'd been drinking and it would never happen again.

Must have been part of the Abuser's Handbook, she thought with a humorless laugh.

If only she'd resisted his charm. Instead, she'd shredded the divorce papers, *relieved* to return to her love.

The second time he attacked her, he'd also shoved a knife in her face and threatened her. Leave him and die.

She'd believed him.

So many times since that horrendous night, she'd *wished* to die. Beatings had become a staple of her life.

She'd survived only because she'd had enough medical training to patch herself.

Today having someone behind her—having *Shivawn* behind her—didn't scare her. She was actually coming to like Shivawn and his gentleness.

Despite everything, even the short amount of time, she'd come to feel safe with him. Proof: earlier, when she'd been holed up in the hobby room, she'd listened to the other women weave stories of sensual exploits, and wanton images had bombarded her. She'd pictured herself doing...intimate things with Shivawn.

Well, not with him, not exactly, but with a faceless man. But she was certain the faceless man was Shivawn. Who else could it be? Not Joachim, that was for sure.

The warrior made her feel dizzy, achy and weak. Completely out of control. Sensations she despised. And yes, at one time, she'd loved them. Once, she'd loved sex and men.

Ethan had killed that love. Until today.

I would have to be a fool to want someone like Joachim. He was nothing like Shivawn. He wasn't kind, and he wasn't gentle. He was a hard, volatile warlord who wasn't afraid to use his fists. Yet even now, thinking about him made her heart race—and not just with fear.

Stop mooning. Get to work.

Right. Silent, she cleaned and bandaged Joachim's wounds, glad to see there were no signs of infection.

He should have been able to leave the bed by now, at least for short periods of time, but he was still too weak.

"If you're going to heal the rest of the way," she told him, "I think Valerian will need to let you...you know."

He arched a brow. "Are you offering?"

"No?" She cleared her throat. "No. Definitely not."

Just as she was finishing up, a new man stepped inside the room. He carried a long, menacing sword; ice crystalized in her veins. She tried to dive under the bed, but Joachim latched on to her and pulled her onto the bed, behind him.

The action surprised and terrified her. Too abrupt! Too suggestive!

A soft whimper escaped her.

"You have nothing to fear, female. Nothing and no one will harm you while I'm with you."

"You're needed in the dining hall, Shivawn," the intruder said.

Shivawn looked at her, then Joachim, ignoring the stranger. He frowned. They weren't under attack? She crawled to her feet and rubbed her side, where she'd been pressed against Joachim. Her skin tingled.

"Did he hurt you?" Shivawn demanded.

Her mind replayed the entire episode, and she shook her head no. She thought...she thought Joachim might have been using his injured body as a shield.

In doing so, he'd reopened his wound.

"Valerian has summoned you," the stranger added impatiently. "Now, not later."

Shivawn flicked the man an irritated glare before closing the distance to give her shoulder a comforting squeeze. "I hate to leave you, but I must obey the king. Do you need to stay here or do you wish to go with me?"

Panic sprouted wings inside her chest. She didn't want him to go, but she didn't want to leave Joachim like this, either.

"I'll stay." She would be brave. And she wouldn't allow Joachim to affect or scare her.

Easier said than done.

Shivawn gave the warrior a brief but dark look,

gently caressed Brenna's cheek before striding into the hallway, following the messenger.

Suddenly Brenna and Joachim were alone.

I can do this. I can! Joachim's too weak to harm me.

Slowly she eased back onto the bed. She was careful not to look into his eyes, those blue, blue eyes that seemed to cut straight to her soul. Her fingers shook as she unwrapped the bandages. New stitches wouldn't be needed; compression could do the trick.

"I'm Joachim," he said, breaking the silence.

"I know." Her voice trembled as much as her hands. "You shouldn't have challenged the king." His nostrils flared in fury but still she forged ahead. "Strength lies in compassion not rage."

A charge thickened the air, and she guessed he would soon be yelling at her. Instead, he changed the subject, admitting grudgingly, "I've thought of you all week." Half pain, half accusation. "I can't seem to get you out of my mind."

Her gaze skipped to his, and she gasped at what she saw. Desire. White-hot desire.

Her hands stilled, remaining poised over his thigh. She had a sheet draped over his middle to protect her modesty rather than his, but that sheet began to tent.

"Every time you come near me, there's fear in your eyes," he said, still speaking low, his voice heated. "But I also detect interest."

She bit her lip and shook her head. She wouldn't admit to any type of interest. That would only encourage him. But...

"Talk to me, Brenna," he said. "Tell me how I can put you at ease. Tell me what caused this fear in the first place."

She never would have expected such a quiet beseeching from such a power-hungry warlord. Her throat constricted, making it difficult to speak.

"Better yet," he added, "tell me everything."

JOACHIM TILTED HIS HEAD to regard Brenna more intently. "I want to know everything about you," he reiterated. Already he knew her smell—the violets and the sunshine he'd encountered too briefly on the surface. He knew her voice—scratchy and harsh but also beautiful.

Now he wanted to know her past. Her likes. Her dislikes. All the things that made her Brenna, the woman who obsessed him more with every second that passed.

Strength lies in compassion, she'd said. He'd wanted to snort but hadn't. There was truth in her words.

"We'll begin with something easy," he said. "What's your favorite color?"

She glanced at the door, as if wondering if she should stay and talk or run. "Blue," she finally replied.

If she were his woman, he would give her all the sapphires he owned. "Do you have family?" A family she missed? Wished to return to?

She shook her head. "Dead."

He shouldn't have felt relieved. The deaths must have caused her pain. "How did you lose them?"

"Mostly of sickness, though I had two cousins die in a car accident."

Car? He was intrigued by a "car" that could kill two people at once. "I'm sorry for your loss, little one."

Features shadowed, she waved a hand through the air. That hand was shaking, he noticed. "Happened a long time ago," her broken voice stated.

He wanted to grab her and kiss her, anything to wipe away those shadows; he ended up fisting the sheets to keep his hands at his sides. "Do you like this new world? Atlantis?"

Her gaze drifted away from him, landing on the wall behind him. She shook her head.

"Why not?" Disappointment hummed through him. He'd hoped she'd already come to love it as he did.

"Scary," she admitted softly. She traced a fingertip over the sheet.

"You are frightened of everyone, not just me?"

She merely shrugged.

"I told you. I'll never hurt you, Brenna." He made the vow as gently as his fierce timbre would allow. "You have my word."

A shiver stole through her. "You might not mean to, but—"

"No. To me, never means *never*."

Shivawn strode back into the room. "What are you saying to her, Joachim?"

Brenna jolted to her feet, looking between them with a resurgence of fear in her eyes.

"Watch your tone, boy," Joachim snapped. "You're frightening her."

Shivawn's features instantly softened. "I'm sorry," he said to her. "Valerian asked me to oversee a search party for oranges, but I'm here now. I'm not angry, I promise you."

BRENNA GAZED BETWEEN the two men, her eyes as wide as saucers. Her...suitors? They were doing everything in their power to comfort her, and they were actually succeeding!

They wanted to kill each other, but her fear was dissipating.

How are they doing this to me?

An image of naked, straining bodies flashed through her mind, and she gasped. Once again, she couldn't see her lover's face; however, the image was so lifelike she could hear the pleasure moans rising from the couple. Nerve endings long forgotten began to stir with new life.

Joachim bared his teeth as he hissed in a breath. "You're aroused. I can smell it on you."

Her cheeks heated to a blazing inferno. He could truly smell it?

"I can, too," Shivawn said with a groan. "Brenna..."

He took a step toward her, but again, there was no fear inside her. *What's wrong with me? What's happening to me?* This wasn't like her. At all!

Joachim eased to a sitting position, and he appeared stronger than he had all week. "You are in need of a man, Brenna, but you are afraid of your desire, yes? You must be, to resist."

"Yes," Shivawn answered for her. "She is afraid."

"Have you ever been with a man?" Joachim asked her.

Unable to breathe, she nodded. Run. She should run.

"Did you like it?" Shivawn asked.

Another nod. She should run and never look back, but part of her was strangely relieved to have this out in the open.

"The man who hurt you and damaged your voice," Joachim persisted. "Did *he* make you afraid of sex?"

She hesitated for a long while, finally opting for the truth. "Yes."

Both men growled low in their throats, as if they wanted to kill Ethan with their bare hands. Still the fear did not return.

"I understand now," Shivawn said. "Once a woman has been forced, any new experience can be difficult for her."

"Yes," Joachim said. "I, too, understand." His voice sounded far away, a lot weaker. The strength he'd rallied had already drained.

"Joachim?" she said, concern for him making her forget all else.

He fell back onto the bed, and his head lolled onto the pillow, his skin draining of color.

She hurried to him to check his vitals. "You'll be okay." She placed a glass at his lips and helped him sip the water.

"Dizzy. Weak," he admitted, the condition clearly enraging him. "Shouldn't have moved."

She could tell the lack of strength did more than enrage him; it also unnerved him. As a fighter, he was probably used to absolute control. Hadn't he admitted to liking and respecting the king, but not wanting to take orders anymore?

At last, bits of her fear returned. Control was something she valued, as well. She couldn't relinquish a speck of hers, no matter how aroused she became. And to be with either one of these men she'd have to give up *all* control.

She beat feet to the door.

When he realized she intended to leave, Joachim uttered an abrupt, "Stay."

A command. Oh, yes, he expected absolute obedience from her. He was to be master and commander and she the slave.

She ignored him, continuing on.

"Brenna," he said. He tried to sit up again, despite his deplorable condition, but strength abandoned him. "I won't always be so weak." There was a warning in his tone. "One day I'll come for you."

She stopped. Just stopped. She stood beside Shivawn.

Her gaze swept over him before returning to Joachim. Both males were so beautiful it almost hurt to look at them. For a moment, she actually wished someone would reach for her...touch her...kiss her...sink inside her.

No, not someone. Shivawn. Only Shivawn. He could give her back everything she'd lost. Hope. Companionship. Passion. But it wasn't green eyes she spied inside her mind, staring down at her.

Her mystery lover's eyes were blue.

She scrubbed a hand over her face, trying to block the image.

How could someone like Joachim arouse her like this when no man had been able to do so for years?

"I won't hurt you," Shivawn said. He held up his hands, all innocence.

"Come to me, Brenna," Joachim intoned.

"No," she told Shivawn, and Joachim grinned.

"No," she told Joachim, wiping away his smugness. Better to be without both of them.

"I want to know you," Shivawn said. His voice was gentle. "I'll keep you safe. I won't let anyone else hurt you."

"Don't allow your need for safety destroy your love of life. I can teach you to conquer your fear and live again," Joachim told her.

Shivawn faced Joachim, and the two squared off. "I can teach her to conquer her fear, too."

"Maybe. But you'll never make her happy," Joachim snapped. "This, I know."

Perhaps neither of them could make her happy. The knowledge overwhelmed her with a keen sense of disappointment. For with the return of his anger, Joachim had reminded her of exactly why she would never give herself to him. If he ever directed that anger at her, he would kill her.

Control, she reminded herself.

Brenna raced out of the room before she did something stupid. Like cry.

SHIVAWN DIDN'T FOLLOW her but remained in the room. For a long while he and Joachim didn't speak.

"I want her," Joachim admitted softly.

Shivawn's hands tightened into fists. He'd known that, but hearing the words… "I want her, too, and she's my woman. Who do you think will get her?"

"I'll challenge you for her," Joachim grated.

"Challenge not accepted. She looked at me with desire, and I find I crave that look again."

"That desire was for me, boy. *Me*. Anything you saw was merely a reflection of that."

Shivawn frowned. Yes, she *had* looked at Joachim with desire. More desire than a woman had ever projected at him, and the realization didn't settle well.

Frustrated, he tossed his arms in the air. "So where does that leave us?"

"Give her to me, and it leaves you alive and well."

"No."

Joachim stroked his chin with two fingers. "I'll not give up. I'll pursue her."

"Is that a threat?"

"Merely a warning. I want her, and I will do anything to win her."

Anger pricked, Shivawn nearly drew his sword. He felt protective of Brenna, wanted her to be happy, and couldn't stand to think of such a delicate creature bonded to this power-hungry warrior. "If you scare her,

I'll kill you. Do you understand me? Unlike Valerian, I'll show you no mercy."

A dark cloud descended over Joachim's face. "I would never scare her."

"Ha! You scared her with your forcefulness. That's why she ran."

"Don't try to pretend you know her or her reasons, and don't pretend you know what she needs. You scared her just as badly or she would have given herself to you by now."

"Perhaps she will. Tonight," Shivawn taunted.

Fury exploded in Joachim's eyes. "No. She'll never give herself to you. That, I also know, because you'll never understand her the way I do."

His teeth clenched. "You? How do *you* think to understand her?"

"That you have to ask proves my point for me."

JOACHIM CLOSED HIS EYES, bringing Brenna's innocent face to the forefront of his mind. Someone had hurt her during sex—someone who would feel the end of his sword one day soon. If he had to travel to the surface, he would.

He would stake his life on the fact that Brenna had once been a woman of passion and vitality. There was a spark in her eyes she just couldn't hide. Deep inside, no matter how strong her fears, she had to crave that type of life again.

The more time he'd spent with her, the more he'd looked at her, the more he'd scented her, the more he'd wanted her. Today he'd begun to suspect...

She was his mate.

No, impossible. He would have known right away. At a glance. A sniff. Yes? She *couldn't* be his.

Unlike other nymphs, he'd never wanted to find his one and only. Relying on a specific person for his strength? Abhorrent! But...he hadn't realized he would like the idea of the woman being reliant on him, as well. Or that she would be his partner. She would always support him. Would choose him above all others. She would love him even when everyone else hated him.

Suddenly he understood the appeal.

He could win her from Shivawn; he knew he could. She'd looked at Joachim with the first tendrils of passion, and he knew she wouldn't be happy with anyone else. He just needed time to prove it to her.

When she'd looked at Shivawn, there'd been no passion. Desire, yes, but it hadn't been sexual. It had been... grateful, like a child with her mother.

She felt safe with the other male—safer than she felt with Joachim.

He wouldn't be able to claim her until he'd reversed the situation. And he would. Whatever proved necessary, he would do.

More than he wanted his own satisfaction, he wanted hers.

Perhaps she *was* his mate. But how could he have missed her importance to him, even for a second? Her fear of him?

Yes. Of course. Had he known what she was to him, he would have pounced immediately. She wouldn't have been ready for him, and he would have frightened her beyond repair. His instincts to protect her had hidden the truth from him.

Strength lies in compassion. Again her words played through his mind. Compassion...something she clearly valued.

Because she herself hadn't received any?

Once he was healed, there would be no stopping his pursuit of her.

"I will have her, Shivawn," he said. "It's me she will always crave in her bed."

A muscle ticked in Shivawn's jaw. "You're wrong. She wants safety. To her, I am calm and you are the storm."

"A man can change."

"Not easily."

No. Not easily.

POSEIDON HUMMED WITH RELISH. Waves whirled and crashed against him, their cerulean beauty lethal to mere mortals. He tasted salt in his mouth, smelled it in his nose—the scent mixed with terror.

No Atlantean was permitted to enter the surface world. Well, that wasn't entirely true. A guardian of the portal could enter, but only to kill anyone who'd escaped the underwater city. None of the nymphs were guardians—and they had entered anyway, it seemed.

Now Poseidon would have to punish them.

"Let me get this straight. You saw nymphs steal human women from the surface world and bring them into Atlantis?" he said, his voice booming across the ocean floor. Sand jumped, floating high in the water; pink and white coral vibrated. Colorful fish darted in every direction, desperate to escape his vicinity.

Two mermaids bowed their heads. Both possessed hair as inky black as the night, the tresses blending together, floating around their delicate shoulders.

"Yes," they said in unison.

"Through the portal?" he insisted. He slammed the end of his trident into the marble base he stood upon, cracking it from one end to the other. This was the most excitement he'd experienced in ages.

"Yes," both women repeated, now trembling.

Poseidon's lips lifted slowly as he stepped from the dais, his white robe dancing around his ankles. From where he stood, he could see the huge crystal dome encompassing the cursed city.

He whisked himself to it, far away one moment, in front of it the next. He needed no portal or doorway to let him inside a world he had helped create. He simply walked through the crystal as if it were not there.

He didn't yet want the citizens to know of his arrival, so he kept himself hidden in a cloak of invisibility. He breathed deeply of the pure, orchid-saturated air. Closed his eyes, enjoyed. Yes, he had turned his back on this land and its people for far too long. A mistake.

Hundreds of years had passed since he'd last entered, and all seemed tranquil. Minotaur children played in mud puddles, centaurs frolicked through thick, dewy grass. Vampires, dragons, griffins, cyclops, Gorgons, harpies and Amazons—they were all present.

How could his brothers think these creatures abominations? Ugly, even. Some of the women of Atlantis were actually quite pretty.

The races even appeared—dare he think it—tamed. And in the taming, stronger. He frowned.

How strong?

Waving his trident, and maintaining his invisibility, Poseidon whisked himself to the palace where Valerian, king of the nymphs, now resided. Within seconds he found himself in a room occupied by three very human women. They were discussing the various positions in which they'd been taken, the various positions in which they wanted to be taken, and how sad they were that Valerian now had a mate and paid them no attention.

Slowly Poseidon allowed his form to appear, though he assumed the guise of a nymph warrior. Dark-haired, vivid blue eyes. Muscled. Tanned. When the women spotted him, they smiled, jumped to their feet and rushed to him.

"Did you come to make love to us?" one asked.

"You're the most beautiful man I've ever seen! More beautiful than Valerian, even."

"Silence," he said, his voice booming. Now was not the time for pleasure. Later, though... "Sit down." He motioned to the mound of pillows behind them.

They sat without question or comment, eyeing him as if he were a delicious platter of chocolate. He settled beside them and allowed them to drape themselves over his legs, stroking him like a prized pet. Hmm. Nice. Very nice.

Nymphs needed sex to survive, the most likely reason they'd stolen the women. Not that it mattered. The law must be obeyed.

Zeus's oracles claimed the Atlanteans would one day destroy the surface.

"First you will tell me exactly how you came to be here," he said. He would hear the damning truth firsthand. "Then you'll tell me all you know about the nymphs."

One of the women kissed his thigh. Another kissed his shoulder. He closed his eyes, a blissful moan slipping from him. Answers, smanswers.

He cleared his throat. "You will tell me later," he said and kissed them back.

Already his venture into Atlantis was doing more for his boredom than a thousand tropical storms.

CHAPTER EIGHTEEN

"LET US BATHE. TOGETHER."

"Bathe? Together?" Dinner was over, and Valerian expected her to strip down and soak? "No, thank you." Shaye stood and backed away from him as if he were poison. Because he was.

"If we're going to date—and I'm not saying we are," she added in a rush. "But. If we're going to date, we've got to do this the normal way. You know, get the Atlantean version of a cell phone and text each other. From a distance."

He stood, unfolding his big body inch by agonizing inch. His pants were tight over his muscled legs, but even tighter over his large erection.

"You said every relationship ends." He stared her down. "Ours won't. You're my mate. Therefore your argument is invalid."

Her eyes widened as he stepped closer to her. She'd wanted him many times since meeting him. Now, faced with the inevitability of having him, she panicked.

"Just…stay where you are, okay. I need time to think about this."

"You've had time. You aren't fighting me, and you know it. You're fighting yourself." His eyelids dipped to half-mast, giving him a slumberous, I-need-a-bed allure. "You're running from what I make you feel when you should be running *to* me."

She inhaled sharply. His scent filled her nose, sexual and fierce. Heat curled from him, wrapping her in sultry coils, squeezing so tightly she had trouble dragging in her next breath. A rush of passion flooded her.

She *did* want to run to him, to take what he offered. But…what if he realized she wasn't truly his mate? What if he dismissed her? What if he turned his attentions to another?

What if, afterward, she craved more of him but he craved less of her? What if she fell in love and lost herself? What if she made a fool of herself?

Every question was a product of the very fight he'd mentioned. And really, the answers were irrelevant. In life, there were no guarantees.

She gulped. "I need more time, Valerian."

His hands fisted at his sides. "How much?"

The wound in his chest had opened, drops of blood on his shirt. *He* needed sex to heal.

"Never mind," he said, and scrubbed a hand down his face. "I won't pressure you."

"I…" *Don't know what to say.* This man unraveled her.

"Would you like to watch me bathe?" he asked, his tone pure silk.

Watch as water droplets trickled down his neck… perhaps catching on his nipples before falling to the ridges of muscle on his stomach. Watch his soap-lathered hands glide over his strength as she'd imagined earlier…

"I…uh…" *Should say no. Definitely.* But…

He was the kind of man women fantasized about but never actually encountered anywhere but a television screen. And he continually offered himself to her as an all-you-can-eat smorgasbord of erotic delights.

"Maybe?" Her heartbeat drummed in her ears, an eternity passing between each one.

"I can't make the decision for you, Moon. But if you say yes, I'll make you glad you did."

STRUGGLING WITH THE POWER of his need, Valerian stalked into the bathing area before he did something foolish. He didn't want to force Shaye to acknowledge her desires. He wanted her to accept them—and him—willingly.

When she'd told him she was virgin, he'd simply reacted. Blood and need had traveled through him at lightning speed. His shaft had hardened painfully. The need to brand her as his woman had sung in his ears like a siren's song. He'd known, deep down, that Shaye had waited for him. He only wished he had waited for her.

However, he *felt* like a virgin with her. Unsure, eager and excited by the possibilities. In such a short time, she'd become everything to him.

Want me. Come to me. Please...

SHAYE'S DESIRES ENGAGED in a knock-down, drag-out battle with her self-preservation.

I like being alone...right?

No. No, she didn't.

The truth slapped her silly.

She craved companionship. But she wasn't her mother, and she wouldn't accept the small scraps of affection some man decided to toss her way.

Nothing Valerian tosses my way is small.

Not yet, anyway.

One day he would grow tired of her, and she would use her desire or even love as an excuse to stay with him despite his roaming eye.

And his eye would roam. Everyone's did.

Her deepest feminine instincts sensed how dangerous Valerian was to her future. If she gave up her virginity, she'd have to give up her home and job next. Then her identify! No longer would she be Shaye Holling. Instead she would be known as "the companion to the nymph king."

The curtain blocking her view of the bathing pool rustled as his clothing fell to the floor.

He's naked.

A splash of water sounded.

He's naked and wet.

Tremors nearly knocked her off her feet.

Steam probably wafted through the room. His skin was probably glistening with moisture.

White-hot desire *consumed* her.

One peek at him wouldn't be so bad, would it?

Her trembling worsened as she moved to the entrance. He couldn't possibly be as exquisite as she imagined. Could he?

She peeled the curtain to the side—Valerian's back came into view. Muscles rippled under tawny skin as he cupped and poured water over himself.

The steam was thicker around him, making him appear gossamer, as if he came from a dream, or a fantasy. As if he were a genie intent on granting her every wish.

Beads of water dripped from the ends of his hair and trickled between his shoulder blades, down the ridges of his spine. She bit her lip. Maybe it wouldn't hurt to be with him once and finally put her body out of its misery. If she guarded her heart, she could use him and be done with him. Right?

He lifted a sapphire glass bottle from the edge of the pool and poured whatever was inside—orchid oil—

over his chest. Oh, to be that oil, she thought, mesmerized, her throat constricting as he rubbed the oil all over. The fragrance mixed with the steam, becoming a summoning finger.

"You can still join me, you know," he said, his voice rough.

She yelped and released the curtain. The material fell back into place, completely blocking him from view. Her cheeks erupted into flames.

"No, thank you," she called.

"Didn't like what you saw? Or did you like what you saw a little too much?"

Before she could think up a response, a panting Brenna burst into the room. Her gaze was wild, her dark curls bouncing around her face. She exhaled a huge sigh of relief when she spotted Shaye.

"What's wrong?" Alarmed, she rushed to the girl's side. "Did something happen?"

Behind her, water splashed and the pound of footsteps echoed. Valerian shoved the curtain aside. He was mouthwateringly, deliciously naked, and completely unabashed.

"What happened?" he demanded.

Shaye's mouth fell open at this first, full-frontal glance of him. He was more muscled than she'd realized, and his erection...

Oh. My. Wow!

Longer and harder than she'd imagined, proudly waving between his legs. Water droplets clung to the crown—

Brenna gaped at him.

"Grab a towel!" Shaye shouted. "Right now! And just know that when I—*if* I—become queen, I'm creating a new law. No twigs and berries on display."

"Ever?" he asked, unperturbed by her outburst. "Or just in public."

She uttered a choking sound.

Brenna's mouth had fallen open, too, and Shaye had to tamp the urge to cover the girl's eyes.

"We're fine." She pointed to a spot over his shoulder. "Go back to your bath. Please! We're going to have a little girl talk and pretend our retinas aren't singed."

He winked at her before disappearing behind the curtain. Only then was Shaye able to breathe again.

"Big," Brenna said in that broken voice of hers, her eyes still wide.

Mine, Shaye almost snapped. She frowned. She had no right to claim him. She'd just turned him down. Again.

Concentrate. "Did someone hurt you, Brenna? Or threaten you?"

Brenna shook her head. "I have a problem."

"What kind? With whom?"

"Joachim."

Her frown deepened. "Is he hurt?"

"No."

"So he did hurt you?"

"No."

Oookay. Shaye clasped her friend's hand.

Was Brenna her friend?

She'd never really had one. Assistants, yes. But had she ever really spent quality personal time with someone else? As a child, she'd been shy and reserved. As a teen, she'd been distrustful of others. As an adult, she'd been too cranky.

Well, whatever Brenna was, Shaye led her to the couch. "What's wrong?" she asked again, settling into the cushions. "Tell me, and I'll do what I can to help."

"Shivawn," Brenna said.

Her brows knit together. "Is *he* hurt?"

"No."

"So *he* hurt *you*?"

"No."

Okay, they were getting nowhere fast. Shaye exhaled with frustration. "I don't understand what's going on. You're going to have to explain."

"I...want." A rosy blush stained Brenna's cheeks. She bit her bottom lip. "I want them."

"You want...them?" Shaye blinked. "As in, the two of them...sexually? Together? With you?"

Her blush intensified, and she looked away. "No. But I think I desire one when I should desire the other, the one who makes me feel safe, and I'm scared. I'm also confused."

"Well, that would scare and confuse me, too." She could barely handle her desire for Valerian. She didn't know what she would have done if she'd felt safer with one of his warriors. "Maybe desire will grow with the one who makes you feel safe?"

Brenna gripped her hands, as if she were in danger of falling and desperately needed an anchor. "Maybe. I just don't know."

"I wish I had an answer for you. These men...these nymphs, they cast a spell over everything female and screw with our common sense." Bitterness seeped through her tone. "I don't like it."

You once mentioned an escape. Brenna mimed the last so there was no chance Valerian would overhear.

Shaye stilled. Escape. What she'd wanted from the beginning. What she wasn't sure she wanted right now, but knew was for the best.

I have a home. A job. Employees who count on me.

"We'll have to make our way to the portal," she said softly. "I tried to leave bread crumbs, removing dust from sections of the wall, but first we have to get to the dusty part."

"I think I know the way," Brenna replied just as softly.

She trembled. "Valerian said I couldn't survive the water alone. We'll have to help each other swim."

"I'm ready."

She glanced to the bathing curtain, saying, "Then there's no better time than now." She had to speak past the sudden lump in her throat. She wished she had time to tell Valerian goodbye, wished she could kiss him once more.

As if attuned to her, Valerian suddenly called, "Shaye!"

Her eyes widened, and Brenna gasped. If they didn't leave now, they would lose this rare opportunity.

"Come on." They sprinted past the front door and into the hallway.

No guards. Valerian hadn't wanted anyone to hear what he'd hoped would be a happy bath time. A very sweet gesture—

Stop missing him and run!

"Shaye!"

He'd given chase!

She increased her speed, and when she blazed around a corner, she plowed into a couple writhing on the floor. A frantic Brenna helped her stand as the couple ignored them, lost in each other.

Lungs threatening to burst from strain, Shaye dared a backward glance. A naked Valerian was closing in on her and…part of her wanted to run *to* him, just as he'd hoped.

"Faster," she shouted at Brenna. "Which way?"

At a fork in the hallway, Brenna swerved right and Shaye followed. If Valerian caught her...

Doorways branched in every direction. They darted past men who regarded them with curiosity, but didn't try to stop them.

Then, suddenly, steal clamps anchored around her waist, lifting her off her feet. She screamed and flailed. Brenna whirled and, spotting Valerian, withered in place.

"You tried to leave me," Valerian grated.

Disappointment and relief mixed, confusing her. She decided to go on the offensive. "For all you know, we were going for a leisurely jog around the palace. No big deal."

"No big deal? No big deal!"

"Oh, good. Your ears are working."

"You tried to leave me," he repeated.

A kernel of shame. "We never agreed to a bargain, remember?"

A growl rumbled from his chest. "When a warrior runs from his commander," he said ominously, "he is punished. Are you ready for your punishment, Shaye?"

CHAPTER NINETEEN

VALERIAN ESCORTED BRENNA to Shivawn without uttering another word. The warrior with beads in his hair accepted her with a frown and a muttered, "Thank you, great king." The entire time, Shaye's warrior carried her under his arm like a sack of potatoes. She'd never been so nervous. This was the first time he'd ever projected such blazing fury in her direction.

And yet, she was still oddly relieved that she'd failed to escape.

"Go back to your duties," Valerian snapped at the soldiers watching in the hallway.

His men jumped into action, looking anywhere but his naked form or Shaye.

"Valer—"

"Do not speak," he interjected.

"Valerian," she persisted. "I told you I would try to escape. You can't say I didn't warn you. At least I didn't lie to you. We'll always be honest with each other, remember?"

"I gave you what you wanted, Shaye. I didn't press you to make love, and yet you ran from me anyway. How am I to treat you now?"

VALERIAN STILL COULDN'T believe his woman's daring.

He stalked to their room and tossed her onto the bed.

She bounced. He stood in place, staring down at her. She didn't try to run again, just regarded him warily.

Light as she was, carrying her shouldn't have affected him, but he was panting. His arms seemed to weigh more than usual and fell to his sides; he was losing strength quickly.

He needed sex.

He needed Shaye.

He'd felt her gaze on him during his bath. Had smelled her desire for him. He'd thought victory was finally within his grasp. And then she'd run. Run! As if he meant nothing to her.

Was the thought of making love *that* abhorrent to her?

"Do you want me?" he said darkly. "A simple yes or no question, requiring only one answer with zero explanations."

She scrambled to the far edge of the bed. Her overlarge shirt gaped open, revealing succulent hints of her breasts.

"I'd rather explain without giving a definitive yes or no," she said nervously.

"You tried to escape me, so we're talking about what I want to talk about now. Do you desire me? Yes or no."

She kept her gaze on his chest, not daring to look down, where he was thick and ready.

A tremble swept through her. In fear? In yearning?

"Yes," she finally whispered. "But—"

"No buts." Something inside him lurched. "Do you want my kiss…my touch…?"

"Yes, but—"

"No buts." Triumph bloomed alongside relief. "You look so beautiful on my bed, Moon, with your hair draped over your shoulders, your legs stretched in front of you. But…"

"No buts," she said.

"In this case, I'll make an exception." He let his hands and knees fall on the mattress. Slowly he crawled forward.

Eyes wide, she tried to scoot back even farther. The wall blocked any escape.

"Did you hate the thought of leaving me?" he asked.

She scowled at him. "Yes, but—"

"No buts."

She pounded a fist into the mattress.

"You feel the connection between us, I know you do. Give me one chance to convince you to stay. If I fail, I'll take you home."

She gasped.

His gaze swept over her, and he suddenly wished he possessed the fire of the dragons so he could burn away her clothing. "I know you've never been with a man, but have you ever engaged in love play?"

Stubborn to the end, she pressed her lips together. "That's none of your business."

He paused, his hands on either side of her knees. The fact that she didn't try to kick him was more telling than she probably knew.

Untouched. His mate was untouched by any man. He would be her first. Her only. He'd be careful with her.

"I like that you're a virgin, Moon."

She flicked a piece of lint off her shirt. "That's hypocritical, don't you think? You've been with thousands."

"I'm sorry that I don't come to you pure." Nymphs never saved themselves for their mates; they were too sexual, their needs too great. But now he wished he'd waited for her. "Perhaps every other woman was merely practice for the day I met you."

She swallowed, bit her lip. "That's, like, the corniest line I've ever heard."

"Is it?"

"For sure."

"Is it, though?"

"Maybe," she conceded grudgingly.

Blood heated to a sizzle inside his veins. Possessiveness and pride stormed him as surely as his army had stormed this palace. No man had ever sneaked past this woman's cool facade to discover the passion underneath, but Valerian was close.

I will give her so much pleasure she'll scream and beg for more.

He crawled the rest of the way up her body, until they were nose to nose. "You fear the unknown. You fear the pleasure I will give you. You think you'll become a slave to it. To me. So I'll dispel your fears or I won't. There's a chance I could screw this up. Ruin it for you. Then you can leave Atlantis with a clear conscience. You gave it your best shot, and the blame rests on me." He placed the softest kiss on her lush mouth. "You want to make an informed decision, don't you?"

Her mouth parted on a gasp—perhaps a sigh. "I'm not dumb. You're working this situation to your favor."

"To our favor, Moon. *Our.*"

Her eyes narrowed in an attempt to hide the emotion banked in their depths. "Yes. Okay? Yes. But are we going to talk all day or are you actually going to get this seduction routine over with?"

"So I have your permission to touch you?"

"You have all the permissions!"

Trying not to grin, he reached out and palmed the fullness of her breast. Her eyes closed, her hips arched slightly, a look of divine pleasure consuming her features.

Satisfaction speared him. He plucked at her nipple with his fingertips. "Do you hate me when I do this?"

A moan shuddered past her lips. "It feels...it feels terrible." He thought she added, "If *terrible* is the new word for *wonderful*," but he couldn't be sure.

He loved seeing her cheeks deepen with rosy color—with arousal. "Just think how much worse it will feel when I suck this hard little morsel into my mouth. I hope you can endure."

She groaned, a sound so laden with need he responded on a primal level, his muscles clenching, his bones vibrating. When he removed his hand—only for the barest of seconds—her groan became a growl. He slid his fingers under her shirt, gliding over the smooth skin of her stomach, surely the softest, sweetest flesh he'd ever encountered.

Rapture glowed from her like a halo, and she trembled.

"Does this make you shudder in revulsion?" he asked, his voice strained. His fingertip brushed the underside of her breast.

"Shudder," she gasped.

"Me, too. Oh, me, too." He held up his hand, his fingers quaking. "I'm *disgusted*."

"Yes, oh, yes. It's the...worst thing...ever," she said, panting. "Don't stop."

I SHOULD SO make him stop, Shaye thought. *Should make him stop...in just a...little while.* This was crazy.

His fingers were white-hot, searing, and everywhere they touched, a fire kindled below the surface of her skin.

Her mind blanked; she was consumed only with pleasure as his hand closed over her bare breast. Instinctively she parted her legs, a silent invitation for him to pin her completely.

He didn't accept. In fact, he lifted slightly.

She almost cursed him.

With his other hand, he inched up the hem of her shirt. "If I cover you, I'll take you," he explained. "I need to see you first."

"Yes," she said, wondering who this passionate creature was. Not Shaye, surely. She wasn't concerned with either of their pasts, or what would happen once the loving was finished; she lifted her hips to give him easier access. His erection rubbed against her belly, and she hissed. He hissed. The absolute pleasure...the wild sensations.

"Mmm, yes," she said. "I like. No, hate. I hate. Stroke it against me."

"Like this." He pressed his erection between her legs and stroked *uuuup*.

Her stomach tightened, quivered. "Yes." She arched her hips for another go.

"That one was free. You want another one, you're going to have to pay for it." Valerian pushed the collar of her shirt beneath her breasts, baring them to his gaze.

Cool air around her—and yet the heat in his fingertips burned her.

"Like this," he rasped, licking his lips. "So beautiful. So perfect."

"Payment through stripping. Got it." She plumped both breasts. "I think I like my job. Or hate it. Yes, I meant I hate it."

His pupils basically exploded. "I have to taste them. Have to have those sweet little beads in my mouth."

She had an unquenchable desire to feel him knead her breasts and slide and pump and grind inside her. To know and understand how people became slaves to their emotions over this one act.

So much better to be informed, just like Valerian had said.

He closed his fingers over her wrist. "What are you thinking about?"

"Passion," she admitted. "Sex."

"Look at me. Show me your passion."

Her gaze jerked to him, and she stilled, amazed by what she saw. He was drinking in the sight of her as if she was the most beautiful thing he'd ever beheld. As if her too-pale skin and her average-size breasts topped his Christmas list.

"I'm thinking that I've never seen a more wondrous sight. Your loveliness captivates me," he said, his tone reverent.

Her mind struggled to believe. "You've been with a thousand women," she reminded him softly. "A thousand times more beautiful than me." He might want those women again after he'd had her—she was going to be a disappointment, wasn't she?

"None are more beautiful than you, love. Now or ever."

"I'm nothing," she insisted. "I'm—"

"Everything." One of his hands cupped her jaw, and his thumb caressed the side of her face. He forced her to look at him, to *see* him. "You are everything to me."

"You don't know…" But he did. He was learning all about her. Her argument that they were strangers no longer held any sway.

It was just…people didn't say beautiful things like that to her.

Tears stung her eyes, and she scrubbed them away. She'd always prided herself on her independence, on her lack of need for another's approval. And she still didn't need someone else's approval; her worth wasn't based on his opinion. But truth was power and the things Valerian said to her…they were truth to him. They mattered. They empowered.

He wiped those tears with his thumbs, his touch gentle.

He was poised above her, his big, hard body illuminated by a golden glow of light. Muscles bunched, strength and arousal exuded from him in mouthwatering waves. His stomach was ripped and hard. His penis stretched toward her center, so thick and hard, reaching for her. A sprinkling of golden hair surrounded the heavy weight of his testicles.

The sight of him, this god of beauty and sex, made her breathless. "You—" she cleared her throat "—aren't bad-looking, either," she said. She'd never given a man a compliment before; she always shoved the opposite sex out of her life as quickly as one entered. And Valerian already had an ego.

His lips twitched. "I'm glad you don't find me ugly."

"Yes. Be very glad."

Inch by agonizing inch, he lowered his head, giving her time to protest, but a gasp of anticipation caught in her windpipe. She could say nothing…finally, blessedly his mouth closed over her nipple, surrounding it with moist heat. When his tongue flicked back and forth against the aching bud, her hand tangled in his hair, holding his head in place. He kneaded her other breast, and the double sensation had her hips writhing.

"Did I not promise you it would feel terrible?"

"Awful, just awful. Don't stop."

"Stop? Oh, no. You make me feel feverish, as if my very life depends on you." He sucked hard, and she groaned at the pleasure-pain of it, then he licked away the sting and she moaned at the heady bliss. "When a nymph makes love with his mate, he becomes completely absorbed in the act, ferocious and bestial. Nothing else matters except the woman in his arms."

I need him the way he needs me, she thought with a yearning she'd never before experienced. *I do. I really do.*

With the admission, something cracked and crumbled inside her. The last vestiges of her resistance? Fear? Doubt? Her anger over her abduction, perhaps? They were suddenly gone, replaced by a need to know him, all of him—in that moment he became more important to her than breathing.

She wrapped her legs around his waist, locked her ankles and jerked him on top of her. All of his weight suddenly pinned her, and it was purely blissful. She savored, reveled in the exquisite press of him. Basked in her first true taste of capitulation. No more denying her needs, no more ignoring her secret wants.

"Shaye?" he said, his voice hoarse. He closed his eyes in sweet surrender, his expression entranced, shocked, awed.

"Valerian."

He nipped at her collarbone, licked up and down her neck. His fingers glided under her panties, to the center of her being.

She nearly screamed as she arched her hips to urge him further.

"Most women think this is the most pleasure-receptive place on their bodies." His fingers pinched her drenched core lightly. And with that one touch, she almost reached the gates of paradise. So close to climax...so close...

"They'd be right," she managed on a pant.

"No, they are wrong." He slid a finger through her damp folds and into the very heat of her. "Small," he said, his voice strained. Sweat trickled from his temples. "Tight. Wonderful."

Had she thought she'd neared paradise before? Not even close. Her feminine walls clamped around him, holding him captive. In and out he moved slowly, and it was sheer torture. She gasped, then gasped his name, then gasped a curse.

"Some women think this rhythm is the cause of their desire."

"Are they...wrong, too?" *Oh, my wow.* She was on fire. Her cells were traveling through her bloodstream at full speed, scorching everything in their path.

"Oh, yes. They are wrong."

He continued sliding those fingers into her, and her stomach coiled, tensed; her leg muscles quivered around him. Orgasm teetered on the sweet brink of arrival.

"Valerian," she beseeched.

"Oh, but I like my name on your lips." His thumb brushed her aching core.

Her head thrashed from side to side. She burned, so hot, nearing explosion. "Show me the most pleasure-receptive place on my body." She had to come. Had to... would die...soon...

"For a kiss," he said, wanting to bargain even now. "I'll give you the world for a single kiss."

"Don't want the world. Want *you*."

"Shaye. My Shaye."

She meshed her lips into his. The moment his tongue collided with hers, his taste filled her mouth. The exquisite sensations between her legs intensified. She unlocked her ankles, letting her knees fall onto the bed, opening herself for whatever he might do.

Lost in passion like this, she was exactly what she'd feared: a slave to it, desperate for it. But she didn't care.

The kiss was hard and hot and only became harder and hotter. Tongues battled, teeth clashed. Valerian's fingers continued to pump her, sinking in and out, as frantic and insatiable as the kiss.

But then, suddenly, he stopped. Stopped the kiss, stopped the motion of his fingers. Her body throbbed, and a sob nearly burst from her lips.

"What are you doing?" she said on a moan. She tangled her hands in his hair and tried to force his mouth back to hers.

Finally she'd allowed herself to enjoy a man, and he stopped?

"Now I will show you where you are most sensitive, where you will verge on climax every time I touch you."

Hmm. Yes. "Hurry."

Sweat continued to trickle from his temples. The lines of tension around his eyes had deepened, bracketing his features. He, too, needed relief, she realized. Did he ache with an almost unquenchable ferocity like she did? Was he desperate, eager? Did he feel like he would blast past the stars if he didn't touch her again?

His lips brushed her softly, once, twice. "Your taste…it's like no one else's, and it's addictive. I think I would die without it."

Darling man.

Touch me. Make love to me. "Valerian, I'm glad you like how I taste, I am, but I shouldn't have to remind you that you've got a point to prove here."

He chuckled. "You're right. I just need to look at you a moment longer and savor the sight of you. Very soon I *will* strip you completely. I'll slide your pants over your legs and feast between them. Until then, I'll concentrate on—"

As he spoke, the image he painted consumed her

mind. There, in her thoughts, he *was* stripping her. He *was* lowering his head to lick her on—

"Your ankles," he rasped. "I bring your foot to my mouth and lick—"

—the arch of her foot, gliding his tongue slowly. His mouth moved up her calf, swirling little hearts over her skin before—

"I'll bite your inner thigh. You'll pant and writhe, like you're doing now, and you'll grow even wetter for me. So wet. You'll bring your own hand between your legs so I can watch you touch yourself. You—"

—circle her finger over her feminine heart, watching him all the while. In her mind, his eyes lowered to half-mast and his hand curled around the base of his length, moving up and down. He told her how much he wanted her mouth to replace his hand, how much he wanted *his* mouth to replace *hers*. Then he kissed her...deep, so deep...but it—

"—isn't enough. I crave another taste of you, Moon. A more intimate taste, and talking about it will never be enough. I'll lower my head between your legs. Your hands will grasp my hair, pulling roughly because you're so far gone with need you aren't able to control your reactions."

She couldn't control her reactions *now*.

Shaye writhed, insatiable. She still wore her pants, but the material actually made her feel as if phantom hands were at work between her legs. As if a phantom tongue licked and lapped at her. She groaned, her breath burning her throat.

"Valerian, Valerian," she chanted. "Valerian, please."

"Please what?" His voice was rough, so rough. Husky, so husky.

"Please finish me."

"But I'm still savoring you."

"Savor later. Show me the most erotic place on my body, right this second. I'm considering killing you!"

"I'm going to die of pleasure anyway." His voice broke with arousal. He pinched her neediness again, and she nearly jumped off the bed. The decadent sensations were acute, almost painful. "I'm going to taste you here before I love you," he said. "And when I love you, you're going to know the most pleasure-receptive place on *my* body."

"Your penis?" she gasped out. She was almost beyond speech. It was too much. He was too much. His words, his actions. His very essence.

"No, my—"

"My king," a voice said urgently.

Valerian stilled. He growled low in his throat, and it was an animal sound. A killing sound.

A moment passed before Shaye realized what was going on. There was a warrior standing at the edge of the bed, his eyes on Valerian, his expression concerned.

Losing her passion haze, she screamed and scrambled for the bedcovers. Mortification bombarded her as she covered her bare breasts. Yet still she ached for Valerian.

"Turn around, Broderick," he growled. His teeth bared in a fierce, lethal scowl. "Or lose your eyes."

Broderick instantly turned. "My apologies, my lord, but—"

"Leave us, or lose your head."

"Decapitate me if you must, but not until after you've heard my news. The dragons," Broderick said. He didn't leave as he'd been commanded. "They're back. They're back with larger forces, Darius, their king, at the helm. They're headed for the palace, clearly intent on war."

CHAPTER TWENTY

VALERIAN COULDN'T BELIEVE someone had entered his private chamber without his knowledge. Even the times he'd gotten caught up in the most animalistic of his desires, his warrior instincts had remained sharp and ready.

Not so with Shaye. He'd been swept up, the rest of the world ceasing to exist.

Such a thing had never before happened to him.

At the moment he battled a fierce torrent of rage and desire. He had Shaye where he'd wanted and needed her for so long, and Broderick expected him to leave her?

But leave her he would.

Her safety would always come before her seduction.

Her safety would always come before his pleasure.

"Gather the others," he told Broderick, the words ripped from him. "Within the next five minutes, everyone will be in full armor and waiting in the arena. I'll be there shortly."

"Consider it done, my king." His second in command rushed off.

Valerian had known this day would come. The dragons wanted a reckoning.

Why could it not have come tomorrow morning?

"Broderick," he called, and the warrior quickly backtracked. "The other females."

"They are being hidden even now."

"Excellent. Go, then. You have your orders."

Broderick stalked from the room a second time, his hurried footsteps echoing off the walls.

"I'm sorry, Moon." Valerian gazed down at the exquisite Shaye. Color flushed her cheeks; pale hair splayed over the bed like ribbons of white silk. Her breasts, covered by the pretty pink sheet, were outlined, her nipples little beads. "I must go."

"You're going to war?" Her voice gave no indication of her emotions.

Only two things she could be feeling: happiness that her trials with him might finally come to an end, or worry. "If war is what's required to keep this palace, then yes, I will go to war."

"But…you're injured."

Worry. She worried for him. "Yes." He pressed a swift kiss to her lips before withdrawing from the bed.

"You shouldn't be fighting. You'll make your wounds worse."

"Don't do this again. Don't doubt my skill. Besides, I'll know you are waiting for me. I'll do whatever proves necessary to survive." He wished there was time, at least, to sate *her* desires, to give one of them relief.

He dressed, tugging on a pair of leather pants, and strapped his armor in place—every piece was stained with blood from today's practice.

He wasn't at full strength. His grip wasn't as tight, and his limbs weren't as steady. But he'd meant what he said. He would survive.

"I thought you fought better without your armor," she said.

"With a single opponent, yes. But the dragons are part of a horde." He laced up his boots, gathered his helmet and shield and slid the Skull in the center sheathe.

She pushed out a heavy breath. "Here's a revolutionary idea. Why don't you just give the dragons back their palace?"

"It's *my* palace now, the only access we have to the portal into and out of Atlantis."

"Oh," she said.

Yes. Oh. Without the palace—the portal—he would never be able to surprise her with a visit topside to see her relatives.

"Our people will never be wanderers again."

"Our?"

"Of course. What's mine is yours, and what's yours is all mine."

The color in her cheeks deepened. With contentment, he hoped.

"Get dressed," he said.

Motions stiff, she straightened her clothing, covering each of her wanton curves. A travesty.

Valerian mourned the loss of her seminakedness. He held out his free hand and motioned her to join him. Surprisingly she did so without protest, smoothing the rest of her clothing in place as she walked.

"Where are you taking me?" she asked.

"To the same place as the other women, where you'll be safest."

"And where is that?" she insisted. "The hobby room?"

"No." Urgency battered at him. He pulled a fur coat from the closet—fur from the were-shifters—and draped it around her shoulders. "Someplace a bit… farther underground."

He led her out of the room, through three separate hallways and down four flights of stairs. Along the way, men rushed past him, nodding in acknowledgment as they headed for the arena.

The air cooled and thickened with moisture; mist curled toward the ceiling. Finally they entered a cave; the walls were rocky and jagged, painted with sensual murals.

A tremor vibrated through Shaye when she spotted the swirling portal. He passed it, careful not to step within reaching distance of the dappled liquid that separated him and Shaye from the sea. Twigs and bones—left over from the time the dragons had owned the palace, killing every human who'd strayed into Atlantis—snapped under his boots.

More than once Valerian had wondered why Atlanteans couldn't survive upon the surface for more than a day or so, and yet humans could come and go through Atlantis as much and as long as they pleased.

"Are those *bones*?" Shaye covered her mouth with a shaky hand. "Gross! How did I miss them last time?"

"I'm sure you were preoccupied by my astounding beauty," he told her dryly.

She snorted. "Yes. That must be it."

"Throughout the centuries, humans have tried to destroy the creatures of Atlantis in an attempt to steal our riches. The dragons did what they thought was right in order to protect the entire kingdom."

Valerian's father had once lamented about a human army that had passed through the portal and not only decimated the dragon army in charge of guarding it, but skulking through the Outer City and slaughtering innocents mercilessly.

Afterward, a new dragon army had taken charge of the portal, and this cavern had become a place of death and destruction. Anyone who'd stumbed through had been killed on sight.

What if Shaye had accidentally passed through when the dragons were in charge?

Easy. She would have been beheaded.

The portal was better off under Valerian's control.

"Is this a test?" Shaye asked. "This feels like a test."

"Will you pass or fail?"

"I guess time will tell. I mean, really. You've proved to be nothing but a tease."

"Me?" he choked out. "*I'm* the tease?"

"Yes, you. You told me you'd make me hate staying here, hate being with you, and you have yet to follow through. I'm outraged!"

His lips twitched with much needed humor. "I'll strive to do better."

The sound of female voices drifted from around the corner. He descended a final flight of stairs, this one hidden in the narrow crevice between two bloodstained boulders.

"By the way," Shaye whispered. "You never told me the most erotic place on a woman's body."

For a moment, he was transported back to bed, this woman splayed underneath him. His blood heated. *Concentrate.* "I haven't and I won't." The mystery would, hopefully, occupy her mind and keep her distracted from the war. "Not until you're naked in our bed."

"You are such a jerk," she grumbled.

"You are such a delight."

They had reached the bottom of the steps and entered a new room. He propped his shield against the wall to slip an arm around Shaye's waist and urged her to his side—if only to prevent her from bolting when she spied the prison cell.

"Um, if I didn't know better, I'd say this is a dungeon."

"It *is* a dungeon."

His gaze skipped over the glowing blue bars in front of cells now bursting with human females. Those bars were made to stop immortals.

"What! No way." Shaye gave a violent shake of her head. "No way you're locking me up like a prisoner."

"I am. For your own good. If any dragons make it inside the palace, through secret passages we haven't yet found, they'll have a difficult time absconding with you." When she opened her mouth to rebuke him, he added, "None of the other women are complaining."

The gaggle of voices suddenly turned into happy coos.

"Valerian, you gorgeous thing! Are you here to pass out free orgasms?"

"Oh! Me first! Me first!"

"Now I understand why royal subjects are supposed to kneel before their king. I'd love to pay homage to your...scepter."

Shaye hurled curses before wrenching from Valerian's clasp.

"Maybe some of the girls are soldiers in the human army," she said. Her dark eyes flashed fire at him. "Did you ever think of that? They can help you. Maybe they are master strategists and they can plan a way out of any battle. Instead of locking them away, use them. Us. Let us help."

"If we weren't fighting dragons, I'd agree with you. You aren't just a pretty face. You have a brain. But we *are* fighting dragons. You know nothing about the fire-breathing race." As he spoke, he backed her into the wall.

She squared her shoulders and raised her chin, the

picture of total defiance. "Try to intimidate me all you want."

"I will. Now that I have your permission," he said, his tone dry.

Her eyes narrowed. "What if you and all your men are killed? Will we die of starvation down here?"

"We won't be killed," he insisted.

"Can you guarantee your survival with one hundred percent certainty?"

"Yes." Fact: Shaye's life depended on him. He would allow nothing bad to happen to himself.

Remaining stubborn, she crossed her arms over her chest. "How can you guarantee such a thing? Are you psychic? Wait. Let me guess. Your nympho visions come only when you're having sex, right? Courtesy of the magic vagina."

Part of him wanted to laugh. The other part of him wanted to howl with frustration. He pointed to the group of warriors standing in front of the prison bars. "If anything happens to me and the others, these men will release you and escort you home. Are you satisfied?"

"No!"

His eyes narrowed. "I'm not surprised. You never are, are you?"

What little color she possessed drained away. "That was a low blow."

"Why? Did I speak an untruth? Because so far, nothing I've done has been good enough for you. You've focused solely on my mistakes, never my successes."

She flinched as if he'd struck her. "Well, you're my captor. What more do you expect?"

Instant remorse. "You're right. I'm sorry."

"Sorry for speaking what you perceive as the truth, or sorry for kidnapping me?" she asked. "Why do you even want to be with me? If I weren't your mate, I'm pretty sure you wouldn't have chosen me."

He softened his tone. "You are a rose worth every prick of thorns. I would choose you *always*."

Her shields began to drop, pure vulnerability staring up at him. She softened against him.

"Valerian," Broderick called.

He gently tapped the bottom of her chin with his knuckles. "Try to keep the other females calm while I'm gone. Will you do this for me? Please, Moon."

For the briefest moment, he thought he glimpsed sheer terror. For him. For his safety. A master at hiding her reactions, she rallied quickly, blanking her expression. His remorse only magnified.

The ice queen was back in place.

"Fine," she said. "I'll do it. But they aren't exactly upset right now. They're freakishly happy to see you."

"We are, Valerian." A brunette gripped the bars, a buttercup-yellow robe draping her lush body. "We're *very* happy to see you. Want to make out?"

Shaye rubbed the back of her neck. "If you don't come back, I swear I'll kill you myself."

"I'll come back." Valerian gave her a swift kiss before nodding to Dylan and Terran, who stood sentry at the cell.

Terran brushed his fingers against the bars, the medallion he wore acting as an on-off switch. The blue dulled until only mist remained.

But one taste of his mate hadn't been enough. Valerian crushed his lips into Shaye's, his tongue swooping inside for a demanding taste, bringing all of his fiercest desires to the surface. She responded violently, brutally, taking everything he had to give her.

When he lifted his head, they were both panting.

Once again, she squared her shoulders. Without further prompting from him, and without ever removing her gaze from his, she stepped into the cage.

Terran removed his hand and the bars reappeared.

One heartbeat passed, two, silence sizzling between Valerian and Shaye.

He hated to leave her and wanted to kiss her again, to linger this time.

He hefted up his shield and stalked from the enclosure, heading for the dining hall. Broderick caught up with him halfway.

"The men are ready."

"Excellent." He pushed Shaye from his mind, determined to act as a warrior: cold, unemotional and lethal. "Where are the dragons now?"

Valerian and Darius had fought only once before, and though Valerian had injured the hulking beast, the end had been a draw, with neither man able to completely conquer the other.

"The Outer City," Broderick replied.

"Have they any allies with them?"

"No. They've come alone."

Their mistake. "I want our best men on the parapet and a group of soldiers strategically placed in the surrounding forest. I want the dragons' every move tracked. If flyers land on the roof, cut them down without mercy."

The two advantages dragons had: their wings and their fire.

Their forces had to be stopped quickly, before they had an opportunity to decimate everything on the ground from a perch in the air, where no one else could reach them.

At least the palace, which had been made for dragons, was fire resistant.

The one advantage the nymphs had: the power to seduce.

Males were not immune, and they, too, could be caught up in the spell of a nymph, becoming a slave to desire.

"Shall I unleash the traps we set around the palace?" Broderick asked.

He considered the idea. "No. Let the dragons reach us without incident. Perhaps we can reach a truce before a single battle must be fought." Whatever would keep the women safest.

Broderick blinked in astonishment before rushing to convey all he'd been ordered.

In the dining hall, Valerian stopped at the wall of windows to peer out. Empty streets greeted him. The citizens who lived in the Outer City must have spied the dragons and run home, fearing for their lives.

Wise.

Valerian spun on his heel and strode to the arena. Broderick was busy instructing the men. As they received orders, they raced to obey.

"May your strength only flourish," he told those who passed him.

"And yours, my king," he heard numerous times.

Those without assignments formed a line and eyed him expectantly. He paced in front of them, saying, "I want you to circle around the Outer City undetected and remain behind the dragons. I want them flanked by nymphs on every side."

They nodded in unison.

"When you receive my signal, close in on them and finally let them know you are there. Now go."

Hurried footsteps echoed as the men rushed to obey. Valerian found himself alone. Gripping his sword hilt, he stood there for a moment, his thoughts drifting inexorably to Shaye. Had she not been here, he most likely would have led a section of his army into the outskirts of the city and attacked the dragons there. As it was, he wanted his forces surrounding the palace. Close at hand. Forming a circle of protection.

All he had to do now was await the dragons' arrival. If a truce couldn't be reached, blood would flood through the city, a crimson river.

CHAPTER TWENTY-ONE

SHAYE STUDIED THE other women who'd been locked inside the cell. Of course, they were the same women who'd been trapped inside the hobby room and attended the wedding. They didn't seem to grasp the danger of the current situation and were, in fact, chatting amicably with one another.

If she stayed in Atlantis, *this* would her life. She would be locked away every time war threatened.

Considering the creatures populating the underwater world, war would always threaten.

Shaye wasn't sure why, but a new card filled her head. One that had nothing to do with her circumstances: *Congrats! You started your period. May you snarl at nothing, cry about everything, eat as many pies as humanly possible and opt* not *to murder your loved ones.*

"—reason I would kick him out of bed," Martina was saying, pulling Shaye's focus out of her head, "was to do him on the floor."

Chuckles abounded.

Another girl said, "I've never been this happy! I mean, who cares if we are being used for sex. Sex feels good. We should only care if we're being used for cooking and laundry."

More chuckles.

Another comment arose from the midst. "I once had

to explain to my ex that sex without foreplay was like going down a waterslide without water. I don't have to explain anything to my nymph."

Okay, maybe the card *did* apply to her circumstances. She wanted to scream: *This isn't you! You're drugged by that stupid pheromone. You're better than this.*

What a nightmare this was. The men were in danger, and no one wanted to talk strategy.

The conversation changed, taking a new direction. Apparently there was a new nymph in residence. One more handsome than any of the others, including Valerian. He liked to ask questions, and he could bring a woman to climax with only a look.

Ugh. Was Brenna here? Shaye really needed an ally. Someone to share her worries with—someone to help her remain calm.

"Brenna," she called.

The beauty shouldered her way through the crowd. "I'm here."

Thank the good Lord above!

At the sound of her raspy voice, some of the women shared pitying looks. Brenna noticed, and her shoulders rolled in.

Shaye considered throwing a pimp hand around. *No one hurts my friend!*

She pulled Brenna into the nearest corner. First things first. "How are you? Did Shivawn punish you for trying to escape?"

"Escape. This again?" A woman named Tiffany tsk-tsked. She leaned against one of the bars. "Please tell me you two aren't trying again. If you are, at least wait until everyone is sleeping and you have a *chance* of success."

"I still don't understand why you'd want to escape, anyway." The redhead who'd left Valerian's room that very first night stepped forward, unabashedly joining the conversation. "He's the best lover in the history of ever. I polled my body parts and they all agreed."

Well, well. Here was one of those testimonials Valerian had considered giving her.

Shaye's hands fisted as…yes, oh, yes—as jealousy speared her. There was no denying it or convincing herself another emotion was at play.

Diamonds were a girl's best friend until Valerian happened.

"I still dream about him," another woman said. Her blade of a nose gave her a regal air. She sighed dreamily. "Does he ever speak of me? I'm Ameena, by the way."

Shaye's teeth gnashed together as images of Valerian and Ameena—naked and straining—consumed her mind.

Jealousy was new to her, and she wasn't exactly sure how to deal with it. "No," she said. "He hasn't mentioned you."

"Oh." Ameena's shoulders sagged with disappointment. "Let me know when he tires of you. I give the best 'get over her and get under me' blow jobs."

When, she'd said. Not *if.*

I will cut first and ask questions never!

But…if Shaye were being honest, she'd admit she feared the same.

How long would Valerian remain interested in her?

Would she lose him soon after he awakened desires that she'd thought buried?

How long until his eye began to rove in search of someone else? Someone sweeter and more biddable?

He was a nymph, after all, and commitment had never before been his jam.

But he hadn't yet met me.

I'm a novelty, that's all.

Valerian *would* tire of her at some point. Already he'd expressed dissatisfaction with her. She complained, never praised.

A fair criticism.

Let's face it. Everyone she'd ever loved had either abandoned her or disappointed her so massively she had never recovered. No one stuck around. No one had ever wanted to work at the relationship.

Yet here she was, falling for Valerian and giving him more of her heart than she'd ever given to another.

Her first instincts had been right. She *needed* to leave him.

The pang in her chest said only one word: stay.

Clinging to hope, like a fool.

Well, it was time to destroy that hope once and for all!

"What makes you so certain he'll tire of me at all?" What did these women see when she and Valerian interacted?

Ameena shrugged. "Don't take this the wrong way, but he's a king and you aren't exactly queen material."

There was a right way to take that?

A dozen new cards took shape in her head. All of them about breaking up.

It's not you, it's me. I've finally realized you're terrible for me.

Don't cry because the relationship ended. Laugh because your ex is now someone else's problem.

Remaining friends after a breakup is like keeping your dog after it dies. FYI we're done.

It's better to love and lose than to live with your scum of an ex.

I almost can't get over how easily I can get over you.

Shaye shook her head to dislodge the rest. Before rage overwhelmed her.

Brenna latched on to her wrist. "If you're thinking about catfighting her, don't. I don't have the tools to patch her."

Deep breath in...out. In, out.

Ameena flipped her hair over her shoulder. "Please. I'm not to be harmed. My man—"

In a lightning-fast movement, Shaye hooked her foot behind her knees. At the same time, she shoved the girl backward.

Between one blink and the next, Ameena dropped.

She lay on the floor, blinking up at the ceiling with confusion.

Shaye pressed her foot against the woman's vulnerable throat. "What your man orders has no bearing on this situation. My word will always trump his. Just ask Valerian. Better yet, don't. You won't even mention his name without first requesting my permission."

Ameena turned pallid.

Point made, Shaye removed her foot. She scanned the cell's occupants and everyone looked away as if suddenly fascinated with the walls and one another.

Enough. She'd had enough.

Determined, she whispered to Brenna, "This is our best chance for escape." The ache in her chest intensified, but she ignored it. "Are you with me?"

Indecision played over Brenna's lovely features. She nibbled on her bottom lip and wrung her hands.

Finally she nodded.

Good. That was good.

Shaye pushed through the crowd, stopping at the bars. Still thick, about the width of a baseball bat, still bright and blue. They were also hot to the touch, she realized as she curled her fingers around two. Not hot enough to blister, just enough to burn.

She tried to rattle them, but they didn't move. How had the warrior caused them to turn to mist?

She replayed the goodbye kiss Valerian had given her—*no shivering!* Terran hadn't had to push a button or use a key to allow her to step into the cage. But, once she'd stood inside, another warrior had waved his hand through mist. That's right! The bars had first become mist. With that wave of his hand, he'd caused the bars to solidify again.

Was an outside touch required? Or had the warrior worn some type of sensor?

Only one way to find out.

"I have a plan," she told Brenna.

Head high, she strode over to Ameena. "You want to get rid of me, then you have to help me." She explained what she wanted the woman to do.

Ameena's eyes narrowed to tiny slits. "You're trying to get me into trouble."

"No, I'm giving you a chance to get rid of me."

"So you plan on leaving Atlantis?"

"Not all of us are happy being sex slaves." Again Shaye's chest throbbed. "But yes. I am."

"In that case, helping you will be my pleasure." Ameena sashayed her way to the front of the crowd. She gripped the bars, smiled sweetly, and called, "Terran, you look so handsome today. I could just eat you up."

He grinned over at her, hungry yearning in his eyes.

"You look handsome, too, Dylan," Ameena added, playing her role perfectly. "Your muscles are so big. May I feel them?"

Both men trudged toward her as if pulled by an invisible cord. What they didn't do: reach for her.

Shaye kept her attention divided between the men and the bars, ready to exit at a moment's notice.

Amenna whispered throatily, "May I lick your neck, Terran? Please. I have to taste you."

He didn't even think of denying her. "Of course." He gripped the bars and leaned into Ameena's waiting lips.

In that moment, the bars turned to mist.

"I want to lick you, too," another woman said.

The entire group surged forward, exiting the prison. Everyone but Shaye and Brenna focused on the two guards, capturing the pair.

Well. The dragons could learn a thing or two. Want to defeat the nymphs? Offer a sexual favor.

Shaye easily and silently slipped away, Brenna beside her. They tiptoed into a section of the cavern.

"All right. Time to return to the cell."

Moans and groans.

"I mean it! Return to the cell. Please." Amid the guards' now-frantic pleas, she and Brenna rounded the corner.

Guilt flared. Before Valerian, sneaky hadn't been her style. But that's what she was doing right now. Sneaking away without saying goodbye. As if he meant nothing to her.

He's something. He's heartbreak waiting to happen.

Strengthening her resolve, she followed the curls of fog wafting through the air and soon reached the portal. Heart racing, she approached tentatively. The center swirled and churned.

Shaye shivered from the cold—not from regret, she assured herself—and wrapped her arms around her middle.

"I can't believe how easy that was," she said. But she didn't take another step.

Brenna didn't respond.

She faced her partner in crime—who was twisting her hands together, her expression tortured.

"What's wrong?" Shaye asked.

"Joachim and Shivawn...they need me."

Ah, crap. The nymphs had brainwashed another one. If Brenna backed out...

"Joachim is healing nicely. You said so yourself."

Brenna bit her lip. "But Shivawn...he's so sweet. He would rather die than hurt me. He keeps me safe."

Understanding dawned. At some point in her life, Brenna had been abused. She'd probably shut down sexually...until the nymphs awakened her desires.

I know the feeling.

Desire alone wasn't the reason for her reluctance. Safe, she'd said. She felt safe. A heady feeling indeed, for someone who'd gone any amount of time without it.

Expelling a sharp breath, Shaye pushed a hand through her hair. "You really want to stay with our captors?"

A moment passed in silence. Without any kind of reaction. Then Brenna nodded. "I think I do. I'm ready to face my fears at long last. No, not ready. We're never really ready for anything, are we? I *will* face my fears. I hate the life I've been living and want a better one. The only way to have change is to make change."

Wow. Talk about a punch to the throat!

Shaye had thought herself content. Until Valerian. He'd opened her eyes to the truth. She'd settled. She'd settled for half a life because it was easier than risking her heart for a full one.

But here she was, running again. Running away from him and the things he made her feel. All because she feared he would one day grow tired of her.

What if he didn't?

What if he meant what he said—she was his one and only, now and always?

What if Valerian was injured during the battle with the dragons? He would need her.

What if he was killed? If she left now, she would never know his fate.

What if she stayed and he fell deeply, madly in love with her?

Her heart fluttered with…longing?

But…she didn't believe in love, right?

Love wouldn't be temporary. Love wouldn't allow someone to hurt another person. Love…

Maybe wasn't what she thought it was?

Like, maybe she'd never actually seen an example of real love. Maybe her mother and father had waxed poetic about lust not love.

Shaye bowed her head and stepped back, away from the portal. "I'm not ready to leave him," she admitted, her voice breaking. He was right. He'd said she would forgive him for abducting her, and she had.

Not that she was okay with his actions. She wasn't and wouldn't be—ever. What he'd done was wrong. But they'd both made mistakes, and she could finally see past his.

Brenna patted her shoulder, a show of solidarity.

She rubbed a hand over her eyes and pushed out a frustrated breath. "I'm afraid," she whispered.

"Of what?"

"Of falling for him, giving up everything to be with him, and then losing him."

"If we do not let go of the past and grasp onto the future, we will regret it for the rest of our lives."

"You're right. I know you're right" She licked her

lips. "And these men could use a queen. I mean, already I can think of a million laws I need to put into motion."

Snorting, Brenna banged her shoulder with her own. "You're doing Valerian a favor, really. Fixing his kingdom."

"I'm a giver."

They shared a smile.

"Ameena is going to be *ticked*," Brenna said.

"Well, she'll just have to get over it."

They shared another smile.

"I don't want to go back to the cell," Shaye said. "Do you?"

"No."

"We can't go into the palace, though." Valerian had asked her to stay down here, so stay down here she would. She wouldn't play the dumb card and inadvertently distract him, placing him in unnecessary danger. Nor would she allow herself to fall in enemy hands, thereby giving the dragons the advantage.

Sighing, she led Brenna through the cave and into the cavern next door to the cell. "We can stay here." The guards wouldn't hear them, the *drip drip* of water too loud.

Wouldn't Valerian get a nice surprise when he came to get her, and she wasn't in the cell? The thought of thwarting him, however slightly, made her want to laugh.

If he survived.

Record scratch.

Time ticked by with agonizing slowness. She spent a good portion of it studying the cave walls in an effort to distract herself.

She traced her fingers over the image of a muscled male body. "The details are exquisite, aren't they?" Something caught her eye, and she examined it more closely.

Realization smacked her, and she gasped. She motioned her friend over. "Brenna, come look at this. They tell a story."

The first picture showed a group of...gods? They were sitting high above an empty world, looking down upon it. The second picture showed a world filled with terrible monsters born from rivers of blood, water and fire. In the third, those monsters were being thrown into an underwater prison. She saw a portal—*the* portal.

No. She saw *two* portals.

The pictures went on to show a human army marching through one of the portals and slaying every creature in its path.

Those humans carried swords and guns, an odd combination of past and present. Perhaps two different armies had marched through the land at two different times, but the images had coalesced into one?

Several of the monstrous races rose up in retaliation and destroyed the human army.

"The violence," Brenna said.

"Yes." What a brutal place Atlantis was—or rather, had been forced to be. Did she really want to stay here, even for a little while?

Valerian's face swam into her mind, reminding her of exactly how beautiful he'd looked when he'd been poised over her, about to enter her. His honey-dark hair had fallen in disarray over his strong shoulders. His crystalline eyes had gleamed with molten desire.

Yes, she thought, she wanted to stay here. Despite the violence, despite the circumstances, she wanted to stay with Valerian.

The corner of her eye snagged on a particular grouping of rocks on the far wall.

"What's that?" she asked, pointing.

Brenna's brow crinkled.

In unison, they moved forward. The closer they came to the grouping, the chillier the air became.

A tremor racked her spine. Once they reached it, she realized it was a hidden doorway.

She gulped and looked to Brenna. "Should we?"

"No. Definitely not."

"I think I'm too curious for my own good. I'm going to check it out." Heart racing, Shaye pushed and prodded until the block had been moved out of the way, and suddenly she stood on the precipice of a dark abyss.

The shuffle of feet pricked at her ears.

Who did Valerian have locked inside?

The first day she'd entered this cave, she recalled how he'd discussed "prisoners" with one of his men.

Curiosity propelled her deeper inside, and she slowly inched around the corner. Torches came to life, lighting her way. Her eyes widened. Several hulking warriors paced inside a cell. They didn't look to be nymphs, for they lacked that air of raw sexuality. They were dark and strong, obviously young, and all had golden, glowing eyes.

One of them spotted her and growled.

She jerked backward with a gasp.

"You," he said. "Let us out of here. *Please.*"

Soft hands suddenly shackled her wrist. "We don't know what these men have done," Brenna said. She'd followed Shaye inside.

They exited the room without another word.

HAD SHE MADE THE right decision?

Brenna had opted not to escape in order to stay with not one but two different men. Men who were possessive and from what she'd seen, disinclined to share. Ever.

She'd never dated two men at once.

Is that what I'm planning to do? Date Shivawn and Joachim at the same time?

Ethan had cause brain damage. Clearly.

Shaye returned to their little room, and her cheeks were pale.

Brenna had spent more time with Shivawn but had never dared to let him kiss her. She'd barely spoken to Joachim, had run away every time he'd tried to start a conversation, but the desire to spend more time with him was undeniable—but only if Shivawn stayed with her. He would protect her. Just in case.

Just in case what?

If she was worried Joachim had a temper, she shouldn't be with him at all.

"I should pick one," she said.

Shaye patted her hand, offering comfort without judgment, something Brenna liked about her. The former maid of honor was her cousin by marriage, and at the wedding, Brenna wouldn't have guessed they would ever be friends. Shaye had scowled the entire ceremony. Her misery plus Brenna's misery, well, two wrongs would never make a right. But the past was the past—a lifetime ago it now seemed.

"I know nothing about love," Shaye said. "Are you in love?"

"I don't know."

Her shoulders dropped. "I was hoping *you* could give *me* advice."

Brenna snorted. Then, sobering, she said, "I was in an abusive relationship."

"I'm sorry."

"I was too afraid to leave. He's in prison now for

attempted murder." And rape, and a handful of other charges. "I don't want to make the same mistake."

"Well. From what I know of Valerian, he would *kill* his men for harming a woman."

"If he found out. Some bruises can be hidden. But… I don't think either man would hurt me. But then, I didn't think Ethan would hurt me, either."

"You remind me of me! I want to trust Valerian, but fear keeps changing my mind." She chewed on her bottom lip. "Can you imagine yourself with one of the guys forever?"

"I don't know if I can handle forever right now. Just one day at a time."

"That's fair. Oh! Just so you know, I'm writing a book, and I just made a decision to change the direction of my plot. You are my heroine." Shaye rubbed her hands together. "I will require daily reports."

Brenna arched a brow and tried not to smile. "What do I get in return?"

She fluffed her pale hair. "The admiration of your queen."

CHAPTER TWENTY-TWO

VALERIAN PACED THE length of the parapet, the rhythmic pounding of his footsteps reverberating in his ears. Waiting for the dragon army proved maddening. He was a man of action. A man eager to finish with business and return to pleasure.

Finally, hundreds of soldiers crested the horizon. That the men had chosen to walk to the palace rather than flying in dragon form meant they were not overcome by rage and did not mean to attack—yet.

With his next step, one of his boots snagged on a fallen branch and he stumbled. He braced his hands on the wall to steady and drew in a shaky breath. The wait had drained more than his patience; the wait had drained his strength. He needed sex. He needed *Shaye*. Soon!

At this rate, he wouldn't be able to win a battle against a bunny, much less a dragon.

"My king." Broderick rushed to Valerian's side. "Are you unwell?"

"I'll be fine." He'd gone a week without sex, something he hadn't done in...ever. Not since his first time. "I'm well enough to do what needs doing."

He must. For Shaye.

The wound in his arm had increased the intensity of his weakness. Had he made love with Shaye earlier, he would have already healed.

But he couldn't regret what *had* transpired between them. For one brief moment of time, she'd softened for him, not only welcoming his kiss and his touch but moaning for more.

"After we deal with the dragons," Broderick said, "we must deal with a stranger who now walks among us. He claims he's a nymph, and he must be, since he's sleeping with all our women. They talk of no one and nothing else. But I've never met him."

A new nymph? Impossible. Valerian knew every one of his people. But Broderick was right. Now wasn't the time.

"If the dragons come within a hundred yards of the palace," he said, "fire a warning shot. If they take a single step after that, fire again and do not stop."

Broderick nodded. "Archers," he called. "Prepare."

The men knelt and pulled their bows tight. Waiting. Waiting. Time ticked by slowly.

Joachim limped onto the parapet, his features contorted by pain. He managed to stay upright as he approached Valerian.

"What are you doing?" Valerian demanded.

"Fighting," his cousin said. "There's to be a war, is there not?"

"You have yet to recover."

"That's no reason to remain in bed."

He searched the male's face and found determination under the pain—he also found a need to make things right and nodded in approval. "Very well. Take your place in the lines below."

Joachim pivoted without protest, ready to do as commanded. Then he paused. Looking over his shoulder, he said, "I won't apologize for challenging you, but I will respect your skill and your leadership from this moment onward. Majesty."

Respect? From Joachim? And even affection?

Reeling, Valerian said, "Thank you," and clapped his cousin lightly on the shoulder.

Joachim turned and pulled him close for a—very manly—embrace. They broke apart a second later and pretended the hug had never happened.

His chest tight, Valerian assumed a battle stance at the wall. He stared down at the field of wildflowers leading to the front entrance of the palace.

Closer and closer the dragons came... Silver armor glinted in the day's light. Trees rattled behind them, the ground visibly shaken. Colorful petals whisked through the air.

Finally the dragon forces stopped and parted; Darius rode his stallion through the center. He held a sword, the long, menacing blade stained crimson from his many kills.

Over the centuries, Darius had become known as a lethal killer. An unfeeling warrior with no conscience.

A worthy adversary, to be sure.

Valerian's hand curled around the hilt of the Skull.

"Hold," he told his men. To the dragons, he called, "Welcome to my home, fire-breathers. You will understand if I do not invite you inside."

Darius scowled up at him. "You know very well the palace is mine."

He tsk-tsked under his tongue. "If you wanted to keep it, you should have sent a stronger battalion to guard it."

"What did you do with the dragons who were inside?"

"Showed them mercy, allowing them to live, and locked them in *my* dungeon."

Blue eyes narrowed to tiny slits. "I have your word of honor they are alive and well?"

"You have my word of honor that *most* are alive and well." A battle had been fought, and a life or twelve lost.

Darius nodded, the action clipped. "My wife has asked that I not slaughter your entire race for daring to steal what's mine. I'll heed her wishes—for now—if you do two things I require of you."

Curiosity got the better of him. "And what are those two things?"

"Release my men and leave the palace. Within the hour. If you refuse, we war."

Valerian laughed with genuine amusement. "Not war. Anything but war."

The nymphs laughed with him.

Smoke wafted from the dragon king's nostrils. "You have no idea what the Guardian of the Portal is required to do with the surface dwellers."

"You're wrong. I know. The guardian is to slay all humans."

"And yet you've allowed a human to sneak into Atlantis. He captured our Jewel of Dunamis."

Yes. Valerian knew the jewel had gone missing.

His friend Layel, king of the vampires, was out searching. Valerian had sent a handful of his troops to scour the land, as well. If the human *was* out there and *did* have the jewel, the two would be found. The one who possessed the jewel, legend claimed, possessed the ultimate power.

"I choose war," he announced.

"Do you know what happens when humans learn of Atlantis, Valerian? They tell others, and soon armies are marching through our land, destroying it—and us."

"Not if you *keep* those humans."

Darius pointed the sword in his direction. "How many other humans have you allowed to come through?"

"I wouldn't call them humans. I would call them *mine*."

The dragon king's eyes glinted with fury. "You are a fool."

A chorus of hissing rose from the crowd of nymphs.

Darius's insult lacked any kind of sting. Being with Shaye was the smartest thing Valerian had ever done.

"One day in the future, when you look back and think about the life you led, you will realize this was the day you welcomed destruction," the dragon king said. "I *will* reclaim the palace, and I *will* take charge of the humans you hold."

Take charge…meaning slay?

He dares threaten my woman? "Try," Valerian said, his jaw clenched, "and I will kill you myself. The portal and everyone who has come through it belong to me. They are mine," he reiterated.

Smoke wafted from the entire dragon army.

Darius regarded him with a strange mix of curiosity and fury. "The rumors are true. You found your mate. A human from the surface."

"Since the dawn of time, nymphs have traveled from one kingdom to the other, living with one race or another, sleeping in their beds, eating their food." His voice rose with his ferocity. "We were good only for pleasure and war. Our women—all of our women—deserve a home of their own."

"As to that—" Darius's lips curled in an arrogant smile "—*I* have your women."

Crackles of fury ignited inside *him*. "What did you say?"

"Your nymphs were on their way to the palace, and we captured them."

"If you've hurt them…"

"No. They are safe."

"I…thank you," he allowed. What Valerian really wanted to do was beat the dragon king until his blood flowed, a river of pain. Those women were *his* responsibility.

"I know your men weaken without sex. The only reason I've allowed you to stay in my palace this week. Are you sure you want to challenge me this day?"

He flashed his teeth in a scowl. "Worry about yourselves. We are plenty strong. You'll soon see."

The dragon released another growl, no longer quite so smug. "Then I suggest a battle of sword skill—between you and me."

Another challenge. One that would save his men from battle. Very well. "Agreed."

"Shall we meet on the battlefield in the morning?"

"Why wait?" He didn't like the thought of Shaye locked away any longer than necessary. He wanted this over and done as quickly as possible. "We can settle this here and now."

"Agreed." Darius grinned, his sharp teeth gleaming. Unlike the others, he wore no armor. "Winner takes the palace and everything inside."

"Winner takes the palace, nothing more, nothing less."

"But my king," Broderick said, sidling up to him and speaking in a low, whispering tone. "You haven't—"

"Worry not, my friend. I will prevail." He always did.

Broderick remained unconvinced. "At least go to Shaye. Take your pleasure. She would hate for you to go down there while—"

"Silence." He held up his hand. He wouldn't have Shaye's first time be nothing more than a quick tumble meant to strengthen him.

No, their first time would be slow and tender. She would be crazed with desire for him, and he would show her the most pleasurable place on her body...then introduce her to his.

"I'll be down shortly, Darius," he called.

The dragon king nodded.

Valerian turned to Broderick and the other men even now circling him.

"This could be a trap." Joachim clutched his sword hilt. "Once you go down, they could close in on you and kill you. That's what I would do."

"Keep the archers in place," Valerian instructed. "If a dragon warrior appears to step out of rank, pin him in place."

Broderick nodded.

"There's something I must do before I meet the dragon." None of his men said a word as he strode away.

They knew what he meant to do—at least, they suspected. They were only partly right.

He exited the parapet and found an empty corner room. While he would not visit Shaye, neither would he fight the dragon king without first doing *something*.

He conjured his mate's pale face in his mind, saw her lips part as desire glimmered in her velvety-brown eyes. As he imagined sinking inside her soft, sweet body, he slipped a hand inside his pants and stroked the thick, hard length.

He could almost feel her hot, wet tightness. Could almost hear her breathy moans and eager purrs. He increased his tempo because she was wild with need and craved a hard slamming.

When she shouted his name in climax, he roared with his own. And with the release, came a wave of strength. It wasn't as intense as if he'd been with Shaye, but it was enough. For now.

He cleaned himself and stalked back to his men.

"Here is your shield," Joachim said. The change in his attitude was remarkable, and more than Valerian had ever hoped for. "The Skull is inside."

"Do you require your spear?" Shivawn asked.

Valerian gripped the shield and cast a glance to Darius, who now stood in the center of a half circle, warriors flanking him. The dragon held a sword. No shield. No spear. He had no need of other weapons really. He would use his teeth, his claws and the fire he spewed.

Valerian in turn would need every weapon at his disposal.

"Yes," he said. "I'll take the spear. The dragon medallion, as well."

Shivawn gathered the items and handed them to him. "May all strength be yours, my king."

Valerian anchored the necklace around his neck and slapped Shivawn on the shoulder. "I finally have something worth fighting for. I won't allow a dragon to keep me from her."

Broderick arched a brow at him. "Her? Do you not fight for the palace, our home?"

"I fight for Shaye. I fight for all of our women, nymph and human, that *they* might have a home."

"Half of the men should come down with you," Joachim said. "We can close the circle with *your* allies."

He nodded. "Excellent idea."

With a troop of nymphs marching behind him, Valerian sliced down the steps lining the edge of the wall and soon stood at the door.

"Open," he said, lifting the necklace. The door instantly obeyed, a crack forming between the white stones and slowly widening.

He and his men filed out, never relaxing their guard. The dragons remained in place, growling at them. Nymphs snarled in response.

Valerian's eyes locked on Darius, the only blue-eyed dragon in existence. Darius had a stern face, harsh and savage. Up close, Valerian could see the scar that slashed down Darius's face—a scar he himself had inflicted.

"Did you beat your shaft like it owed you money, nymph?" a dragon warrior called.

Laughter abounded.

"Three cheers. The nymph king released many handcestors today. The children never to be born because he spilled on his hand."

More laughter.

This. This was the kind of teasing he'd lived with his entire life. Nymphs were nothing but whores and jokes to most of the other races.

"Careful," Joachim said, his voice as cold as ice. "I can have every one of you begging for it within seconds." The pheromone wafted from him and carried to the dragon army.

The laughter died. Several men stepped backward, widening the distance between dragon and nymph.

"This is amusing, really," Valerian told Darius.

The male arched his brows in a menacing salute. "And why is that?"

"You took a human woman for your mate, same as I, and now you think to scold me. *You* are the fool. I will fight to the death—your death—to keep my woman safe."

The dragon regarded Valerian with something akin to understanding. "Long ago, I was ordered never to enter the surface and never to bring humans here." He spewed a stream of fire at Valerian's feet. "I fear you will bring the wrath of Poseidon to us all."

"Me? What of you?" Valerian leaped forward, stabbing his spear at Darius's middle.

Darius jumped out of the way at the last second, spraying more fire along the way. Valerian rolled from its path of destruction, the flames barely missing him. The scent of charred hair filled his nose.

No matter. He used the momentum of his roll, stabbing at Darius again.

The spear *whooshed,* hitting only air. Another miss. Darius's wings expanded in a burst, the thick length of opalescent membrane allowing him to hover.

Valerian popped to his feet and immediately had to dodge left, away from another blast of fire. He spun on his heel, pretending to lunge. In truth, he swung his spear behind him to stab forward from the opposite side. The sharp tip grazed Darius's thigh even though he still hovered in the air.

The other dragons hissed; their king had been injured.

Darius gave no outward reaction. He simply opened his mouth and unleashed a terrible inferno.

Valerian raised his shield in the nick of time, blocking—but it wasn't long before the metal began to blister his hand. *Can't stay down here.* He leaped up and swung.

Clang. Metal vibrated against metal, swooping up his arm and stinging the wound in his arm. He blocked the pain, moving with the impetus, and twisted, slicing his spear through the air to force Darius to duck.

But Darius didn't duck; he charged. Valerian had to block and lunge, block and stab.

"I can do this all day," Darius growled. "Can you? Already you are drenched in sweat."

Valerian gouged his spear at a downward angle, hoping to slice into Darius's other thigh. If he could hobble the dragon, forcing him to rely only on his wings, Valerian could gain the advantage. But Darius flew up and dropped quickly, snapping the weapon in two.

Valerian slid the Skull from its scabbard inside his shield. A two-step run, a jump, and he cut downward. This time Darius didn't move quickly enough and the blade sliced into his arm.

Once again the surrounding dragons hissed, and once again Darius gave no reaction. It was as if he was impervious to pain. Unfortunately, Valerian was not any longer. His wounded arm throbbed, and his legs were growing shaky. If the fight didn't end soon…

Distantly he heard his men cheering for him.

"For Shaye," Broderick shouted. "Shaye. Shaye. Shaye."

Her lovely face flashed before his mind, and he gathered his strength. Rallied. He'd been pushed to the brink before. There had been times he'd gone without food and water, his people without shelter. He could prevail.

Perhaps he should change his battle strategy. Instead of forcing Darius to fly, perhaps he should cut into Darius's wings, grounding him?

The dragon king slammed into him, knocking him down and hacking at his chest armor. Valerian tasted dirt, felt warm blood ooze down his face, and kicked backward. Darius soared over him—taking Valerian's shield with him.

Valerian didn't bother rising this time. He spied Da-

rius from the corner of his eye and simply extended his
sword, jabbing the tip at his enemy, stabbing Darius between his arm and a rib.

A collective gasp from the dragons, as if they
couldn't believe what had just happened. A hearty cheer
from the nymphs.

Victory is...mine?

With a growl, Darius hit the sword with his own,
proving the tip had actually slid through air rather than
flesh.

Valerian anchored his feet and leaped up while
swinging behind him. *Clang.* Quickly he pivoted,
swinging again. *Clang.*

"Go now, and I'll let you keep the women," Darius
said. *Clang.*

"And how will we shelter them without the palace?"
He drew in a deep breath—and noticed the scents of
blood and death that now thickened the air.

"Vampires," the dragons hissed in unison.

Darius stilled. Valerian could have struck him. A
blow while the male was distracted would win him
the battle. But...too much did he respect the dragon's
strength.

*Will win with honor. No one will ever have the right
to question my victory.*

He could see the vampires were interspersed with
the contingent of men he'd sent to the rear of the dragon
army.

"You tricked me," Darius snarled. "This wasn't to
be a fair fight, after all. You planned the vampires ambush all along."

"I didn't ask them to come, but I certainly won't send
them away. They are my allies. You and I, we can finish this fight here and now."

"As if I'll trust the vampires not to attack while I'm distracted. We will leave now, Valerian, but we aren't finished with you and yours. You have my word."

Black-clad vampires closed in fast, floating rather than walking, constantly hurling curses at the dragons. The dragons, in turn, mutated into their bestial forms, wings sprouting from their backs, ripping every piece of their clothing. Scales consumed their skin, green and black and menacing. Fangs grew in place of their teeth. Tails sprouted from their lower backs.

The beasts didn't engage the vampires or nymphs in any way. No, they sprang into the sky, moving higher and higher, before disappearing from sight altogether.

They would be back, just as Darius had promised. The next fight would be brutal. Violent. Nothing like the mild display today.

There would be a bloodbath between races.

LAYEL, KING OF THE VAMPIRES, came to an abrupt stop in front of Valerian. As the dragons disappeared from view, his men cheered.

"Good to see you again, my friend," Valerian said when the cheers died down.

"I heard the dragons were marching toward you and decided to help."

Valerian clapped him on the shoulder. "Last time we crossed paths, you were holding court with the demon queen. Do you ally yourself with her still?"

Layel smiled with slow deliberation. He knew the reason the nymph asked. Valerian despised the demons, as he should. As all of Atlantis should. They were the scourge of the land.

"I never allied myself with her," he admitted. "I used

her, and then I killed her. I haven't forgiven her people for what they did to mine."

Rapes. Tortures. Murders.

Layel's motto: *Repay with interest*.

"My king." One of his soldiers—Alyssa—approached. A distant relation, she had pale hair and blue eyes, just like Layel, though her features were much softer.

I am as hard as nails inside and out.

Usually Layel commanded his females to maintain distance with the nymphs. He made an exception for this one. She desired a specific male, but wouldn't kill other women simply to win him, thereby igniting a war with the only friend Layel had.

"Alyssa," he acknowledged with a nod. Not exactly a fond greeting—he liked and respected Valerian, who'd helped him through the worst time of his life, and no other—but not exactly cranky, either.

He'd just sent a dragon army running for cover. Today was a good day.

"Permission to break rank, Majesty." She avoided glancing at the warrior she'd come here to tempt, holding Layel's amused gaze.

"Granted." *And good luck.* Shivawn, the one she "needed more than blood," paid her zero attention.

That. That was the crux of life. What you wanted, you couldn't have. Or, if you *were* able to acquire it, you soon lost it, guaranteed.

VALERIAN STUDIED HIS FRIEND, the brutal, violent vampire most of Atlantis feared. Layel appeared more aloof than usual, the shadows in his eyes hiding the grief and sorrow he'd carried since the murder of his wife.

"You and yours are welcome inside. Come." Valerian

strode toward the palace. The door sensed the dragon medallion around his neck and opened automatically.

Layel kept pace beside him, the others staying close to their king.

"Did you ever find the Jewel of Dunamis?" Valerian asked as they entered the main hall. "I know you were on a crusade to unearth her. Darius claimed a human now has possession of the girl."

"He's correct. She escaped us with the help of the human."

"She's on the surface, then?"

"Yes."

Unfortunate. If the girl were to stay here, no army would dare attack, even a dragon army, and Shaye would be safe. "Is there any way we can get her back?"

"None, I'm afraid. We don't know the surface world well enough."

He wished he could trust Shaye to return to her world, find the jewel and come home to him. But...

The fact that Shaye would choose to remain topside began to bother him. If she wanted to leave him, shouldn't he let her go?

He scrubbed a hand down his face. He would ponder this later. Right now, he was weak and tired.

"Broderick," he called. "See that guards are stationed around the entire palace, top and bottom, inside and out."

"My men can help," Layel offered.

"I accept your generous offer. Thank you." He would never decline protection for Shaye. "Dorian, show the vampires to their posts."

Layel's brows winged toward his hairline. "There's something different about you, my friend."

"There is." He wanted to beat at his chest—a chest even now puffing with pride. "I found my mate."

The shadows in Layel's eyes darkened. "Then you are both blessed and cursed," he said softly.

"Yes," Valerian agreed with a sigh. "I am."

Taking pity on him, Layel waved him off. "Go. Go and be with her. There's no need to keep me company. I'll treat the palace and everyone in it as if I'm lord and master."

With any other male, Valerian would have taken the words as a threat and attacked. With Layel, he snorted.

"Your kindness overwhelms me." He slapped the vampire on the back and rushed off.

I hope you're ready for me, sweet Shaye.

CHAPTER TWENTY-THREE

SHAYE KEPT HER BACK pressed against the wall farthest from the door—as far away as she could get from the prisoners. She didn't want to accidentally release them. They'd begged and pleaded relentlessly, and she'd tried to distract herself with new anti-cards. Well, not really *anti*. All her ideas were for a new, not-so-anti collection. Things like, *I think I'd enjoy spending more time with you.* And, *Being with you isn't so bad.*

"Let us out!" one of the prisoners called. Again.

Beasts, Valerian had once labeled them. *Killers*.

The handsome men—or rather, boys—didn't look like killers. They looked cold, their lips tinted blue.

Brenna paced in front of her. "They're little more than children. Can we truly leave them inside a freezing cell?"

"Can we let them out and risk the lives of the nymphs?" she countered.

"Please," the youngest beseeched. "My name is Kendrick. Let us go. We have no plans to hurt you. We would never hurt a woman."

Yes, but what of the men?

"Perhaps we can help each other. I will help free you from the nymphs' spell," he rushed on, his voice suddenly dripping with hate, "and you can let me go. Just touch the bars. That's all you have to do."

She and Brenna shared a look. Kendrick's hatred settled the matter. The boys stayed in the cell.

"You're speaking English. How did you learn? And why were you imprisoned?" Brenna asked.

His eyes narrowed. "Our king married a human. And we're here because we're dragons. Why else? Because this is *our* palace and the nymphs stole it."

Just as she'd suspected. "They fought for it and won it. There's a difference." The moment the words left her, she flinched. *Was* there a difference?

Valerian would say he'd fought for her and won her, and she would say he'd stolen her from her home.

That man is turning me inside out!

"Sorry, boys. I feel for you, I do, but I can't help you. Not at this time. However, I'll speak with Valerian about releasing you into the wild. Alive. And un-injured." Better to cover all the bases so there were no misunderstandings.

Brenna nodded in agreement.

"Don't you see?" The bars rattled; a feat Shaye hadn't been able to accomplish. The strength the dragons must possess... "You're under Valerian's spell. Fight it or you'll remain his slave for all eternity."

Under Valerian's spell...how true those words were. She hadn't been herself since she'd first laid eyes on the sexy man.

Had his nymphness enchanted her, though, or was Valerian the man responsible? She suspected the latter, because none of the other nymphs appealed to her in any way.

"Even still." She squared her shoulders, determined. "I'm leaving you in there. Setting you free would en-danger too many—"

"Where is she?" The shout sounded from beyond the cavern, the words filled with terror and fury.

Valerian!

Her heart sped into a too-fast rhythm, beating against her ribs like a broken drumstick. Heat infused her cells. "Gotta go," she told the boys. "I won't forget you, I promise. Come on, Brenna."

"Shaye!" Valerian bellowed, unashamedly frantic. "Shaye!"

"Don't leave us here," Kendrick pleaded. "Fight against his allure. It's the only way—"

She raced from the enclosure, Brenna right behind her. They rounded the corner and bypassed the back side of the portal.

"I'll return as soon as possible," Valerian said to someone.

He was about to step into the portal, she realized. About to search for her on the surface. Warmth spread through her.

"I'm here, Valerian." She moved into his line of vision. "I'm here."

Their gazes locked, and shadows of relief couched his features...followed quickly by a blaze of fury.

He braced his arms over his chest. A battle stance. It was then that she saw what rested in his hand, and she almost cried. An orange. He held an orange.

A barbed lump filled her throat. She had mentioned that she wanted one, and even in the midst of war, he'd found one.

Her knees shook. Her nerve endings sizzled as she accepted the gift from him. "Thank you," she said softly.

His hair was sweat soaked and hanging in sand-coated tangles at his temples. Streaks of blood covered his face and arms, and his turquoise eyes shot sparks at her. Of the fury, yes, but also of lust.

Lust that kindled the need inside her.

A deep gash bisected his chest, and she gasped, horrified. "You're hurt!"

"I'm fine. Tell me how you escaped the cell." The quiet statement crackled with menace and was far more ominous than if he'd shouted. When Brenna stepped beside her, he added, "I'd also like to hear your reasoning for endangering your friend."

Shaye, too, assumed a battle stance. If he wasn't worried about the wound, she wouldn't be, either. "We were never in danger. And for your information, I got out with a little thing called ingenuity."

He ran his tongue over his teeth. "How long have you been free?"

Chin up. "Long enough to go through the portal."

He sucked in a breath. Then, bit by bit, his expression relaxed. "You could have gone through...but you didn't. You stayed. Why?"

Because...she wanted to pick up where they'd left off. She wanted his tongue on her and in her. Wanted, finally, to know the most erotic place on her body. Wanted him to bring her to a shuddering climax. Twice.

She wanted to drip orange juice on his skin and lap up every drop.

He must have read the desire in her eyes. His long legs ate up the distance between them as he backed her against the wall. Cold rock behind her, hot man in front of her. Goose bumps broke out.

Dylan and Terran entered the enclosure, ushering the rest of the women from the cell.

"Take this one, as well," Valerian said, motioning to Brenna without removing his gaze from Shaye.

"No," Brenna said, shaking her head. "No touching."

"Take her, but do not touch her," he corrected.

Brenna squeezed Shaye's hand before joining the group.

Ameena spotted Shaye and frowned. "Why are you still here?"

"Changed my mind," she said—to Valerian.

He flattened his palms at her temples, caging her in, becoming all she saw...all she wanted to see.

Business before pleasure! "Listen. I was chatting with the captured dragons and—" She pressed her lips together.

His nostrils flared. "You *chatted* with dragons?"

Uh, maybe now wasn't the best time for this conversation.

"I put you in that cell to protect you, Shaye. Not only did you escape, you visited with dangerous dragons."

She drew herself to her full height. "That's right. I did. So? I won't tolerate being locked away. I told you that. Where's my thanks for staying true to my word? Where's my thanks for staying down here when I could have gone back to the surface?"

"Your thanks? *Your thanks?*" He pounded a fist into the wall, cracking the rock. "The dragons could have spewed fire at you."

The heat drained from her cheeks. Well, crap! She'd never considered *that*.

"Did they touch you in any way?" he demanded.

"No. I'm fine," she said, using his own words against him. "And since we're on the subject, I think you should let them go. They're just boys, Valerian."

He straightened, backed away from her—as if he feared what he would do to her—and smoothed a hand down his face. "They are dragons, Shaye. You shouldn't go near them."

"So give them back to their king. Problem solved."

"That's my plan," he said, throwing his arms in the air. "I'm going to trade them for the nymph females Darius captured."

Oh. *Maybe I should have had faith in my man?* "Good."

"Good," he mocked. Then he sighed. "I like that you are stepping into your role of queen, and I even like that you are advising me and issuing orders. But you are in dire need of a tongue-lashing, woman."

Erotic shivers danced through her. Her eyes lowered. "Tongue-lash me, then. Go ahead. Do it. You know how much I hate it."

Any lingering hint of his anger evaporated in an instant, leaving only white-hot lust in his gaze. "You hate it? Truly?"

"So much," she whispered. Her stomach clenched. This man...despite their separation, he'd never stopped making love to her, had he?

Her desires had simmered, waiting for the perfect moment to rise up and consume her...

Every moment with Valerian was perfect.

She, the woman who'd so often prided herself on remaining distant from everyone and everything, could no longer fight the nymph king's...what had the dragon boy called it? Allure.

Once she'd found comfort in a frosty attitude. Now she quaked with potent vulnerability, desperate and needy, raw and emotionally exposed.

She had no defenses with this man. With Valerian, she didn't need defenses. The girl who'd once felt as if she were standing on top of a mountain, screaming and begging for love and affection she'd never received, was now cherished.

Slowly, never breaking eye contact, she closed the small gap between them. This was the first time she'd ever willingly gone to him without being asked, and the closer she came, the hotter the air became, chasing away the chill. Her nipples beaded, as if reaching for him, definitely yearning for contact.

"You want me?" he asked, his voice as rough as sandpaper.

"I do."

His pupils flared, like ink spilling over an ocean. "I won't stop this time." A warning. "Not for war. Not even if the fortress burns down."

"Good. We agree about something else." *Touch me.* She didn't care that people were just beyond the rock. She only cared about Valerian. Finally they would assuage the ache they'd ignited in each other.

"Run," he said softly.

She blinked, certain she'd misheard him. "What?" Was he sending her away? Without—

"Run. Run to my room. Right now. Do not stop."

"Wh-why?" The breath in her throat snagged. She backed away from him, her heart skipping a beat. His expression was intense, savage and utterly wild.

"Run," he repeated. "Now."

Clutching the orange, she sprang forward, racing around him, careful not to touch him. Her arms pumped at her sides as she pounded up the stairs. She remembered the path to the room and whipped around the proper corners.

Soon, footsteps began to echo behind her.

Excitement bubbled in her veins. He was chasing her. Warriors roamed the halls, collecting their bed partners. Panting, she barreled past them. Thankfully no one tried to stop her. Valerian's intensity had been frightening. And arousing. And startling. And arousing.

There! The door to his suite. She made it inside but didn't stop. She passed the outer bathing pool. What was he going to do to her when he caught her?

The door slammed closed.

Valerian!

She squealed as she darted into the bedroom— a hard weight slammed into her from behind. She soared through the air, dropping the orange as Valerian wrapped his arms of steel around her. Just before they hit the bed, he twisted, absorbing the bulk of impact.

In one second, only one, he flipped her over, so that she lay on top of him, and stripped her of everything but her panties.

"Why did you chase me?" she asked between panting breaths.

"Fastest way to get you in bed." With his hands under her arms, he lifted her, placing her breasts directly above his mouth. He sucked a nipple into his mouth.

Pure heat engulfed her, her gasp of surprise turning into a moan of pleasure.

Somewhere along the way, he had abandoned his armor. She scraped her nails over his chest, mindful of his injuries. His silver nipple ring proved cool to the touch yet somehow burned her in the most delicious way.

Tingling all over, nearly drunk from the avalanche of sensations he roused, she straddled his waist and anchored her weight on her knees. As her hair cascaded down to create a curtain around them, pulses of electricity arced across her skin.

"I'm going to kiss you here." His fingertip grazed

a fiery path along the center of her panties. "Then I'm going to pleasure you the way I've wanted to from the first moment I saw you."

"Yes." She rubbed against the hard, hot length of his shaft. "Pleasure me. Do it." Please!

"Nothing will stop me."

"Except this conversation? Because I'm hearing a lot of talk but not seeing enough action."

He pressed his thumb in the new center of her world, and she cried out with bliss.

He rolled her over, ripping her panties from her body and discarding the tattered remains. Cool air kissed her where she burned.

Completely naked and unabashed, she reached between them and did her best to unfasten his pants. But her motions were clipped, eager, even more desperate, and she made no progress.

"I can't get them off," she said, beating at his chest. "Help me!"

Within seconds he had the material peeled away, and she was peering at paradise made flesh. Mmm. He was magnificent. Bronzed perfection. Strength personified. And big. Really, really big.

"You're so soft," he praised. He traced a path along her collarbone, then nipped at her neck, grazing her overly sensitive flesh with his teeth.

Every point of contact, every move he made, proved masterful. Exactly what her body needed. He lit her up from the inside out.

He readied her.

And oh, she could feel the girth of his massive arousal on her belly, a white-hot band of steel. Staying still wasn't an option. She arched against it, already needing it inside her.

"Now," she said. "Before I change my mind."

A mock growl. "You won't change your mind, Moon."

No. No, she wouldn't. "More! Gimme! Obey your queen."

His shaft jerked against her, and his teeth bit more sharply. "Kiss first," he said hoarsely. He licked down her body, exploring her breasts again, lingering at her stomach before flicking his tongue in her belly button.

His mouth worshipped her until she thrashed against the pillows.

"Grip the top of the bed," he demanded.

She'd been reaching down, intent on threading her fingers through his hair. "But—"

"Do it. Grip the bed."

She obeyed. In this, she trusted him completely.

The moment her fingers curled around the ivory base, his tongue glided over her molten core. An avalanche of pleasure rolled through her. She screamed. Her hips shot up, and she gasped his name.

With one hand, he opened her fully. With the other, he glided a finger into her, probing her, stretching her. But his tongue never stopped working her, and the combination of sensations shattered her.

Another coast of his tongue. A pump of his fingers.

This man knew what he was doing.

He sucked at her and increased the tempo. She cried out. She sobbed for more…less…more, please more. Oh, the bliss! Her legs locked around his shoulders. Her hands clutched the headboard so tightly her knuckles could have snapped into pieces.

Her eyelids squeezed shut. In her mind she saw him between her legs, his tawny hair falling onto her thighs. The muscles in his back knotted as he reined in his own need.

"Valerian! I can't take any more. It's torment."

"By the end of the night, you'll have taken everything I have to give."

"Give me…let me come. Mercy, just this once."

She writhed. On the verge. So close, yet not close enough. He slid another finger into her, and it was a tight fit, stretching her further. Filling her up. And it was so much better…and so much worse.

He flicked his tongue over her aching bundle of nerves, showing absolutely zero mercy. Not that she wanted any, no matter how much she'd begged for it. This was everything she'd ever dreamed, everything she'd needed without knowing she did.

"I'm going to sink into you, Shaye. You're going to spread your legs and welcome me, take every inch."

"Yes." Oh, yes. The thought of this man inside her hurled her over the sweet edge. Pleasure exploded inside her, and her inner walls spasmed around his fingers, clenching them tight. A scream, a sob as flashing white lights blinked behind her eyes.

He loomed above her, spreading her legs to open her fully. To expose her completely.

He poised himself on the brink of penetration.

"Wait! What about children?"

"I took a potion. I can't get anyone pregnant until it wears off."

Good, that was good. She wasn't ready for a family.

"Once I'm inside you," he said, "you will be mine. Say it."

"I'll be yours." There was no denying it. She *was* his. Now, this moment…forever?

Like an animal, he growled his approval. His wild eyes glittered with heat and possession.

She reached up to tangle her fingers in his hair…

draw him closer. *Will never push him away again.* His chest pressed against hers, and she could feel the fine-grained sand that still clung to him from the fight, adding friction, another depth of pleasure.

"Kiss," she beseeched.

His head swooped down, and he claimed her mouth. The moment their tongues touched, he slammed inside her. No waiting. No gradually letting her become accustomed. He was simply in her fully, as if he couldn't go another minute without being one with her.

She cried out in his mouth, still so aroused, so slick with desire. She'd been prepared for him, but a slight sting remained.

He stretched her erotically, filled her inexorably, but didn't move. *Now* he allowed her to become accustomed to him.

On and on the kiss continued. She tasted herself on his lips. Tasted him, the heat of him, and the passion. In and out his tongue probed…eventually, his body began to move in sync. In and out. Slowly, then quickly, hurtling them both toward the stars.

"Can't…slow…down," he panted. "Need…"

"More."

Tension coiled in her stomach, in her blood. He twisted his hips, hitting her in a new spot, and she screamed, exploding for the second time.

"Shaye!" he roared. He pumped into her. "Mine."

Mine, she silently repeated.

The climax gripped her, more intense than the first, making her shudder against him. Her knees clenched on him, and to the heavens she soared. High, so high.

He joined her there as he gave a final, pounding thrust, his eyes squeezed tight. Bliss consumed his features.

"Now. Time for round two," he growled.

VALERIAN HAD NEVER felt more powerful. Strength radiated from him, filled him, pulsed and sizzled inside him. He always felt invigorated after sex, but this... No, never like this.

And with Shaye it hadn't been sex, he thought. It had been lovemaking. A union. Total and complete. Especially the second when they'd licked her favorite fruit off each other.

Mine.

The word refused to leave him. He'd never felt so possessive of another person. Actually, he'd never felt so possessive of anything, including his cherished sword. Including the palace. She'd tasted like no other woman. Erupted like no other woman. Pleased him like no other woman. Strengthened him like no other woman. All of his injuries were healed.

He was the nymph, and yet it was she who wrapped him in her sensual spell. She who enslaved him.

She snuggled into his side, nestling her curves against him. He could feel the soft exhalations of her breath and thought he would die without this woman. He would simply perish. Cease to exist.

He wanted to give her the world, wanted to offer her everything her heart desired.

Keeping the palace had been the right decision. He would not have his woman homeless, staying in whatever shack he could find for them.

I will cherish her always.

When he'd returned to the dungeon, and she had not been inside the cell, his heart had stopped beating. Panic, dread and fury had consumed him. He'd nearly hacked Dylan and Terran to pieces. Then, when he'd seen Shaye as relaxed and at ease as if she hadn't a care in the world—while standing next to the portal—he'd panicked again.

How close he'd come to losing her.

Then she'd begun issuing orders with bravery and wisdom, acting every bit the queen she was meant to be, and he'd been struck by love for her.

Love. The all-consuming kind. It gave rather than took. It protected.

Somehow, some way, he would gain her oath to stay forever. Because, he could never let her go.

CHAPTER TWENTY-FOUR

AFTER HE'D SATED himself on another round of scrumptious female and listened to their tales about the surface world, Poseidon had whisked himself to the nearest river, a crystal stream of tranquillity. Lilies floated on the surface. He blended into the water itself, flowing with it, absorbing its coolness.

The nymphs had indeed broken the law. He needed to punish them quickly, before others thought to do the same. And he knew just what to do.

When he reached a fork in the river, he stopped. The water stilled, as well. No waves, no ripples. Wind whistled, and the patter of nearby animals echoed.

The bank to his left suddenly flooded with enraged dragon warriors, their wings flapping as they landed. Still, the water did not ripple.

Poseidon watched as their dragon forms faded, leaving a human facade. Skin instead of scales. Silky hair. Teeth instead of fangs, their tail vanishing. Of course, they were now naked, wearing only dragon medallions and holding swords.

As the warriors drank from the stream, angry chatter bounced between the trees. Poseidon scanned the masses until he came to Darius. The leader of the dragons barked orders to several of his men, his expression fierce.

He hadn't liked abandoning the palace. His instincts

demanded he stay and fight the nymphs—Valerian in particular. But Darius was a warrior who weighed the odds, studied the situation and calculated the percentages. He'd been severely outnumbered, and he hadn't wanted his men injured when a sneak attack could work in their favor and even the odds.

A very smart man. Exactly what Poseidon needed.

Come to me, he said, his voice carrying on the wind.

Darius paused and stiffened. He searched the surrounding wooded area, gazed over the river, saw nothing and returned to his men. His shoulders remained stiff, however, his posture erect and his hands clenched tightly on the hilt of his sword.

Come, Poseidon said again.

Darius's attention whipped to the river for the second time. His eyes narrowed.

The water provided only a reflection of Poseidon's image, a glint in the fading light. Still, Darius obeyed at last, long strides leading him to the river's edge. The men he'd been speaking with frowned, clearly confused.

"Is something wrong?" a hulking blond giant asked.

The dragon king never looked back. "Rest a while, Brand."

When Darius stood alone, he said, "You called, Poseidon?"

He recognizes me, and yet he shows no reverence.

Annoyance caused the water to churn. "You know me, then."

"I know *of* you."

"Then you know the consequences of speaking to me in such a manner. You know the suffering I can mete out."

Darius gave a clipped nod. "I do."

And still the dragon did not bow.

Admire his courage or strike him down?

Admire. Why not? He'd hated his life so much he'd come here to set a new course. *Want different circumstances, do different things.*

"I've learned some disturbing things since my return, Darius, and I am not pleased. Because of this, I have several tasks for you."

A muscle jumped beneath his eye. "Then I am at your command, of course."

Excellent. "First, you will return to the palace."

There was a heavy pause. "That isn't *my* plan."

"No, you wish to gather more men. That will take time, and I want my will obeyed now. This moment."

Darius stood firm. "That will place dragon lives in unnecessary danger, and *that* I will not do."

A refusal. Admiration dwindled fast. "Sneak inside, and there will be no danger to you and yours."

"I do plan to sneak inside. But there *will be* danger if the nymphs and vampires outnumber us ten to one."

Poseidon grinned slowly. "O ye creature of doubt. You will destroy half of the nymph and vampire forces before you even reach the palace hallways."

Darius's brows arched, interest sparkling in his eyes. "Tell me how that's possible."

He thinks to give the orders now? Poseidon's hands fisted. "There's a doorway. A secret entrance *below* the portal."

"Below?" He sounded faraway, as if he was already breaching it in his mind. "How did I not know of it before now?"

"Not my problem. You'll sneak inside, gather the humans and return them to the surface, with their memories wiped clean."

Poseidon continued. "To get the women in one place,

you'll send an army back to the palace, as if they meant to fight. The women will be hidden below."

"Done."

"Once they are returned, you will focus on the nymphs. They'll be weak without their daily dose and easy for you run down. Six nymphs dared to enter the surface world, so six nymphs will die."

"What happens next?"

"Easy, you take back the palace and slaughter the rest of the nymphs. A cautionary tale for any who think to follow their lead."

Darius balked. Interesting. A warrior should enjoy taking down his enemy.

"You have done such deeds before, Guardian. This should be no hardship for you. But, if you think to refuse me, I'll have *your* wife sent back to the surface. You acquired her from there, did you not?"

A blaze of fury sparked inside the dragon's eyes, revealing the merciless killer he had once been. "I won't allow Grace to be taken from me. She is mine, a daughter of Atlantis now, pregnant with my child."

"The child is the only reason I'm allowing you to keep her," Poseidon informed him. "For now."

Fury blazed in the dragon's eyes. "I'm so...grateful you have finally decided to take an interest in your people."

"Is this sarcasm something you acquired from your bride?" Poseidon wasn't a fan. "Watch your tongue, or I'll feed it to the vampires. Go now," he said. "Return to the palace. I'll be there waiting, and I'll show you the way inside."

"Wait. Before you leave," Darius said, irreverence still blazing in his eyes, "perhaps you could be a dear and gift us with clothing."

"Of course. It will be my pleasure." As a slight punishment for Darius's impertinence today, Poseidon blew his breath upon the dragon army, spraying them with a fine mist of sea…and leaving them dressed in women's scarves.

Their hisses of shock rang in his ears long after he left them.

BRENNA'S HANDS TWISTED together. She stood just outside the dining hall, observing Shivawn while waiting for him to notice her. He was speaking heatedly with a female she'd never met—a white-haired beauty with blue eyes and bloodred lips.

Brenna watched the interaction with only mild curiosity. What would happen to her if Shivawn decided to be with another woman? Would Brenna be given to someone else?

Joachim, perhaps?

Her stomach quivered.

Would she be jealous or irritated if Joachim talked so heatedly with another woman?

Her stomach quivered *harder*.

But…she still feared Joachim. Didn't she? He was everything she should despise: controlling, dominant and violent.

Why did she have to desire him at all? Why could she not want Shivawn, and only Shivawn?

She sighed. Like she'd told Shaye, if she had any hope of forging a better future, she had to let go of the past.

Would one of these men help her reclaim a life of contentment and joy?

The feminist part of her being screamed *You can reclaim your life without a man!*

And at any other time, she would have agreed. But men were the foundation of her fear. By cutting one—or two—from her life, she merely perpetuated that fear.

I'm going to do it, then. I'm going to sleep with someone. Today!

Joachim's image barreled into her mind. Probably because the man himself was forceful!

He lay in bed, his finger motioning her over, a silent request for her to join him.

She shivered. One way or another, she *was* going to dive headfirst into a relationship: sexual, emotional and uncomfortably intimate. But which man would she pick?

Life with Shivawn would be sweet and tender.

Life with Joachim would be turbulent…and possibly exciting.

Shivawn shook his head and snarled something to the now-scowling woman. When his gaze met Brenna's, he jolted with surprise. Why? Because he hadn't sensed her the way Valerian always seemed to sense Shaye?

He stalked toward her, clasped her hand and dragged her from the room. Thoughts of him—of being with him—failed to heat her blood.

Was he taking her to his room?

Would she trace her hands all over his body?

Her body gave no reaction, and she wanted to scream with frustration.

They weren't heading toward his room, she noticed a moment later.

"Where?" The walls surrounding his room were in a different state of repair than the ones here. These had…

The murals that led to Joachim's room. Her eyes widened. They were going to Joachim's room, where menacing weapons hung on the walls, a blatant reminder of why she couldn't want a man like him.

Now her blood heated with a mixture of apprehension and anticipation. "Is Joachim okay?"

"He's well, yes."

That meant...what?

They arrived at the door a moment later. Shivawn didn't pause or announce himself, just strode inside. He released her hand and marched to a side table, keeping his back to her as he poured a drink.

The first thing she noticed? The weapons were gone. Why? Why had they been removed?

Her gaze flicked to Joachim. He sat on the bed, his legs over the side, his elbows resting on his knees. His gaze devoured her.

"Brenna," he said, her name a sensual caress.

Instantly her blood heated another degree. Her nipples hardened further, and need pooled between her legs.

They must have come to the same conclusion she had: it was time to choose.

Last time she'd run from this, and from her feelings. Now she squared her shoulders. It was *past* time. Because, honestly, there would never be a right time. Not with fear at her back, holding a knife at her throat. There was only here and now.

The other women in the palace were well satisfied. They always grinned, never experienced a single fear. So badly she wanted to be one of them.

She *would* be one of them.

No, there would be no more running. But could she risk the safety she was sure to find with Shivawn for the passion she was sure to find with Joachim? There would be no going back once she'd voiced her preference. These men were too possessive, too determined to be "the one."

Shivawn focused on her. "I've sensed your readiness," he said, once again at her side. He gently gripped her shoulders and turned her to face him. "I know you want more."

She licked her lips, nodded.

Satisfaction in his eyes. "I will never allow another man to hurt you. I will take care of you, pleasure you, make you so happy you'll forget ever being sad."

The perfect response. The words she'd always longed to hear—because he meant them. She knew he meant them.

He added, "The man on that bed will never be kind or gentle or any of the things I sense that you need." He turned her again, this time making her face Joachim.

Their gazes locked, his heated, and her stomach quivered.

"Look at him," Shivawn said. "Even now there's a wildness about him that you cannot deny. He will never be able to control his temper. He will never be able to destroy the demons that plague you."

Shivawn's final words were supposed to comfort her, to assure her that choosing safety over passion was the right decision. But in that regard, they failed. Because there was no stronger warrior than Joachim. He did have a temper, and he did appear wild. Yet, if anyone could fight and destroy the demons of her past, he could. He was just so...*vital*.

Joachim didn't utter a sound. He simply pulled four strips of cloth from underneath his pillow and draped them over his knees.

A tremor swept through her.

"What are those for?" Shivawn demanded.

"Tie me to the bed, Brenna," Joachim said.

She glanced down at the material in puzzlement... and desire. "What?"

"Tie me to the bed. Know that I have never allowed another woman to do this to me, never will. For you, I make an exception. Because you are important to me."

Her gaze swiftly returned to Joachim. His expression was hard, resolved and hot with arousal. So much arousal. Desire blazed in his blue eyes, burning her inside and out.

"Why?" she asked. "I don't understand."

"I'm not going to tell you that you'll hate yourself later if you decide to be with Shivawn. You could probably be happy with him, and you would always feel safe. But he can't fill the void inside you, and he can't give you the life I know you've dreamed of having. I can. All you have to do is trust that I'll never hurt you. Never. I would die first. These ties will allow me to prove it—you will have the power in our relationship."

"Joachim," Shivawn snarled.

But he wasn't done. "Tie me to the bed, and you'll be in control of everything that happens." His jaw was clenched. "I'm giving you complete...control over me, allowing you to take back your own."

Bondage. During sex. Her wild gaze darted between the two men. "Shi-Shivawn?" What did he have to say about this?

He remained stiff and silent, radiating fury.

"I noticed how you jolt every time someone comes up behind you," Joachim said, "so I'm going to show you the pleasure of having a man there. Later. This time I want to show you the pleasure of being in control."

This big, strong warrior was willing to give up control—his precious control—to be with her. A tremor worked through her. The revelation startled her, *strengthened* her. She'd wanted passion, she'd admitted that to herself already. No one could give her more passion than Joachim. She'd admitted that, too, but she'd been scared of it. Scared of him. And so she'd done her best to fall for Shivawn. She might even have convinced herself of it. For a little while. Eventually, she would have had to accept the truth.

All along, it had been Joachim she'd desired. She simply hadn't wanted to want him. He was trusting her with his life. She could do no less for him.

I'm not going to be scared anymore.

Eyes filling with tears, she looked at Shivawn. He was so sweet, so kind and giving. But as she looked at him, she realized he was exactly what she didn't need anymore. A bodyguard. She could take care of herself now. She'd been in this palace for over a week and hadn't been hurt. She'd faced down the warriors, and she hadn't been attacked or even disrespected.

"You can walk away from both of us," Joachim said, his voice rough. "We won't stop you."

Run, and stay locked in her safe little world. No feeling. No pain. No pleasure. *I'll never run again.*

"I'm so sorry, Shivawn," she said, chin trembling. "I wanted it to be you. I did. But..."

"Stop. Please. Just stop." He studied her for a long while, his jaw locked tight. Then he slowly turned to Joachim. "She is yours. I relinquish all claim to her."

"Thank you," Joachim said tightly.

Shivawn flicked her one last glance, nodded and strode from the room, leaving her alone with Joachim.

Before she would have run after her guard. Now she gulped and held her ground. Gathering her courage, she faced him.

Her man.

Fear would never rule her life again.

She'd chosen him, and she was only sorry it had taken her so long to realize the depth of his honor.

He'd made a play for the crown. When he lost, he could have vowed vengeance against Valerian. Instead, he accepted defeat and pledged his services to the king.

Underneath the rough exterior, he was a good man.

Ready to finally move on with her life, Brenna walked forward. With every step, she felt an invisible chain fall off her. Her heart raced erratically. She stopped in front of him.

Joachim stood, grasping the ties in his fists.

His gaze was hard, unrelenting. "Did your attacker use his hands or a weapon? If he used a weapon, I would like you to use the same on me."

At first, she didn't answer, didn't want the memory to intrude on this precious time. "Only hands," she finally managed on a trembling breath.

He nodded and gave her the bonds. Slowly, very slowly, he unfastened his pants and pushed them from his hips. They pooled on the floor, and she was given a glimpse of her very large, very aroused male.

"We go at your pace," he said, lying on the bed. "When you're ready, tie me."

Her hands shook as she tied his wrists to the posts, then his ankles. Then she stood at the side of the bed, staring down at him. Utterly amazed by him.

Silent, Joachim watched her with mind-blowing intensity. Her knees almost buckled; she knew what he expected, what he wanted.

My turn to strip.

After the attack, she'd stopped working out, unwittingly trying to make herself as unattractive as possible to other men. If they didn't come around, she didn't have to worry about them. And she had scars. Ugly scars. What if Joachim found her body undesirable?

Then he isn't worthy of my time.

Easily said. Hard to accept.

She reached up with shaky fingers and undid her robe's shoulder ties, revealing her breasts. She continued to gauge Joachim's reaction. There was no disappointment in his eyes. Only desire. She lost a little of her uncertainty. Delicious bumps broke out over her skin as his gaze skimmed over her, his nostrils flaring with the force of his arousal.

"You are beautiful, Brenna. More so than I ever realized."

With her robe completely loosed, the material fell from her body to join Joachim's pants on the floor. Finally she was naked. Her cheeks heated as Joachim's eyes raked over her once again. At one time, the thought of joining a man on a bed would have paralyzed her. This time, her hormones were too busy rejoicing.

"Close your eyes," he said.

She didn't think to argue.

"Imagine me behind you. Imagine my hands caressing your shoulders and cupping your breasts. Imagine me rolling your nipples between my fingers."

Yes. Yes! She saw it in her mind, only this time the image was crystal clear. Her head fell onto his shoulder, her hair tickling them both. His fingers roved over every inch of her.

"Are you wet?" he rasped.

Unbearably so. She nodded.

"I want to lick you. May I?"

"Yes," she said breathlessly.

"Then come to me. Please."

She climbed onto the bed without hesitation and straddled him, her knees at his waist, his erection resting between her legs, touching her intimately but not entering her. The decadence! She moaned.

"Lean forward," Joachim urged roughly.

He might be tied, but he was still a warrior. For the first time, a small kernel of fear sprouted. *You're safe. You're protected.*

"Please," he added.

Slowly she crawled up him…until her breasts were poised over his waiting mouth. Her black curls fell over her line of vision as he eagerly sucked on her, dissolving her fear, filling her with pleasure. Contact with his hot, hot mouth was like nothing she'd ever experienced, volts of electricity lancing through her body.

She groaned, the sound broken and rough.

While Joachim sucked her, she continued to imagine. Had his hands been free, he would have traced them over her back, over the ridges of her spine. Over the curve of her bottom. Yes, yes! She saw it happening, somehow felt it. Everywhere his phantom hands touched, his mouth followed, his phantom tongue laving her skin. She writhed against him, so wet she slid back and forth with ease.

"You taste like heaven," Joachim said.

In her mind, his big hands circled her and urged her to straighten, allowing his fingers to sink into her moist, hot center. Yes, oh, yes!

Why had she tied him? she mused.

He sucked her nipple with delicious force.

"Yes," she gasped out, unable to say anything else. "Yes."

"Do you want me to lick between your legs?"

"Yes." She didn't try to deny it or play coy. She

wanted Joachim's mouth there. She wanted it fiercely. Madly.

"Come here," Joachim said. Sweat beaded his brow. His jaw was tense.

She crawled forward until she was poised over his face, the apex of her thighs mere inches from his beautiful lips.

"Lower," he commanded, a rough snarl.

"Joachim," she said, sinking into him and in the next instant he devoured her with tongue, lip and teeth.

She screamed at the intense sensation, the heady pleasure. Her hips ground against him.

"Come, Brenna. Come for me," he said, and she obeyed.

Her pleasure exploded. Erupted. Her entire body shook and trembled with her climax, propelling her to new heights. Joachim drank her up until she thought she could take no more.

"Take me," he said. "Put me inside you."

Limbs weak, she straddled his waist without hesitation. As she rose up, she placed his shaft at her entrance.

Am I ready for this?

Her gaze met Joachim's. His lids were half-closed His pupils completely overshadowed his irises. His lips were stretched taut over his teeth. Sweat glistened on his skin, and a pleasure flush darkened his cheeks.

This man...he was all in. Metaphorically speaking.

I'm ready.

"What about a condom?" she asked.

"Can't get you pregnant."

Now? Or ever?

Whatever! They'd work out the particulars later.

She sank down on him, accepting every inch he had to give.

All in, literally now, she thought, and wanted to burst out with a joyous laugh. He was big, and it had been so long. He stretched her, but it was a wonderful feeling. For the first time in years, she was alive.

"Joachim..."

He roared.

She rose up, panting his name. "Joachim." She slid down. "My Joachim."

She was safe. She was sated—and she would soon find release again. Her nerve endings were already sparking with renewed life.

"My Brenna. Faster. Go faster."

She anchored her hands on his chest. Their faces were inches apart, his breath a part of hers and her breath a part of his.

"Kiss me," he said. "Please."

Her mouth meshed against his, and she gasped in pleasure; he swallowed the sound. Hard, hot, gentle, fast, slow, his tongue sparred with hers and she rode him, meeting his tempo. Total ravishment. Total bliss.

The kiss became savage, and in turn, the loving became savage. Her teeth banged his; her body slammed up and down. She purred and groaned and gasped some more.

"That's it," Joachim praised. "Take it all."

"Yes."

"No more fear."

"No more," she panted.

"Come for me, sweet." He nipped her collarbone. He strained against his bonds. "Show me how much you like having me inside you."

At that point, she could no longer hold back, could not prolong the pleasure. She erupted for the second time, the new orgasm so intense a black web clouded her vision. She was dying slowly, quickly, unable to breathe, yet so alive she could have stayed exactly where she was forever.

"Joachim," she screamed, and for once she didn't care how broken her voice sounded.

"Brenna." He roared loud and long and reared up, sinking deep, deeper than she'd ever thought possible.

When he stopped shuddering against her, he collapsed on the mattress and she collapsed onto his chest.

"Thank you," she panted. "Thank you."

"Untie me," he ordered harshly.

She didn't think to deny him—though she would bet he could have busted free very easily. Blindly she reached up and removed the bonds. His arms instantly wrapped around her, pulling her close and holding her tightly, cherishing her.

"No more fear with me," he said again.

"No more," she agreed. She would have agreed with anything he said just then. Marry him—yes. Be his slave—well, maybe. His heat surrounded her, enveloped her, beckoned her.

"Mine," he said.

"Yours," she breathed. "Joachim's." Her eyes closed, her lids growing heavier and heavier with every second that passed. Sleep summoned, a peaceful sleep she'd needed for so long but had been too afraid to take. "Don't let me go."

"Never."

As oblivion claimed her, she was smiling.

SHIVAWN STOOD IN the hallway for a long while. He wished Brenna had chosen him, but it had been Joachim her eyes had heated for. Joachim she'd probably wanted all along. He was angry, so very angry. She was beautiful, passionate and kind. But she wasn't his. He knew that now. No matter how much pleasure Shivawn could have given her, no matter how safe he could have made her feel, she would always have wanted Joachim.

The two were meant to be together. They were mates. How could he have missed the signs?

Now he was alone.

Perhaps one day he would find a woman who wanted him above all others.

He blinked when he realized vampire Alyssa had glided into the hallway and now stood a few feet away from him.

He scowled. She frowned.

"You smell like a human," she said, her tone flat. "Have you been with one? Is she your one and only?"

Always she asked him a thousand questions. What was he doing? What did he like to eat? What made him happy? Sad? Would he like to kiss her?

He told her what he'd always told her. "What business is it of yours?" He leaped into a quick stride in an effort to escape her.

She followed, keeping pace beside him. "Is she?"

"No," he snapped.

"See! I told you she wasn't. I told you! Because *I* am. I and I alone can attend to your needs," she snapped back. "You should have come to *me*."

"And I told you how wrong you are."

His mate would not be vampire. He'd never shared Valerian's love for the race, and he never would.

Alyssa was beautiful, and as usual Shivawn even felt himself stir for a taste of her, but he would never touch her.

Vampires survived on blood, and they sometimes took more than a donor wished to offer. Or often took without asking permission. He'd made the mistake of bedding a vampire only once and had almost died for it. Never again, he'd vowed. Alyssa knew that, but she always sought him out whenever she came to visit.

"Goodbye, Alyssa," he said, and strode away from her.

She wasn't content to remain behind. She never was.

She rushed after him, even jumped in front of him, her eyes aglow. Determination radiated from her. "I've always known I would have you one day, Shivawn, and I've decided today is that day."

She threw herself at him, her lips slamming into his, her tongue forcing its way into his mouth. The taste of her filled him in an instant. Not a taste of blood and death, but of woman. Sweet, needy woman.

His body responded.

He might hate himself in the morning, but she could help him forget his loneliness.

"One night," he growled. "That's all I'll give you."

Triumph blazed in her eyes, and her red, red lips curled in a sensual smile. "That's all I'm asking for. For now."

CHAPTER TWENTY-FIVE

SHAYE LOUNGED AT the edge of the bathing pool. Hot water lapped at her ultrasensitized skin. The scent of orchids filled the room, sweetly perfuming the air with sultry ambiance. She inhaled deeply and savored. Her body was sore, but her spirit was invigorated.

Valerian sat behind her, massaging her shoulders. His magical fingers worked her muscles expertly. He knew exactly where to rub, the precise amount of pressure to apply for optimum enjoyment. Her head lolled back, resting on his shoulder. Steam coated them both.

"Have I thanked you for gifting me with your virginity?" he asked.

"Only a thousand times." She should probably be the one thanking him. She'd never enjoyed herself more. Had never thought losing all control, all sense of her cool facade, could be so blissful.

In the pleasure-filled hours they'd just spent together, she'd realized a few things. She'd given Valerian more than her body; she'd given him pieces of her heart, just as she'd feared. She hadn't meant to, and had tried to guard against it, but it happened regardless.

No matter. Everything would be okay.

He was a nymph, and nymphs liked sex. Lots of it. She would be the one he came to, always; she was going to trust him. Not love him, she assured herself, still distrustful of the emotion itself—but trusting *him*.

It would be hard, she didn't doubt that, but all the best things were. To keep him in her life she was willing to try anything.

"This means you've forgiven me," he said. A statement not a question.

She gave a mock pout. "I guess it does."

He banged his chest like a gorilla, making her giggle like a girl. "Me man. You woman."

"And that's why I couldn't maintain my mad," she said, glancing over her shoulder. "I'm a sucker for caveman theatrics."

A glint in his eye...

She laughed. "I was kidding, only kidding! Do not turn into a caveman in an effort to please me."

"But I want to please you. I *like* to please you."

Uh-oh. His voice had lowered. She had better change the subject before he seduced her again.

"I'm too sore," she told him. "But at least your wounds finally healed."

"I believe I mentioned they would heal the moment you surrendered to me."

Lookie there. The nymph version of *I told you so.* "In romance novels, the heroines always have magic vaginas. I guess with nymphos, it's actually true."

He snorted. "I insist we read these romance novels together."

"Maybe I'll let you read mine. I've already written the opening."

"Well, I just figured out what I want you to give me for my six hundred and fourth birthday. Your first romance novel."

She nearly choked on her tongue. "You're six hundred and three? Years old?" Just to be clear.

Mind...can't...handle...

She backed away from that subject. For now. "Never mind. My head might exploded if we discuss our age difference. You have the strength to tell me the secret spot on a woman's body," she pointed out. "The place that brings maximum pleasure. So tell!"

"I'll tell you—" he nuzzled the side of her cheek "—for a kiss."

Ah, she loved his bargaining. "Only one," she said throatily, grinding against the erection pressed against her lower back.

He hissed in a breath. "Keep doing that, and I'll tell you anything you want to know. Even my deep, dark secrets."

Up, down she moved. "Start with the pleasure spot."

His hands tightened on her waist. "Close your eyes," he commanded softly.

They'd made love only an hour ago, but it felt like an eternity. She needed him inside her again. Addicting…that's what he was.

"Shaye." He tsk-tsked. "Close. Your. Eyes."

Her eyelids fluttered shut. Darkness blanketed her mind. His hands glided over her shoulders, caressed her neck, then dipped to her breasts, kneading.

"Picture what I'm doing to you."

"I thought—"

"This is how I'm going to tell you, promise."

Picture it, he'd said, so she did. In her mind, she could see the thickness of his hands covering the pale mounds of her breasts. Her nipples, pink and pearled, peaked through the crevices of his fingers. Pleasure spiraled through her, hot and needy. Seemingly unquenchable.

Unbidden, her legs spread, silently begging for his

attention. A single touch, a pinch, something. Anything. She ached, oh, she ached.

One of Valerian's hands glided down her stomach. She felt it, yes, just the way she'd wanted it, but more than that she continued to *see* it in her mind. Another picture of them. Valerian behind her, this time with his hand between her legs, parting her wet folds. But he didn't touch her where she needed him most. Not yet. He stayed poised, inches above her entrance.

"What do you picture?" His voice was strained, as if he required all his strength to remain still.

"You. Me."

"Do you see me licking you here or sliding my fingers into you?"

"F-fingers," she managed.

"Are they moving slowly, savoring or pounding in and out?"

As he spoke, images flooded her. Yet he didn't do anything, didn't do what she needed. Her hips moved forward, seeking. Back, seeking. Forward, back. Writhing and arching.

"Touch me, Valerian. Please."

"I thought you were too sore."

"But now I'm *dying* for you."

His warm breath fanned her skin. "Tell me. What do you see right this second? Are my fingers moving slowly or quickly?"

"Quickly. Hard." Her breath caught. Water sloshed over the pool's rim. "So hard."

He pinched her nipple, and a lance of desire hit directly between her legs. She cried out, loving the amazing torment.

"Shaye. Moon. Your mind shows you the things your body needs before you actually know you need them."

No more talking, she wanted to shout. *Make love to me.* But still she said, "I don't understand."

"The most erotic place on a woman's body is her mind. By giving her the right images, a man can increase her pleasure a hundred times over." He bit her ear. "Lean forward for me, Moon. I'll give you fast and hard."

She did, and even that served as a stimulant. The water stroked between her legs, making her shiver.

"Hold on to the ledge," Valerian said.

Angling forward a few more inches, she curled her hands as instructed. Her breasts and hips were out of the water now, granting Valerian a full view of her from behind.

A long while passed in silence. She stayed where she was, anticipating the first touch. Wet hair tumbled down her back and shoulders. Some of the ends trod the water's surface.

When would he caress her? She needed him to caress her. "Valerian?"

"You are magnificent," he said, his voice heavy with awe. He traced the tattoo on her lower back.

A shiver danced through her.

"I like this," he said. "A skull with a pretty bow on top. It's a mark that says you are both warrior and woman." His lips brushed the tattoo; the hot wetness of his tongue traced it. He kissed his way up her spine and grazed the back of her neck, smoothing her hair aside to get to her.

"The first time I saw you," she said, "I thought you were a god, rising from the sea."

"And I thought you were the thing I needed most in my life."

His words acted with the heady intoxication of a

caress. She licked her lips, then bit into them to tamp down a loud, long scream of pleasure when his shaft pressed into her opening.

"So tight," he praised.

"More. Hard and fast, like you promised."

He gave her another inch. "Is this enough?"

"No! Give me more."

Another inch, but it still wasn't enough. "And now?"

"More, more, more."

With a roar, he pounded all the way in. She gasped. He groaned. But he didn't move, just left them both at the edge.

"Hard! Fast!"

He ignored her, saying, "Do you know the most erotic place on a man's body, Moon? His heart," Valerian said.

His heart...

She had an orgasm in that moment, exploding, throbbing, throbbing so hard. Screaming and sobbing. The force of it raked her, causing bone to vibrate and hum against muscle, every part of her affected.

Valerian slid out and pounded forward. Over and over, driving hard and deep, just as she'd commanded.

He rode her until another orgasm caused her spirit to leave her body. An out of body experience. She was raw sensation. A phantom forever climaxing.

"Shaye," he roared, shuddering into her a final time. "Love. You." His hands dug into her hips. Gripping, bruising deliciously. "Love you so much."

"Talk to me," Valerian said a long while later. He lay on the bed, Shaye had wiggled out from under him a few minutes ago and though she hadn't gotten up, she maintained stiff and distanced on the bed. "Tell me what's wrong."

"You said...never mind."

What? "That I love you?"

She nodded but didn't look his way.

And the emotion bothered her? "I vowed to always be honest with you."

"Yes, but... I feel like I need to protect you from yourself. Love feeds your soul to someone else."

"You're wrong. Love feeds your soul. Period."

A tremor swept through her, and he pulled her against him. After a minute, she sighed and cuddled against him.

Much better. They were both naked, and he was tempted to remain that way for the rest of eternity.

He loved her, and he loved the way her curves fit against him. As if she were the last piece of a puzzle, and they were perfectly matched.

"I'm being rude to my guests," he said a little while later.

She yawned. "What guests?" she asked, her breath fanning his chest.

"Vampires. They helped us with the dragons and bought us a bit of a reprieve."

"Vampires." She shuddered. "I should run screaming from this room, but I'm too tired to be afraid of bloodsuckers."

"No one will be sucking your blood but me."

She chuckled. "Do you *regret* being rude to them?" Her fingertip slid along the ridges of his stomach.

"I'm with you. I regret nothing," he said roughly, aroused by her touch *and* her words. She was adapting to life here. Maybe even coming to love it as he'd always craved.

Her finger looped through his nipple ring, and she chuckled again. "Such a naughty boy. The bad boy mommas warn their daughters about."

He liked the sound of her laughter and realized he'd never really heard her amusement before. "How old are you?" he asked, wanting to know everything about her.

"Twenty-five. Way too young for you."

He frowned.

"Are you going to live forever? Do you never age?"

"I age, just slower than humans."

Her entire body tensed. "Wait, wait, wait. I just had a thought. I'm going to grow old while you continue to look like *that*. No! Absolutely not!"

"You are in Atlantis now, love. Your aging process will slow, as well."

"Oh." Little by little, she relaxed. "That's okay, then. Unless I still end up aging faster than you. The moment, the very second, I can pass as your mother, I'm out of here."

Too bad, so sad. I'm never letting you go. "Do you miss your surface life as intensely as you did before?"

She released another sigh. "That's a tough question to answer."

"Quite easy, actually. A yes or no is all that's required." He didn't want her to miss her old life. He wanted her happy, completely, with him. If she did miss it...

What would he do? His two greatest desires would be at war with each other—the desire to keep her with him and the desire to see to her happiness, always, no matter the cost to himself.

"I'm not sure if I miss it or not. I mean, I'm not close to my family. I never have been, really, but closure would have been nice."

"Why exactly were you not close with them?" He couldn't imagine such a thing with his brother if Ver-ryn had lived.

"They wanted me to be something I wasn't," she said.

"What?"

"Sweet."

He snorted. "You *are* sweet. You like to pretend otherwise, but you are most definitely the sweetest morsel I've ever sampled."

Shaye bit him on the shoulder and licked away the sting. "I think you see into my soul—the one you're feeding whether you realize it or not. I think you see the woman I've always secretly wanted to be. Something my own mother hadn't been able to do."

"How can your family not see how sweet you are? Well, it's their shame, not yours."

She raised her head and cupped his cheeks with her palms. "Thank you for that."

Valerian's chest tightened. This woman possessed his heart, and he wanted hers. He would fight for it. The greatest battle of his life. "Have you been able to make your anti-cards here?"

"Yes."

"If you were to make one for me right now, what would it say?"

"Well…let's see." She rested her head on his shoulder. A minute ticked by, then another. "Are you sure you want to know?"

Yes. No. "Yes."

"If I were going to make and send you a card, it would say…" She paused, frowning as she drummed her fingers against his chest. "I'm trusting you not to break my heart. If it gets even a little scratch, I'll break your face."

His lips twitched. "Break my face?"

"That's right. You heard me."

Break his face if he broke her heart... Her heart. Valerian stilled, the significance of what she'd said finally registering. Even his blood ceased flowing and breath froze in his lungs. A wave of dizziness hit him as one emotion after another crashed through him.

"You are trusting me with your heart?" He was almost afraid to ask, and prayed he hadn't misunderstood.

He, a warrior who had laughed at danger his entire life, was afraid this tiny, pale woman wouldn't love him the way he loved her.

"Kind of," she said. "I'm giving you a piece of it. Just a little piece. I mean, I'm not saying I'm head over heels in love with you or anything like that. You're the only one who's fallen into the deep end. Okay?" A layer of panic coated her words. "But I'm trusting you not to be with anyone else while we're together. In case I wasn't clear, that means no other women."

"Moon, I desire no other save you."

"Now you don't. But what about later, when the novelty of me wears off?"

As she spoke, he heard her vulnerability, and it unmanned him. He rolled her to her back to stare down at her. "You are my mate. I've told you that, but I don't think you understand what it means. None arouse me anymore but you. None tempt me. None appeal to me. Only you. When a nymph takes a mate, that's the way of it. Always. For the rest of his existence."

Her gaze softened, and he knew she wanted to believe him. "Yeah, well," she said, putting on a brave face. "We'll see what happens in the coming days."

"So you want to stay with me?"

Radiating vulnerability, she whispered, "Yes."

Joy burst through him, full but not complete. Not yet. "You want to stay with me, but you don't want to love me?"

"Right. Love is complicated and messy."

"Is it? I love the way your nipples are pushing into my chest. That isn't complicated."

Her lips pursed. "That's not what I meant, and you know it. Loving someone gives them permission to do bad things to you because they know you'll forgive them."

A pinprick of anger. "What kind of bad things have been done to you by those you loved?" The question emerged quietly, lethally.

He would slay anyone, man or woman, who had dared hurt this woman.

"I've been abandoned, rejected, dismissed and forgotten," she said, and he tensed. "Plus, I saw the way you pushed aside the women who came before me."

"I didn't expect you, Moon. You were a surprise. I cannot undo what I've done in the past. But you have my vow of honor that I'll never tire of you. In time, you'll realize this for yourself." He paused, intent. "I know you said you would stay, but I'd like your vow. Promise me you will give me time to prove myself and my intentions toward you."

Her eyes searched his face, probing. Whatever she saw in his expression must have comforted her because she gave him a slow smile and nodded. "You have my vow."

He breathed a sigh of relief, his joy renewed.

Then she added, "If we're going to do this—"

"We are."

"You can't watch me sleep." She shuddered.

"Why? You're beautiful when you sleep. Or so I assume," he hastily added.

She rolled her eyes. "You've already done it, haven't you?"

"Only twelve times."

Only. "I've been here, what? Eight days. So you suck at math, but that's hardly your fault. A man as gorgeous as you are can't have brains, too."

He snorted.

"Also," she continued, "you can't obsess over me. You can't make all my troubles go away. You've got to let me get myself out of my own messes. You can't throw jealous fits of rage, and you can't ever, under any circumstances, call me your old lady, your ball and chain, or your property. I belong to myself. I'm loaning you my time."

"You. Are. Wonderful. Never change." Leaning down, he brushed his lips over hers. His hands found hers, and he intertwined their fingers before anchoring them above her head. The action lifted her chest and pressed her breasts deeper into him. She licked her lips as her eyelids lowered.

"While you've seen only the bad side of love, I have seen the best. My mother and father were mated and completely devoted to each other."

"Where are they, your parents?"

"They died many years ago. My father died in battle and my mother's sadness took her not long after."

"Wow. To be so devoted to someone you actually die without them, simply lose the will to live. It's like something out of a movie, yet a part of me doesn't want to acknowledge such devotion is possible. It frightens me…but it also excites me for the first time in forever."

He translated: hope was not lost.

"I'm sorry about your parents," she said softly.

"Uh-oh. There you go, showing your sweet side again."

She grinned. "How dare you say such a thing? I'm hard-core!"

"And you hate the things I do to you."

"Hate them," she agreed with a laugh.

His breath tunneled into her ear, followed by his tongue. Her hands tangled in his hair as she trembled.

"Just like you hate me," he breathed.

"Yes," she whispered. "I hate you so very much."

"That's good. Because I'm going to hate you until you can't imagine life without me."

He thought she might have whispered, "Too late," as he slid inside her.

CHAPTER TWENTY-SIX

LEAVING SHAYE ASLEEP in his bed—*their* bed, Valerian amended—was the hardest thing he'd ever done...while he was the hardest he'd ever been. He only wanted more! Her soft, pale tresses tapered over the violet sheets, as ethereal as a dream. Her features were relaxed, the sandy length of her lashes casting shadows over her cheekbones. Her lips were plump and rosy from his kisses.

Will never get enough of this woman.

He'd already dressed, had hastily tugged on a black shirt and pants before he'd lost his resolve to leave. As king, it was his duty to see to his guests. But more than that, he wanted to see to the palace's defenses and ensure they were well fortified and strong enough to withstand the most violent of attacks.

This peaceful reprieve the vampires had given them wouldn't last long, he knew. Darius would be back. Valerian only hoped the dragon would arrive later rather than sooner. The longer he had to solidify his bond with Shaye, the better. She strengthened him in ways he'd never thought possible.

He placed a chaste kiss on the tip of her nose—which proved to be a mistake. She muttered under her breath, an airy gurgle of unintelligible words, one of which might have been his name.

Must have. Now, now—

Leave. Safety first.

Right. Valerian forced one foot in front of the other and finally exited the room. Now that Shaye had decided to stay with him, she would begin to make the palace her own, gifting every inch with little touches of her personality.

He couldn't wait!

Would she fill the rooms with the colorful bouquets he planned to buy her? Hang her favorite paintings on the walls, select hand-carved furniture, add beaded pillows to the couches? He would take her into the Outer City and purchase everything she fancied. All the things humans used to make a home, well, a home. She would want for nothing, her every wish his to grant.

His jaw hurt from grinning too wide as he entered the dining hall. Vampires surrounded the table. Most clutched goblets filled with some type of blood, he was sure. Several nymphs were here, though most were on duty and if not on duty, they were most assuredly having sex, preparing for battle. There were no females present.

Layel, who had claimed the head of the table, spotted him and motioned him over.

"Acting as king of the place, already?" Valerian said, his grin only widening. He plopped onto the now-vacant spot beside his friend.

"Of course." Layel sipped at his goblet. "I don't think you've ever looked so sated, nymph."

"Mated life agrees with me, vampire."

A curtain of sadness flittered over Layel's expression. "Ah, yes. I remember mated life very well."

Layel had lost his mate years ago. She'd been a human, descended from those first banished from the surface and dropped into the city as punishment.

When other races had hunted those humans as sport,

the nymphs stepped in and protected. Layel spotted her—Sara—and challenged Valerian for rights to her.

They'd nearly killed each other, their strength evenly matched. But in the end, the girl had wished to go with Layel and Valerian had acquiesced.

Soon afterward Layel had wed her, and soon after that, a rogue group of dragons had raided the village where she had been living, raped her and burned her to death.

Not Darius—he'd been a child then—but a contingent of his tutor's men. Still. It didn't matter to Layel that Darius was innocent. The vampire king despised all dragons and would stop at nothing to destroy them all.

Valerian recalled in vivid detail the devastation Layel had endured upon discovering his lover's charred remains. His grief had been severe and gut-wrenching. Still was.

The experience had changed him. From merciful to cold, kind to callous. A fact Valerian understood in a way he never had before. Were he to lose Shaye in such a manner...

His hands fisted. *I will never lose her.*

"The dragons have captured a group of nymph females," Valerian said, "and that's something I cannot allow to stand."

"It would be my pleasure to retrieve the females for you," the vampire king said with relish.

And risk his army over Valerian's mistake? "No. I'll send my own men and ask you to stay a while longer to make up for the loss here. If you are able."

Layel didn't hesitate. "If you need us, we stay. That's how this thing works between us. There's nothing more to discuss."

Loyal Layel, always willing to give of himself and

his valuable time. That was one of the many reasons Valerian prized his friendship. There were not many men who would fight for another race as passionately as they would fight for their own.

Those who had earned the vampire king's wrath, however, were enemies for life. Layel lived for their suffering. He never forgot a wrong.

"Thank you, my friend." Valerian clapped him on the back. "If you ever need me, I'm here."

Layel's face was usually as pale as Shaye's, yet a rush of color had suffused his cheeks. "You are cherished, Valerian. Know that."

"I say the same to you." He stood. "Take what animals you need. But if your men have need of female companionship, which I'm sure they will, they'll have to visit the Outer City. Those here are happy with their lovers."

Layel gave a booming laugh. "The dark seduction of a vampire could rival the creepy stalkering of a nymph, but we'll do our best to hide our irresistible magnetism."

Valerian snorted. "Your ego is almost as big as your...humility."

Layel barked out a laugh. "That is it."

"We'll talk again soon." Valerian stood. "I must see to the palace's defenses."

"Ha! I know you. You might see to the palace's defenses, but your true goal is to get back to your bed."

He knew his grin came with a wicked glint. "Yes, you do know me well."

WHISPERS DRIFTED THROUGH Shaye's mind, attempting to rouse her.

"—haven't moved the humans to the dungeon."

"We arrived sooner than anticipated. We can't wait. We'll be spotted. We have to act now."

A hard, callused hand slapped over Shaye's mouth. She came awake instantly, a scream lodged in her throat. A scream that emerged as nothing more substantial than a quiet murmur. The hand didn't belong to Valerian. It smelled different, wasn't as erotic and didn't remind her a brewing storm. There wasn't a single spark of awareness inside her.

Vampire, perhaps? Valerian had mentioned the vampires were inside the palace. But why would an ally have snuck inside her bedroom?

Panicked, she swung her fist—connected with something solid. Her captor grunted.

"Not another move, woman. We don't want to hurt you."

But they would if they felt they had to?

Undeterred, she thrashed and kicked.

"Why can't you be a good girl and listen?"

Oh, no, he didn't!

Her narrowed gaze darted throughout the darkness. What she wouldn't have given for a flashlight. Scratch that. What she wouldn't have given for a stun gun or a knife. With no other recourse, she wrapped her fingers around the thickness of the man's wrist and jerked.

He grunted. "If I must, I'll render you unconscious, and neither of us will like the way I do it."

Dang him! A threat she couldn't overlook. She forced herself to still. Unconscious, she would be completely vulnerable with no way to break free when the time arrived. And it would. She had to believe it would.

"Good," the man—vampire?—said. "Now, I'm going to remove my hand. If you scream to draw your lover in here, we'll kill him without hesitation. Understand?"

We'll. We will. There were at least two in the room with her. Good to know.

She offered an affirmative nod, even though her mind screamed "No!" over and over again.

Somehow, she had to warn Valerian without luring him into an ambush. What could she do?

Think, Shaye, think.

As promised, the man removed his hold on her mouth. She dragged in a shaky breath. "Who are you? What do you want?"

"We are dragons, and we are going to take you home."

Dragons. The enemy. *They will ravish you and burn you*, Valerian had said. She shook her head, tendrils of hair slapping her cheeks. "I *am* home."

She was, wasn't she? She'd finally found the place she belonged. Not just temporarily but forever.

"That's what the others said, as well, but they didn't sway us from our purpose, and you won't, either."

"You can't take me. I won't let you." She'd promised Valerian she would stay. She would not break her word.

Valerian! her mind shouted. Slowly her eyes adjusted to the dark. She counted four silhouettes, each larger than the last. Weapons of all shapes and sizes were strapped to their bodies.

"We can do whatever we want," one of the men said, clearly amused by her spirit. "Sit up, dearling. Slowly."

He was one of *those*. The Hero of Sexist Elitism.

She did as instructed, clutching the sheet to her chin.

"I'm naked," she snapped. "I need clothes."

"Here," said a man to her left. "Put this on."

A gown was shoved over her head, surprising her.

"Why are you doing this?" she demanded, quickly pulling the garment the rest of the way down. Gossamer silk, practically see-through. Whatever. It would do.

"Poseidon has returned to punish the nymphs for breaking our laws. Now stand up. Keep your arms at your side."

Poseidon. The Greek god of the ocean. He was in Atlantis? Determined to dish out a few spankings. Unease churned in her stomach.

She inched from the bed as quietly as possible, hoping the dragons wouldn't sense her exact location. The door was to the left, and she inched one step forward, two. Then she broke into a full run.

Strong arms anchored around her before she reached the door, bringing her to a dead stop.

"You'll pay for this," she grated as she flailed. "Let me go."

"Woman, I warned you."

Knowing he meant to knock her out, Shaye increased her struggles. She used moves she'd learned in self-defense class, slamming her elbow into his stomach, stomping on his instep, dropping, but to no avail. "I hope you're cursed!"

"No worries. I am." A heavy sigh. "I'm sorry to do this, but you've given me no choice."

"Liar! We always have a choice!"

His hold on her tightened.

One of the other dragons snapped a stream of words she didn't understand and her captor loosened his hold. A moment later, someone else approached her. This one muttered a new series of unintelligible words, and a wave of lethargy swept through her. Her eyelids drifted shut, so heavy she could no longer hold them open. Sleep beckoned her, as alluring as any nymph.

Help, she tried to scream, knowing this moment—this might be her final moment in Atlantis. If she fell asleep, she would be taken from Valerian.

Help...sleep...sleep...no! She shook her head. *Scream!* She opened her mouth, but no sound emerged.

And still sleep called to her, luring her.

"She's a fighter, this one," someone said, his awe clear.

"I've never seen such determination."

"She should have dropped by now."

"Sleep, woman. On the morrow, you won't remember any of this."

What! No. No, no, no.

She prized her memories of Valerian. He'd gifted her with her first taste of contentment. First taste of pleasure. Her first taste of hope...

Strength abandoned her limbs, slowly or quickly, she wasn't sure. Time had ceased to exist. Utter darkness continued to creep gnarled fingers inside her mind.

Fight...fight...can't leave him...can't forget him... can't...sorry, so sorry...

She knew nothing else.

CHAPTER TWENTY-SEVEN

WITH HIS DUTIES COMPLETED, the palace fortified, his guests welcomed properly, Valerian raced back to his bedroom. Urgency filled him. He wanted Shaye again. He hungered for her. The more time he'd spent apart from her, the more crazed he'd become. He needed her.

And he sensed that she needed him, too. A moment ago, he thought he'd heard her voice in his mind, calling out to him.

He quickened his pace, speeding through the hallway, through the door. He would strip and crawl into bed beside her, if that's where she was, and awaken her with his mouth between her legs. She would scream his name, and the sound would echo between—

He stopped abruptly. He stood at the edge of the bed, golden rays of light streaming over its emptiness. Only rumpled sheets remained.

"Shaye," he called.

When silence greeted him, he spun, searching other areas. She hadn't been in the bathing pool; he would have seen her when he passed.

"Shaye?"

Again, there was only silence. Thick, frightening silence.

Where had she gone? He didn't want her roaming the halls without a guard. He wanted nothing taken for granted where her safety was concerned.

He didn't allow himself to panic—yet. Her scent permeated the air—she'd been here very recently—but there were other scents… His nose crinkled, and he frowned.

Dragons?

He hurried through the entire palace: the dining hall, where he received curious glances, the training room, the weapons room in case she'd gotten lost. He'd been remiss in his duty toward her. He should have taught her the layout of the palace.

Everyone he encountered, he demanded to know if she had been spotted. No one had seen her. In fact, several warriors were looking for their women, as well.

"I can't find Brenna," Joachim said, worry thick in his voice.

So, Joachim had taken Brenna from Shivawn—or maybe Shivawn had given her to the man. Valerian didn't know and at the moment he didn't care. All that mattered was Shaye.

"I can't find my bed partner," another said.

"I can't find my human." Still another.

Hearing this, Valerian finally allowed his panic free rein. He sprinted to the cave. Surely Shaye hadn't led all the women into the portal. She'd promised to stay. She'd told him she desired time with him. She had been so close to giving him her love; he'd sensed it.

Had she changed her mind?

Sweat trickled from his skin. Tension thrummed and pulsed.

Had she lied in order to trick him into lowering his guard?

No. No! She wouldn't have left him willingly. She wasn't a liar.

The last time he'd seen her, she'd worn a soft, sated

expression. Vulnerability had glinted in her eyes as she vowed to trust him. She'd said she craved fidelity from him, and those weren't the words of a woman intent on leaving.

That meant only one thing. She had been taken. But where? And by whom? Had his enemy returned more quickly than he'd anticipated? If so, why had they taken the women and not killed a single nymph?

Battle strategy. Take the ones response for strengthening the nymphs, leaving the nymphs weak and vulnerable to injury.

Hands fisted, Valerian swung around and backtracked, heading to the top floor, leaving the coldness of the cave behind. He ran into Broderick.

"Something's wrong." Broderick scrubbed a hand down his face. "The women. They've vanished."

"They've been taken. It happened within the last few hours, so there's a good chance they're still here. Keep searching, and send a full contingent to the portal."

Where else could he look? He'd searched the palace from top to bottom.

Valerian stalked into the dining hall. Layel had returned to the table, staring into emptiness, sadness radiating from him.

If the women had been taken out of the palace and into the Outer City... It wasn't a place for unarmed females. Demons would eat anything, for they survived on fear and carnage. And demons would most definitely view the women as succulent treats.

"Layel," he said. He knew the vampire and his people had no responsibility in this. He trusted the male without question. "I need your help."

His friend jolted upright. "It is yours."

"How many of your people can withstand the light?"

"Most of us can."

Vampires could scent humans like no other race. "Please, I'm begging you. Take your vampires through the forest and into the city to search for our women. The dragons have taken them."

In a movement so fluid it was almost undetectable, Layel stood. "I will do as you've asked. Do you stay or do you go?"

Valerian debated. If he stayed and Shaye was in the city, she wouldn't know Layel and would fight him, perhaps getting hurt in the process. But if Valerian left, and she was still inside the palace, perhaps being hidden and held against her will, the dragons waiting for the opportunity to push her through the portal, he would never forgive himself for leaving her.

Indecision and frustration ate at him. Go? Stay? "I will go," he finally said. He'd posted guards at the portal. The dragons would have to fight nymphs and females to get through. "Ready your men."

Layel nodded and rushed off.

Valerian raced into his room and gathered the dragon medallion he'd tossed aside when making love with Shaye. He stuffed it in his pocket before hunting down Broderick, who had another contingent of armed warriors stomping through every room, questioning other nymphs and vampires. "I'm going into the city. Send a messenger if the women are found…whatever condition they're in," he added starkly.

Broderick gave a stiff nod.

Alone, Valerian paused and…cried. He wanted Shaye surrounded by a hedge of protection, wanted her back at his side, healthy and whole.

He would trade his own life for hers. Gladly. Without hesitation.

Stop blubbering like a baby. Go and fight for your woman!

He grabbed the Skull and raced outside. The vampires possessed an unnatural speed. They would move much faster without him, and as much as he wanted to reach Shaye first, he would rather not hinder them.

At the outer gates, the vampires had already gathered, preparing for the search. "Don't let me slow you," he told Layel. "Move as quickly as you can, and I'll make my own way. Gather any human females you find."

Layel's eyes glowed bright, vivid blue. "We will find her, Valerian. I won't rest until we do."

Valerian turned away before he broke down a second time, just fell to his knees and sobbed. Loss wasn't new to him, but this particular loss would kill him.

"Go." The single word was hoarse, scratching his burning throat. "Go."

The vampires leaped into action; one moment they were there, the next moment they were gone. Valerian entered the stable and mounted Henry the centaur. They raced around trees and quicksand, and he continually shouted Shaye's name. Sometimes he paused to listen for a response.

Finally he concluded she wasn't in the forest.

She wasn't in the Outer City, either. None of the humans were, and none of the residents claimed to have seen them. He scoured every shadow, home, hill and valley until dusk. With every second that passed, his frustration magnified. So did his fear.

Where was she? She wasn't...dead. No, no. He could barely even think the hated word. He would have sensed it. As her mate, he would have known the moment death came for her, just as he'd known when his twin had died, all those years ago.

He left Layel and the vampire army in the city with instructions to continue the hunt—they could see in the dark while he could not. Valerian returned to the palace.

When he reached the gates, he dismounted and ran inside without a word. As he ran, he withdrew the dragon medallion from his pocket. The crystal door opened before him and closed behind him.

The palace was eerily silent, his men nowhere to be seen.

"Broderick," he called. "Joachim. Shivawn."

He ground to a halt, the fine hairs on the back of his neck standing at attention. He sniffed, encountering the same faint scent from his bedroom.

The dragons were here.

Valerian quickly withdrew his sword from the sheath at his side.

"Your men are otherwise occupied," a voice said above him.

Darius.

Lips thinning in a fierce scowl, Valerian looked up. There, circling him from the second-floor parapet, was the entire dragon army.

"What did you do with my woman?" he demanded.

"By the time you discovered her missing, it was too late. We had already sent her home, nymph."

CHAPTER TWENTY-EIGHT

"WAKE UP, SHAYE." Shake. "Wake up."

Shaye heard the voice from a long, dark tunnel. *Yes*, she thought. *Must. Wake. Up.* Trouble was nearby. Trouble for her and for Valerian.

Consciousness gradually worked through her mind, chasing away the darkness.

"Wake up."

Slowly she cracked open her eyelids. Sunlight glared down at her, and orange-gold spots danced through her vision. Dry cotton filled her mouth. Sand and salt coated the rest of her. Her dress was stiff, as if it had been soaked and dried right on her. The sound of lulling waves greeted her ears, soothing, familiar. Yet…wrong. The smells weren't right, either. Yes, she smelled salt, but not orchids or storms.

"Valerian," she called. Her throat felt raw, scratchy. "Valerian."

"Do you want the herb, honey? Someone. Help! Get me valerian root!"

"No. I want the man. My man." Her attention veered to the speaker. Her… "Mom?" She rubbed at her eyes. "What are you doing here?"

"I've been haunting the beach since you were taken. Are you—" her mother gulped "—okay? Did they hurt you?"

"I'm fine." From the corner of her eye, she saw

Ameena kneeling in the sand, dark hair hanging in tangles around her face. Dirt smeared her blade of a nose and the sharpness of her now gaunt cheeks.

Shaye crawled to her. "What's going on?"

"I want to go back," she said, never looking Shaye's way. "I'd give *anything* to go back."

Go back… Understanding clicked. Yes. The dragons had invaded Valerian's bedroom, had threatened to take her to the surface, wipe her memory, then had rendered her unconscious.

Well, the memory wipe clearly failed.

She hugged the woman and shoved to her feet. Her equilibrium was off balance, and she swayed. Her mom wrapped an arm around her waist.

"Are you sure you're okay?" Tamara asked.

"Yes, yes. I'll be fine." Shaye massaged her temples to ward off the dizziness. She scanned the area. Other women were scattered across the beach. Some sitting up. Some still lying down. Others were walking around, frowning and obviously confused. "Ameena, help me talk to the others. Any who want to go back, we'll try together."

When the world finally righted itself, she cataloged her surroundings. White-gold sand stretched as far as the eyes could see. Waves crested to the beach, leaving sea foam in their wake. The sun shone brightly, no hint of crystal.

"I was here when you arrived," her mom explained, realizing the direction of her gaze. "I've questioned everyone who awoke. Most can't recall their own name, why they're here, or even how they got here."

"There was a boat docked over there." Her mom pointed to the right. "The men inside helped get you to the beach, but they didn't know anything, either. I did see the initials *OBI* on the side, though, whatever that means."

"I still don't understand why you're here," Shaye said, pinning her with a frown.

Tamara's expression contorted. "After you disappeared, the police arrived at the tent. They didn't believe us when we told them what had happened. They laughed at us, said you girls had probably paid strippers to pretend a mass abduction. All I could think was that you were gone, I'd never see you again, and the last words between us had been harsh."

"I—" Shaye had no idea what to say. Her mother had never shown her such a vulnerable, repentant side.

"I haven't been the best mother. I know that," the distressed woman rushed on. "And I know things will probably never be comfortable between us. I'm just glad you're okay."

Tears burned Shaye's eyes as she wrapped her arms around her mom. "Thank you for that."

Tamara hugged her back, expelling a shaky breath.

"So you're happy?" Shaye asked her.

"Now that you're here? Yes." Her mom drew back and wiped at her own tears with the back of her wrist. "I think Conner truly is the love of my life, and Preston seems to like me. They're at opposite ends of the beach, passing out flyers with your picture and asking if anyone's seen you."

Wow. For the first time in her life, her mother was acting like a loving mother. As if they were part of a real family But…she had a new family, too. "I have to go back, Mom." She wanted—needed—Valerian. He probably thought she'd left him on purpose. If he wasn't— No! She wouldn't think of him as dead. He was strong, the strongest man she'd ever encountered. He would have gathered his army and defeated the dragons.

"I have to go back," she repeated.

"Go back where, exactly?"

She didn't have time to explain. "Just...find Conner and Preston and tell them I'm okay. Tell Preston I'm sorry for the way I acted at the wedding. I'll return if I can. If not, know that I'm happy and that I've found the man of my dreams, too."

"But—"

"Trust me. Please." Shaye gave her mom one last hug and moved toward the water. The rest of the women were awakening. Ameena had already spoken to a few of them.

Everyone wore different colored robes. Beachgoers probably assumed they'd come from a costume party, intoxicated, and gone for a swim.

"You ready to do this?" Ameena asked, moving to her side.

"Yes."

"Me, too," Brenna said, joining them.

"Anyone else?" she asked.

"Only three," Ameena said.

Those three rushed over.

The others walked away, acting as if they had no idea who Shaye was. They probably didn't.

Well. Their loss. Shaye had no desire to live without Valerian.

She loved him. She loved him with all of her heart. A heart she'd once thought too cold to care for anyone. But she couldn't deny her feelings any longer. He'd melted her ice and left her with fire.

His love fed her soul, just as her love fed her soul. And his! He'd been right. Love gave, it didn't take.

Fear had led her for far too long. But no more! Today, love took over.

Water lapped at her ankles, sand squished between her toes. Rising, rising, the cool liquid soon hit her calves, her thighs. If those dragons hurt her man in any way, she'd hunt them down and *destroy* them.

She swam as far as she could, all the women with her, then dived under the water. No luck. She had to come up for air.

Again and again she repeated the action. Hours passed, exhaustion settled in, but they never gave up their search.

"Why are we doing this?" Ameena panted as she treaded water beside her. "I… I can't remember."

"Atlantis." Shaye swallowed a mouthful of salty liquid. "The nymphs."

"The who?" Ameena's face scrunched in confusion.

The same transformation overcame the others—except Brenna. She possessed an aura of determination, just like Shaye.

"I hate to swim," one of the women said. "I'm going home."

"Me, too."

"This is stupid."

"I don't even know how I got here. Wasn't I at a wedding?" On and on they muttered as they swam back to the beach.

They were forgetting, just as the dragons had promised, and Shaye was suddenly afraid of the same thing happening to her. Already Valerian's face had begun to blur in her mind.

"I won't forget," she wheezed between labored breaths.

"We have to get back," Brenna wheezed right back. "They need us."

They swam under and up for an hour longer. By the end, Shaye felt as if she'd gained three hundred pounds of water weight. She could barely move.

Tears of frustration and fury streamed down her cheeks. If she didn't return to shore, she would drown here. And she would take Brenna with her.

But the needed to try one more time to get back to... what was his name?

No! I won't forget. Valerian. Yes! That was it. His name was Valerian, and she loved him.

"One more dive," she told Brenna.

Brenna was gasping for breath, but she nodded. "Yes. I...need....Joachim."

If they failed to find the portal this time, they would swim back to shore and try again tomorrow. Try every day until they succeeded.

When Shaye went under, the salt stung her eyes. But she pushed herself farther than ever before, while Brenna remained at her side.

Her arms and legs shook violently. Fish brushed against her. Her lungs burned. Brenna stopped moving, her hands and feet stilling, as if she'd lost all control of her body.

Shaye grabbed on to her and switched directions, angling upward—but it was too late. She'd pushed herself too far and didn't have the strength to swim the rest of the way up. Especially with Brenna's added weight.

She might have a chance if she released her friend.

No way was she releasing her friend.

At first she panicked, flailing, opening her mouth, desperate to fill her burning lungs with oxygen. She swallowed more water instead. Still she retained a grip on Brenna, doing her best to get them both to the top despite the obstacles.

A strange blackness, began to weave through her mind, thicker than any darkness she'd ever encountered. Then a flash of light sparked in her line of vision. A bubble floated in front of her, growing, growing, until it completely surrounded her and Brenna.

She spit out a mouthful of water and gasped for breath. Miraculously, she sucked in actual air. Wet hair clung to her face, but she didn't brush it aside. Couldn't. Too weak.

Was she dreaming? Dead?

She dropped to her knees in front of Brenna, who lay unconscious. She'd never performed CPR, but she'd seen it done and now mimicked the motions.

"Come on," she panted. "Come on."

After a long while of pumping and breathing for her friend, Brenna coughed up a river. Her eyes remained closed, but she, too, sucked in a breath of air.

Depleted, Shaye sagged beside her.

"Foolish human," a deep, thunderous voice growled. "Why are you doing this? You nearly died, both of you. And for what?"

Her exhausted gaze circled the bubble. Water churned around it, but she couldn't see a person—not inside or out. "Where are you? *Who* are you?"

"An insulting question. I am Poseidon, king of the sea. Obviously."

Another king. The one who wanted to punish the nymphs. "Take me to Valerian," she demanded.

He laughed. "A command from a human. Your sense of humor pleases me. Unfortunately, your lover is already dead."

"No." Fierce despair tried to sink sharp claws inside her. "No. He can't be."

Colorful sparks appeared just in front of her, solidifying into a male form. He was beautiful, more so than even Valerian. White hair framed an utterly masculine face. His eyes were as blue as the ocean, a liquid crystal, utterly hypnotic. They were almost neon, glowing, pulsing with energy and power.

"Valerian disobeyed the laws of Atlantis. He brought humans into the city."

"He doesn't deserve to die for that," she snarled at him, trying to gather the strength to rise. She could only lie there.

Poseidon smiled at her, an amused twitching of his sensual lips. "I had forgotten how fierce you humans can be when someone you love is threatened. It is quite entertaining."

"Take me to Valerian. Right now!"

He quickly lost his smile. "And now I remember how *annoying* it can be. Do you wish to die? With your every word, you are begging me to slay you."

"Please." She nearly curled into a sobbing heap. "I just want to be with Valerian."

Poseidon studied her face for a long while before turning his attention to Brenna. His expression never softened. "I told you, he is already dead."

"No. I won't believe you until you've shown him to me. That's right. Until I see him, I will continue to dive this ocean, continue to plague you."

Silence. Even the water refused to make noise.

Then, "What would you give me if I allowed you to see him? To go to him?"

"Anything. Everything." A huge black-and-white whale swam past them, its majestic body consuming the area. She watched in amazement as it lowered its head to Poseidon.

"Your own life?" the god asked.

That wasn't even a question. "Yes."

He blinked in surprise.

"Have you never been in love?" she asked. "Have you never craved another person so much you would rather die than be without them?"

"No," he admitted. "The concept is laughable at best." Slowly he circled her, his hair like a curtain, ribboning in the air. His body was fluid, rippling like waves.

She maintained eye contact.

"I'm not evil, but to send you back into Atlantis and allow the nymphs to live will make me appear soft. My people will continue to break the law."

Joy thrummed through her because, with his words, he'd confirmed the nymphs were not yet dead; that there was still time.

"Or," she said, "they'll think you merciful and sing your praises and be happy to obey your every whim."

His eyes narrowed, but not before she saw sparks of pleasure flickering in their depths. "You think you are clever, don't you?"

"I'd argue the word *think*." Pushing too hard? Yeah. Probably. "I just want to be with my man."

There was a long pause. "Watching one such as you battle with the nymph king *could* be amusing," he said absently.

He wanted to be amused, did he? "I'll give him nothing but trouble," she promised. "I'll turn his life upside down. I'll create absolute havoc."

As she spoke, Poseidon's expression became more

and more excited. Visions of the coming trouble were rolling through his mind; she could see it in his eyes.

"Very well," he said, and there was relish in his tone. "I'll allow you to reenter Atlantis."

Her joy tripled, an avalanche of incomparable force. "Thank you, thank you so much. Brenna, too, right?"

"I suppose." He sighed.

"You won't regret this, I promise you."

"However," he continued as if she hadn't spoken, "I won't stop the course I have set. I'll allow the dragons to fight the nymphs. If the dragons win, and they will, for even now they have the nymphs at their mercy—a mercy they do not possess—Valerian will die and you will be forced to live in Atlantis without him. Because, by returning, I will never allow you to leave."

She licked her lips, nodded. "Agreed."

The bubble burst in the next instant, and water suddenly barraged her. She reached for Brenna but couldn't find her. Water shot inside her nostrils, her mouth and lungs. A dark void closed around her, spinning her in every direction. Stars winked in and out.

Then, oh, blessedly then, the water was sucked away, leaving only a tunnel.

She coughed and sputtered as she fell, tumbling headlong into an abyss. She wasn't frightened, though. She knew Valerian awaited her on the other end. Valerian. Her love, her life.

Impact! Her feet hit a solid foundation, jarring her all the way to her bones. She swayed, but managed to right herself and crack open her eyes.

Never had she seen a more welcome sight. The stark walls of the cave closed around her, crimson-stained, decorated with those beautiful murals. Cool air slithered from every corner.

Home. She was home.

She heard a moan and glanced down. Brenna was sprawled out and just opening her eyes.

"We did it," Shaye told her. She couldn't stop grinning. "We did it."

Eyes lighting, Brenna eased to her feet.

The sound of angry male voices suddenly hit her awareness, and she whipped around. The nymphs must have been placed in the cells.

Trembling, she motioned to Brenna to be quiet, and her friend nodded.

Just in case dragons were guarding the area, she sneaked along the walls. Brenna tiptoed behind her. They remained in the shadows. Leaning forward, she peeked at the cell. It was overcrowded, positively bursting with nymphs. She looked for Valerian but didn't see him. Still, she didn't allow herself to become upset. He was here, and he was alive. She knew it.

There was a single dragon guard, probably because the fewer men outside the cell, the fewer who could be tricked into opening it.

Game time.

Shaye picked up the largest rock she could find and mouthed for Brenna to run for the cell and free the men on her signal.

Eagerness danced through her as she silently held up her fingers. *One. Two. Three.* In unison, she and Brenna burst inside. Shaye managed to surprise the guard— three cheers!—and smash his temple with her rock.

He roared, but he didn't fall. At the same time, Brenna grabbed hold of the bars. They misted and the nymphs immediately surged out, toppling the guard.

"Brenna!" a male voice shouted.

YOUR PARTICIPATION IS REQUESTED!

Dear Reader,

Since you are a lover of our books – we would like to get to know you!

Inside you will find a short Reader's Survey. Sharing your answers with us will help our editorial staff understand who you are and what activities you enjoy.

To thank you for your participation, we would like to send you 2 books and 2 gifts – **ABSOLUTELY FREE!**

Enjoy your gifts with our appreciation,

Pam Powers

SEE INSIDE FOR READER'S SURVEY

For Your Reading Pleasure...

We'll send you 2 books and 2 gifts
ABSOLUTELY FREE
just for completing our Reader's Survey!

YOUR READER'S SURVEY
"THANK YOU" FREE GIFTS INCLUDE:
- ▶ 2 FREE books
- ▶ 2 lovely surprise gifts

PLEASE FILL IN THE CIRCLES COMPLETELY TO RESPOND

1) What type of fiction books do you enjoy reading? (Check all that apply)
- ○ Suspense/Thrillers ○ Action/Adventure ○ Modern-day Romances
- ○ Historical Romance ○ Humor ○ Paranormal Romance

2) What attracted you most to the last fiction book you purchased on impulse?
- ○ The Title ○ The Cover ○ The Author ○ The Story

3) What is usually the greatest influencer when you <u>plan</u> to buy a book?
- ○ Advertising ○ Referral ○ Book Review

4) How often do you access the internet?
- ○ Daily ○ Weekly ○ Monthly ○ Rarely or never

5) How many NEW paperback fiction novels have you purchased in the past 3 months?
- ○ 0 - 2 ○ 3 - 6 ○ 7 or more

YES! I have completed the Reader's Survey. Please send me the 2 FREE books and 2 FREE gifts (gifts are worth about $10 retail) for which I qualify. I understand that I am under no obligation to purchase any books, as explained on the back of this card.

191/391 MDL GLPE

FIRST NAME	LAST NAME

ADDRESS

APT.#	CITY

STATE/PROV.	ZIP/POSTAL CODE

NO POSTAGE
NECESSARY
IF MAILED
IN THE
UNITED STATES

BUSINESS REPLY MAIL

FIRST-CLASS MAIL   PERMIT NO. 717   BUFFALO, NY

POSTAGE WILL BE PAID BY ADDRESSEE

READER SERVICE

PO BOX 1867

BUFFALO NY 14240-9952

Brenna squealed happily and rushed forward. Joachim wrapped his big arms around her.

Shaye searched for Valerian. *He's here, he's here, he has to be here.* The crowd of nymphs was parting, but she didn't see him.

"Valerian? Valerian!"

Where was he?

CHAPTER TWENTY-NINE

"VALERIAN!"

He heard his name being called, and his stomach clenched with joy. Shaye's voice. His head shot up; his mouth fell open. "Shaye? Where are you?" Before the last word left him, he spotted her in front of the cell.

He leaped up, their gazes locking.

A grin split her entire face, jubilant. Radiant.

"You came back." He pushed past his men. Tears burned his eyes—and he didn't care. He ordered Broderick to free the nymphs from the other cell, but his man had beaten him there.

She threw herself into Valerian's arms.

He kissed her and nipped at her chin. "I thought you were lost to me." His voice shook.

His arms tightened around her, lifting her feet off the ground. She wound her legs around his waist, kissing him with the same ferocity.

"I promised to stay, didn't I?" she said.

He breathed deeply of her scent, letting it fill him, strengthen him. "I'd planned to come for you. I was going to help my men retake the palace, then go to you. Live with you up there. One day with you would be better than a lifetime without you."

"I love you, Valerian. I love you so much. And I'm sorry I didn't tell you sooner. Sorry I let fear—"

He squeezed her so tightly she couldn't finish her

sentence, could only laugh. "I love you so much, my sweet moonbeam. I'm still in shock you came back to me."

"I'll always come back to you."

"What of the others?" Broderick had completed his mission and strode over. "Did they return, as well?"

"No. Only Brenna and me," Shaye told him as gently as possible. "I'm sorry."

Broderick gave a stiff nod.

Valerian faced his men—without releasing Shaye. He wasn't ready to let her go, couldn't stop touching her.

"As your queen, I'm ordering you to reclaim our palace," Shaye said before he could speak.

Several of the warriors smiled at her.

Valerian flicked her a grin of his own. "That's right." He placed a kiss on Shaye's soft lips, lingered far longer than he should have, savoring her taste, then sighed.

"Where are the vampires?" Broderick asked. "They could help us."

"I sent them into the city. By the time they returned, the dragons had already regained control and barred them from entry." His stare became hard, penetrating as he peered down at Shaye. "I want to leave you down here."

"No," she said. "No way."

"Shaye."

"Valerian."

"She's queen," Broderick said, clearly entertained. "You won't be able to command her."

Valerian sighed. "Promise me you'll duck and hide when the fighting begins."

"Promise," she said. "I'm not looking to get hurt. Just looking for an opportunity to help if possible and if necessary."

His hand closed around hers. He loved the feel of her. "Men, we go in hard, and we go in fast."

"Like Broderick does with his women," someone joked.

Male chuckles abounded.

"Where's Shivawn?" Brenna asked.

"No one has seen him," Joachim replied, hugging her closer. "He probably left the palace before the dragons arrived, sleeping off the night's excess in the city."

"Just...try not to kill the dragons," Shaye said. "They could have killed us—and you—but they placed us on the surface unharmed and only locked you away. You owe them the same consideration."

"My mate is very wise," Valerian said. "Listen to her."

After confining Valerian and his army inside the cells, Darius had looked him in the eyes and said, "I've been ordered by Poseidon to execute every nymph who journeyed to the surface...before killing everyone else. Perhaps I bring his wrath upon my own head, but I don't think your race deserves annihilation. You will remain here until I decide what to do with you."

A man of his caliber didn't deserve to die. No matter how much Layel despised him.

As quietly as possible, Valerian crept up the stairs, Shaye behind him, the army behind her. They were without weapons, yet they were determined. This was their home, and they weren't giving it up.

When they reached the top, Valerian softly ordered everyone to split.

Lines of men branched in every direction. Joachim had kept Brenna with him, as well, Valerian noticed. Couldn't tolerate a moment away from her?

Know the feeling.

Surprise was their biggest advantage right now. Their

footsteps tapped lightly, barely echoing from the walls. Torches glowed, heating the air and lighting their path.

"This way." He led his contingent into the dining hall.

A group of dragons came into view. They stood at the table, discussing their best course of action.

"Kill them and be done with it," someone growled. "I don't wish Poseidon's wrath upon my family."

"By doing Poseidon's will in this, we give him complete control of our lives," Darius said. "What if, tomorrow, he wishes us to kill our own women?"

"If we disobey him, we may not live long enough to find out."

"There's a reason the Greeks have never slain us, a reason why they sent us back into this palace instead of destroying the nymphs themselves." Darius again.

"What reason?"

"I don't know, yet knowing there *is* a reason gives us leverage. All I am saying is that we can't become Poseidon's servants."

"Agreed," Valerian answered. His signal.

Weaponless, the nymphs swarmed forward. Valerian wished he held the Skull, but he couldn't postpone this fight to retrieve it.

Streams of fire suddenly spewed from the dragons. Valerian shoved Shaye behind a small side table and leaped forward. He and Darius met midair. That the dragon king had retained his human form meant he wasn't enraged. Yet.

They grappled to the ground. Valerian landed a hard punch into his opponent's face. Blood trickled from Darius's mouth, yet the cut healed quickly. He gave another punch and rolled, then kicked out his leg, hitting Darius's stomach.

The dragon king flew backward, but immediately righted himself and spun. His tail had sprouted, and it slashed at Valerian's face, cutting deep. He felt the sting of it but didn't let the pain affect him.

All around him nymphs and dragons warred. Their grunts permeated the air.

"I agree with what you said about Poseidon." Valerian lunged, punched. Contact. "Must we be enemies?"

"Yes!" Darius kicked again, and his foot slammed into Valerian's side. "You allowed the Jewel of Dunamis to escape to the mortal world."

Spinning continuously, he lashed out at Darius again and again, landing four successive blows. "I won't give up this palace. It belongs to us. *You* already have a home."

"For the safety of Atlantis, the portal must be guarded. How can I trust you to do this? To not use it for your own gain?"

Valerian paused.

Darius did the same.

They stared each other down, both panting.

"When we win the nymph females back from you," Valerian said, "we will have no more need of the surface world."

Around them, the battle still raged. Valerian ducked as a stream of fire was launched his way. The heat singed him, even though the flames never touched him.

Darius said, "The law claims only guardians are to use the portals to travel to the surface, that any one else deserves punishment. If you were a guardian..."

"I would do my duty." Valerian studied Darius's face. That scar slashed from eyebrow to chin. His eyes were swirling blue, determined to kill if he must, but hoping to find another way.

"The portal I guard leads to a jungle on the surface.

The portal here leads to an ocean on the surface, as I'm sure you know. If you stay here," Darius said, "human travelers *will* come through. Most often they swim too deeply, are innocent, but they will be yours to either memory wipe and return or destroy. The Outer City will be yours to guard, as well. I'm ready to relinquish this duty as it was never meant to be mine. I've enough to do handling the Inner City."

"I will protect it with my life," Valerian vowed. "This is the only home we have ever known."

"Then kneel."

Valerian knelt without hesitation. Even though the dragon could betray him. For a chance at this alliance...

He stared up at Darius, who sliced a thin cut down the center of his chest, and offered a blood oath to always guard the portal, to keep the city safe.

Around them, the fighting ceased at last. The men stopped to listen and watch. Shaye approached Valerian's side, and he stood. He linked their fingers. He should have scolded her for leaving the safety of the table, but too much did he like her where she was.

Darius's gaze flicked to her and widened with surprise.

"I told you I wouldn't leave him," she said with a proud tilt of her chin. "I found a way to return."

His lips twitched. "My Grace would have done the same."

"Shall we trust each other, dragon?" Valerian waited impatiently for the answer. Everything he'd ever wanted hovered just beyond his grasp.

Darius's gaze became piercing. "Yes," he finally said. "We shall trust each other. And battle Poseidon together if necessary."

Valerian held out his hand. Darius eyed it for several seconds before clasping it with his own. The truce was sealed, and Valerian had no idea how he would explain it to Layel.

"Let us hope we live long enough to regret this." He turned to Shaye and gathered her in his arms, where she belonged—where he planned to keep her for all of eternity.

"This is the most unhappy I've ever been," she said, grinning at him. "I've never hated you so much."

Softly he kissed her sweet, sweet lips. "You don't hate me as much as I hate you."

"You hate each other?" Darius asked. "I'm confused."

Valerian ignored him. "Oh, Moon, we are going to have a long, happy life together. I know it."

EPILOGUE

"HOW MUCH IS THIS ONE?"

"That one will cost you a kiss. A big wet one. Probably a ten-second Frencher."

Valerian pushed away the basket of oranges he always kept in his room and studied the card Shaye had made for him.

It read: *Without you, I'm nothing.*

With each day that had passed, her cards had become more and more poetic. Which was a good thing, since his men were going to need those cards to lure the female nymphs from their pique. Seemed they weren't too happy about being left with the dragons for so long.

But the sweet cards also meant that Shaye's past hurts were being soothed. She'd even written her romance novel. An erotic tale about two women who fell deeply in love with nymph warriors.

She was adapting to life in Atlantis admirably, amusing herself by selling cards to the residents of the Outer City, where she'd set up shop. Valerian ensured she was always guarded from demons and other forces, of course.

Even the dragons bought a card or twenty when they came to visit—Darius had needed one for his pregnant wife. The vampires, too, bought them, though they didn't visit often. Layel was upset by the alliance between nymphs and dragons.

Valerian was now determined to unite the two races.

So far Poseidon hadn't returned. Or rather, he hadn't made himself known.

Maybe he would, maybe he wouldn't. No reason to waste energy worrying. Whatever happened, happened.

Valerian had Shaye, and that was all that mattered. He could handle anything else. He'd even promised Shaye he would find a way to take her to see her mother. And he would. What Shaye wanted, Shaye received.

Life, at the moment, was all that he'd ever dreamed.

Joachim was mated to Brenna, and the little woman had become their healer—for children and the nymphs who were single. She patched those in need with a smile, followed by a lecture about "acting like babies" when the fearless warriors whimpered at the sight of her needles.

Shivawn was his only reason for upset. The man's mood grew blacker and blacker every day. He'd been spending more and more time in the vampire camp, most likely stalking Alyssa.

They'd slept together once—or so Valerian suspected—and afterward the girl had then rejected him. Her reasons remained a mystery.

But the two would find their way. Of that Valerian was sure. If he had to lock them in a room together until they worked out their differences, he would.

He would consider it inspiration for Shaye's cards and stories.

"Well, do you like it?" she asked, pointing to the card in his hand.

"I love it. But a kiss is too low a price, Moon." She sat behind a table and he leaned over it, placing them nose to nose. "You should demand sex and nothing less."

She chuckled. "Your men would buy more if I did."

He growled with mock ferocity. "I will pay my men's debts. In fact, I owe you for several Joachim purchased, and it's time I paid up."

"Then close the shop." Her arms wound around his neck. "Take me to bed, Valerian."

"That will be my pleasure."

"And mine, love. And mine."

* * * * *

*If you enjoyed THE NYMPH KING,
you will love Gena Showalter's
LORDS OF THE UNDERWORLD series,
featuring immortal warriors possessed by demons
and the women who bring them to their knees.
Look for the newest Lords book,
THE DARKEST PROMISE,
coming soon from HQN Books!*

THE BEAUTIFUL ASHES

Jeaniene Frost

To JBA, now more than ever.

CHAPTER ONE

I'M TWENTY, AND ALREADY, I've got nothing left to lose. That's why I didn't care that Bennington, Vermont, looked like a postcard for autumn in the country. The two-story bed-and-breakfast I pulled up to was no different. It even had a white picket fence and a steady swirl of sunset-colored leaves drifting down from the many trees in the yard.

My picturesque surroundings were in stark contrast to how *I* looked. If I hadn't been exhausted from grief and stress, I might've cared that my brown hair now resembled greasy mud. Or that my breath was in desperate need of a Mentos, and don't get me started on the coffee stains decorating my WMU shirt. Since I had more important things to worry about, I didn't even bother to cover my head against the downpour as I left my car and ran into the bed-and-breakfast.

"One moment!" a cheery voice called out from farther inside. Then a heavyset older woman with graying red hair came down the hallway.

"Hello, dear. I'm Mrs. Paulson. Are you—oh, my, you're soaked!"

"It's nothing," I said, but she bustled out of sight, returning moments later with a towel.

"You sit down and dry yourself off," she ordered in the same *tsk*ing tone my mother had used a million times before. A surge of grief had me dropping into the chair she waved at. The things you didn't realize you'd miss until they were gone…

"Thanks," I said, determined not to cry in front of a total stranger. Then I pulled out the Ziploc bag I'd carried around most of the day. "I'm looking for two people who might've stayed here the weekend before last."

As I spoke, I pulled out a picture of my sister, Jasmine, and her boyfriend, Tommy.

Mrs. Paulson got a pair of glasses from her apron pocket. Then she sat behind a large antique desk and accepted the picture.

"Oh, what a pretty girl," she said, adding kindly, "just like you. But I've never seen either of them before, sorry."

"Thanks," I said, although I wanted to scream.

I'd spent the day showing Jasmine's picture to every hotel, motel and inn in Bennington, yet no one had recognized my sister. She'd been here, though. The last texts she'd sent came from Bennington, but the police already hinted that they thought she'd sent them while driving through. To them, Jasmine was an impulsive eighteen-year-old who'd gone on a road trip with her boyfriend. My sister might be impulsive, but she wouldn't have disappeared for over a week unless she was in real trouble.

I stuffed her picture back into the plastic bag and rose, so upset that I barely registered what Mrs. Paulson was saying.

"…can't let you go back out in that, dear. Wait here until the rain stops."

I blinked in surprise at her unexpected kindness. Every other proprietor had been anxious for me to leave once they knew why I was there, as if losing a family member could somehow be contagious. My eyes stung with a sudden rush of tears. Maybe it was. My parents' funeral was the day after tomorrow.

"Thank you, but I can't," I said, voice husky from emotions I couldn't let myself feel yet. The shock helped with that. Ten days ago, my biggest concern had been making a bad impression on my Comparative Revolutions professor after my text message alerts kept going off in his class. Then I read Jasmine's texts, and everything had changed.

Mrs. Paulson gave me another sympathetic smile. "At least let me make you a hot cup of tea—"

A dark, hazy double image suddenly appeared over the reception lounge, making it look as though it had aged over a hundred years in an instant. I stifled a groan. Not *this* again.

The pricey antiques vanished, replaced by broken-down furniture or nothing at all. The temperature also plummeted, making me shiver before movement in the hallway caught my eye.

A blonde girl walked past the decrepit-looking reception lounge. Her face was smudged with dirt and she was bundled up in a tattered blanket, but I didn't need a second glance to recognize her.

"Jasmine," I whispered.

Mrs. Paulson came around the desk and grabbed me, coiling shadows suddenly darting across her face as if she had snakes trapped beneath her flesh. Jasmine continued to walk by as if she wasn't aware that we were there. If not for the innkeeper's surprisingly strong grip, I could have reached out and touched my sister.

"Wait!" I cried out.

The house blinked back into elegant furnishings and warm, cozy temperatures. Just as quickly, Jasmine disappeared. Mrs. Paulson still held me in a tight grip, although the shadows on her face had vanished. I finally managed to shove her away, heading down the hallway where I'd glimpsed my sister.

Before I made it three steps, pain exploded in the back of my head. It must've briefly knocked me out, because the next thing I knew, I was on my knees and Mrs. Paulson was about to hit me with a heavy picture frame again.

Get out! The single, emphatic thought was all my mind was capable of producing. My body must've agreed. I don't know how, but I was suddenly outside and slamming the door shut on my Cherokee. Then I sped away, wondering what had made Mrs. Paulson turn from a kindly old lady into a skull-smashing maniac.

I drove back to my hotel as though on autopilot. After I parked, I sat in the car with the engine off, trying to fight back nausea while I figured out my next move. I could call 911, but I didn't want to admit that I'd had another weird hallucination right before Mrs. Paulson attacked me. If I told anyone *that,* I'd be signing up for a stay in a padded room. Again. Second, the cops in Bennington already didn't like me. As soon as I'd arrived this morning, I'd bitched them out for not doing enough to find Jasmine. They'd probably take Mrs. Paulson's side and assume I'd done something to provoke her.

I paused. Had I? I didn't remember getting away from Mrs. Paulson. What if I'd done something else I didn't remember? Maybe something that had scared her so much, she'd hit me in self-defense? The idea that I might be having blackouts in addition to hallucinations soured my already bleak mood. I got out of the car and went to my hotel room. Once inside, I dropped my purse as though it were a fifty-pound anchor, then flicked on the light.

Everything in me stiffened. The couch should've been empty, but a guy with hair the color of dark honey sat there, his large frame taking up most of the space. Strong brows, a straight nose, high cheekbones and a sensual mouth made up a face that was striking enough to adorn billboards. He didn't look startled by my appearance, either. In fact, if I didn't know better, I'd swear he'd been expecting me.

Gorgeous guys do not spend their evenings waiting around for me. That's why I thought he was another hallucination until he spoke. My hallucinations had never spoken to me before.

"Hi," the stranger said, his deep voice tinged with an accent I couldn't place. "Sorry to tell you, but you're about to have a really bad night."

I knew I should turn around, open the door and run, preferably while screaming. That was the only logical response, but I stood there, somehow unafraid of my intruder. Great. My survival instincts must've secretly made a suicide pact.

"If you knew the week I'd had, you'd realize that whatever you had planned could only make it better," I heard myself reply, proving my vocal cords were in on the death wish.

Then again, I wasn't wrong. My sister? Missing without a trace after texting me help and trapped! last Monday. Parents? Died in a car accident two days after they arrived in Bennington trying to retrace Jasmine's steps. Me? In addition to losing my whole family, I'd nearly gotten my head bashed in. By comparison, being robbed sounded like a vacation.

A grin cocked the side of my intruder's mouth. Whatever response he'd been expecting, it hadn't been that.

"If I win? Probably. If I lose, things are about to get much, much worse," he assured me.

"What's the contest?" I asked, wondering why I was having a conversation with my intruder. Brain damage from the head wound?

He rose. Despite my baffling lack of fear, I flinched as he came nearer. He had to be a foot taller than my five-six height, with shoulders that would fill a door frame and muscles no bulky overcoat could hide. The only thing more striking was his eyes: a deep blue rimmed with gray so light, it almost gleamed.

"The contest is to see who walks out of here with you," he replied, that silver-and-sapphire gaze sliding over me.

"What if I don't want to go anywhere?" I countered.

"It's too late for that," he said softly, reaching out and drawing my attention to the fact that he wore leather gloves.

I darted away. For some reason, I still wasn't consumed with terror—wake up, survival instincts!—but I wasn't about to let him grab me. He didn't try to stop me as I ran past him into the bedroom. Then again, I realized with an inner groan, why would he? Now he stood between me and the room's only door.

He came toward me, and my heart started to hammer. Why hadn't I left when I had the chance? And *why* wasn't I screaming for help right now?

Three hard raps on the door startled me. Then I couldn't believe it when I recognized the voice.

"Miss Jenkins, could you let me in? It's Detective Kroger. We met this morning at the police station."

A cop when I needed one? Miracles *did* happen!

To my shock, my intruder turned around and opened the door. The two men stared at each other, and though the intruder had his back to me, I saw Detective Kroger size him up.

"He broke into my room," I said, making a "do something" gesture.

Kroger's brow went up. "Is that so, mister?"

"Guess you'd better take me in," my intruder drawled.

I expected Kroger to reach for his handcuffs. Instead, he came inside, shut the door, and turned off the lights.

"What are you doing?" I gasped.

"Move over to the couch," Kroger said, and I didn't know if he was talking to me or my enigmatic intruder.

I wasn't going to remain in the dark to find out. I felt around the bedroom until I reached the nightstand, then turned on the lamp. Light flooded the room, showing that my intruder was still in the mini lounge area with Kroger. In fact, it didn't look like either man had moved an inch. What was going on?

"Why aren't you arresting me, Detective?" the intruder asked in his silky, accented voice.

"Good question," I added.

"Shut up, bitch," Kroger said harshly.

My jaw dropped. Before I could respond, Kroger's fist shot out, punching the bigger man in the shoulder. Then he frowned, as if surprised that it had no effect. The intruder caught Kroger's fist when he swung at him again.

Kroger stared, disbelief creasing his features as he tried to yank free and couldn't. Then, understanding seemed to dawn.

"You must be Adrian," Kroger spat.

"In the flesh," my intruder responded lightly.

I was about to ask what the hell was going on when shots rang out. I dropped down right as one of the men hurtled toward me, too fast to see who. I managed to leap away without getting flattened, though I took out the nightstand in my wild lunge.

The room went dark as the lamp broke. My heart pounded at the instant blindness. I hadn't been afraid before, but I was now, trapped in a room with two men who clearly wanted to kill each other. I began to feel my way around the bed again, and this time, stumbled on something big. That something grabbed me, and I freaked out, kicking, punching and clawing to get free.

Then I was yanked away and shoved viciously into the wall. Pain exploded over me, and when I swallowed, I tasted blood. I started to fall, dazed, when a rough grip hauled me up.

A beam of moonlight landed on my attacker's face, and I recoiled. Shadows flickered like snake tongues across Kroger's skin, turning his features into a sickening mask of evil. Worse, I knew I wasn't hallucinating. The pain I felt was too real.

"You want to know what happened to your sister?" Kroger's voice was harsh. Guttural. "You're about to find out."

Without thinking, I punched him as hard as I could. He looked surprised, but the blow didn't even make him flinch.

Suddenly, he was snatched backward and then flung straight up. As Kroger fell back down, Adrian kicked him hard enough to send him crashing through the bedroom window. Before I could even scream, Adrian leaped after him. Then all I heard were thumping noises and groans before a distinct snapping sound made something primal tense inside me.

One of them had just died, I knew it. But which one? A dark form rose in the gaping hole where the window had been. I began to back away, every movement painful, when I saw something silvery gleam in the moonlight.

Adrian's eyes.

"Looks like you're coming with me after all," he said while vaulting through the window.

I wasn't bothered by his casual tone or the fact that he'd just killed someone. I was too busy trying to absorb what I'd seen on Detective Kroger's face, let alone what he'd said.

You want to know what happened to your sister? You're about to find out.

Hope clawed through my reeling emotions. If the snakelike shadows on Kroger's face were real, then maybe so was my vision of Jasmine at the bed-and-breakfast!

"We need to…get Jasmine," I managed to gasp, feeling something wet where I clutched my abdomen.

Adrian pried my hands away and sighed.

"You're hurt. Sorry, he was one of Demetrius's dogs, so he was harder to kill."

He picked me up. Despite Adrian's touch being far gentler than Kroger's, I couldn't stop my pained moan.

"Don't worry, you'll be better soon," he said, carrying me toward the door.

We need to get Jasmine! I wanted to insist, but my tongue seemed to have gone on strike. The tingling in my limbs and buzzing in my ears probably wasn't a good sign, either.

"What's your name, anyway?" I heard Adrian ask, his voice now sounding very far away.

I managed one word before everything went dark.

"Ivy."

CHAPTER TWO

A FAMILIAR SONG was playing, but I couldn't remember the name. That bugged me enough to open my eyes. A wall of black met my gaze, slick and smooth like glass. I reached up to see what it was, and that's when I realized my hands were tied.

"Silent Lucidity" by Queensryche, my mind supplied, followed immediately by, *I'm in the backseat of a car.* One that was well taken care of, going by that flawless, shiny roof. With those details filled in, I also remembered what had happened right before I'd passed out. And who I was with.

"Why are my hands tied?" I said, heaving myself into an upright position.

For some reason Adrian didn't have a rearview mirror, which was why he had to glance over his shoulder to look at me.

"Does anything make you panic?" he asked, sounding amused. "You're tied up in the backseat of a cop-killer's car, but I've seen people get more upset when Starbucks runs out of Pumpkin Spice flavor."

Anyone normal would panic, not that it would do any good. Besides, I ran out of "normal" a long time ago, when I realized I saw things no one else did.

Speaking of which, why wasn't I in pain? The lump where Mrs. Paulson had whacked me was gone, and my shirt was red from blood, but aside from a mild kink in my neck, I felt fine. When I pushed my shirt up, some-how I wasn't surprised to see smooth, unbroken skin on my abdomen. Well, that and a bunch of crumbs, like I'd eaten a dessert too messily.

"Why does it look like I have angel food cake on my stomach?" I wondered aloud.

Adrian snorted. "Close. It's medicine. You were in-jured."

"You can tell me how I'm not anymore," I said, hold-ing out my bound hands, "after you untie me."

Another backward glance, this one challenging.

"You may be the calmest person I've ever been sent to retrieve, but if I tell you now what you want to know, that will change. So pick—the truth, or being untied?"

"Truth," I said instantly.

He let out a laugh. "Another first. You're full of sur-prises."

So was he. He'd just admitted that he regularly kidnapped people—which was how I translated "re-trieve"—so I should be trying my damnedest to get free. But more than anything, I needed answers. Besides, I still wasn't afraid of him, and somehow, that had noth-ing to do with him magically healing me.

"Truth, Adrian," I repeated.

He turned once again and his gaze locked with mine, those odd blue eyes startling me with their intensity. For a moment, I could only stare, all thought frozen in my mind. I don't know why I reached out, awkwardly touching his arm to feel the hard muscles beneath that bulky jacket. If I'd thought about it, I wouldn't have done it. Yet I couldn't make myself pull away.

Then I gasped when his hand covered mine. At some point, he'd taken off his gloves, and the feel of his warm, bare skin sent a shock wave through me. The touch seemed to affect Adrian, too. His lips parted and he edged over the back of the seats—

He yanked on the steering wheel, narrowly avoiding another car. A horn blared, and when the driver passed us, an extended middle finger shook angrily in our direction. I leaned back, my heart pounding from the near collision. At least, that's what I told myself it was from.

"Dyate," Adrian muttered.

I didn't recognize the word, and I was at a loss to place his accent. It had a musical cadence like Italian, but beneath that was a harsher, darker edge.

"What's that language?" I asked, trying to mask the sudden shakiness in my voice.

This time, he didn't take his eyes off the road. "Nothing you've heard of."

"I picked truth, remember?" I said, holding up my bound hands for emphasis.

That earned me a quick glance. "That is the truth, but you don't get more until you meet Zach. Then we can skip all the 'this isn't possible' arguments."

I let out a short laugh. "After what I saw on Detective Kroger's face, my definition of 'impossible' has changed."

Adrian swerved again, but this time, no other car was near.

"What did you see?"

I tensed. How did I explain without sounding insane? No way to, so I chose to go on the attack instead.

"Why were you in my hotel room? And how did you heal me? There isn't even a mark—"

"What did you see on his *face,* Ivy?"

Despite his hard tone, when my name crossed his lips, something thrummed inside me, like he'd yanked on a tie I hadn't known was there. Feeling it was as disturbing as my inexplicable reaction to his clasping my hands.

"Shadows," I said quickly, to distract from that. "He had snakelike shadows all over his face."

I expected Adrian to tell me I'd imagined it, a response I was used to hearing. Instead, he pulled over, putting the car in park but keeping the engine running. Then he turned to stare at me.

"Was that the only strange thing you saw?"

I swallowed. I knew better than to talk about these things. Still, I'd demanded the truth from Adrian. It didn't seem fair to lie in return.

"I saw two versions of the same B and B earlier. One was pretty, but the other was old and rotted, and my sister was trapped inside it."

Adrian said nothing, though he continued to pin me with that hard stare. When he finally spoke, his question was so bizarre I thought I'd misheard him.

"What do I look like to you?"

"Huh?"

"My appearance." He drew out the words like I was slow. "Describe me."

All of a sudden, he wanted compliments? I might have finally met someone crazier than me.

"This is ridiculous," I muttered, but started with the obvious. "Six-six, early twenties, built like Thor, golden brown hair with blond highlights, silvery blue eyes... you want me to go on?"

He began to laugh, a deep, rich baritone that would've been sensual except for how angry it made me.

"Now I know why they came after you," he said, still chuckling. "They must've realized you were different, but if they'd known what you could see, you never would've made it out of that B and B."

"You can stop laughing," I said sharply. "I get that it's crazy to see the things I do."

Lots of kids had imaginary friends growing up. I had imaginary places, though at first, I hadn't known I was the only one who could see them. Once my parents had realized that what I kept describing went far beyond childhood fancy, the endless doctor visits and tests began. One by one, diseases and psychoses had been crossed off until I was diagnosed with a non-monoamine-cholinergic imbalance in my temporal cortex.

In other words, I saw shit that wasn't there for reasons no one could figure out. The pills I took helped a little, though I lied and said they got rid of all my hallucinations. I was sick of doctors poking at me. So whenever I saw something that no one else did, I forced myself to ignore it—until Mrs. Paulson and Detective Kroger had tried to kill me, of course.

Adrian did stop laughing, and that unblinking intensity was back in his gaze.

"Well, Ivy, I've got good news and bad news. The good news is, you're not crazy. The bad news is, everything you've seen is real, and now, it'll be coming for you."

CHAPTER THREE

EVEN ON A GOOD DAY, I hated when guys were cryptic. Those of the Testosterone Persuasion already came with a mountain of senseless tendencies—did they really think they needed to add purposefully vague statements on top of that?

The fact that Adrian refused to elaborate on his enigmatic warning *while I was tied up in his backseat* made it unbearable. As the time ticked on, I consoled myself by imagining hitting him in the head with something heavy. Or leaning over the seat and choking him with the band of duct tape around my wrists. If the back of this vehicle had had a cigarette lighter, I might've gotten creative with fantasies about that, too.

Guess being kidnapped turned me into a violent person.

"Are you a sex slaver?" I asked abruptly.

"Someone's watched *Taken* too many times," Adrian said, and the amusement in his tone grated on my last nerve.

"Why wouldn't I think that?" I shot back. "You saved my life, but you're taking me somewhere against my will, and you refuse to untie me."

"You picked truth, remember?" was his infuriating response.

I swear, the first heavy object I got a hold of...! "You didn't give me *that,* either."

"Yes, I did." He said it with a heavy-lidded, backward glance that would've made me straighten up and smile if he'd done it while we were sitting at a bar. "Just not all of it, but don't worry. We're here."

With that statement, Adrian turned down a long road that led to a set of soaring, elaborately carved gates.

"Wait a sec while I open the gates," he said, turning the car off and taking the keys with him.

I waited…until he was far enough away for me to make my move. Then I leaped over the seats. When I yanked on the driver's side door, however, a large hand on the window prevented it from opening.

"Why am I not surprised?" Adrian said with irony dripping from his tone.

I stared at his hand, as if that could explain how the rest of him was attached to it. A second ago, he'd been in front of those barbarically ornate gates, doing something that caused them to swing open with a mechanical moan.

No one could move that fast. Or, more accurately, no one *should* be able to move that fast.

"What are you?" I breathed.

His teeth flashed in a smile that was predatory and sexy at the same time.

"A couple hours ago, I wondered the same thing about you."

Me? Before I could ask what he meant, he opened the door and let me out. Ice raced through my veins when I saw the knife in his other hand. That was also the moment when I noticed the sign on the gates: Green-Wood Cemetery.

"Don't," I gasped.

He raised a brow, cutting through the duct tape

around my wrists. "You're the one who wanted to be untied."

My arms fell to my sides while relief roared over me, replacing the surge of fear-fueled adrenaline. Just as quickly, something snapped inside me. All the grief, anger, fear and frustration of the past ten days hurtled through my defenses, turning me into someone I didn't recognize.

A rage monster.

My hand cracked across Adrian's face with enough force to make it tingle and burn, and still, it wasn't enough. I began beating on his chest, part of me horrified by my actions, but the rest urging me to hit him harder.

"What is the matter with you?" I yelled. "You pull out a knife with no explanation? I thought you were going to *kill* me!"

Adrian grabbed my hands. Any sane person would have recognized how overmatched I was and calmed the hell down, but I was way past sanity. With my hands out of commission, I kicked his shin hard enough to send pain shooting up my leg. He grunted, backing me up until I was pressed against the car hood. Now I had a wall of steel behind me and a wall of muscled flesh on top of me.

"Stop it," Adrian ordered, his strange accent thicker with his vehemence. "I *promise,* I'm not going to hurt you!"

My breath came in pants. Adrian countered my attempt to drop down and wiggle free by pressing his thigh between my legs. I stopped *that* course of action at once, which was the same as admitting defeat. I couldn't use my arms to push him away. He felt more solid and heavy than a stone gargoyle.

"Get off me," I said between ragged breaths.

"Not until you calm down," he replied sternly. Then the barest grin tugged at his mouth. "Feel free to take your time."

I glanced down, only now registering that my breasts were pressed against his chest just as tightly as his thigh was wedged between my legs. Any movement on my part caused an embarrassingly personal friction, as if inhaling each other's breaths while we panted wasn't intimate enough.

I tried to slow my breathing, not to mention my galloping heartbeat. If not for his grin, I wouldn't have known he thought anything of the compromising position he had me in.

If nothing else, he didn't seem angry that I'd slapped, kicked and pummeled him. Now that my reckless rage had passed, I realized how stupid I'd been. One punch from his massive fist would've meant lights-out, but he hadn't hit back. Instead, he'd promised that he wouldn't hurt me. Despite his kidnapping me and his refusal to give me answers about what was going on, I decided to believe him.

"Sorry I attacked you," I said, my voice no longer shrill.

He shrugged like he was used to it. "Don't worry. You were overdue for a breakdown, anyway."

Just how many people have *you kidnapped?* I almost asked. Since I didn't really want to know, all I said was, "Can you get off me? You're heavy."

He slowly uncurled his body from mine, but that silvery blue gaze stayed glued to me. I shivered, suddenly aware of how cold it was, now that I wasn't covered by over two hundred pounds of warm-blooded male.

Adrian shrugged out of his coat, revealing a crewneck black shirt that hugged his physique like it was paying homage. Of course he'd noticed the shiver. I wondered if anything escaped those piercing eyes.

I put it on. The hem had been midcalf on him; it pooled on the ground with me. I'd never felt dainty around a guy before. I was comfortable at a size eight because I didn't have to starve to maintain it, and my five-six height meant I could usually wear heels without being taller than my dates. Next to Adrian, however, I seemed to drop twenty pounds while also shrinking a few inches. Of course, his bulk was all muscle. Feeling him on top of me had made that clear....

I nixed that line of thought before it led to other, more dangerous musings, and tightened his coat around me.

"If we're not here so you can kill me and bury my body in an empty plot, what else is there to do at a cemetery?" I asked with admirable calm.

He laughed, the deep, masculine rumble teasing something inside me that was too stupid to realize kidnappers were off-limits. That's why I refused to notice the chin dimple it revealed, or how his lower lip was fuller than the top one.

"Lots of things, but we'll get to that later."

"Sure there's going to be a later?" I challenged him.

"Of course." Another tantalizing smile. "Since you and I are from the same line, you'll be seeing a lot more of me."

Line? "You think we're *related*?"

His gaze brushed me like a physical caress. "Not like that, thankfully. That would make our first date awkward."

I stared at him in disbelief. "You're *hitting* on me?" I finally managed. "Do you have any idea how twisted that is?"

He shrugged. "I don't do subtle, it wastes time. Besides—" the silvery part of his eyes gleamed like liquid moonlight "—if you say you don't find me attractive, I'll know you're lying."

Under other circumstances, I might have blushed at being busted ogling someone I'd just met, but my *kidnapper* was hitting on me! Should that make me more afraid, or less? He'd already saved my life once and had had plenty of chances to harm me since, yet he hadn't.

Plus, I wouldn't be much fun as a date if I was dead.

"How about we hold the date talk until you give me the answers you promised?" I said, part of me wondering if tonight could get any stranger. The other part felt happy for the first time in over a week. Stupid ovaries. *Down, girls, down!*

Adrian's expression turned serious. "I'm taking you to the person who can give you those answers."

"Zach?" I asked, remembering Adrian mentioning the name.

"That's him. This cemetery is almost five hundred acres, so if you don't want to spend hours walking around in the cold—" he went over to the passenger side of the vintage-looking muscle car and opened the door "—get in."

He was giving me a choice. Or at least, the illusion of one. If I ran, we both knew he could catch me.

The car's interior light showed a hint of stubble trying to break through the smooth skin along his jaw, shadowing it in a way that was far too attractive. His exotic accent wasn't helping, either. If I was ever kidnapped again, it had better be by an old, ugly guy. That would be less confusing to my emotions.

And less embarrassing. What idiot got caught lusting

over her kidnapper? No wonder he'd asked me out. He must have thought I gave "easy" a whole new definition.

I walked over, thinking that even if I could run away from him, I wouldn't. My sister was trapped in a place that shouldn't be real, yet somehow was, and Adrian was my only ally because he could see the same crazy things that I did. More importantly, Adrian had proven that he was able to kill those things.

If he was able to help me save my sister, I'd not only take him up on his date offer. I'd pay for everything and seriously consider putting out.

I got in the passenger side, hearing the door lock as soon as he shut it. I tried to open it. Nothing. My sense of unease returned. What kind of person saved people just to kidnap them, and had a vehicle you could only exit from the driver's side?

Then again, as Adrian slid into the seat next to me with an almost spooky fluidity, I realized what kind of person he was might be less important than *what* he was.

CHAPTER FOUR

WHOEVER HAD DESIGNED Green-Wood Cemetery must have done so while puking drunk since it lacked a single straight road. I felt like we were driving through a child's maze game with all the twists and turns. Then again, maybe lots of cemeteries were laid out like this. I wouldn't know. I'd never been in one before. My parents' funeral wasn't until the day after tomorrow, both sets of my grandparents had died before my birth, and neither of my parents had siblings or cousins. Until ten days ago, I hadn't lost anyone close to me.

Now, I'd lost everyone, and while I buried my grief with the same determination I'd used to ignore seeing impossible things, it wasn't enough. When Adrian drove by a large tomb engraved "Beloved Parents," the ache that had burned in my throat since their deaths grew into an impassable boulder.

Adrian stopped the car at the same time that I suddenly found it difficult to breathe.

"What's wrong?" he asked urgently. "You see something?"

I shook my head, managing to draw in a breath despite that awful squeezing in my throat.

"Ivy." A large hand cupped my face, forcing me to look at him instead of the headstone. "What is it?"

Right then, I was glad that Adrian was so hot. Thank

God for the deep hollows under his cheekbones, those sapphire eyes, and the blondish-brown hair that looked like it had been tousled from too much sex. If I hadn't had his looks to distract me, I might've had to focus on how bad it hurt to lose two people who'd never let me down, even when I'd been a stranger to them.

"It's just…my parents died five days ago."

My voice was husky from the emotions I kept trying to shove back, but the strangling tightness had eased. Another few deep breaths, and all that was left was a familiar burn.

"I'm sorry," Adrian said, taking my hand and squeezing it.

I'd heard those words from friends and fellow students a lot in the past week, often with an added cliché about all things happening for a reason. Adrian didn't say any of that crap. He just kept holding my hand while looking at me with an understanding that transcended compassion, as if he knew what it was like to lose everything within a brutally short amount of time.

"Thanks." I drew in another breath, blinking away the tears. Crying felt like giving up, and I wasn't doing that because I needed to find a way to bring my sister back home. "That's why I need answers, because I'm not about to lose my sister forever, too."

He let go of my hand and looked away, his jaw tightening. "Answers don't mean miracles. I heard what that cop said to you. If they have your sister, I'm sorry, but she's as good as dead."

"Bullshit," I snapped, instantly angry. "I know where she is. I just need a…way in."

Adrian sighed. "You see things no one else does, yet you're still in denial, aren't you? The creatures that have your sister are too strong, Ivy. Even if you got in, you'd never get out."

Creatures? Before I could respond, something flashed ahead, as if a spotlight had briefly turned on. Adrian began driving toward it. A few minutes later, we pulled up to what looked like a tiny castle, with circular turrets on the four corners and a tall, windowed dome blooming out of the center.

Adrian parked, going around to my side to let me out. "Welcome to Green-Wood Chapel."

The door was ajar, soft light emanating from within. Adrian entered and I followed, hugging his coat around me as though it were a protective shield. I was so disturbed by what he said that the equally ornate interior was lost on me. He must've meant "creatures" in a metaphorical way, my logic argued.

A young African-American man stood at the end of the pews, his face partially concealed by the blue hoodie hanging over his bent head. I would've thought he was praying except that he faced us, not the altar, and his hands were at his sides instead of folded in the universal gesture for piety.

"Ivy, this is Zach," Adrian said. "Zach, meet Ivy, the girl you sent me to rescue."

Zach looked up, his hoodie fell back, and—

Light exploded around him like thousands of camera flashes. My eyes burned, unable to adjust to the blinding intensity, and yet I couldn't close them. I stared, stunned, as the glow around him became even brighter, until I saw nothing except Zach. A multitude of voices roared through my mind, deafening me to everything except their beauteous, painful crescendo. My body vibrated, caught in the thunderous echo, until it felt like my flesh would be shaken right off my bones—

"Don't be afraid."

The church morphed back around me, Adrian standing a few feet away like he'd been before. Zach hadn't moved, either. I had, though. Somehow, I was on my knees, hands raised, my face wet from tears I didn't remember shedding.

"Don't be afraid," Zach repeated, coming toward me.

I staggered to my feet. The lights around him were gone, as was the terrible noise that had made my whole body ache. Right now, Zach looked like half the guys around my campus, but I knew, with every fiber of my being, that he wasn't human. He was something else.

A creature, like Adrian had said.

I kept backing away, but then strong hands settled around my shoulders, gripping me with protective gentleness.

"Don't worry. He's not one of the bad ones," Adrian said softly. "Zach plays for the other team."

"The creatures have teams?" I choked out.

"Yes, they do," Adrian said, a note of grimness coloring his tone. "And both sides play for keeps."

I stared into Zach's walnut-colored eyes, seeing the *otherness* beneath the facade of a twentysomething man with closely cropped hair, thick brows, and smooth, dark skin. I didn't need Adrian to tell me he could rip me limb from limb if he wanted to. An instinctual, animalistic part of me knew that. In fact, I was painfully aware of how easily my bones could shatter, how little my skin protected the vulnerable parts beneath, and how useless my average strength was to defend myself. Fear made me want to edge farther into Adrian's embrace, but I forced myself to stay where I was.

Zach might terrify me, but Adrian said he fought

against the things that had Jasmine. That made him my new best friend.

"I think freaky shadow people kidnapped my sister," I said, proud that my voice wasn't shaking. "So I need to know how to get her back."

"Did I mention she could see beneath demon glamour?" Adrian asked in a wry tone.

My stomach clenched at the word *demon,* but I didn't do anything embarrassing, like puke. Okay, so demons had my sister. Not much different than saying that freaky shadow people had her, right?

I might puke after all.

"Of course she can see through it," Zach replied, as casual as if he were noting that I liked chocolate more than vanilla. "It's in her bloodline."

I was standing so close to Adrian, I felt it when his whole body stiffened. "You knew what she was?"

A faint smile touched Zach's mouth. "I've always known."

"What do you mean, what I am?" I wondered.

Adrian ignored that and strode over to Zach, his height forcing the shorter man to look up in order to meet his eyes.

"You lied to me," Adrian bit out, his finger stabbing Zach in the chest with each word. "You said that I was the last of my line, yet you knew all along about Ivy?"

I couldn't believe Adrian kept jabbing Zach like he was a roast that needed tenderizing. Didn't he sense the blasting power beneath Zach's average-guy disguise?

"She's not a descendant of your line," Zach said, his hand closing over Adrian's with enough strength to hold it immobile. "You *are* the last of that, but she sees past the disguises of this world because she is the last descendant of David's."

"Last of whose?" I began, then stopped, stunned into silence as Adrian turned toward me.

Horror didn't begin to describe the look on his face. Adrian stared at me like I'd crushed his world, ground it up and then forced it down his throat until he died choking on its remains. If my skin had suddenly been replaced by scales oozing poison, I still wouldn't have thought I deserved such a look.

"Last of a line of rulers dating back to ancient times, when King David sat on the throne of Jerusalem," Zach replied.

History was my major in college, but I'd also been a fan of the arts since I was a little girl.

"King David as in the guy from Michelangelo's famous marble statue?" *The naked one?* I mentally added.

"The same," Zach agreed, a slight arch of his brow making me wonder if he'd guessed what I hadn't said out loud.

"Nice story," I said flippantly, "but all anyone knows about my biological parents is that my mother was an illegal immigrant who left me on the side of the road after the tractor trailer she was hiding in jackknifed."

In some ways, I couldn't blame her. All the illegals who'd survived the accident had run, and disappearing in a new country would have been harder with a newborn. The Jenkinses, who'd also been caught in the multicar pileup, had found me, and after a series of court battles, officially adopted me.

Zach shrugged. "Your disbelief doesn't change the truth."

Adrian was suddenly at the back of the church, his silhouette a dark outline against the stained glass panels.

"If you knew she was the last Davidian, how could you send me to get her?" His voice lashed the air like a whip. "How could you let me anywhere *near her,* Zacchaeus?"

Now I knew what *Zach* was short for, but that wasn't why my mouth dropped. "What is your problem?" I sputtered.

Adrian turned away as if he couldn't stand the sight of me. Amidst my disbelief, I felt a sliver of hurt. Why was he acting like I was viler than the cop he'd killed with his bare hands?

"You have to be near her," Zach replied in an implacable voice. "You cannot escape your fate."

At that, Adrian whirled, fists clenched, shoulders rigid and anger roiling from him in palpable waves.

"Fuck my fate," he snarled.

I didn't see him pass me. He moved too fast again. I only knew that he'd left when the chapel door slammed behind me.

CHAPTER FIVE

THE SUN WAS up by the time Zach returned. He'd gone after Adrian, but since he came back without him, that must not have gone well. My mood was pretty foul, too. I'd only waited in the church because I still didn't have the answers I needed. All I knew was that Adrian now hated me, demons existed, and Zach was…well, with the light show he'd given off, I could guess what sort of creature Zach was, but it was too unbelievable to say out loud.

"We're also known as Archons," Zach said, throwing me a sardonic look. "Is that word easier for you to handle?"

Once again, he'd guessed my thoughts, and I was starting to believe it was more than luck. No, I was in the presence of a creature with untold supernatural abilities, and unless I wanted to spend more time crying on my knees, I had to deal with that.

I'd start with the challenge he'd just thrown down.

"It's not my fault that you don't match up with the brochure," I replied flippantly. "You could've paired that hoodie with a harp and a halo, at least."

He smiled, reminding me that every species except humans showed their teeth to convey a threat.

"This mortal shell conceals my true nature. Because you and Adrian are the last of your lines, you see beneath it, but the rest of humanity does not."

I shrugged as though my already-careening world

hadn't been turned upside down within the past several hours.

"Or I'm hallucinating again. I missed taking a couple doses of my meds—"

"Makes no difference, they're placebos," Zach informed me.

I stared at him, my lips parted, but my brain processing too many thoughts to speak.

"That's why your adoptive parents always filled your prescriptions for you," Zach went on, as if each word wasn't blasting apart what was left of my life. "Your psychologist provided the placebos as part of your therapy, but there is nothing medically wrong with you. Your adoptive parents were going to tell you the truth when you turned twenty-one—"

"Liar," I whispered.

A thick brow arched. "Demons lie. My kind does not. If you require proof, take one of your pills to a pharmacist for analysis."

My knees wobbled, but I didn't sit down. If I did, I might not be able to get back up. Zach might be a mind reader, but he couldn't have known that my parents always filled my prescriptions because I hadn't been thinking of that. He also couldn't know something that I didn't—if the pills were really placebos instead of actual meds.

Adrian was right. Despite everything I'd seen, I still hadn't accepted that it could actually be *real*. Now Zach was destroying my denial one revelation at a time.

"Your real mother didn't leave you because she was running from the police," Zach went on pitilessly. "She did it to save you, just as your dream revealed—"

"Stop!" I shouted, my breath now coming in pants. No one knew about that dream. I hadn't told my parents, Jasmine or the countless therapists I'd been to.

How could Zach know, unless he was exactly who—*what*—he claimed to be?

"Enough."

Adrian's voice cracked through the chapel, startling me. I hadn't seen him come back in. I turned toward him, glad for anything that kept me from hearing revelations that were too incredible to be real.

"Don't mind Zach," Adrian said, an edge coloring his tone. "Archons have no tact when it comes to delivering big news."

Zach shrugged. "She asked for the truth. I gave it to her."

Adrian came nearer, his gaze glittering with anger. "Yeah, well, you want me to play this fate thing through? Then from now on, *I* tell Ivy what's what, not you."

My mind still felt like it had been thrown into a blender, but at that, I stiffened.

"Don't talk about me like I'm not even here."

Adrian turned that darkly jeweled gaze my way. "Believe me, Ivy, I know you're here."

The flat way he spoke somehow gave his words more weight, but this time, Adrian no longer looked at me with horror. Instead, he stared at me like I was the most dangerous person he'd ever met, which, all things considered, was ridiculous.

"You want to save your sister?" he asked evenly. "You'll need something strong enough to kill demons."

This was too much, too fast. "Like holy water? Or crosses?" I asked numbly.

His look became pointed. "Those are for vampires, and they don't exist. To take down demons, you need one of three weapons, and the second and third ones will probably kill you."

"Okay, so we skip those," I muttered, part of me

wondering if I was really having a conversation about how to kill demons. Placebos or not, right now, I missed my meds.

"Right," Adrian said, a glint appearing in his eyes. "Problem is, the first weapon is lost somewhere in one of the demon realms."

"Of course it is. Shopping for it on eBay would be too easy."

His lips curled, as if he knew my glibness masked a rising sense of disbelief. "You've already seen one demon realm. They appear as creepy, dark duplicates of the same place, just like that bed-and-breakfast you described."

If that was true, I'd seen others over the years, but they all had the same problem.

"How do we enter one long enough to save Jasmine? After a few seconds, they seem to disappear."

At that, Adrian shot Zach a frustrated look. "If her abilities are so weak that she only sees the other realms for a few seconds, she's nowhere near ready to do this."

I'd be offended if I didn't agree. My athletic skills were limited to occasionally dancing all night, as if *that* was any advantage in a demon fight. Still, ready or not, I didn't have a choice. Jasmine had no one else to come for her.

"I'll do whatever it takes," I said firmly.

The hardness in Adrian's stare made me wonder if I'd regret those words. Then he smiled, wolfish and challenging.

"All right, Ivy. To answer your question, you get into a demon realm the same way you get in anywhere. Through a door."

I WANTED TO start looking for the demon-killing weapon at once, but Zach insisted that we sleep. Due to my exhaustion, I didn't argue until Adrian showed me my "bed." Being in an underground mausoleum was bad enough, but sleeping in one of the tiny rooms that contained a body?

"Hell no," I said.

Adrian rolled his eyes. "What's dead can't hurt you. Living demons can, and they can go anywhere except hallowed ground."

"Then I'll sleep in the church" was my instant response.

"Tourists visit the church," he replied inexorably. "They don't visit the catacombs, so we're sleeping here."

As he spoke, he gestured to another crypt that also had a sleeping bag in it. I looked back at my crypt. A small spider descended from the ceiling and landed right on my sleeping bag.

"I'll just sit in the hallway," I said grimly.

Adrian sighed. "Zach?"

I felt a tap on my shoulder. When I turned around, Zach was behind me. Before I could say anything, he touched my forehead, and like a switch had been flipped, everything went dark.

When I opened my eyes, I was in Adrian's car, my head resting against the cool glass of the passenger window. Lights blurred by, and with mild shock, I saw that it was evening.

"Wh-what happened?" I mumbled, sitting up.

Adrian didn't look away from the road, but his mouth twitched. "Zach compelled you to sleep."

Memory returned with a vengeance. "In a spider-infested crypt?" I began slapping at my clothes. If I saw anything with eight legs, I was launching myself out of this car.

A stronger twitch of his mouth. "Nothing beats an Archon sedative."

"You think this is funny?" I unlocked my seat belt, took off his coat, and threw it into the backseat. With luck, now I wouldn't have things crawling all over me.

That earned me a slanted look. "You want to fight demons, and you're freaking out over spiders. That's *damn* funny."

Put like that, he had a point. "Speaking of, uh, them—" would I ever say *demons* without feeling like I should be in a straitjacket? "—why do we need this special weapon to save my sister? You killed Detective Kroger just fine without it."

"Kroger wasn't a demon, he was a minion. Demons can't tolerate our realm for long, so they take willing humans, mark them, and send them out to do their dirty work. They have their own signature marks, too. The shadows you saw on Kroger meant he belonged to Demetrius. Marks make minions a lot tougher than humans, but compared to their masters, they're easy to kill."

I hardly knew where to begin with my questions. "Our realm? You mean…this?" I asked, waving at the scenery we drove past.

"Yeah, this," he said, the words heavy with emotion. Regret? Resolve? I didn't know him well enough to be sure.

"And we can see demon marks and demon realms because we're the last of King David's line," I said, trying to piece the impossible facts together.

Adrian stiffened, his mouth tightening until white edged his lips. "You are. I'm not."

That's right, Zach had said he was the last of another line. "What are you, then?" I asked softly.

The look Adrian pinned me with seemed to compress me, until every breath I drew felt like a hard-fought victory.

"I'm something else," he bit out.

I was glad when he glanced back at the road. My heart was thumping as if I'd been jogging. Whatever Adrian was, he didn't like it, and if a man who wasn't afraid of demons didn't like what he was, then I should be scared shitless of him.

So why did I have a strong urge to smooth away the hardness in his expression? I swear, my reactions to him made *no* sense. I never went for the tortured bad boy because I had enough issues of my own. On top of that, Adrian had made it clear that, given his choice, he'd be nowhere near me. Whatever strange pull I felt toward him, I had to get rid of it. Fast.

"Where are we headed?" I asked in a neutral tone.

"Gold Hill, Oregon," he replied, his voice equally emotionless.

All the way across the country? "What's in Oregon that makes it so special?"

His grunt sounded grimly amused. "A door to multiple demon realms."

CHAPTER SIX

I LEARNED A few things over the next twenty hours. Not about demons or the mysterious weapon—Adrian refused to talk about those—but about him. Like, for example, his pathological hatred of mirrors.

Every time we stopped to refuel, Adrian would smash the mirror in the ladies' room before he let me inside to pee. I was convinced he'd be arrested, but I soon found out another fact: no one but me could see what Adrian really looked like.

"He's five-eight, skinny, with black hair," the gas station attendant snapped into his phone, his Spanish accent thickening as he yelled, *"Pendajo!"* at Adrian for destroying his bathroom mirror. "And he's driving…*a mi Dios!*"

That last part was screamed when Adrian moved with his incredible speed, yanking away the shotgun the attendant had pulled out. Then he broke it over his knee and handed the two pieces back with a growled, "Have a nice day."

"Diablo," the attendant moaned, sinking behind his counter.

I didn't think Adrian was a devil, but I still didn't know what he was. The fastest way to get the silent treatment from him was to ask again what "line" he was from. He did explain that Archon glamour masked his appearance, so he wouldn't be recognized by minions.

Now I knew why Detective Kroger's first punch had hit Adrian in the shoulder. He thought he'd been striking a much shorter opponent. That was also why Adrian had demanded that I describe him soon after we met.

"You could see through demon glamour," he'd explained, throwing me one of those hooded looks. "Minions can do that, too, but only humans from one of our lines can see through Archon glamour, so I needed to find out what you were."

"What if I'd failed to describe you accurately?" I'd asked.

A shrug. "Then you'd have been a minion, and I'd have killed you."

Between that admission, the compulsive mirror smashing and his impenetrable secretiveness, I was well on my way to getting over my attraction. Adrian wasn't just damaged goods, he was *deranged* goods, and coming from someone with a history of psychosis, that was saying something. By the time we pulled into a motel at the halfway point of Kearney, Nebraska, I would've been happy never to see him again.

I called shotgun on the bathroom as soon as we entered the hotel room. Adrian obliged after smashing the mirror—he had to have ten thousand years of bad luck by now—then finally, I was able to take a shower. Thank God the motel had complimentary bottles of shampoo and conditioner because I wasn't about to ask Adrian for any. For all I knew, the bulky duffel bag he'd brought in was filled with severed minion heads.

After I showered, I washed my clothes, making a mental note to insist that we shop before hitting the road tomorrow. With everything I owned now hanging to dry, I donned Adrian's coat over my towel before leaving the bathroom.

He stood in front of the motel door, flicking something from a glass vial onto it. He did the same with the window, all while muttering in that strange, harshly lyrical language.

He probably wouldn't tell me, but I asked anyway. "What are you doing?"

"Setting supernatural locks," he replied, with a jaded glance at me. "This motel isn't on hallowed ground, so we have to demon-proof this room. I don't think we were followed, but I'd rather you weren't murdered in your sleep."

I swallowed. I'd rather that not happen, too. "So, that stuff you're sprinkling around is like demon-mace?"

His mouth twitched, making me wonder if he fought back a smile. "Close. Know how a priest blesses water and then it's considered holy? This is the Archon version of blessed oil, which briefly renders any place it touches as hallowed."

"How brief is 'briefly'?" I wondered.

A shrug. "Long enough for us to sleep."

"If it hallows out any place, then *why* did we spend last night in a spider-infested crypt?" I asked at once.

Now I was sure he was fighting back a smile. "You looked like you slept there just fine to me." At my instant glower, he added, "I can only get this stuff from Zach, and he's stingy with handing it out. This is the last I've got, so after tonight, we'll need to sleep on real hallowed ground until he decides to show up and give me more."

A stingy angel. Now I'd heard of everything. Guess I'd better enjoy the real bed tonight. Who knew what I'd be cuddling up next to tomorrow. Speaking of that, I needed to handle some things before I went off the grid any longer.

"You have a phone I can use? I need to call my room-mate, Delia. Tell her I'll be gone for…a while."

Adrian's expression changed from suppressed amusement to stern refusal. "Not a chance. No calls, texts or emails."

Who did he think he was, my new father? "Let me rephrase—I'm *calling* my roommate, either with your phone or with someone else's."

I couldn't just disappear on Delia. I, of all people, knew how awful it was to wonder if someone you cared about was alive or dead, and she wasn't just my room-mate. After Jasmine, Delia was my best friend.

"You call her or anyone else you know, you're mak-ing them a target," Adrian replied coolly. "Not many people escape a demonic kidnapping attempt. The ones that do are usually helped by me, so that makes the de-mons extra mad. By now, minions have combed through every aspect of your life, and they're waiting for you to connect to someone so they can use that person against you."

Nothing changed in the room, but it suddenly felt smaller, as if the walls were edging toward each other.

"What's the point? They already have my sister," I said, anger and despair sharpening my tone.

Adrian leveled that gemstone stare at me. "Right, so don't give them anyone else."

I sat down on what I guessed was my bed, since Adrian's duffel bag was on the other. The zipper was open, revealing nothing more sinister than clothes and toiletries. And here I'd been so sure about the severed minion heads. I did give the toothbrush a longing look. This motel didn't have those as freebies, and my breath could probably slay a dragon.

"Help yourself," Adrian stated, nodding at the bag. "Zach packed supplies for both of us."

He didn't need to tell me twice. I went to his bed and began to rummage through the bag. Thanks to his large build, it wasn't hard to distinguish what was meant for Adrian and what was intended for me. The only surprise was that Zach had guessed my size, even on the intimate items.

"What kind of angel notices cup size?" I muttered under my breath as I added a bra to my pile.

Adrian's bark of laughter let me know that I'd said it too loud. "Zach is nothing if not detail-oriented."

"You sound like you've known him a long time," I observed.

His face closed off in a now familiar way. I could let it go, like I had most of the drive here, but I was getting tired of his frequent bouts of silent treatment.

"I get that you don't want to be here and you *really* don't want to talk about whatever it is that you are, but if we're going to be fighting demons together, I should at least know more about you."

Adrian walked toward me, a hard little smile twisting his features. Then he bent down until his face was level with mine. His eyes looked even more vivid in the overhead light, and he was so close, I could see that his lashes were dark brown instead of black.

"Here's the most important thing you need to know. I hate demons more than you do, so you can trust that I'll help you kill them. But, Ivy—" harsh laughter brushed my skin in its own caress "—whatever you do, don't trust me with anything else."

The last time we'd been this close, he'd had me pinned to his car. He wasn't touching me now, but somehow, his gaze made the moment equally intense. The scary part was, I liked it. Without thinking, I moistened my lips.

His gaze dropped there, and I sucked in a breath at the hunger that flashed across his face. So finding out about my supposed lineage *hadn't* killed his attraction to me! With that knowledge, things lower down began to tighten. Adrian was maddening, confusing, dangerous…and what would I do if he tried to kiss me?

Suddenly, I saw a blur of motion and then he was gone, the door vibrating from his exit.

I AWOKE TO the wonderful smell of hot, greasy food, and the even more tantalizing aroma of coffee. When I opened my eyes, a bag of McDonald's was on my nightstand. I hadn't heard Adrian leave to get it, but then again, I hadn't heard him come back last night, either. He must have since his bed was mussed, and from the sounds of it, he was now in the shower.

I fell on the food like a starving animal. A candy bar and a small bag of peanuts had been all I'd eaten over the past two days. Getting yelled at by multiple gas station attendants after Adrian broke their mirrors hadn't made me want to browse for more substantial fare. After I finished, I quickly put on new clothes, not wanting Adrian to come out while I was half-naked. Things were strange enough between us already.

My necklace snagged on my sweater as I yanked it over my head, reminding me there was one mirror Adrian hadn't smashed yet. Since the shower was still running, I opened the locket, a pang hitting me when I saw my sister's picture on one side and a small mirror on the other.

This way, we'll always be together, Jasmine had said when she'd given it to me the night before I left for college. She'd cried a little then, and I never admitted it, but when I was alone in my room that night, I did, too. Sure, we fought like mad sometimes, but no one was closer to me than Jasmine. With everyone else, I had to keep faking so they'd believe everything was fine. For my parents, it was so they wouldn't worry about me. For my psychologist, it was to avoid more tests or inpatient stays. For my friends and the occasional boyfriend, it was so I wouldn't have to explain things they probably didn't want to understand. With Jaz, I could be myself because whoever that was, she was okay with it.

"Nuts, normal, doesn't matter," she'd said years ago when I was upset after my psychologist told me I might never be cured. "You're my sister, Ives, so no matter what, we're stuck with each other."

As I stared at her picture next to my own reflection, her loss hit me all over again. It took everything I had to hold the tears back. After several hard blinks, her image became less blurry. As I looked at her, I silently made her a promise. *No matter what, I will find you.* She'd never given up on me. I sure as hell wouldn't give up on her.

Vow made, I could look at her picture without tearing up again. We didn't resemble each other, of course. Jasmine was a blue-eyed blonde like my adoptive parents, and I had hazel eyes and brown hair. My greenish-brown eyes, light skin tone and other markers had caused my pediatrician to speculate that one of my parents had been Caucasian. We guessed the other was Hispanic because that was the nationality of the immigrants who'd been unable to flee the tractor-trailer accident, but who knew?

Thinking about my biological parents made Zach's words steal through my mind, though I'd done my best to forget them. *Your real mother didn't leave you because she was running from the police...she did it to save you, just as your dreams revealed...*

"Good, you're up."

Adrian's curt voice made me jump. I snapped the locket shut, glad my back was to him so he couldn't see what I tucked under my sweater. He was *not* smashing the last gift my sister gave to me, mirror phobia or not. With the locket safely hidden, I turned around.

"Thanks for...breakfast."

I couldn't help my pause. Some things should come with a warning label, and seeing Adrian stalk through the room wearing only a towel was definitely one of them. I hadn't known ab definition like that existed without airbrushing, and the network of muscles on his arms, back and chest rippled as though dancing to a song that reverberated beneath his flesh.

Michelangelo had it wrong, I thought, tearing my gaze away. With that body, Adrian was the one who needed a marble statue made in his image. Good thing he was so fixated on shoving his things into his duffel bag, he didn't notice my admiration.

"We're leaving in ten minutes," he stated, still in that brusque tone.

After he'd stormed out last night, I told myself it didn't matter if Adrian was still attracted to me. I needed to rescue my sister, not start something with a guy who'd warned me he wasn't trustworthy, let alone all the other reasons why Adrian was off-limits. No matter the dazzling packaging, he was six feet six inches of undetermined supernatural bad news, so his coldness now suited my purposes.

His barked orders, however, didn't. We needed to get a few things straight before we went any further.

"Just because you're pissed about our little road trip doesn't mean you get to keep taking it out on me," I said. "For whatever reason, you chose to come, and we don't need to be friends, but you do need to quit acting like my boss. So we're not leaving in ten minutes, Adrian. We're leaving in twenty because I'm taking a shower, too."

He swung around, arms crossing over that muscled chest in obvious annoyance. I continued on as if I didn't notice.

"It's not my fault if you've never had a serious girlfriend, but believe me when I tell you that it's impossible for a girl to get ready in less than twenty minutes."

"Fine," he said, his tone only slightly less rude.

"You may want to wait until I'm in the bathroom to get dressed, too," I said airily. "If you drop that towel now, I'll think it's your way of telling me you still want that date."

I didn't wait for his response before disappearing into the bathroom. All jokes aside, if he *did* drop that towel, I might forget all the many reasons why I should stay away from him.

CHAPTER SEVEN

TWENTY MINUTES LATER—OKAY, twenty-five, but close enough—we climbed into his car. I wasn't much for old muscle cars, but I had to admit that his Challenger was in great shape. Still, I'd kill for a satellite radio. This only had AM and FM.

"You don't need to drive the whole way. We can take turns," I offered.

"No," he replied at once.

"So you're one of those," I muttered.

His brow went up. "One of what?"

"Guys who think a girl can't handle their precious metal babies," I said, rolling my eyes.

At that, he laughed. "I rebuilt this car from the axle up, so yeah, you can call it my baby. But no one, male *or* female, drives it except me."

"So you're an equal-opportunity control freak?" I replied without missing a beat.

"You have no idea," he said, voice lowering while his blue eyes slid over me in a phantom caress.

My breath caught. Until that moment, I hadn't realized he'd avoided looking at me since he stormed out last night. Now, his gaze moved over me as if he already knew which parts to touch first and which parts to leave until I was breathless and begging. My heart began to beat faster. How could he affect me so much when we barely knew each other?

Then, like a switch had been flipped, he looked away as though the sight of me had burned his eyes. His whole demeanor changed, too, as if he were angry for revealing something that was supposed to remain hidden.

"When should we arrive in Oregon?" I asked, needing something, anything, to break up the tense moment.

He revved up the car and glanced at the clock. "Three a.m., if we don't get caught in traffic."

Nineteen hours until I crossed into one of the places that countless doctors had sworn were merely figments of my imbalanced mind. Once again, I had so many questions, I hardly knew where to begin.

"Have you been to this particular 'realm door' before?"

"Yes."

One tightly spoken word that warned me to drop the subject, if I didn't want another round of the silent treatment. I stifled a frustrated sigh. I needed more information, and he was moodier than a tween girl with her first PMS attack.

"How did you know minions were trying to kidnap me the other night?" There. Total change of subject, and something I'd been wondering about, anyway.

Adrian didn't look at me as he pulled out onto the road. "Zach told me. He's the one who sent me to retrieve you."

I'd have to drag everything out of him, wouldn't I? "Okay, how did Zach know?"

He grunted. "Archons get information about future events. Every so often, they interfere to change the outcome."

"Every so often?" I repeated with angry disbelief, thinking of Jasmine's kidnapping and my parents' deaths. "Why not every time? Or do Archons have days where they're just not in the *mood* to save people from harm and death?"

Nothing changed in his expression, but his tone hardened with what I thought might be remembered pain. "That's the million-dollar question, isn't it? I don't have an answer, and when I asked Zach the same thing, all he said was something about 'orders.'"

"That's such bullshit," I muttered.

"I couldn't agree more," Adrian said dryly.

Neither of us spoke for a few minutes. Not strained silence like before, but silent, shared reflection while both of us thought of things that we wished had turned out different.

"So that's what you do?" I finally said. "Rescue people for Zach after he tells you that minions are after them?"

He shrugged. "Gives me a chance to piss off demons."

"Most people would *avoid* doing that," I pointed out, suppressing a shudder. If not for Jasmine, you wouldn't catch me near a demon, minion, realm or anything freakily supernatural. Why did Adrian run toward the danger instead?

"You and I aren't most people, Ivy," he said softly. "Because of what we see, we don't get to pretend the world is a beautiful place where monsters don't exist."

I was the one who looked away that time, unable to handle the truth of his statement or the intensity in his stare. Until a few days ago, I *had* been doing that. Even as a child, as soon as I'd realized no one else saw the things I did, I'd wanted it to stop. I hated feeling like something was wrong with me, so after I'd jumped through almost a decade of medical hoops looking for a cure, I started pretending that I'd found one.

I told my parents, the doctors and even eventually Jasmine that I no longer saw the strange, dark worlds hanging like nightmares over regular places. I certainly never told Delia or my other friends about them. I said the pills I took were for a hormonal imbalance, and all my doctor appointments were for that, too.

Lies, lies, lies, all because I wanted to pretend I was normal. According to the gorgeous stranger across from me, I wasn't then and never would be.

"What happened with you?" I asked, my voice low as if we were sharing secrets. "I hid from what I saw, but you started hunting down the things everyone told me couldn't exist. You must've had proof that they were real, so what was it?"

He closed off so fast I was surprised I didn't hear a sonic boom. I shut my eyes, letting out a sigh as I tried to settle myself more comfortably into my seat. Looked like the question-and-answer segment of our time was over.

Eventually, as afternoon slid into evening during the long drive, the late hour and boredom lulled me into drifting off.

A thunderous boom woke the black-haired woman. Her baby began to wail at the multiple crashing noises. She left the baby in the backseat, walking through the brush that hid her car.

On the nearby highway, a tractor-trailer was on its side, multiple cars piled up around it. Each passing second brought a new screech of tires and, more faintly, screams. Then the back of the trailer opened, and people stumbled out, some disappearing into the tall grass

*that lined the road, others limping a few feet before col-
lapsing onto the road.*

*The black-haired woman hurried back to her car,
but as she began to strap her baby in the car seat, she
paused. Then she turned around and stared. Sunlight
broke through the clouds, streaming down to the side
of the road about fifty yards from the accident. The
woman began to shake.*

"No. No, I can't leave her," she whispered.

*The light grew brighter, and another sunbeam ap-
peared, illuminating the same spot. Tears streamed
down her face, but after a minute, she picked up her
child and walked toward it.*

*"Promise me she'll be safe," she choked out, setting
the baby in the grass. Then she kissed the child, whispering, "Mommy loves you. Always," before running
to her car and driving away—*

"What is that?"

Adrian's voice startled me. For a second, I was disoriented, the dream clinging to me as it always did. Yes,
I was in a car, but I wasn't the unknown woman driving
away from her baby. That wasn't real. The glare Adrian
leveled at my chest was, though.

"Is that a mirror?" He sounded horrified.

I looked down. My locket was open, the mirrored
side facing me. At some point while I was sleeping, I
must've opened it. Adrian's hand shot out, but this time,
I was too fast for him.

"Don't you dare," I snapped, holding it out of his
reach. "It's the only picture I have of my sister after you
left everything I own back at that hotel in Bennington!"

He lunged again, actually letting go of the steering
wheel to reach the side of the car where I held it. With
a sharp yank, he wrested the locket from my hands. I

tried to snatch it back, but he shoved me into my seat with one hand, finally grabbing the steering wheel with the other.

"Are you crazy?" I shrieked. "You could've gotten us killed!" If this hadn't been a lonely stretch of desert road, our careening into the next lane might've had permanent consequences.

"You're going to get *yourself* killed," was his chilling response. Then, still pinning me to my chair with that single hand, he held my locket up.

I gasped. Something dark poked out of the small mirror, like a snake made of blackest smoke. It disappeared when Adrian smashed the mirror against the steering wheel, but an eerie wind whistled through the car, ruffling my hair and stinging my nostrils with its acrid scent.

Adrian muttered a word in that unknown language, and I didn't need a translator to tell me it was a curse.

"What was that?" My voice was hoarse.

He threw me a pitying glance, which frightened me even more. If he wasn't angry, we must really be screwed.

His next words proved that. "Brace yourself, Ivy. You're about to meet a demon."

CHAPTER EIGHT

I DIDN'T CONSIDER myself religious. My parents used to take Jasmine and me to church on Christmas, but it was more a social event than a pious one. Hearing we were about to be attacked by a demon, however, made me pray like I'd never done before. I just wished I knew if anyone was listening.

Adrian wasn't praying. He was cursing up a storm, if I correctly translated the spate of words coming from his mouth. He'd also lost that pitying expression, because the looks he shot me now were distinctly grim. It wasn't the right time, but I couldn't stop myself from asking the obvious.

"How did it find us?"

Adrian stomped on the accelerator, and the muscle car shot forward like it had rockets in the engine.

"Through the mirror," he said shortly. "For stronger demons, mirrors act as portals, and you've been number one on their Most Wanted list since you escaped them in Bennington."

I gaped at him. "Maybe you should have *told* me that?"

"You think I smash every mirror near you because I don't want you to get conceited?" Then his tone softened. "You're barely holding it together with what you *do* know, Ivy. I'm not about to tell you what you can't handle yet."

Anger flared, which felt better than the fear that made my blood seem like it had been replaced by ice water.

"No, I wasn't ready to know that demons used mirrors as portals. I also wasn't ready to know demons existed, or had kidnapped my sister, or that my parents were dead, or any of the horrible things I've dealt with in the past two weeks. But that didn't stop them from happening, so quit protecting me from the truth, Adrian! It doesn't help a damn bit!"

Adrian glanced at me, a gauntlet of emotions flitting across his features.

"You're right. If we survive, I'll apologize."

My laughter was bleak. "You? Say you're sorry? Now I *really* want to live."

To my surprise, he laughed as well, though it was colored with dark expectancy.

"Hold that thought. You'll need it."

Before I could respond, something filled the road in front of us. I would've said it was storm clouds, except clouds don't sweep along the ground like a heavy fog rolling in.

"Shut your vents," Adrian said, flipping the tiny levers on his side. I did the same, more apprehension filling me as he turned the entire air-conditioning system off. No, those weren't low-hanging clouds. They were something far more ominous.

"Turn around," I said, my voice suddenly breathy.

"It wouldn't matter" was Adrian's chilling reply. "He'd only follow us. I need you to find hallowed ground, Ivy."

I couldn't take my eyes away from the billowing clouds in front of us. They were so dark, they seemed to devour the beams that came from Adrian's headlights.

"All right," I mumbled. "Give me your phone, I'll look up the nearest church or cemetery."

"It's too late for that," he said, stunning me. "You need to find it yourself."

"How?" I burst out. We were almost at the line of black clouds. The temperature in the car plummeted, making my skin feel like it had turned to ice.

"It's in your bloodline," Adrian said, swinging off the road so sharply that the back end began to fishtail. "You can sense hallowed ground, so find some, Ivy. Now."

"I don't know how!" I shouted.

The car shuddered over the uneven terrain, bouncing so much I almost hit my head on the roof, but I didn't tell Adrian to slow down. That wall of darkness filled up the rear window of the Challenger until I couldn't see the glow of our taillights anymore.

"Yes, you do." A growl that sounded comforting compared to the horrible hissing noises coming from outside the car.

"I don't!" What was that flash of white on my side of the car? Or that new, ripping sound? Oh God, were those *teeth* scraping away at the metal on my door?

"It's getting in, it's getting in!"

"He can't get in the car."

Adrian's strong voice broke through my panic. I stared at him, my eyes starting to burn from the acrid stench that crept in through parts of the car we hadn't been able to seal.

"I warded it against demons a long time ago," he went on.

I felt better about that for three seconds, which was how long it took before the car lifted up on one side like a gargantuan hand had swatted it. For a paralyzing moment, I wasn't sure if we were going to flip completely over. Then we crashed down hard enough to make the windows shatter, and I tasted blood from my jaw snapping shut on my tongue.

"'Course, that doesn't mean he can't tear the car apart around us," Adrian said, stomping on the gas as soon as all four wheels were on the ground. "We're running out of time. Where's the hallowed ground?"

"I. Don't. Know," I screamed. My heart was pounding out of my chest from terror. If I knew a way out of this, I'd take it.

"Yes, you do," he insisted, those sapphire eyes searing me when he glanced over. "Tell me which direction you want to run. That's the right way, I promise."

Which way did I want to run? In whatever direction this living nightmare wasn't! The car lifted again, and everything in me braced for another impact. That awful hissing noise grew into a roar, and Adrian's gaze met mine. In those darkly beautiful depths, I realized these would be the last moments of our lives if I didn't use an ability I'd never heard of before.

In the seconds before the car came crashing down, I closed my eyes. Concentrated on which direction I wanted to flee to, and tried to ignore the pain as flying glass pelted me from all sides. My instincts were screaming at me to run from the horrible thing outside these crumbling metal walls, and I let those instincts consume me, filling me until I couldn't focus on anything else. I needed to get out of here. I needed to leave right now and go...*there*.

"That way," I said hoarsely, opening my eyes and pointing.

Adrian's hand closed over mine, his grip strong and sure. Then the car crashed down hard enough to make my vision go black and my whole body ache, but he didn't hesitate. As soon as the worst of the impact was over, he grabbed his coat, yanked me into his arms, and then flung us out of the car.

His body took the brunt of the impact, but it still felt like I hit the ground with almost the same force as the car crashing down. My yelp was swallowed up by a tremendous *boom!* as Adrian threw something at the fog that rushed us. White flashed, more bright and brilliant than a lightning bolt. Those hideous clouds recoiled with a scream as though they were in pain.

Adrian leaped up, still holding me in his arms. Then he began to run in the direction I'd pointed, leaving that ugly, writhing darkness behind us.

Even without the nightmarish clouds surrounding us, I could barely see. Nothing but desert stretched out in front of us, and the headlights from Adrian's car were now too far away to do any good. That strange flash of light was gone, too. Even the moon seemed to hide, but Adrian's incredible strides never wavered. It was as if his eyes had night-vision technology built into them.

His speed had startled me when I was only an observer of it. Now that I was locked in his arms, hurtling through the night like I'd been strapped to the front of a bullet train, it filled me with terrified awe. His heart pounded next to my cheek, but he *couldn't* be human. No mere mortal could move this way. Hell, some hybrid cars couldn't go this fast.

"Where is it, Ivy?" he yelled, the wind snatching away his words almost before I could hear them.

I wasn't sure anymore. All the darkness had disoriented me, and it wasn't like there was a neon sign that said Hallowed Ground This Way. I didn't say that, though. What I saw when I glanced over his shoulder froze the words in my throat.

That roiling mass of evil was right behind us. I shouldn't have been able to see it against the midnight-soaked desert, but I could. The shadows forming it were filled with such seething malevolence that their darkness gleamed. Then something like a huge mouth gaped open, teeth long and razor-sharp.

"Adrian!" I screamed, tightening my arms around him.

He didn't look back, though his grip on me turned bruising. "Tell me where to go, Ivy!"

I forced myself to look away from the appalling sight, but I couldn't look ahead. Sand-filled wind stung my eyes from how fast Adrian ran. I couldn't see, but maybe I didn't have to.

I closed my eyes like I had back in the car. Concentrated on my need to be as far away from the formless death monster as I could. My concentration broke when something sharp lashed my legs before digging in as though trying to claw its way up my body. I screamed again, and Adrian snarled, somehow increasing his incredible speed. With a final slice, the claws left my body, but something hot and wet ran down my legs.

I choked back my next scream, my heart pounding as fast as the booming beneath my cheek. Then I concentrated again, pain and panic finding the switch in my mind that I hadn't realized was there.

"That way," I said, pointing without opening my eyes.

Adrian changed direction, the hard pumping of his legs shooting pain into me from the endless impacts, but I didn't care. Another roar sounded behind us, growing closer, until I could almost feel its icy breath on my cheek. My legs throbbed, anticipating more claws slicing through my skin, and though I knew I shouldn't, I opened my eyes.

It was *right there,* faceless except for those grotesquely large teeth that snapped mere inches from my head. I stared, too horrified to scream again. It stretched, growing even bigger, until I couldn't see anything except the wall of evil that was about to come crashing down on us—

It split through the middle, breaking around us like water parted by rocks. An unearthly howl shook me, blasting my ears and blowing my hair back. Just as abruptly, Adrian slowed down, coming to a complete stop a couple dozen feet away from the thing, which surged and recoiled as though trying to break past an invisible barrier.

I didn't understand for the first few breathless seconds. Then I saw the faint shimmers coming up from the earth and heard the faraway echo of long-dead voices chanting prayers. We'd made it to the hallowed ground, and the demon might rage along its perimeter, but it couldn't cross it to get to us.

CHAPTER NINE

NOW I KNEW why people who'd escaped certain death broke into laughter. It had always looked strange in the movies, but I hadn't realized how quickly adrenaline turned to relief, the change hitting your bloodstream like a dozen tequila shots. For a few seconds, I didn't even feel any pain as I laughed from the wild, wondrous exhilaration of still being alive. I wanted to hug Adrian. I wanted to spin in circles. I wanted to scream, "Take *that!*" at the swirls of dark clouds that stormed along the edge of our supernaturally impregnable walls.

Adrian didn't laugh, but his wide smile conveyed both victory and savage satisfaction. He stared at the living darkness a short distance from us and said something in that strange, harshly melodic language.

To my surprise, the clouds began to shrink, dissipating as quickly as a fog machine in reverse. Soon, nothing remained except an inky pool on the ground, like the shadows had been transformed into liquid.

"What did you say to make it disappear?" I asked, my brain adding numbly, *and why didn't you say it sooner?*

"He's not gone," Adrian said, his tone edged with an emotion I couldn't name. "He's just shedding his disguise."

Those fluid shadows suddenly began to rise, forming

into a pillar. Then they changed, coiling and swirling until a slender girl with long blond hair broke through them as though she'd been expelled out.

Jasmine hunched in fear as she looked around. When she saw me, she collapsed on the ground in relief.

"Ivy," she said, her hands trembling as she reached out. "Please, help me!"

I didn't need Adrian to keep holding me to stop me from going to her. This wasn't my sister. It was a *thing* wearing her image like a coat, and it infuriated me.

"Fuck you," I replied, all my fear and hatred rolled into those two words.

Jasmine's form blurred, turning into slithering shadows again. Out of those, a man emerged. He was almost as tall as Adrian, though not as thickly muscled, and he moved with snakelike grace as he prowled along the edge of the barrier. Long black hair hid most of his face as the wind tossed it around, but I caught a glimpse of pale skin, burning black eyes and a dark pink mouth that opened as he said—

"I can see why you like her, my son."

I barely noticed Adrian stiffen. I was too busy being shocked by the thing's identical, exotic accent and how he'd addressed the man holding me. *My son.* Was this the secret Adrian refused to talk about? It would explain his superhuman speed—

"Don't call me that." Adrian's voice lashed the air with palpable hatred. "I was never your son."

The demon sighed in the way my father used to do when I was a child and he was explaining why some things, like dental visits, were unavoidable.

"Not by blood, but you're mine nonetheless. Now, Adrian, your little rebellion, while amusing, has gone on long enough. Carry her out to me. It will save us all from a lengthy, boring fight before the inevitable occurs."

Adrian's smile reminded me of a tiger baring his teeth. "I live to fight you, Demetrius, so it's never boring for me."

Demetrius. Wasn't that the demon who'd sent Detective Kroger after me? I started to squirm, wanting out of Adrian's arms while I processed this, but his grip only tightened.

Demetrius noticed, and the look he flashed Adrian was both knowing and cruel.

"Every moment you spend with her will strengthen the bond between you. Break it now, before it destroys you when you fulfill your destiny."

A noise escaped Adrian, too visceral to be called a snarl. "My 'destiny' won't happen if you're dead. How much did the Archon grenade hurt? Not nearly as much as David's slingshot will, I hope."

Demetrius laughed, sending shivers of revulsion over me. If evil came in audible form, it would sound like that.

"Now that I've seen the last of David's seed, I'm even more confident of my people's success. You must be, too. That's why she has no idea what we're talking about." Another mocking, repellent laugh, then the demon's face turned serious. "Come home, my son. I miss you. Obsidiana misses you. You don't belong with them. You never did."

Adrian's grip hardened until it felt like I was encased in steel. "I'd rather die where I don't belong than live another day with you," he gritted out.

Demetrius shook his head. "So slow to learn," he said sadly. Then he looked at me, a smile playing about his lips.

"I make your sister scream in pain every day," he said in an offhand way. "If you want to save her, say my name in a mirror. I'll trade her life for yours."

My reply contained every filthy word I knew, plus a few I made up. Demetrius only laughed again. Then, with a swirl of shadows, he disappeared. Or did he?

"Is he really gone?" I asked hoarsely.

"He's gone. I told you, demons can't tolerate our realm for long. Even strong ones like Demetrius would be dead after an hour here."

As he spoke, he let me down, which was good, since I didn't want him touching me. The words *my son* kept resounding in my mind. Biologically related or not, the demon imprisoning my sister had close ties to Adrian— a fact he'd deliberately kept from me. Worse, Demetrius seemed very confident that their ties would be restored soon.

"So Demetrius is your stepdad?"

He sighed at the acid in my tone. "The simplest explanation is that Demetrius was…my foster parent."

The slight hesitation before those words told me he was hiding large chunks of the truth. Again.

"And Daddy Dearest misses you. How sweet."

Adrian's expression darkened so much, I half expected to see shadows appear beneath his skin.

"I get that you're pissed, but don't ever call him my father again. I was a child when he took me. Not all of us were lucky enough to end up with kind, *human* foster parents."

His raw tone melted away some of my anger. He might still be hiding something, but I couldn't imagine the horrors of growing up at the mercy of a demon.

"Why did Demetrius take you?" I asked with less rancor. "Does it have to do with your mysterious bloodline?"

As I watched his lips tighten in that familiar way, I knew I was right—and that he still wasn't going to tell me what he was. Not part-demon, evidently, and I doubted he was part-Archon. If he was, Demetrius would've killed him, not raised him as his "son."

"Your legs are injured," Adrian stated, changing the subject. "Sit. I've got medicine in my coat."

If they hadn't been throbbing with pain for the past several minutes, I would have refused until Adrian told me the rest of what he was hiding. Since our car was busted and we probably had a long walk ahead of us, I sat, wincing when he pulled at the tears in my jeans. The wounds had already started to stick to the fabric.

After a few moments, Adrian let out a soft hiss. "Lots of gouges, and deep. Take your pants off."

"Geez, buy a girl a drink first," I said to cover my dread over how much that would hurt.

His lips curled as he retrieved a flask from his coat. "Ask and you shall receive."

"You've had liquor on you this whole time?" I didn't know whether to laugh or cry. "I could've really used some, oh, *every day* for the last few days!"

I snatched the flask and took a gulp, welcoming the burn that made my eyes water, and forced a sputter after I swallowed.

"Not a bourbon girl?" Adrian asked dryly.

"That's bourbon?" I let out a choking cough. "I thought it might be prison brew!" Still, I took another throat-scorching gulp. Beggars can't be choosers.

His snort was soft. "No, but let's just say the recipe doesn't come from a normal brew company."

"I'll bet," I muttered, then coughed out a protest when he took it from me. "Wait, I'm not done!"

"That's much stronger than regular bourbon," he

said, putting it back in his coat. "Trust me, you've had enough."

When he started tugging my jeans down, the pain shooting through me made me want to argue, but I didn't. I hadn't eaten in hours, and I didn't want to add puking to all the other reasons why this night had been awful. Once my jeans were off, I stayed silent for a different reason.

Savage swipes had ripped open my flesh in at least a dozen places. I saw white in some of the gaping spaces, making my fear of vomiting a real possibility. If I'd been thrown into an angry bear's den, I probably would've fared better. How had I managed to even *stand* with injuries like this?

I must've said that last part out loud, because Adrian answered me.

"Shock and adrenaline, plus your bloodline. You're stronger, faster and tougher than you realize. You just didn't know it before because you never needed to be."

With that, he pulled a sealed plastic bag out of his coat. No wonder he'd made sure to grab it when we fled the car; liquor and medicine were necessities in any survivalist's book, not to mention the Archon grenade that had made cloud-Demetrius scream.

If I'd known then what I knew now, I'd have savored that scream. His taunts about Jasmine tormented me, as he'd intended them to. If I had any confidence that a demon would keep his word, I'd be tempted to trade my life for hers. Finding the weapon and taking on Demetrius might get me killed anyway, and then my sister would *really* be doomed.

Adrian scooped out some of the bag's contents, interrupting that bleak line of thought. The medicine looked like mashed-up macaroon cookies, and I tensed as he held that sticky mixture over the deepest gouge on my thigh. His eyes met mine, their silvery perimeter gleaming.

"Take a deep breath, Ivy."

I did, and still almost screamed when he brought his hand down. The medicine hurt more than when Demetrius had made the wounds, but I bit my lip and didn't cry out. Adrian was trying to help. The less I distracted him, the faster this would end.

I repeated that like a litany while he smeared the agony-inducing substance on all my deeper gashes. He worked with quiet efficiency, thankfully not commenting on the sweat that beaded my forehead or how my breath came in pants.

"Almost over," he murmured in sympathy.

Something strange began to happen. The pain changed, turning into a tingling that reminded me of what it felt like when my foot fell asleep. Adrian finished with the final gouge and leaned back, watching my legs with an expectant expression.

The wounds began to close, expelling the now red-smeared medicine as smooth flesh filled in what had been gaping tears. Within minutes, the only marks left were shallower grazes that I could've made while shaving. I could hardly believe it.

"What is that stuff?"

His mouth curled. "Manna."

Where had I heard that word...? "The mythical bread that fed the Israelites when they wandered in the desert?"

His half smile remained. "As you see, it has a lot of uses. Now, turn over so I can get the other gouges."

I did, thinking it was a good thing that Zach had done

my recent shopping. I normally wore thongs, but now, my ass was more modestly covered by bikini briefs.

Once I was on my stomach, Adrian's large hand covered a wound high up on my hip. Though the initial pain was just as sharp, something else flared through me. Maybe it was because I knew the harsh sting would soon fade. Maybe the bellyful of superpotent liquor contributed to the urge I had to see his expression as he dragged his hand over my skin, or perhaps it was the way his touch seemed to linger longer than medicinally necessary.

I could've told him to stop. Insisted on dressing the wounds myself; I could reach them, after all. But I didn't. He didn't speak, either, and as his hands continued their path down my body, treating and then smoothing over newly healed skin, the pain was a price I willingly paid to keep feeling him touch me.

It was wrong, of course. I kept telling that to my rapidly beating heart and the shivers that followed every stroke of his hands. He was danger wrapped in secrets tied with a bow of bad intentions, and it was totally unfair that no one had made me feel this way before.

"Almost over?" I asked, hating how much he affected me.

"Yeah."

He sounded angry, which made me flip over before he'd finished smoothing manna over a shallower cut. My quick movement must've surprised him, because it took a second for his expression to close off into that familiar, jaded mask.

In that brief, unguarded moment, I learned I wasn't the only one who'd been affected by his touching me. Suddenly, it seemed like a very good idea to put my pants back on.

CHAPTER TEN

ADRIAN MADE A fire out of plants, scrub and other things I wouldn't have thought to use, starting it by rubbing twigs together fast enough to get a spark. I huddled as close as I could to the fire without catching myself ablaze. Even so, my breath made tiny white clouds with every exhalation. Who knew a desert could be so chilly at night?

"How long do we have to stay out here?"

Adrian glanced back at me. He didn't appear bothered by the cold temperatures, or his pacing was keeping him warm. He hadn't stopped since he quit treating my injuries.

"Until morning. We can't risk another demon ambushing us if we leave the hallowed ground before sunrise."

"They can't enter our realm in daylight?" Interesting.

"Didn't I tell you that?"

"No, you didn't," I replied, adding, "along with a lot of other things," in case my tone hadn't been pointed enough.

He snorted, the slight breath pluming in the frigid air, too. "I'm not keeping secrets to make things worse for you, Ivy. I'm doing it to help you. One thing I can say is that Demetrius is full of shit about your sister."

"How?" I asked instantly.

He came closer, until the firelight revealed every nuance of his intensely beautiful face.

"Right now, she's the safest, most well-treated human in all the realms. Your sister is the only leverage the demons have over you, and they might be evil, but they're not stupid enough to kill, maim or emotionally break their only advantage."

My sigh whooshed out, as if the part of me that had been holding its breath for days finally relaxed enough to release it. Even as relief seemed to blend with the liquor in me, creating a lethargic sort of high, a new question arose.

"Thanks for telling me, but…why did you?" He'd made it clear that he'd rather not be here, and keeping me scared about my sister's treatment was motivation for me to find the weapon as quickly as possible.

Adrian looked away, his jaw tightening. "Demetrius said it to hurt you, and I don't like to see you hurt."

The simple statement made me wonder all the more about him. Who was the real Adrian? The oddly charming man who'd asked me for a date right after he kidnapped me? The heroic one who'd saved my life two times in four days? Or the surly one who acted like I was a venereal disease he couldn't wait to be cured of? I didn't think the night was long enough to find out, but it might be too long for other things.

"What if Demetrius sends his minions after us?" I shivered as I looked around. "It's so dark, we wouldn't even see them coming."

"I would."

Two quiet, steely words that reminded me how different Adrian was from a normal person. To prevent myself from wondering for the umpteenth time what he was, I kept talking.

"What kind of hallowed ground do you suppose this is?" The ethereal shimmers coming up from the sand marked an area roughly the size of a football field.

Adrian shrugged. "This part of the Oregon desert? Indian burial ground maybe."

"That would explain the chanting," I said, cocking my head and listening. "I don't hear it anymore. Do you?"

His features tightened, but his tone was light. "I never heard it, Ivy."

I stared at him, understanding slowly dawning. "You don't see the shimmers coming up from the ground, either, do you?"

"No. Only you can sense hallowed objects." The smile he flashed held an edge of darkness. "My talents lie elsewhere."

I let out a short laugh as more pieces fell into place. "That's why you came with me even though you didn't want to. The demon-killing weapon is hallowed, isn't it? So you can't sense it, but with my abilities, I can, if you get me near enough."

That hint of menace didn't leave his smile. "I've wanted to kill Demetrius for years, but I've never had the means to. With you and that weapon, I finally will. Like I said, Ivy, when it comes to my hatred of demons, you can trust me completely."

"But once you kill Demetrius, all bets are off?" I filled in, a touch of anger coloring my tone. Adrian wasn't just some guy I was way too attracted to. He was also the only person who knew what it was like to see things that made everyone else believe you were crazy, until you believed it yourself.

Adrian stared at me, his smile wiping away. "I said I don't want to hurt you, and I meant it. So if we live through this, Ivy, I'm getting away from you as fast as I can."

I tried not to show how much that stung. What had I done that he relished the thought of never seeing me again? I'd think it was my hiding a mirror that almost got us killed, but Adrian had acted that way since Zach told him I was the last descendant of King David's line. I'd never forget the look he gave me when he found that out.

I paused. Maybe it wasn't what I'd done, but what someone else had done. After all, I hadn't misread some of the *other* looks Adrian had given me. Not every part of him wanted to run away from me as fast as he could.

"Did my ancestor do something terrible to your ancestor?" I guessed.

He looked shocked. Then he let out a laugh that was so bitter, I thought I'd finally stumbled on the truth. That was why his reply stunned me.

"No, Ivy. It was the other way around."

Despite my many attempts to get him to elaborate, he refused to say anything else.

ONCE DAWN BROKE, I found out that manna could heal more than human injuries. Adrian spread a thin layer over his busted-up Challenger, and the vintage vehicle knit itself back together like I was watching an episode of *Counting Cars* on fast-forward. After that, we just had to brush the shattered glass out of the interior, and we were on our way.

When we made our first pit stop, I insisted on going into the ladies' room alone. Adrian kept getting caught destroying mirrors because it drew attention when a man entered a women-only area. He made me swear not to even peek at the mirror until after I'd shattered it. Demetrius might not be able to enter our realm during the day, but we didn't want him spying on us so he could ambush us once night fell.

That was how I found myself looking fixedly at the dirty tile floor as I approached the mirror in the Gas-N-Go restroom. Adrian had also given me a rock and a pair of oversize work gloves, so I didn't worry about cutting myself when I hit the glass with a hard bang, glancing at it only after I saw shards hit the floor. *Take that, Demetrius,* I thought, seeing only splinters of my reflection in its remains.

A flush sounded, and then the nearest stall door opened, revealing a fiftyish woman who looked back and forth between the ruined mirror and the rock in my hand.

"Why'd you do a thing like that?" she demanded.

Nothing I said would make it appear less crazy, so I might as well live up to her expectations.

"Ever have one of those days when you just *hate* your hair?" I asked, widening my eyes for maximum disturbed effect.

She didn't even wash her hands before she left. I made sure to be quick about my business as well, not surprised to see her talking to the store clerk once I exited the bathroom.

"Hey, girlie," the bald clerk said sharply. "Did you—?"

"This is for the damage," Adrian interrupted, slapping a handful of blank papers in front of the clerk. My confusion increased when the man snatched them up, his scowl turning into a grin.

"No problem," the clerk said, actually giving me a cheery wave. "Take care, girlie!"

I waited until we were outside before I said, "What was that?"

Adrian's mouth curled into a sardonic smile. "Zach's here."

That's when I paid attention to the hoodie-clad guy next to Adrian's car. Zach turned around, thankfully not projecting a blinding array of light as he faced us.

"I understand you ran into some difficulty last night," he stated, as if we'd only gotten a flat tire.

I blamed my response on being frustrated, under-caffeinated and hungry. "Yeah, and I hope you were too busy to show up because you were saving a bus full of nuns!"

A shrug. "I wasn't sent to you until now."

"Are you serious?" Incredulity sharpened my tone. "Is your boss in a bad mood, or does He suffer from time-delay up there?"

Zach's face turned stony, but it didn't escape me that Adrian's smile widened.

"You don't know how many times I've wondered that," he murmured, nudging me in a sympathetic way.

Zach had a different response. "Why do you expect someone else to solve problems you are capable of handling yourselves?"

Adrian grunted. "Get used to hearing that. It's his favorite line."

Then you must want to punch him a lot, I thought before Zach's pointedly arched brow reminded me that my musings weren't private. That might not be all bad, though. I seized my chance.

Tell me what Adrian is, and why he's so determined to get away from me once this is over, I thought, staring at Zach.

"No," he said out loud. "I gave Adrian my word, and as I told you, Archons do not lie."

"What am I missing?" Adrian said, casting a suspicious look between both of us.

Don't you dare! I thought, but Zach was already replying. "Ivy sought the answers you are still refusing to give her."

Adrian's gaze swung to me. "Don't do that again," he said in an ominous tone.

"You bet your ass I will," I flared. "My life and my sister's life are on the line, so I have a right to know what's going on. Besides, after the fallout from your mirror omission, you said you'd quit hiding things *and* that you'd apologize."

Zach smirked at him. Actually smirked, and said, "I will enjoy witnessing this." There went another note under my ever-growing list titled Things I Didn't Expect From An Archon.

Adrian gave both of us such a cold glare that I was sure he'd refuse. Then he spoke.

"I'm sorry, Ivy, for not telling you about the mirrors. There's your apology, and here's information you didn't know—because you can see through Archon glamour, you saw me hand blank pieces of paper to the clerk. *He* saw a stack of hundred dollar bills, and we're using the same trick to fly to Mexico because we can't use the Oregon vortex to enter multiple realms through the same gateway anymore."

At my indrawn breath, Adrian went on. "Demetrius will guess that's where we're headed since we were in the Oregon desert when he caught up with us. Zach's here to refill our manna supply, glamour your appearance and remind me that we're on our own once we enter the demon realms. The two sides can't cross into each other's territories, so if we're captured, Zach can't help us even if he wants to."

I was openmouthed by the time he finished, but I quickly recovered. "And you are *what?*" I asked, wanting to know that more than all the other details.

Adrian smiled. "I promised to share secrets and I did. I never specified which ones."

Zach smirked again, and this time, it was directed at me.

"I'll remember that," I replied, giving Adrian a look that promised retribution.

If he thought I'd give up my quest to find out what he was, why he acted so hot and cold around me or what Demetrius had meant when he said that every moment "the bond" would strengthen between us, he was dead wrong. Now, the real trick would be to make sure that none of us ended up *really* dead before I got my answers.

I turned my back on Adrian, giving Zach my full attention. "You're going to change how others see me? Fine. I've always wondered what it would be like to be a blonde."

CHAPTER ELEVEN

THE AIRPORT TELLER'S name was Kristin. I handed her two blank paper stubs and a stack of equally blank Post-it pages, hoping I didn't look as guilty as I felt.

"One round-trip ticket to Durango, Mexico, please," I said.

Kristin looked at the blank stubs and pages. I tried to smile, but my face froze. Adrian swore that she and everyone else would see a driver's license, a passport and lots of cash in the Post-it note pile. All I saw was my imminent arrest, if the Archon glamour didn't hold up.

After what might have been five seconds but felt like ten years, the teller snapped up the two stubs from the pile, starting to type with crazy quickness on her keyboard.

"Anything to declare?" she asked.

Yes. I'm a total criminal right now. "Uh, nope."

The next flight to Durango had two stopovers, and only first-class seats available. I looked at the Post-it pages. Damned if I knew what monetary denominations they were supposed to be.

"Take it," Adrian said softly from behind me.

"Sold," I told the teller, pushing the pile toward her. If I didn't have enough pretend money in it, I'd get more from Adrian or play up the dumb blonde stereotype as an excuse for not being able to count.

After more brisk typing, the teller handed me the two blank stubs, most of the blank pages—my change, I supposed—and a ticket with the fake name I'd chosen for myself. Adrian bought his ticket, then we checked our bags and proceeded to our gate.

That's when my last shred of denial ripped away. Some tiny part of me must've still been clinging to the idea that everything I'd seen was a hallucination, just like countless doctors over the years had assured me. But after a TSA official ran our blank stubs through a computer that authenticated them as valid IDs, the truth was undisputable.

I wasn't experiencing a psychotic break with another equally crazy companion. The fact that even computer systems were fooled by Archon glamour proved that this was nothing short of a supernatural phenomenon. Archons—*angels*—were real. Demons were, too, and I was going to enter into their world to find a weapon so Adrian and I could kill them.

To say I was in way over my head was an understatement.

This time, I was the one who brooded in silence over the next couple days of layovers and long flights. When the plane finally touched down in Durango, I'd come to the same realization I had in Bennington over two weeks ago.

I had nothing left to lose. My whole family had been taken from me, and I didn't have someone special waiting back at college. Truth be told, there had never been anyone special. I used to blame my lack of romantic enthusiasm on the medication I took, but now that I knew the pills were placebos, I had to admit the problem was me. I even kept my roommate and my other friends at arm's length, so while they'd miss me if I never came back, it wouldn't leave a big hole in their lives. Sure, we had fun hanging out, but no matter how many parties we went to or how many nights we stayed up talking, part of me hadn't really been there. I think they must have sensed that because while I didn't lack for friends, I'd never been anybody's *best* friend. That took the kind of trust and honesty I'd only shared with Jasmine. With everyone else, I was too busy pretending not to catch glimpses of things only I could see, or worrying if I was living the college life the way everyone expected me to. Most days, I worked harder at faking "normal" than I did on my grades, friendships or the few-and-fleeting relationships I'd had. So while I was scared shitless, the only person who'd really care if I didn't make it was Jasmine, and my doing this was her only hope of surviving.

It kinda sucked seeing how little my life mattered in the big scheme of things, but then again, that was also my biggest advantage. People with nothing to lose were dangerous, and since I was taking on demons, I needed to be as dangerous as I could.

As we disembarked, Adrian grasped my arm, the contact sending a familiar shiver through me. He was the only guy who'd made me feel everything I'd been missing all these years, and for reasons he refused to discuss, he wanted nothing to do with me. Figured.

"I know I deserved it, but are you done paying me back for all the times I've given you the silent treatment?" he asked.

I looked at him, taking in his height, muscular build and devastating good looks that were invisible to everyone but me. Then I spoke the first words I had in over a thousand miles.

"Yeah, I'm done, and more important, I'm ready."

WE SPENT THE night in a hotel in Ceballos, one of Durango's smaller towns. Adrian spoke fluent Spanish, which helped with checking in and getting dinner. Jet lag and my new resolve ensured that I slept well, and in the morning, I found out that we weren't driving to the entrance of the demon realm alone. Two guys approached us as soon as we entered the hotel parking lot, exchanging backslapping man-hugs with Adrian.

"Ivy, this is my friend Tomas," Adrian said, indicating the tough-looking Hispanic man with a scar curving from his neck down to his upper arm.

"Hola," I said, wishing I'd taken more than two years of Spanish in high school. Tomas accepted my outstretched hand, shaking it firmly.

"Hola, senorita." Then his stoic features cracked, and he flashed a wide smile at Adrian. *"La rubia es caliente! Hora de que empieces a salir de nuevo, mi amigo."*

"It's not like that," Adrian said in English, though I'd translated enough to get the misassumption. "Ivy and I aren't dating. We're...friends."

I stiffened at his pause. No, we weren't besties, but did he have to make it obvious that I was an unwelcome acquaintance? Something reckless stirred in me. Adrian might not want me around, but he wanted some things from me. Plus, I might die before sundown and I wasn't sure I'd really lived during the past twenty years. Time to change that.

I gave Tomas a wide grin as I wrapped my arms around Adrian's midsection.

"Don't mind him, he's in denial over how crazy he is about me," I said glibly. "You should've seen him rubbing my ass the other night. It's like he was trying to polish it shiny."

Adrian gazed at me in disbelief. Tomas choked back a laugh, and the guy I hadn't been introduced to yet let out a low chuckle.

"Looks like you have more on your plate than just demons, Adrian," he drawled, his accent sounding Mediterranean.

Adrian's hands flexed on my back, as though he was having trouble deciding whether to push me away or mold me closer. His gaze had changed, too. Disbelief turned to something darker and infinitely more enticing in those silvery sapphire depths.

"You have no idea what you're toying with," he said, the growled words barely audible.

"What if I want to know?" I replied, and shivered as his grip on me began to tighten.

I'd started this as a game, but it felt very serious now. His stare burned into my eyes with more than the lust I'd called his bluff on. Secrets, promises and lies seemed to swirl together, drawing me in and warning me away at the same time. When he pulled me closer, those warnings collapsed under the explosion of sensation as he pressed against me, and when his hand coiled through my hair, pulling my head back with a strong, possessive grip, I didn't just shiver. I shuddered.

"Do you and your *friend* want to postpone our trip until tomorrow?" an amused voice asked.

Adrian released me as suddenly as if I'd become scalding. Maybe I had. My whole body felt feverish, and if my heart beat any faster, I might be in danger of a coronary.

"We're leaving now," he said in a strained voice. "Get in the black Jeep, Ivy. I'll be right there."

I would've argued if I didn't feel like I needed a moment to compose myself. I walked toward the black, open-topped Wrangler that had four machine guns in the back. No seats, though, and the front ones must be for Tomas and our as-yet-unnamed companion. Looked like Adrian and I would be standing.

Adrian. The thought of how close he'd come to kissing me made that feverishness sweep through me again. Why did he keep pulling away at the last minute? Was it the secret he thought was too terrible to reveal? He wasn't a demon or a minion, and he worked with an *angel,* so how bad could it be?

Adrian's arrival with the two men cut my musings short. He jumped into the back of the Wrangler, grasping the bar that the machine guns were strapped to.

"This is Costa," Adrian said, indicating the handsome young man with the wavy black hair and dark brown eyes. "Get in, Ivy."

I climbed into the back, accepting Adrian's hand up. He held mine a second too long, as if reluctant to let me go. I felt the same way, though I grasped the metal railing between the seats when Adrian did. Was it me, or did something *happen* when we touched? Something more than lust, although I had that bad, too. Could this be the supernatural bond Demetrius had spoken of? If so, he was right. It was getting stronger.

"Hi, Costa," I said, trying to refocus my attention. "You mentioned demons, so I take it you know what we'll be doing?"

Costa snorted. "Yes, though I wish you didn't have to. No one leaves the dark realms the same way they entered them."

Tomas gunned the Jeep, and bracing to stay upright made me almost miss the look on Adrian's face. From the way his features tightened, Costa wasn't referring to different exits. Adrian had told me the demon world was awful, as if I couldn't figure that out for myself. From his expression and Costa's words, maybe I hadn't prepared enough. I drew in a deep breath. *Think about Jasmine,* I reminded myself. If she could survive being trapped in one, I could survive searching however many I needed to in order to save her.

"I'm tougher than I look" was what I said.

Adrian's hand brushed my back, the brief caress wordlessly promising that I wasn't doing this alone. Then he nodded at Costa, supporting my statement. I held on to that as tightly as I did the metal bar that kept me from being vaulted out of the car from Tomas's crazy driving. Jasmine needed me, and Adrian believed in me. I wouldn't fail either of them.

I couldn't.

CHAPTER TWELVE

THE VORTEX WE were headed to was located in a section of desert called *La Zona del Silencio,* or the Zone of Silence. I found out why they called it that after Tomas turned off the highway and started driving on the barren terrain. After a hundred yards, the radio station he'd been blasting abruptly went silent. Costa held out his cell, showing me the screen going blank as though the phone had powered down on its own.

"Technology doesn't work here," he stated. "Most people don't know why, but it's the vortex. It's one of the bigger ones on the planet, so it drains everything around it."

Our surroundings reminded me of where Demetrius had attacked us. Like that sliver of Oregon desert, the endless landscape of sand was interrupted here and there by cacti and other scrub. It had more mountains, though, sometimes narrowing the path Tomas drove through. Every so often, Adrian would call out directions. He seemed to know exactly where he was despite the lack of roads or signs. I tried to pay attention to our route in case I needed to come back in the future, but after half an hour, I gave up. "Turn left at the rock" wouldn't work because all the damn rocks looked the same, and once you've seen one cactus, you've seen them all.

Finally, after my muscles ached from hours of the

Jeep's rough jostling, Adrian told Tomas to stop. Then he jumped out of the back, unloading his bulky duffel bag with him.

"We're here?" I looked around, squinting in the bright sunlight. "I don't see any older, rotted versions of what's around us." Plus, the only landmark for miles seemed to be an oblong piece of rock sticking out of the ground.

Adrian flashed me a challenging look. "You can sense hallowed ground. I can sense gateways to the dark worlds."

I jumped down, too. "How can you do that?"

His smile was dangerous and beautiful, like the caress of sunshine right before it became a burn. "A gift of my lineage, same as your abilities."

Wasn't that a not-so-subtle warning? If sensing demon realm gateways was one of his "gifts," he was letting me know that he wasn't the last descendant of Mother Teresa's line. Still, why should his family tree weigh so heavily on him? Our previous conversation replayed in my mind. *Did my ancestor do something terrible to your ancestor?... No, Ivy, it was the other way around...*

Did Adrian keep pushing me away because he felt guilty for what his ancestor had done? If so, could his big, awful secret actually not be about *him,* but about his long-dead relative?

"I don't know who my biological parents were," I said in an even tone. "Or who their parents were, and so on. I do know it has no bearing on who *I* am, beyond genetic leftovers like hair color, eye color, and apparently, an ability to sense hallowed objects and see through supernatural glamour. Same goes for you. Regardless of who your ancestor was, your decisions make you who *you* are, and aside from being a dick sometimes, you can also be pretty great. Maybe, if you dropped whatever your ancient relative's baggage is, you'd like who you were, too."

Adrian's expression was as hard as the grayish rock behind him, but Tomas gave me a thumbs-up, and Costa started to smile. Guess I wasn't the only person to think that Adrian's biggest issue might be Crap Family syndrome.

"I wish I believed you, Ivy," he said roughly. "But believing you is part of the fate that I can't allow to happen, for both our sakes."

Without waiting for me to respond, he opened the duffel bag and tossed a ski jacket, thermal pants and gloves at me.

"Put these on."

I gestured at the scorched landscape, as if he hadn't realized we were in the middle of a desert with high noon approaching. "Are you serious?"

"These, too," he said, adding a pair of fleece-lined boots to my pile.

I gave him a level look. "Either you're trying to kill me, or the realm we're about to enter is really cold."

"They're all cold," Tomas said, accompanied by a grim snort of agreement from Costa.

I was shocked. "You two have been in one?"

"We were trapped and Adrian pulled us out," Tomas said, only to be cut off by Adrian's, "Now's not the time."

I marched over to Adrian and jabbed my finger in his chest.

"You told me there was no way to get Jasmine back without this mysterious weapon, but you got *them* out of a demon realm?"

"Ivy," he began.

"Don't! You said the only thing I could trust about you was your hatred of demons. If you want me to find that demon-killing weapon, you're going to tell me *right now* why you could rescue Tomas and Costa, but you can't help me save my sister yet!"

I planted my feet, my glare promising that I wasn't moving until I had an answer. Tomas and Costa looked uncomfortable, and Adrian looked angry enough to deck both of them, but all he did was let out a sharp sigh.

"I wasn't lying when I said we needed the weapon to save your sister. The only reason I was able to save them without it was because I took them with me when I left."

My scoff was instant. "A bunch of demons just let you waltz out of their realm with two of the humans they'd captured?"

"Yes," he said, his tone now flatter than a polished mirror. "I grew up in that realm, so they were used to me doing whatever I wanted in it."

I don't know why the words hit me like a punch. Adrian had told me that Demetrius took him when he was a child. I guess I'd just assumed minions had raised him in this world, and Demetrius had…checked in on him frequently.

"You were raised in a demon realm," I said, my anger changing into something else. "And they trusted you, so you must've, um—"

"Lived just like they did," he supplied, an icy bleakness filling his tone. "Still think I'm pretty great?"

I didn't know what to think. Part of me was appalled and the other part was weeping. How old had Adrian been when Demetrius yanked him out of this world and raised him in a demon one? If he'd been very young, would he even have known that everything he saw—or did—was evil if it was all he'd ever seen of "normal"? Maybe finding out was what had made him switch sides and work with Zach. Maybe that was why he hated demons with such pathological single-mindedness now.

And maybe his twisted upbringing, combined with whatever his ancestor had done, made Adrian feel like fate had doomed him. In some ways, I couldn't blame him.

"I still think you are what your decisions make you to be," I said at last. "I also think if these guys made it out of a demon realm, then my sister can, too, so let's do this."

With that, I pulled the ski jacket over my tank top, slipped the thermal pants over my shorts, replaced my sandals with the knee-high fuzzy boots and put on the gloves. Finally, I released my long brown hair from its ponytail. If it was cold enough to warrant ski wear, my ears would need the covering.

All Adrian did was toss the now-empty duffel bag into the back of the Jeep.

"You're wearing that?" I said, gesturing to his long-sleeved T-shirt and regular jeans.

A diffident shrug. "I'm used to the cold."

I left that alone, forcing a smile as I glanced at Tomas and Costa. "See you guys soon, hopefully."

I didn't get a chance to hear their response. Adrian wrapped his arms around me, walked us rapidly toward the tall, oblong rock and then plunged us through it.

I'VE ALWAYS LOVED roller-coaster rides. The wild exhilaration of being propelled through turns and loops so fast that your face felt heavy and your body molded to your seat was second only to the rush of relief when the ride was over. Being transported through a gateway into a demon realm was sorta like that, only with a lot more noise and nausea. It took a few moments to settle my heaving stomach once we were on the other side, and during that time, I was grateful for the icy air. Then I opened my eyes and realized I still saw…nothing.

"Adrian?" I said, panic setting in when rapid blinking didn't make the blackness disappear. "Something's wrong. I'm—"

"You're not blind," he said, his deep voice almost as comforting as his hand closing over mine. "Sunlight doesn't exist in demon realms. That's why they're so cold, too."

I'd never been in total darkness before. It wasn't just frightening and disorienting—it was dangerous. For all I knew, we were standing on the edge of a cliff. Even if everything around us was flat, I couldn't judge the length of my steps because I couldn't see the ground. When I tried to walk, I ended up staggering.

Adrian's arm went around me, clasping my left side to his right one.

"Close your eyes and concentrate on moving with me," he said, the confidence in his tone easing my fears. "Don't worry. I can see where we're going, and I'm not going to let anything happen to you."

We began to walk, first in hesitant steps while I learned to trust the feel of his body instead of my sight, and then at a normal pace. Surprisingly, it did help to keep my eyes closed. Since I wasn't trying to see, I focused on his smooth strides, the flexing muscles that preceded a change in his direction, and the reassuring way he instantly adjusted his hold to support me if I faltered.

It didn't take me long to be grateful for the parka, boots, gloves and pants, too. Even with them on, the cold seemed to seep into my bones, but just like the darkness, it didn't appear to bother Adrian. He didn't so much as shiver in his light clothing, and his hand felt warm in mine. How many years had it taken for him to adapt to this dark, frigid wasteland? Once more, my heart broke for the child he'd been. Even without demons, growing up in a place like this would have been awful.

After what felt like an hour, Adrian paused. I did, too, of course, sniffing at the new, fuel-like smell in the air.

"You can open your eyes," he said. "The town's up ahead."

At first all I saw was a black-and-gold spotted blur. After a few blinks, my eyes adjusted, and I made out a blaze of light in the distance, showing lots of smaller structures surrounding what looked like a wide, soaring building.

"Thank God," I breathed, so glad to be able to see that I didn't care if I was looking at a demon town.

"Don't say that. It's a real giveaway that we don't belong."

Adrian's face was hidden by darkness, yet his tone made me imagine that he said it with one of his wry smiles.

"Good point, but aren't we avoiding the town?" I asked, whispering in case someone was out in the blackness with us.

"Can't. What's known of the weapon's location is that it was hidden in a wall, and the only walls are in town."

"Is that all we know, or do the demons know exactly where it is?"

He snorted. "No. If they did, they would've used it for themselves a long time ago."

"Why didn't the demon that hid it do that?"

Adrian paused, seeming to choose his words, which meant I'd just be getting part of the truth again. "As it turns out, only a few people can activate the weapon's true power. Minions can't, and neither can the average demon. Zach said that the demon who hid it was on his way to tell a more powerful demon about it when Zach killed him."

"Wait. You said demons could only be killed with the weapon *Zach didn't have*," I emphasized.

A shrug I felt but couldn't see. "Archons don't need it to kill demons, and other demons don't need it to kill their own. The rest of us do, which includes you and me."

Figures. "Couldn't Zach have gotten its location before he silenced its hider forever?"

Another pause, longer this time. My temper flared. "Could you for once just answer me with the *whole* truth?"

"Fine." His tone thickened. "For all I know, Zach did find out where the weapon was. Even if he didn't, his boss knows, yet here we are. Know why? Because neither of them really cares if we live or die trying to find it."

His brutal analysis stunned me. "But that's…they're… they're on the *good* side," I sputtered.

His laughter was like glass grinding together. "*They* win or lose this war, Ivy. Not us. We can only depend on each other, because to Archons and demons, we're just pawns that they move around for their own purposes."

"But Zach's your friend," I argued softly.

"You don't understand Archons. They're not fluffy beings sprinkling supernatural happy dust everywhere they go. They're soldiers who've been relegated to the sidelines until the pesky issue of humanity has been settled. Frankly, I think Zach's reached the point where he doesn't care what happens to our race, as long as he finally gets to fight."

What Adrian described couldn't be true. Good couldn't give a complicit shrug to evil, and the faith of billions of people from every race, background and creed couldn't be worthless to whoever the Archons' "boss" was.

"You're wrong," I said, still softly but with an undercurrent of iron. "We *do* matter to them. It just might not look that way sometimes, from our side of the fence."

The harshness was gone from Adrian's laughter, replaced by a despairing sort of anger.

"That's why I still hide things from you, Ivy. If you can't accept the way the board's set up, you're not nearly ready to learn the endgame yet."

"Maybe you're the one who's not ready," I replied, my sense of resolve increasing. "I get why. You've had it bad for so long, all you see is darkness even when the lights are on."

"Bad?" His voice changed, becoming a whisper that seared me even in the frigid temperature. "You don't know the meaning of the word, but you're about to find out."

CHAPTER THIRTEEN

I HAD BRACED MYSELF, but no amount of mental preparation would've been enough. At least, when I finally did throw up, it matched the reaction any human would have at seeing how demons lived inside their own world.

At first, the town reminded me of a medieval fiefdom, with the overlord's manor overlooking the serfs' much cruder lodgings. In this case, wigwam structures were laid out in tight clusters along the lowest part of the hill. Smoke billowed from their open tops, reminiscent of pictures I'd seen of sixteenth-century Native American life. Very few people seemed to be in the wigwam village, and the ones we passed looked away when they saw Adrian. They were also skinny to the point of appearing wasted, and their clothes consisted of shapeless leather tunics that couldn't have been nearly warm enough in these frigid temperatures.

"This area is for laborers, the lowest level of human slaves," Adrian said tersely. "Next are overseers' and merchants' quarters."

Those must have been the plain but sturdy huts that dotted the hill about a hundred yards higher than the wigwam village. Torches were interspersed among the narrow paths between them, and their interiors glowed from what I guessed were fire hearths. They looked like ancient Southwestern pueblo houses, with the addition of leather flaps covering the doorways and windows to keep the heat in. Once more, no one attempted to stop us as we walked through. In fact, anyone we passed seemed to avoid eye contact with Adrian, and he strode by as though he owned the place. I practically had to run to keep up, and since the hill was steep, it was quite a workout.

After we ascended about three hundred yards, we reached gray stone gates that surrounded what was clearly the town's epicenter. Torches lined the exterior of the gates, but I smelled fuel and heard the unmistakable hum of generators, which explained how this area appeared to have electricity. The added lighting made it easier to see, and once I did, I stared.

This wasn't a mini city located at the top of a hill. The city *was* the hill. The closest thing I could compare it to was a gargantuan pyramid. The base had to be a mile long, with courtyards I couldn't fully see from my lower vantage point. Massive balconies with elaborately carved stone columns showed people milling around inside the pyramid, and one entire side of it seemed to house a huge stadium.

Further up, the corners had huge faces carved into them. One was a lion and one was an eagle, with the predators' mouths open as though about to devour their prey. The very top of the pyramid blazed with so much light that it looked like a star had landed there. I couldn't make out much detail, though. It had to be as high up as the sphere on the Empire State Building.

I was so awed that I didn't realize someone had come up to us until I heard Adrian speaking in that poetically guttural language. My gaze snapped to his left, where a dark-haired, muscled man now stood. It wasn't the metal breastplate over his brown camouflage clothes that caught my attention, although *that* fashion mis-

take should never be repeated. It was the man's face.
Light rolled over his eyes like the passing of clouds,
and inky black wings rose and fell beneath his cheekbones, as if he had a tattoo that could magically appear
and disappear.

My staring seemed to annoy him, so I looked away.
He said something sharply to Adrian and then grabbed
my wrist hard enough to bruise me. Adrian moved with
that lightning quickness, putting Camo Guy in a headlock with his arm bent at the wrong angle before I could
even say, "Let go."

"I told you, she goes straight to Mayhemium,"
Adrian said, speaking English this time. "And if you
delay me again, I'll rip your head off."

I didn't know if it was Adrian's dangerous tone
or how quickly he'd broken Camo Guy's arm, but he
grunted something that must've been an agreement.
Adrian let him go, smiled as though they'd exchanged
a friendly hello, and then half dragged me through one
of the openings in the wall.

Lots of stone steps later, we reached the pyramid's
lower courtyards. At first glance, it looked like an average street market. Vendors hawked various wares inside their booths, food cooked on open grills, and people
milled around, either buying or window-shopping. But
every other person had that strange roll of light over
their eyes, and when I got a closer look at some of the
vendors' wares, my legs abruptly stopped working.

"Keep moving," Adrian whispered, half lifting me
so it wasn't obvious that shock had frozen me where
I stood.

I forced my suddenly numb limbs to keep working.
It helped that Adrian took us quickly through the market section and into a side alcove that had a drain in the

floor. Even though his large frame blocked most of my view of the courtyard, I still couldn't stop the grisly images from replaying in my mind.

Along with a few slabs of cow and pig, food vendors also sold human body parts. For customers who wanted fresher meat, their human selections were slaughtered on the spot.

"Why?" I choked, unable to say more because words couldn't make it past the bile in my throat.

"There's no sunlight here." Although Adrian's tone was matter-of-fact, something haunted flashed across his expression. "That means no grass, grains, vegetation or animals. Minions and pampered human pets get to have regular food imported from the other side, but the slaves have only one thing to eat. Each other."

That bile turned into vomit that I couldn't hold back. At the same time, I was shaking with rage. Now I knew what all the leather garments and doorway flaps were probably made of, too.

Adrian didn't mock me for puking, or tell me to pull myself together. He held back my hair, his other hand moving over my shoulders in a comforting caress.

"We can leave," he said low. "The realm's not going anywhere. We'll come back another day to search it."

Laughter drifted down from one of the pyramid's balconies, its sound an abomination. No one should laugh here. No sound should be made except screams of horror at what was going on in this lightless pit of evil. I wanted to run back to my world as fast as I could and never, ever return, but if I did, I'd be condemning Jasmine to spending the rest of her life in a similar hellhole. I'd rather die than do that.

Resolve mixed with my rage, helping me get control of my stomach. I wiped my mouth with a gloved hand

and gave Adrian a look that reflected the new hardness creeping through my soul.

"Take me deeper inside this place. I'm not leaving until I check every frigging wall for that weapon."

I LEARNED MORE about demon life than I ever wanted to know as Adrian guided me through the pyramid's many levels. First, generators supplied heat as well as light to the massive structure, so my extra clothes were now slung over my arm. Second, the inside looked like someone had taken the Great Pyramid of Giza and pimped it out with modern—albeit barbaric—amenities.

The large stadium section was for gladiator-style fights to the death, a popular form of entertainment here. "Pets," which was how Adrian referred to humans who'd caught the eye of demons, lived above the courtyards. Minions lived above them in condo-styled units, and of course, the best, most luxurious quarters were reserved for the supernaturally sadistic rulers of this realm. Adrian said we'd be avoiding those places unless I sensed something, but so far, I hadn't picked up a hint of anything hallowed in this opulent, stone-and-brick nightmare.

I also found out how Adrian was able to escort me around without arousing suspicion. For one, he spoke the language, and every light-show-eyed guard who stopped us only used that to communicate. For another, Adrian's cover story was that I was a newly arrived "pet" for Mayhemium. From the knowing looks that garnered, whoever Mayhemium was, he had a lot of "pets."

I'd figured out Adrian's final trick after noticing how quickly every human looked away from him when we passed. The only other people they treated that way were guards, and since they didn't all dress alike, that left only one other thing.

"Zach glamoured your eyes to shine like the guards' eyes, didn't he?" I whispered once we had a moment alone in one of the pyramid's many stairways.

The barest smile cocked his mouth. "That's right."

"Why do theirs do that?" Also whispered, but wheezier. I must've climbed two miles in steps by now.

"Part of the perks of being a minion. Along with increased strength and endurance, demon marks give them the supernatural version of *tapetum lucidum*." At my raised brow, he added, "The extra layer of tissue in animals' eyes that allows them to see in the dark."

That explained the odd shine, but… "You don't have that, and you see as well as they do." *And move faster,* I mentally added.

I couldn't read the look he threw me. "I've already told you why."

Right, his mysterious lineage. He might've told me some of the whys, but he hadn't spilled the "what" yet. The more secrets he revealed, the more I burned to know his biggest one.

"That's the gift that keeps on giving, then," I said, trying not to sound like I was probing, which I was.

His jaw tightened until I swore I heard cartilage crack. "I'd give anything not to have this lineage." Sapphire eyes seemed to burn as they swept over me. "Especially after meeting you."

If we weren't inside a demonic version of the Luxor hotel, I would've demanded that he elaborate. He'd already told me more since we'd arrived than he had in the week leading up to it, but "bad timing" didn't begin to cover our current situation.

Of course, that meant it was about to get worse.

The hairs on the back of my neck rose before I saw her. Apparently, my "hallowed" sensor could also pick up on the presence of pure darkness, because with one glance, I knew the woman coming down the staircase was a demon.

It's not that she had "Evil!" stamped on her forehead, or obvious supernatural indicators like Demetrius's shifting shadows. Maybe it was the way she moved, as if every muscle instantly coordinated with the others, turning her walk into a graceful, predatory glide. Maybe it was her hair, each wavy lock either midnight black or a burnished copper shade. Her pale skin was also telling, but it was her face that sealed my suspicions.

No one could be that incredibly, perfectly beautiful unless they'd had a million dollars in plastic surgery or had made a deal with the devil, and my money was on Option B.

Even Adrian couldn't tear his eyes away, which hurt in ways I didn't even want to acknowledge. Yes, she was gorgeous, but did he need to stop walking and stare like he'd been transfixed? He hadn't been affected enough to pause in his stride when they were slaughtering people in the courtyards!

I either made a sound, or my instant hostility caught her attention because dark topaz eyes slid over me as she passed. Just like with Demetrius, I fought the urge to wipe my clothes, as if her gaze had left a tangible trail where it landed. She said something in what I now referred to as Demonish and Adrian responded, his voice much raspier than normal.

He couldn't even talk right around Her Evil Hotness? I quietly seethed, but when she disappeared down the stairwell, Adrian let out a sigh that almost blew the lid off my temper.

He was actually *sighing* after her. Guess when he said he hated demons, he meant only the males or the ugly ones.

"How much more ground do we have to cover?" I whispered acidly, hating him and hating myself more for caring.

His attention snapped back to me. "You still don't sense anything?"

Only your hard-on for evil incarnate. "Nothing."

"Then we're done. You sensed the burial ground at half the distance from what we've covered, so it must not be here."

Good, we could leave. Not soon enough for my tastes, either. This realm wasn't where the weapon had been hidden, I'd already have nightmares from the horrors I'd seen, and now I wanted to punch my only ally in the face. Lose-lose all around.

We made it out of the pyramid without incident, and I looked down as we exited through the courtyards. No one stopped us at the stone gates, and we navigated the pueblo-like village with nary a word spoken in acknowledgement. Once we'd cleared the edge of the wigwam village, however, our luck ran out.

"Hondalte," a commanding voice ordered.

Adrian paused. I did, too, schooling my features into a blank mask despite the hairs standing up on the back of my neck. When I turned around, I saw that my demon radar hadn't been malfunctioning. The lanky, blond-haired man approaching us had two tall, dark arcs rising out of his back.

Not arcs, I realized when he drew nearer. Pitch-black wings. Then he spoke, causing my stomach to flip-flop in fear.

"If she is a new pet for me," the winged stranger said in English, "tell me, why are you leaving with her?"

CHAPTER FOURTEEN

"My lord Mayhemium," Adrian said, bowing formally. "I have discovered that this one is too flawed for you."

The blond demon came closer. I tried not to stare, but he had *wings*. Were they real or a type of illusion, like Demetrius's ability to transform into shadows and other people?

"What is so flawed about her?" Mayhemium asked, and my skin felt like it was trying to crawl away as his gaze slid over me.

"I have crabs," I blurted out, saying the first gross thing that came to mind.

The single glare Adrian shot my way said that I wasn't helping. "She's mentally defective," he replied, his tone implying that it should be obvious. "I'm taking her to Ryse's realm. He doesn't mind less-than-superior pets."

Mayhemium's gaze swept me again. From his expression, Zach had glamoured me into looking as gorgeous as Adrian's disguise was plain. Then the demon waved an imperious hand.

"I'll take her anyway."

Adrian let go of my arm and stepped away. I tried to conceal my shock, but I wasn't that good of an actress. Yes, we were deep in enemy territory and outnumbered by a thousand to one, but was he really going to let Mayhemium take me?

The demon thought so. My breath sucked in at the gleam that appeared in those inhuman eyes. Now I knew what death looked like when you stared it in the face. Then Adrian straightened, abandoning his subservient posture.

"I never liked you, Mayhemium," he said in a tone so flat, he sounded bored. "At least you're so arrogant, you came alone."

Before the last word left him, he hit the demon, moving so fast all I saw was his usual blur. Mayhemium stared at him, something inky leaking out from the side of his mouth.

"Adrian?" he asked in disbelief.

"Ivy, leave," Adrian ordered, urgency now replacing the flatness in his tone.

Mayhemium's head whipped around, and he stared at me with understanding that turned into unbridled savageness. "The last Davidian," he hissed.

Adrian punched him so hard, I expected a dent to appear in the demon's face. It didn't, but more incredibly, Mayhemium shattered, his body transforming into dozens of large crows that flew straight up before diving in a furious arc toward me.

My arms rose to shield myself, but Adrian was suddenly blocking them, his large body absorbing the stabs from beaks sharpened into knifelike points. With lightning-strike quickness, Adrian snatched the largest crow out of the air and then crushed it in his fist. Mayhemium materialized at once, howling in apparent agony, his long black wings now broken.

"Think I didn't remember how to neutralize your trick?" Adrian's purr dripped viciousness as he punched the demon hard enough to knock him over again. "What's wrong? Can't fight without your wings?"

Mayhemium snarled something in Demonish that turned Adrian's face into a mask of rage.

"No," he spat. "I'll never do it."

"You will," Mayhemium roared. "It's your destiny!"

"Not today." With that, Adrian landed a kick that snapped the demon's leg when he got up again. When Mayhemium bent low and staggered, Adrian smashed a knee into his face, crunching bones with an audible sound. Then Adrian's fist drove through the demon's neck, briefly disappearing up to his wrist before he yanked it and a handful of something pulpy out.

Yesterday, the sight would've made me gag, but after touring the pyramid, all I wanted to do was cheer, especially when Mayhemium fell and didn't get back up.

Adrian strode over, yanking my arm with a hand now coated in what looked like motor oil.

"What part of 'leave' did you not understand?" he snapped.

"The part where I left you alone with a pissed-off demon," I replied, feeling dazed. "Is he dead?"

"Of course not." Adrian propelled me into the darkness, running so fast I had trouble keeping up. "For the tenth time, humans can only kill demons with the weapon we don't have yet."

"You're not human," I panted, my strides no match for his.

"I'm as human as you are," he said, shocking me. "And you need to run faster. He'll wake up soon and send every minion in this realm after us."

"I can't…run faster." I could barely talk, I was huffing and puffing so much from our frantic pace.

"Yes, you can." He hauled me closer, his body a guide in the stygian darkness. "We're the last of the two most powerful lines in history, and our ancestors passed down all their supernatural abilities to us. If you try, you can do everything I can do, except sense demon gateways. It's in your blood, so *use* it."

The source of his incredible abilities was also in *my* blood? Impossible. I wasn't superwoman; I was the girl who'd hated gym class because of all the times I'd gotten picked last for teams.

"I'm running as fast…as I can," I gasped out.

He only yanked harder on my arm. "Not yet, and you need to. I can protect you from a few demons, but not all of them. Do you know what will happen if they catch you? Death will be the best part. Before that, they'll hurt you worse than they've hurt anyone else. Rape won't be enough. Torture won't be enough—"

"Stop!"

"—and they'll make you watch as they do the same to your sister," he continued ruthlessly. "You'll die knowing that everything she suffered was your fault, so *run,* Ivy!"

Something snapped in me. I'd already failed Jasmine by leaving her in that B and B when I should have stayed until I found a way to get her. The last time I'd seen my sister, I'd been running away, and she had no way to know that I was coming back for her—

"That's it," Adrian yelled, his grip on me loosening. "Faster, Ivy, you can do it!"

I didn't feel any change in my body. My legs didn't work harder, my lungs didn't suck in more air, but I was somehow ahead of Adrian, running flat out into the impenetrable darkness. Once again, I flashed to that day at the B and B. Mrs. Paulson had attacked me, and I'd made it into my Cherokee without knowing how. Right now, I did. I must've run just like this, with a speed no human should have, but I somehow did.

Was Adrian right? Had ancient legacies and inherited abilities been simmering in me this whole time?

He drew even with me, his hand a brand on my chilled flesh, guiding me in directions I couldn't see. At some point, I'd dropped the ski gear, but I was glad I didn't have it. All that padding would've hindered me, and the cold spurred me on. In my mind, it was now tied to this place, so I hated it. I ached to be back in the sunshine where it was warm and demon-free, and all I had to do to accomplish that was to run faster.

So I did, my legs pumping with the same velocity as Adrian's. When he grabbed me and I felt the body-bending force of hurtling through one realm into another, then found myself facedown with a mouthful of hot sand, I smiled.

We were back in the Zone of Silence.

Adrian didn't give me time to celebrate by kissing the ground, which I wanted to do. He also didn't pull me back through the gateway so we could search another demon realm through the vortex's version of a revolving door. Not with Costa and Tomas waiting here like sitting ducks. Instead, Adrian hauled me up into the Jeep, barking something to Tomas in Spanish that had the brawny Mexican and the handsome Greek scrambling for their machine guns.

"Vamonos!" Tomas shouted, starting the Jeep.

Adrian practically flung me into the back, jumping in after me and grabbing the third gun. To my surprise, he shoved it into my hands, barking out quick instructions.

"Hold it tight. It'll still fire if you drop it, then you'll blow your own head off. Stay down, but if anyone gets too close, shoot them until you see ash."

He grabbed the last gun, hooking his other arm

through the railing behind the seats. I did, too, after Tomas's rapid acceleration almost pitched me out the back. I'd just gotten a good grip on both the automatic weapon and the metal bar when a stream of people hurtled out of the oblong rock behind us.

"Incoming!" Adrian yelled, and started firing. Costa did, too. The noise was like explosions going off in my ears, but when the minions began running after us as if they had rockets strapped to their asses, I didn't care if I'd go deaf.

They moved like Adrian did, and they were armed, too.

Adrian shoved me down at the first hail of bullets. The back of the Jeep shuddered, but the rounds didn't penetrate. Now that I was eye level with it, I saw how thick the back door was, and that extra metal plating couldn't have come standard.

"Didn't I tell you to stay down?" I heard Adrian snap, then another barrage of gunfire stole his voice. The Jeep bounced madly from Tomas's speed, but Adrian and Costa held on to the rails as they fired and ducked in a frenetic display of violence and defense.

"You gave me a gun, let me help!" I protested.

"No," Tomas yelled, whipping the Jeep around so fast that I hit my head on its side panel. "Stay down! You're who they most want to kill!"

Me? Then I remembered Mayhemium's look of loathing, and what he'd hissed right before Adrian hit him. *The last Davidian.* Did the demons want me dead because I was the only one who could locate a weapon that could kill them?

It didn't take long to get my answer. Despite the hail of gunfire Adrian, Costa and even Tomas leveled at the minions, they kept trying to get to where I crouched.

My little corner became dented from all the bullets fired at it, and every so often, minions would hurtle themselves into the Jeep kamikaze-style. Adrian threw them out with his incredible speed, but I was soon covered in blood, bruises and cuts. And they kept on coming, until I was convinced that the whole realm had emptied in their attempt to kill us.

Or kill me, specifically.

When Tomas had to slow down to get through the tight passage between the mountains, five minions managed to jump onto the Jeep. Adrian got clobbered by three of them, and Tomas and Costa sounded like they were in their own life-and-death struggles. Their bulky machine guns were a hindrance in a close-contact fight, but I still had mine. I got up, raising it with grim determination.

Out of nowhere, another minion grabbed the barrel and used it to yank the gun from my hands, delivering a brutal kick to my midsection at the same time. I fell back into the corner, and for a split second, our eyes met. His were cerulean blue, and he grinned as he raised his own gun. Unarmed and wedged between the door and the seat, there was nothing I could do to save myself.

A knife suddenly slammed into the top of his head, twisting with vicious force. My would-be killer abruptly went cross-eyed and dropped his gun. I snatched it up, clutching it but not firing. Adrian was now right in front of me, and I didn't want to hit him, plus my would-be killer looked really, really dead.

Adrian yanked his knife out and the minion began to fall. As he did, his body transformed, turning dark as pitch and then dissipating altogether. What landed on the blood-spattered floor wasn't a man. It was a pile of ashes that coated me when the Jeep bounced from Tomas's wild acceleration as we finally cleared the mountain pass.

Adrian knelt, one hand roughly cupping my face while the other searched me for injuries.

"Thank God you're okay," he breathed.

For some reason, hearing Adrian thank a deity he mostly seemed to despise shocked me as much as seeing my would-be killer disintegrate before my eyes. I stared at Adrian, the ashes covering me and then the horizon. No more leaping, murderous minions appeared, and since Costa and Tomas had stopped firing, I assumed we were finally in the clear.

But with the sun hanging lower into the sky, we wouldn't be clear for long. Night was coming, and with it, demons.

CHAPTER FIFTEEN

WE DIDN'T GO back to our hotel in Ceballos. Tomas drove straight to an empty, ancient-looking monastery, and we passed through the gates right as the last rays of sunlight disappeared. I staggered into the abandoned sanctuary with relief so intense, it felt like a cheap high. Who knew that entering a church would be my new favorite thing?

"Hide the Jeep," Adrian ordered. "How're we on ammo?"

"Nearly out," Tomas said, running a red-splattered hand through his hair. "I'll make a call, try to get more."

"Costa." Adrian threw the bag of manna at him. "Here."

The curly-haired man winced as he reached up and caught it. "Thanks. Bastards got me."

When Costa lifted his shirt and I saw two oozing holes in his abdomen, I ran over to him. "You've been shot!"

Mentally defective is right, I immediately chided myself. Talk about stating the obvious.

"Let me help you," I added, tucking my shoulder under Costa's arm so he could use me as a crutch. Adrian shook his head, muttering something unintelligible as he left the gutted sanctuary. I led Costa to an alcove, seating him on the groove.

"You know what you're doing with that?" Costa asked, sounding pained yet amused.

"Scoop 'n slap, right?" I replied, digging my fingers into the mushy substance. Out of everyone, my hands were the cleanest, but I still left bloody smudges in the bag.

Costa grunted. "That's it." Then he visibly braced as I held my manna-smeared hand over the first entry wound. "Do it."

I pressed it against the bullet hole, wincing in empathy as his whole body jerked. After a few minutes, his harsh breathing eased, so I pulled my hand away.

No more blood oozed from the hole, which was growing smaller before my eyes. After another minute, it disappeared entirely, leaving a smooth, shiny patch of skin in its place.

"One to go," I said, reaching for more manna.

"Did your hands get shot, too, Costa?"

The question startled me. I hadn't noticed Adrian return, but there he was, standing where the doors would have been, if the sanctuary entrance still had them.

Costa lifted one shoulder in a shrug. "Only a fool turns down attention from a pretty girl."

Adrian's expression hardened even more than his current scowl, which made no sense. First, having your bullet wounds treated could hardly be counted as flirting, and second, why would he care even if Costa *was* flirting?

"I'm trying to help," I said, placing manna over the second bullet hole, which effectively silenced Costa. "I didn't prove too useful with a gun, but this, at least, I can do."

Adrian's stare went from my face to my hand on Costa's abdomen and back again. "Oh, I'm sure he appreciates it."

After those quietly growled words, he disappeared.

Costa's brow rose. I lifted my free hand in a "don't ask me" gesture. Maybe his rudeness was just another side effect of having been raised by demons.

"I don't think he likes you touching me," Costa said, his mouth curling. "Adrian, acting jealous. That's a first."

"He's not jealous," I muttered, wiping my hands on my shorts after I confirmed that his wound had healed. "He keeps reminding me that he can't wait to get away from me."

"That's not about you." Something dark flitted across Costa's expression. "That's about him."

Tomas returned, stopping me from probing more. "Jeep's hidden," he announced, "and more guns are on the way."

Relief swept through me. Who knew that guns would be my *second* favorite thing after hallowed ground?

"What're the odds the demons won't find us until we get those guns?" I asked, hoping for a high percentage.

"Fifty-fifty," Tomas replied, dashing that. "They know you can't have gotten too far by sundown, so they'll have minions search every hallowed site within a hundred miles."

"Right, they want me dead because I'm the only person who can find a demon-killing weapon," I said wearily.

"That's not—" Tomas began, then shut his mouth at the warning look Costa gave him.

"Not what?" I asked, suspicion replacing my fatigue.

"If Adrian hasn't told you, he must have a reason," Costa said, landing himself right after Demetrius on my shit list.

"Yeah, because he's pathologically secretive," I snapped. "I'm getting sick of being the only person who doesn't know what's going on, so one of you had better talk."

Tomas exchanged another look with Costa, then he leaned back against the wall.

"You know what it was like for us in the realms?" he asked in a conversational tone. "We were beaten, forced into cannibalism, worked almost to death...and that was on a good day."

Sympathy tempered my anger. "I am so sorry," I said, meaning every word.

Tomas's dark brown stare held mine. "Don't be. We survived. Know how Adrian was treated before he started fighting demons? Like a prince." He paused, letting that sink in. "Anything he wanted, he got. He didn't even have to ask. They practically worshipped him, and when demons want to shower someone with adulation, *créeme,* they make it rain. Beautiful women, more gold than Fort Knox, power to rule any realm he entered—"

"Why?" I whispered, stunned.

"Because of his lineage, they believe he's going to do something that will make demons unbeatable in their war against Archons."

It's your destiny! Mayhemium had roared at Adrian. Demetrius had said something similar when he caught up with us. Even Zach had told Adrian he couldn't escape his fate, but Zach was an *Archon,* so he couldn't believe Adrian was destined to help demons win the war against them. If he did, why wouldn't Zach kill Adrian as a preemptive strike? The demons sure wanted to kill me, and all I could do was find one ancient weapon....

I sucked in a breath, realization shattering me. "It's the weapon, isn't it? Adrian said if the demons knew where it was, they'd have already used it for their own purposes. I didn't think it through at the time, but that means it must do a lot more than just kill demons."

Tomas's mouth thinned into a straight line. Costa got up, dropping a hand briefly on his friend's shoulder.

"You've heard of David and Goliath?" Costa asked evenly. "Thousands of years ago, a shepherd boy killed a giant with nothing more than a slingshot and blind faith, thus David's fame was born. You are the last Davidian, so in your hands, that ancient slingshot has the onetime power to overcome any and all odds. In short, whatever you point it at, it will defeat."

That sounded too good to be true, so there had to be more. "What can the demons do with it?"

Costa's smile was grim. "Goliath was no ordinary giant. He descended from demons, and some of his originating bloodline lives on. If one of *those* demons gets the slingshot, they get a onetime ability to overcome unbeatable odds, too. So with it, demons think they can win the war against Archons in a day."

My head was starting to pound, probably from trying to process information that was too incredible—and horrible—to believe. If I hadn't crossed through to a different realm today or seen multiple examples of supernatural phenomena all my life, I would have called Tomas and Costa crazy.

Unfortunately, I knew they weren't.

"Is Adrian descended from Goliath's line?" was what I asked. "Is that why the demons think he's their savior? Because if he gets the weapon, he can use it against Archons?"

Tomas and Costa exchanged another look, then Tomas let out a deep sigh.

"No, Ivy. Adrian's the last of another line."

"Whose?" I asked in a steely voice, my glare daring them not to tell me.

"Get out, both of you."

Adrian's voice cut through the silence. Like before, he'd come in without anyone noticing. Tomas and Costa rose at once, leaving without another word. When I saw the expression on Adrian's face, part of me wanted to follow them, but the rest wanted the truth so much, I didn't care about the consequences.

"Whose line are you the last of?" I said, refusing to back down. "Tell me now, or I leave that weapon lost, and after what I just heard, 'lost' is probably where it should stay."

He smiled, the seductive curve of his lips not taking away from the lethal hardness in his jeweled gaze. His jaw was shadowed from not having shaved recently, and that hint of darkness only made his high cheekbones look more pronounced, giving an edge to his already unforgettable features. Even in his bloody, torn clothes, I'd never seen him look more gorgeous, and for the first time, I was also afraid of him.

"Haven't you guessed?" he asked, his voice caressing the words like silk draping across daggers. "Who in history committed such a heinous act that it made his name forever synonymous with betrayal?"

"I don't know," I said, backing up as he came toward me with slow, stalking steps.

"Yes, you do."

A rough, throaty whisper, and then he was in front of me, his arms a cage that blocked me in while the wall behind me made retreat impossible. Despite my fear, I shivered as he leaned down, his mouth only inches from mine and his hands sliding to rest on my shoulders. The last time we'd been this close, he'd almost kissed me, and God help me, I still wanted him to. My feelings for him defied logic, sanity or safety, and judging from the intensity in his gaze as he wound one hand through my hair, it was possible he felt the same way.

Then his mouth lowered, but not to my lips, though they parted in reckless anticipation. Instead, he kissed my cheek, whispering his darkest secret at the same time.

"I'm the last descendant of Judas, and like my infamous forefather, my fate has been, and always will be, to betray the children of David."

CHAPTER SIXTEEN

I FELT LIKE I couldn't breathe. His mouth was still pressed to my skin, caramel-colored hair like rough silk against my forehead, breaths teasing my ear with soft heat. Add that to his revelation, and the wall was the only thing holding me up.

"Adrian," I began.

"Don't." His hand tightened in my hair. "Everything that's happened since we met only proves how entangled in our fates we already are. Judians and Davidians have always been drawn to one another, but then Judians betray and destroy Davidians. Thousands of years and countless betrayals later, we're the only ones left."

His hand stroked from my shoulder to my face, moving over it in a caress that made my skin burn.

"Maybe being the last of our lines made what we feel for each other so much stronger. I'm not just drawn to you, Ivy. I've wanted you since the first time you touched me. It was as if you reached inside and claimed something that had always been yours." He drew back to stare at me as if he was trying to memorize my features. "That's why I thought you had to be a minion. Nothing but dark magic had ever felt so powerful, and when I touch you, it's a thousand times worse. You're the light I can never have...and I'm the darkness you'll never succumb to."

His hand dropped, leaving my skin feeling cold.

"That's why it would never work between us, so now you understand why I need to get away from you, Ivy. Before I betray you like everyone else in my line has betrayed Davidians. I refuse that part of my fate, and it's not just to spite Demetrius anymore. It's because I can't stand the thought of hurting you."

Before my next breath, he was standing in the sanctuary entrance, the night surrounding him like a cloak.

"So do what your ancestors weren't able to," he rasped. "Save yourself by never believing you can save me."

Then he was gone, leaving me with questions I had no answers to and emotions I couldn't seem to control.

TOMAS SAT IN the sanctuary with me, his cell phone screen providing a small circle of light. Adrian and Costa were on the roof, watching out for any unwelcome visitors. Even if Adrian wasn't the only one who could see in the dark, he still wouldn't have stayed down here. His decision to avoid me didn't take into consideration my wishes on the subject.

For now, I'd let him get away with that. My emotions got in the way when Adrian was near, so this gave me a chance to separate fact from feeling. Unfortunately, that hadn't helped.

Fact: Adrian had lived like a demon for many years. Feeling: with how he'd been brought up, he wouldn't have known it was wrong. Fact: he felt doomed to repeat the mistakes of his ancestors. Feeling: to hell with them, everyone was responsible for their own choices. Fact: I didn't want to be betrayed. Feeling: Adrian wouldn't do it. Fact: I shouldn't fall for a borderline psychopath with demonic daddy issues. Feeling: something special was brewing between me and Adrian, and it had nothing to do with Adrian being the last Judian or me being the last Davidian.

The sound of a car interrupted my thoughts. I ran over to the window, but Tomas said, "Don't worry, it's my friends."

"How do you know?" I couldn't see anything except headlights.

"Because they just texted me, 'Don't shoot, we're here.'"

Okay, then. Tomas went to tell Adrian and Costa, and I stayed in the sanctuary, watching through windows that hadn't seen a pane of glass in decades. A worn Chevy pulled into the monastery, two people in front and one in the back. They got out, speaking Spanish so rapidly I only caught the names Tucco, Danny and Jorge. They'd brought a bunch of weapons, though, and that made them a welcome sight.

Adrian was in the middle of checking the scope on a rifle when he paused, staring into the distance. "Are there more of you coming, Tucco?"

"No, *por qué?*" the shorter man replied.

Adrian cocked the rifle. "Take positions on top of the church," he said curtly. "We've got company."

I didn't see anything, but I believed him. So did the others. They scrambled to unload the rest of the guns, then at Adrian's command, parked the truck in front of the sanctuary. Now the vehicle blocked the largest entrance to where I was, although the windows were big enough for someone to get through.

Adrian proved that when he vaulted through one, angling his big body sideways to fit.

"Here," he said, pressing a small caliber gun into my hand. "This'll be easier for you to use. It's cocked and ready. All you have to do is pull the trigger."

"And not get it yanked away," I said grimly.

Adrian flashed me a smile. "Second time's the charm."

I hoped so. "Adrian, before you go—"

"No matter what happens, stay here," he said, cutting me off. "They can't cross hallowed ground. The gun's for emergencies, but Tomas'll be with you. Stay down so the minions don't see you. We'll be on the roof, keeping them from getting too close."

"No," I protested, but he was already gone. Tomas jumped through the window Adrian had just vacated, his dark gaze flicking to me as he accepted a bundle of automatic weapons from Costa.

"You want to help, *sí?*" At my vigorous nod, Tomas gestured to the weapons. "I'll show you how to change the magazines. When I run out, you replace them."

In the short time it took me to learn, three cars began bouncing across the desert terrain toward the monastery, their headlights the only illumination for miles.

"Any chance they're lost tourists?" I asked with a fake chuckle.

Tomas shrugged. "Could be members of a local drug cartel."

"Oh, let's hope."

When they were close enough to notice the truck blocking the entrance, the vehicles screeched to a stop. A barrage of gunfire from the roof cut off the instant chatter of Demonish, dashing any chance that these were drug runners looking to hide their stash.

As instructed, I stayed low while the minions returned fire. Then again, these ocher-colored walls were already in bad shape; I doubted they'd stop bullets for long. Maybe we should've tried to hide. As soon as I thought it, I rejected the idea. Would minions sent on a murder mission by demons really be content to shine a flashlight around and then call it a night?

"This one's out," Tomas said, dropping one rifle and snatching up another. Quickly, I replaced the magazine, trying not to flash back to the last firefight when I'd been almost killed. Easier said than done with the rat-a-tat-tat-tat! of gunfire going off. If I lived through this, I'd never be able to watch a war movie without risking a PTSD attack.

Right now, I channeled my anxiety into replacing Tomas's ammunition as fast as he needed it. The pile of magazines seemed to be shrinking at an alarming rate, and the sanctuary walls were beginning to look like Swiss cheese from the hits they were taking. Every time a bullet penetrated, a small cloud of stone dust puffed out. There had been so many, the air was starting to get chalky.

Worse, it sounded like fewer guns were firing back from the roof. I tried not to think about what that meant, or drive myself crazy wondering if Adrian was okay. Every so often, a shout would rise above the other noises, but I couldn't tell who made it. The roof had stone arches, carvings and a bell tower to hide behind, but if they were sustaining as much damage as the sanctuary walls, things were getting dire.

And we were down to only two clips of ammo.

"How many minions are still out there?" I asked Tomas, needing to shout to be heard above the gunfire.

"Four more carfuls just pulled up," he yelled back.

Four! An irrational urge to start screaming built, but I choked it back with forced optimism. We'd survived a minion attack before. If we hung in there, we'd survive again—

Tomas spun around, clutching his chest. Horrified, I saw a new hole in the wall right where he'd been standing. I barely managed to catch him before he crumpled, crimson leaking out between his fingers.

I set him down and rushed across the room to retrieve the manna Adrian had left. Something burned in my leg, but I ignored it, zigzagging to avoid more bullets on my way back.

"No," Tomas groaned, coughing up blood with the word.

I tore open the bag and, pulling his hands away, clapped a large glob of manna onto his chest. He coughed up more blood, then his lips stretched into a grisly imitation of a smile.

"Doesn't work...mortal wounds."

My eyes welled, causing his features to blur. "You're not dying," I insisted, pressing another handful to his chest.

"Can't save...me." His breathing became labored, and blood continued to stream through my fingers, soaking the manna.

"Don't talk," I said, desperately trying to stem the flow. "You need to save your strength."

Tomas stared at me, and for a second, the agonized haze left his vision and his eyes became clear.

"You need to save Adrian," he said distinctly. Then his eyes rolled back, and his body convulsed before he went limp.

"Tomas!" I screamed.

No response. His chest didn't rise for another breath, and the gush of blood between my fingers slowed to a trickle. I didn't need to check for a pulse to know he was gone. Slowly, I lifted my hands from his chest and sent a single glare upward that wasn't directed at the men on the roof.

Why? I thought furiously. *He was fighting for Your side! Don't You even care?*

No response again, not that I expected any. Maybe Adrian was right and we were nothing more than collateral damage to both sides. Fine. If the Archon's boss wouldn't do anything to help, I would.

I picked up Tomas's gun, barely noticing how hot the metal was from his repeated firing. Every part of me was consumed by guilt and rage. I'd stayed down like they told me to, and Tomas had died. No more. I'd fight and live, or I'd fight and die, but either way, I was fighting.

I braced the barrel against a hole in the wall like Tomas had done and started firing. For the first few rounds, my aim was terrible, and I hit the cars the minions hid behind instead of them. Stone exploded near my face as they returned fire. I ducked low until it stopped, then began firing again, aiming for the flashes of light I'd glimpsed from the minions' guns.

I didn't hear a yelp, but one of their weapons abruptly went silent. I felt nothing except grim satisfaction, which surprised the small part of me that hadn't been irrevocably changed by the past two weeks. I kept firing, scooting over when the wall became too pocked with holes for sufficient protection. I'd just replaced the magazine clip with the last full one when a thunderous boom shook the sanctuary.

Sand rolled in like a fast-moving fog. Between that and the sudden glare of headlights, I was momentarily blinded, but the noise and the shuddering ground kept me moving. I ran toward the back, keeping low, which was a good thing. The sickening rushes of air over me had to be gunshots I barely avoided.

"Ivy!" I heard someone scream before a frenzy of gunfire drowned out the sound. Then another, more ominous noise swelled. Metal screeched, stone groaned, and the ground shook like I was in the middle of an earthquake. Frantically, I blinked the sand out of my eyes, finally able to see enough to realize the sanctuary was crashing down around me.

CHAPTER SEVENTEEN

I RAN FOR the window, pain exploding over me as I was pelted by chunks of the roof. Then I dove through it right as the walls folded, releasing a thick cloud of crushed stone from the tremendous impact. My knees and arms tore, but I forced myself to keep moving through the rubble. Through the chalklike fog, I saw something dark rush toward me. I raised my arms before realizing I no longer held a gun. Sometime during my mad dash to escape the collapsing sanctuary, I'd dropped it.

I tried to run—and was grabbed before I made it a step. Then I recognized the large body I was pressed to. Felt rough, hot hands race over me, seeking out signs of injury. I hurt everywhere, but the pain faded at the knowledge that Adrian was still alive. I threw my arms around him and, for a blissful second, felt him hug me back with equal vehemence. Then Adrian thrust me behind him fast enough to make my teeth rattle.

"Hondalte!" a voice rang out.

Stop, I mentally translated, recognizing the Demonish word from our time in the realm. The thick cloud dissipated, revealing the cause of the sanctuary's demise. One of the minions had rammed their truck into the side of the building, taking down the gunfire-weakened walls. What I saw when I peeked around Adrian looked equally ominous.

Half a dozen minions were silhouetted against the vehicles' headlights. Demetrius stood in the middle, his black hair merging into the shadows that trailed behind him like a cape.

"Adrian, enough," the demon said in an annoyed voice. "Move aside. I have no wish to hurt you."

"Sure you don't," Adrian mocked. "All those bullets aimed my way were just you trying to say hi."

Demetrius's gaze raked over him. "Those were to limit the damage you inflicted on my people, but you, more than anyone, know why we want you alive. In fact, Mayhemium is being punished for not instructing his people to take care with you earlier."

I hadn't thought a demon was capable of telling the truth, but right now, I believed Demetrius. For starters, six guns were trained on us, yet at the demon's command, no one was firing. As for Adrian, blood dripped down him from multiple wounds, staining his clothes and turning his hair auburn, but when I'd held him, he had felt whole. Sad that I was learning to tell the difference between seriously injured and moderately hurt.

"Ah, but if she's dead, then you don't need me anymore," Adrian countered.

Good point, and a very frightening one. I glanced down. We were still on hallowed ground, from the faint luminescence drifting up, so Demetrius couldn't get to us. Of course, with all the guns pointed our way, he didn't need to.

"You're still my son," Demetrius said quietly. "Give us the Davidian, and I will gladly welcome you home."

Adrian's whole body tensed. "Stop calling me that," he said, each word vibrating with hatred. "And you're only getting Ivy over my dead body."

Demetrius sighed, resignation flickering across his

pale features. "If you insist on dying for her, so be it." Then his black eyes gleamed. "I will, however, raise you back up so you can fulfill your destiny."

Adrian's breath hissed through his teeth. "You don't have the power to."

The demon's laughter sent shivers of revulsion through me. "All your overdoses, son? I already have. Many times."

Six guns rose with lethal purpose. Amidst a surge of fear, I also felt sheer resolve take hold of me. I couldn't save myself, but no one else was dying for me tonight.

I shoved Adrian aside as hard as I could. Whether it was adrenaline or the determination of a last wish, I actually succeeded in knocking him over. Right as his shocked gaze met mine, multiple loud cracks sounded. I tensed, waiting for the pain…and then a cool, familiar voice spoke.

"Is this a bad time?" Zach asked dryly.

Shock froze me with my muscles still bunched and eyes mere slits from the process of squeezing them shut. It took a second before I registered that I was not, in fact, dead. I wasn't shot, either, unless you counted my leg, but that was from earlier and felt like a flesh wound, anyway.

Bullets were lined up in front of me, though, close enough to reach out and pluck them from the air. They hung as if someone had pressed Pause on a remote control, and I stared at their hollow points in morbid fascination. Then another series of loud cracks sounded.

My firing squad fell in a row, their bodies dissipating into ash as soon as they touched the ground. Not even their clothes or shoes remained. Only their guns were left, the sand absorbing the impact as the weapons dropped with muffled thuds.

"Archon." Demetrius's voice was a barely controlled growl. "You should not be here."

What do you do when you have a demon staring down an angel while the ashes of dead minions blew between them? You get out of the way, of course.

I slunk sideways, clearing that path of bullets in case they suddenly reactivated. Adrian got up, grasping my arm and moving me toward the shattered sanctuary. Zach didn't look at either of us. His piercing dark gaze was focused on the demon, whose shadows stretched and grew ominously large behind him.

"You should leave," Zach stated in a mild tone.

I was in full agreement, but he was talking to Demetrius. The demon let out another growl, his shadows increasing even more. Then they began to spin, forming into multiple funnel clouds that whipped up the sand and caused the cars nearest him to slowly slide and spin.

"The Davidian is mine," Demetrius hissed.

"Uh, time to go, Adrian," I said nervously.

"Our cars are smashed," was his grim response.

"Stop the theatrics, Demetrius," Zach said, still in that calm tone. "You can't defeat an officer of the Most High."

"If that's what you are," the demon responded with luxuriant hatred. "I know all the officers, because once, I was one, yet none of them are named Zacchaeus." Then he cocked his head as if curious. "You could be concealing your identity behind that name and your human shell, but if you are what you claim, why not smite me along with my servants?"

"Those weren't my orders," Zach replied indifferently.

Why not? I wanted to yell, but kept backing away with Adrian. We were now even with the ruined sanctuary, the desert spreading out like a blank canvas behind us.

"Orders." Scorn dripped from Demetrius's tone. "Don't you ever weary of those?"

Zach's mouth curled into the faintest of smiles. "Some days."

"Then free yourself," Demetrius commanded. "Live under your own rule as we do, my brother."

Then he said something in a language that reminded me of Demonish, if you took out all the harsh syllables and replaced them with lyrical exquisiteness. Zach replied in the same language, and I almost closed my eyes in bliss. Nothing had ever sounded so beautiful. Of course, if he was accepting Demetrius's offer, we were both dead.

"Do you know what they're saying?" I whispered to Adrian.

He kept backing us away. "Demetrius said his people would soon claim this realm, and he urged Zach to join them. Zach refused."

That had pissed off the demon, clearly. I watched with dread as Demetrius's funnel clouds grew into what looked like F4 tornados, tossing up debris from the crumpled sanctuary. One of the minion's cars flipped over, setting off an alarm.

"Are you able to run, Ivy?" Adrian asked, his voice barely audible over the wind and whooping car alarm.

I felt like I didn't have the energy to crawl, but if my life depended on it? Yep. "What about Costa and the others?"

"They're dead," Adrian replied flatly.

Despair made me stumble. I didn't even remember all their names, and they'd died because of me. How many more would die if I kept going after that weapon to save my sister?

"Go now," Adrian urged, releasing my hand.

What about you? I was about to ask, then light crashed around us, briefly illuminating everything with noonday clarity. I saw arms and legs amidst the rubble, the back end of the truck that had demolished the sanctuary, piles of ashes blowing away and every nuance of Demetrius's shocked expression as his wall of tornados abruptly dissipated.

Zach's hand dropped, but light still pulsed beneath his skin, as if his veins had been replaced with streaks of electricity. "Leave, Demetrius," he said in the sudden silence.

"Who are you?" the demon almost whispered.

Zach's stare didn't waver. "This is your final warning."

Demetrius disappeared, taking the wispy remains of his ruined shadows with him. I would've let out a triumphant whoop if I wasn't so upset by the senseless loss.

"Everyone else is dead," I said, my tone as flat as Adrian's. "Why didn't you show up before, Zach?"

"I wasn't sent," he replied, the answer making me want to scream. "Besides, not all are dead. Some are asleep."

With that, he walked over to the rubble and grasped a dirty, limp hand. Costa came up from the rocks with a gasp, his gaze darting around as if expecting an attack.

"Don't be afraid," Zach stated. "You are safe."

And uninjured, judging from how easily Costa moved once he was free from the rocks. I stared, disbelief turning to amazement. No way had he only been "asleep." He still had bullet holes in his shirt, not to mention he'd been buried under a stone building; yet now, he looked in better shape than me.

One glance at Adrian's face confirmed it. He stared at Zach while his expression changed from shock to expectancy.

"Wake the rest of them up," he said with barely contained vehemence.

Zach didn't reply, but he did go over to another motionless body part and then pulled up a perfectly healthy Tucco.

"What happened to the minions?" Tucco asked, shaking the dust and debris out of his hair.

"Ashes," Adrian responded in a terse tone.

"Bueno," was Tucco's reply, followed by, "Where's Tomas?"

"In the sanctuary," I said, my voice catching on the next word. "Asleep."

"Not asleep. Tomas is dead," Zach corrected, no emotion in his tone.

Adrian strode over, gripping Zach by the collar of his pullover sweater. "Wake. Him. Up," he said through gritted teeth.

Zach's handsome features stayed in that serene mask. "He is dead," he replied, spacing out the words like Adrian had. "Neither your demands nor your anger can change that."

"But you can save him," I burst out, rushing over to grip the Archon's sleeve. *"Please,* save him."

Zach looked at Adrian and me before brushing our hands aside. "His time had come, as with the other two. It is done."

Then he walked away, adding, "There are others you can still save, if you haven't given up. Tickets are waiting at the Durango airport. Whatever you decide, don't remain here. Demetrius will soon find his courage and return."

As Zach disappeared, one of the formerly silent cars revved to life. The four of us stared at it for a moment, and then, by unspoken agreement, climbed inside.

I didn't know if the rest of them were motivated by survival instinct, but I knew why I got into the car, and it wasn't just because I wanted away from the sanctuary of death behind us. I might be angry, confused and in desperate need of a shower, but I still wasn't ready to give up.

CHAPTER EIGHTEEN

ADRIAN USED THE last of the manna he'd stuffed in his pocket to heal our injuries on our way to the airport. Tucco got off on our first layover in Mexico City. Costa, Adrian and I continued to our plane's final destination of Miami, Florida. I'd learned on the flight there that Costa and Tomas lived in Miami, and they'd journeyed to Durango to help Adrian after he called them. Now only Costa had survived to make the trip home.

Their house was a former church located only two blocks from the beach. It even had a steeple with a cross on top. When Costa showed me around, I realized that he and Tomas had closed in that soaring, pointed ceiling, turning it into the house's second floor. That was where I stayed, in Tomas's old room, and for the first day, all I did was sleep.

The second day, I went to the beach. I wasn't trying to work on my tan, but the sun, heat and tropical scenery made it the exact opposite of the demon realm, and I gratefully soaked up the differences. Already, I couldn't stand the cold or dark. I'd kept the lights on when I slept, something I hadn't done since I was child, and if the air-conditioning dipped too low, a feeling of dread washed over me.

Costa said that no one left the realms the same way they entered them. Adrian had warned me, too. They were both right.

I stayed at the beach the whole afternoon, moving under the shade of the pavilion when my skin began to redden. Late October in Miami felt like June in Virginia, but the beach wasn't crowded, probably because it was a Thursday. Back at WMU, Delia and the rest of my friends would be making their weekend plans. They knew which bars had a strict ID policy and which didn't, plus there were always parties on or around campus. I'd joined them on the classes-parties seesaw for the past two years, but it almost seemed strange to realize I'd be doing that again if I went back home. I'd often had to fake my enthusiasm for going out, and that was before I knew the freaky things I saw were real. Now? I couldn't pretend to be impressed by some drunken guy pulling off a keg stand. Kick a demon's ass, *that'll* impress me.

Speaking of guys, a few hit on me throughout the day, which would've been flattering under regular circumstances. These were anything but. For starters, they were hitting on my blond disguise, not *me*. More importantly, when I wasn't thinking about Tomas's death, my sister's imprisonment or the awfulness of the realms, I thought about Adrian. Flirting with cute strangers was the last thing on my mind.

Three of the guys took my rebuff like men and went on their way. The fourth, however, was being a little bitch about it.

"Come on, sugar, have *one* drink with me," he urged.

"Again, no," I said, not adding "and I'm not your sugar" only because simple phrases already seemed too much for him.

He grinned, showing off nice teeth. He wasn't bad-looking, either, with his short black hair and a leanly muscular build, but even if I was looking for a date, he wouldn't be it. Years ago, I'd dated another guy who didn't understand the word *no,* and I'd ended up breaking an empty beer bottle over his head on prom night. *That,* he'd understood.

Mr. Pushy grabbed my hand, tugging on it with that same smug grin. "Bar's right up the street. You'll love it—"

Being snatched backward and flung to the sand ended his grabby sales pitch. Adrian stood over him, his foot grinding into the guy's back. Somehow, I wasn't a bit surprised.

"You've been spying on me all day, haven't you?" I said. "I told you I needed some time to myself, Adrian."

He glanced down at Mr. Pushy. "Good thing I didn't listen."

I rolled my eyes. "Like I couldn't handle him? If nothing else, you should've known that I'd be able to out*run* him."

"…'et me…up," the guy said, his words garbled, trying to spit out enough sand to talk.

Adrian hauled him up, though a hard cuff almost sent Mr. Pushy sprawling again.

"Get lost," he said curtly.

The guy looked at Adrian with surly confidence, reminding me that he only saw the disguise. Not the hulking, six-six man who'd ripped the throat out of the last person who touched me without my consent.

"I should kick your ass," the guy muttered.

"You should run while your legs still work," I told Mr. Pushy. To Adrian I said, "He's not worth the police report, so don't do whatever you're thinking of."

Either the guy sensed the danger in Adrian's glare, or he suddenly remembered another girl who wanted to go to the bar. Whatever it was, with another mutter, he left, still brushing sand off himself as he climbed up the pavilion staircase.

Once he was gone, Adrian and I stared at each other. Moments ago, he'd been poised to strike; now he looked almost hesitant, like he didn't know what to say.

"Costa's making dinner," he told me, as if that had anything to do with why he was here. "It'll be ready in half an hour."

My annoyance began to evaporate. I'd seen Adrian look angry, vengeful, bitter, confident, lethal and seductive, but this was different. He almost seemed... shy. Was it because I'd busted him for spying on me? If so, he must not have been doing it only out of concern for my safety.

"So what's for dinner?" I asked, my voice soft.

He smiled. "Burnt moussaka, probably. Costa loves to cook, and I don't have the heart to tell him that he sucks at it."

I laughed. "Thanks for the heads-up. I'll play along and clean my plate, too."

Adrian chuckled before he looked away. The sea breeze blew his longer bangs back while the setting sun turned his blondish-brown hair into different shades of red. His shirt molded to him from the wind, and his shorts showed off those shapely, muscular legs.

"You did really well in the realm," he said, still not looking at me. "I meant to tell you that before, but..."

"Everyone died and Zach only brought a couple back," I filled in, grief chasing away my other thoughts. "Thank you, by the way. I didn't get to say that before, either. I wouldn't have made it out of there alive without you."

Or out of the desert, the monastery, the other desert,

Bennington… Because of Adrian, I was turning out to have more lives than a cat.

He looked at me then, sadness making his eyes appear a deeper shade of blue. "Did Tomas… Was it quick?"

I drew in a shuddering breath, remembering that awful wound and Tomas's last words. "It was quick."

He nodded, returning his attention to the water, but I glimpsed the grief he was trying to hold back. I moved closer, sliding my hand into his without even thinking about it. His fingers curled around mine, and the sense of rightness I felt hit me like a wrecking ball. Had I fallen so hard, so fast?

"I'm glad you were with him," he said, his tone faintly hoarse. "Dying's hard enough. Doing it alone is worse."

I couldn't imagine all the death Adrian had seen growing up in the demon realms. I'd suffered so little by comparison, and some days, I still felt like I couldn't take it. Today had been one of those days. All the warmth and sunshine I'd tried to soak up hadn't put a dent in the icy darkness rising inside me. But holding his hand did, and that scared me as much as I silently marveled at it.

"Do you really think I'm strong enough to keep searching the realms until I find this weapon?" I asked, my voice barely audible as I spoke my greatest fear aloud.

His hand tightened on mine. "I know you are," Adrian said, turning to look at me once more.

It wasn't the words, though I'd needed to hear them. It wasn't even his voice, though it vibrated with surety. It was his eyes. I'd never read so much from a person's eyes before, but Adrian's seemed to spill all the secrets he still refused to tell me. In those sapphire depths, I knew he meant what he'd said. I might not believe in me, but he did, and right now, it gave me hope that we would make it through. All of us.

I reached out, trailing my free hand down his arm. "Thanks," I said softly.

He stepped closer, brushing my hair back, and I closed my eyes. I felt so safe with him, which he'd say was the last thing I should feel. Still, if nothing but betrayal loomed ahead, how could Adrian be the only person I trusted? And how could he be the only person who made me feel alive if he was destined to be the death of me?

"I believe in you, too," I told him, not opening my eyes. "You'll beat your fate. I know you will."

He let out a strangled sound, and my skin felt cold from how fast he let me go. When I opened my eyes, I wasn't surprised to see only surf-soaked sand in front of me.

Once again, Adrian had vanished, but like all the other times, he wasn't really gone. Whether by destiny or by choice, neither of us could completely walk away from the other.

Not yet.

CHAPTER NINETEEN

THE NEXT MORNING, I awoke to a strange man sitting on the end of my bed. His back was to me, and I would've screamed if I hadn't recognized his faded blue hoodie. Good thing I'd caught myself. Adrian and Costa would've run in with their guns drawn.

"What are you doing here?" I asked Zach.

The Archon set down a picture of Tomas as a boy with his father. Family pictures occupied most of Tomas's room. I hoped looking at them made Zach feel guilty. He could've saved Tomas, but he'd chosen not to for reasons I still didn't understand.

"I am here to glamour your appearance," Zach replied, ignoring the thought I knew he'd heard. "Adrian has chosen the next realm for you both to search, and demons will be more watchful of blonde women."

I ran a hand through my hair, remembering that only Adrian, Zach and I saw its deep brown shade. As for my face, well, I hadn't seen that clearly in almost two weeks. Not being able to look in a mirror without risking a demon attack cut back on any feminine urges to check my appearance.

"Don't overdue the hotness factor this time," I said. "We might have made it out of that realm without a fight if Mayhemium hadn't gotten a hard-on over my glamoured looks."

Zach nodded. "I will make appropriate changes."

Then he placed his hand on top of my head. Like last time, I didn't feel anything, but when he said, "It is done," I knew I now looked completely different. Pity I couldn't see my disguises. When I looked at my reflection in shiny surfaces, it still looked like the "real" me.

"Okay." I got out of bed, put on a robe and went to the door. "I'm making coffee. Don't suppose you want any?"

The side of his mouth twitched. "I'm trying to cut back."

Had he just cracked a joke? I looked sharply at him, but that twitch was gone and his expression was back to its normal, placid mask. Deciding I had more important things to worry about, I left the bedroom.

"Zach's here," I announced on my way to the kitchen.

Costa's door flung open, and he stared at me, shock creasing his features. "Ivy?" he asked with disbelief.

I waved a hand. "I know. Zach gave me a makeover, so minions and demons don't recognize me from my old disguise."

"They sure won't," Costa croaked, his lip curling in a way that said Zach had taken my admonition seriously by beating my new appearance with an ugly stick.

I gave a mental shrug. I was shallow enough to care if Adrian saw me that way, but he didn't.

Speaking of Adrian, his door opened as we passed. He'd been in the process of pulling on a shirt, which gave me a glimpse of his muscled chest and ripped abs before the loose material covered them. I swallowed, glancing away. With a mind-reading angel in the house, now *really* wasn't the time to dwell on how much Adrian affected me.

"Zach." Adrian's voice was brisk. "We need more manna, plus a new appearance for me, too."

Costa said something in Greek that had Adrian whipping around to stare at me. Then he let out a snort of amusement.

"Nice," he told Zach, the edginess gone from his tone.

Had Zach given me Halloween-style warts, too? I lifted my nose and started making coffee. Some of us were too mature to worry about things like unattractive fake appearances.

"Where are we going this time?" I asked.

Zach remained standing, but Adrian and Costa sat at the kitchen table. I pulled three cups out from the cabinet. None of *us* were trying to cut back on our coffee habit.

"Roanoke, North Carolina," Adrian replied.

Not another desert, at least. "There's a vortex there?"

"No." The edge was back in Adrian's tone. "No more vortexes."

I turned around, still holding my empty coffee cup. "Why?"

"Demetrius now knows the weapon is hidden in a demon realm," Zach answered for him. "He'll expect you to try vortexes, since they are the most efficient means of entry into their realms."

Adrian's shrug conveyed, *What he said.* Costa still seemed to be reconciling my new appearance with who I was, but I was focused on the information no one had told me before.

"You mean the demons didn't know the weapon had been hidden in one of *their* realms before they caught us looking for it?"

"That's right," Adrian said, with a sidelong glance at Zach. "It'll be a race to see who finds it first, and you can bet they'll be searching their worlds from top to bottom."

"Do you know where it is?" I asked Zach bluntly, remembering Adrian's accusation about the Archon.

As if he knew the source of my question, Zach gave Adrian a measured look before he responded. "No."

Archons don't lie, I reminded myself. Then again, I only had an Archon's word on that, so it wasn't exactly unbiased.

"But your boss knows," I prodded. "Right?"

The faintest smile curled Zach's mouth. "He would not be much of a 'boss' otherwise."

"How about we save a lot of lives by having him tell us where it is, then?" I asked, barely holding back my sarcasm.

Zach gave an infuriating shrug. "If that were His will, you would already know its location."

The coffee cup in my hand shattered. I yelped, both at the pain and the clattering sound as pieces hit the floor. I hadn't been aware of tightening my grip, but in my anger, I must have. Adrian started forward, but I waved him back with a frustrated swipe of my hand.

"Sorry," I muttered to Costa, bending to pick up the pieces. To Zach I said, "Then your boss sucks. It's to *His* benefit that I find the weapon before the demons do, but instead of helping, *He's* grabbing popcorn to sit back and watch."

"Get used to it," Adrian said dryly.

"Isn't that what *you* would rather do?" Zach replied, his gaze flashing as it swept over me. "If your sister's life wasn't tied to this weapon, would you risk yourself searching for it?" Before I could respond, he started in on Adrian. "And if it wasn't the key to your vengeance, would you risk your fate to help her? No," he answered for both of us. "Therefore, sit judgment on your own sins before you presume to judge others'."

Now I was glad I'd broken the thick glass cup. Otherwise, I might have thrown it at him. "There's nothing wrong with wanting to save my sister's life," I almost snarled.

"Untold thousands are trapped in the dark realms. If hers is the only life you care about, something is very wrong," Zach responded at once.

"That's out of my control and you know it. If I could save all of them, I would!" I snapped back.

Absolute silence fell. For a second, it seemed like the traffic noise outside Costa's house vanished, too. Adrian closed his eyes, anger and resignation skipping over his features. Light briefly gleamed in Zach's gaze, and he stared at me with such intensity that a wave of foreboding swept over me.

Something significant had just happened, and as usual, I was the only one who didn't know what it was. Also per usual, none of them were going to tell me about it.

Whatever. I'd get it out of them eventually. I threw the last of the shattered cup into the trash and then ran my hand under the tap, washing the cut one of the shards had made.

"When do we leave for Roanoke?" Costa asked, breaking the loaded silence. "And before you argue, Adrian, I *am* going with you. Tomas died fighting for Ivy's chance to find that weapon. I'm seeing this through until she does. Then my best friend can finally rest in peace."

I'd started this to rescue my sister, but in a short amount of time, the stakes had grown much larger. Now more than Jasmine's life hung in the balance. So did Adrian's revenge, Tomas's justice and Costa's tribute to his friend, all hinging on my ability to find and successfully use a supernatural weapon, if the demons hunting us didn't kill us first.

No pressure, right?

Adrian's gaze moved to Zach, and the two men exchanged a look I couldn't read. Whatever it was, it wasn't happy.

"Did you bring my car?" Adrian finally asked.

An oblique nod. "Of course."

Adrian went over to the now-full coffeepot, downed a steaming mug like it was a single shot and then flashed the rest of us a grimly expectant smile.

"We leave in an hour."

CHAPTER TWENTY

A GLIMPSE INSIDE Adrian's trunk explained why we were driving to North Carolina instead of flying. It looked like an NRA gold-member kit, with row upon row of handguns, regular rifles and assault rifles. We barely had room for luggage, not that I had much to bring. Aside from the clothes and basic hygiene items Zach had gotten me, all I owned was a lipstick, gum and face cream, all stuffed inside a tiny, clear travel bag.

I took that bag out to put my lipstick on during our first pit stop. Costa wasn't the only person who stared as I contorted my head in order to see a distorted reflection in the chrome from Adrian's empty side mirror. Not that I cared. I wasn't doing this to look prettier for Adrian, Costa or even myself. I did it because it was my last link to a semi-normal life. Everything else had been turned upside down or taken away, but this small feminine ritual was my silent promise that one day, if I survived, I'd get it back. No matter how long it took, or what I might change based on truths I now knew.

"That looks...disturbing," Costa said when I was finished.

I smacked my lips at him, unperturbed. "I'll get better at doing this without a mirror. Now, pass me the rock and gloves. I'm hitting the ladies' room before we leave."

"Uh, I don't think—" Costa began, only to be cut off by Adrian's "Don't. This I have to see."

I gave them a questioning look as I accepted the gloves and rock I'd need to smash the mirror. That turned to suspicion when they followed me into the gas station, not even pretending to browse as they watched me enter the bathroom. Jeez, had I screwed up my lipstick *that* badly?

This time, I glanced under the stalls before I broke the mirror. No one, good. After I kicked the worst of the shards out of the way, I answered nature's call. I was in the process of washing my hands when the door opened and a squeal startled me.

"That was already broken," I began to lie, only to be interrupted by the heavyset African-American woman saying, "You are in the *wrong* place, Grandpa!"

What? As I goggled at her, the woman's gaze dropped to my lips, then to the glass on the floor.

"You okay, sir?" she asked in a less scandalized voice.

"I'm not a man," I protested, then stopped at the sudden burst of laughter from inside the store. Uh-oh.

Costa's look of disbelief when he first saw me. Adrian's amused comment of "Nice" to Zach. Both of them following me to the ladies' room. This woman calling me "sir" and "Grandpa."

"I look like an old guy, don't I?" I asked resignedly. "An old guy wearing lipstick, no less."

Concern pinched her features. "Is someone here with you, sir? Or is there someone we can call?"

"Yeah." My voice was wry. "Call the angel with the warped sense of humor, because this is all his fault."

Now she *really* looked concerned, but I brushed by

her, saying, "Fun's over, sonnies. Time to take Grandpa for a ride!" to the two grinning guys waiting for me.

WAY BACK WHEN, Roanoke Island had been the site of a Colonial-era settlement that mysteriously disappeared. Today, parts of the island drew visitors by marketing that event. Take Festival Park, a tourist attraction complete with a structural re-creation of the Lost Colony, a play about it, several Elizabethan-styled games, and people wandering around in sixteenth-century costumes.

Costa didn't drop Adrian and me off here so we could join the festivities. In the glimpses I caught of the demon realm, the north side of Roanoke Island was surrounded by ice instead of water, with barren earth replacing the pretty oak and myrtle trees. Some of the pre-Colonial huts from Festival Park were there, though, looking not much different from the ones that duplicated the village in the former Lost Colony.

"It's like the realm swallowed this place," I murmured to Adrian, glad someone else could see what I did.

"That's exactly what happened," he responded, his voice low. "Realms start out as duplicate reflections of our world, with everything we build here getting mirrored there."

"Everything?" I tried to absorb the staggering thought that demon realms had duplicated the entire world.

"As reflections," Adrian stressed, leading me into the trees behind the Visitor's Center. "They're not tangible yet. That only happens when demons get powerful enough to absorb an area. When they do, the place, along with everyone in it, gets sucked into a new realm in the demon world. So in effect, they swallow it. Then what's left in our world is an empty shell."

For a second, I closed my eyes, thinking of the two versions of the bed-and-breakfast Jasmine was trapped in. "But that shell can be rebuilt."

"It can." Adrian looked around, his mouth curling. "Absorbed places carry negative imprints of what happened, even if people don't understand why they don't want to build there. Festival Park is at the back end of the demon realm. The main part looks just as beautiful in our world, but it isn't crawling with shops and hotels like these sections of Manteo."

He was right. The part of Manteo we'd rented a room in had nearly wall-to-wall bed-and-breakfasts, inns, restaurants and stores. Compared to that, the place where the former Lost Colony had been located was largely undeveloped.

"So what was our version of Mayhemium's realm, before he swallowed it?" I asked, no longer whispering since we were a hundred yards into the woods by now. "It looked like bigger versions of the Sun and Moon pyramids in the Avenue of the Dead."

He gave me a tight smile. "You know your history."

"It's my major," I said, remembering that the ruins of Teotihuacan were thousands of years old on our end. The demons had had plenty of time to keep building on their side of the realm. By comparison, the colony at Roanoke had been recently swallowed, and it was far less impressive than sucking in the third-largest pyramid in the world.

"Why'd the demons want this place?" I wondered.

Adrian gave me a jaded look as he held back a low-hanging branch so I could duck under it.

"Same reason every conqueror wants more territory. The person with the most usually wins."

Duly noted. "And you think the weapon might be here, why?"

He stopped in front of a tall tree stump that had been halved, as though a lightning strike long ago had split it in two. The dark wood rising up behind him reminded me of Mayhemium's wings, and I shifted uncomfortably. What horrors would I discover in this new realm?

"It's led by a weak demon," Adrian said. "All I know of the demons from Goliath's line is that they're very strong. That rules out the weapon being hidden in one of their realms. Otherwise, the demon who stole it would've just given it to that realm's ruler instead of hiding it while looking for someone who could wield it."

I stared at him, incredulous. "You're saying that Mayhemium was a *weak* demon?"

His snort was contemptuous. "Oh, yeah. Total pussy."

"Sure. Because who can't transform into dozens of killer crows, am I right?"

His mouth quirked at my shrill tone. "You freaking out, Ivy?"

Yes. If Mayhemium was the demon-lite version, we were so screwed! "I'm just…absorbing this."

That quirk deepened. "Sorry, time's up. Here's the door."

With that, he grasped me and then dropped us backward into the V in the tree stump. Instead of hitting the long-dead wood, the realm-piercing roller coaster started, leaving me with a familiar sensation of nausea when it spit us out into a dark, freezing version of Festival Park.

This time, lights from the realm's residents were close enough that I didn't feel like I'd been struck blind.

Of course, it also meant that we were stopped by a minion before we'd been here less than five minutes. The slide show of white in his eyes matched the furs he wore over his leather-and-metal outfit, making him look like he'd gotten it at a Viking surplus store.

I'd heard enough Demonish to know that he said a variation of "Stop! Who goes there?" to Adrian, but his reply was lost on me. It seemed to satisfy the minion guard, and the way he barely looked at me made me glad for Zach's old-man disguise.

"What was your excuse this time?" I whispered when the guard was far enough away not to overhear us.

Adrian's mouth tightened. "I told him you were food."

Right, because that, forced labor and forced sex were the only things demons imported humans into their realms for. A sick sort of rage swept over me. *Jasmine.* Despite Adrian's assurance that the demons were treating her better than anyone else, I couldn't help but wonder what horrors she'd gone through while I was fumbling around looking for this weapon.

I forced those thoughts back. They only led to more rage and feelings of helplessness, which wouldn't do my sister any good. Finding the weapon would, and to do that, I needed to concentrate on abilities I was just learning to use.

We passed some old wooden huts that were covered by a thick layer of ice. Human slaves occupied them, and it was all I could do not to give away my warm jacket, boots and gloves when I saw them shivering in their paltry coverings. I couldn't, of course. That would be announcing myself to the minions and demons here, and though there were a lot less of them than in Mayhemium's realm, there were a lot more innocent bystanders on our side of Festival Park. Costa waited with our arsenal in the parking lot, but starting a firefight at a tourist attraction was the last thing we wanted to do.

After the wooden huts, we walked along what seemed like a mile-long line of igloos. The igloos made sense, I supposed, since ice was the only material in large supply here, and demons had absorbed this realm before anything substantial was built. Light inside made the igloos glow, and while I was sickened by all the trapped people they denoted, I was grateful for the extra illumination. Did I mention I'd come to hate the dark?

"Sense anything?" Adrian asked.

"No," I replied, and he grunted as though he'd expected that. Guess the last place he thought the weapon was hidden was in the wall of a slave hut.

About three miles into our hike, I had a question, too. "Why are demon headquarters so far away from realm entrances?"

Adrian shot me a slanted look. "Tactical advantage. They want to see an army coming, if someone's after their realm."

"Demons fight each other for control of the realms?"

Adrian's mouth curled into a sardonic grin. "Humans don't have a monopoly on land grabs, Ivy."

Guess we wouldn't. Compared to all the demons' other cruelties, snatching each other's kingdoms seemed almost a benign activity.

After ten minutes of brisk walking, a castle came into view. The walls glowed with different colors, faint but ethereal, reminding me of a small, multicolored version of the Emerald City in *The Wizard of Oz*. When we got closer, I saw the gates were adorned with ice sculptures that looked like mermen and mermaids. A long staircase bordered by ice-carved waves led up to the castle, and the front doors resembled huge seashells.

More guards were stationed around the gates. In addition to metal, some of their weapons seemed to be forged from ice. It was as though we'd stepped into a demonic version of Poseidon's Frozen Paradise, and the more I stared, the less I wanted to remember. I hated that it was so beautiful when I knew what horrors lurked beneath the exquisite exterior.

After exchanging a few words with one of the guards, Adrian took us around to the back of the castle. There, we were stopped again, and Adrian relayed the same cover story as before. One of the guards shook his head as he gave me a rough cuff, and I didn't need to know Demonish to guess that he was disparaging my proposed edibility. I hunched my shoulders and tried to look terrified while I hoped Adrian's darkening expression didn't mean he was about to deck the guard. I still hadn't sensed anything, but we hadn't entered the castle, and I wasn't leaving until I'd given it a supernatural once-over.

Thankfully, Adrian didn't do anything violent, and we were finally allowed into the back of the castle. The narrow hallway looked more igloo-like than Icy Emerald City, but I guess fanciness wasn't required for the slave entrance, although the floor was a pretty shade of deep pink—

Adrian's grip on my arm tightened until it should have been painful, but I barely felt it. The floor of the room we entered resembled a layer of rubies. The reason for that became abhorrently clear as I saw a cloudy-eyed minion mop up a pool of blood, its crystallized stain adding another layer of red. The blood came from a nearby ice slab, where another leather-clad minion carved out sections from the body lying on it.

This wasn't the slave entrance. It was the slaughterhouse.

Mopping Minion said something in Demonish to Adrian. He responded in a harsh voice, dropping his hand from my arm, but I wasn't focused on him.

A bound, naked boy lay on the floor. At first, I thought he was dead, too. Then his gaze slid from the dripping slab to me, and the absolute hopelessness I saw in it shattered me. He wasn't silently begging for help. As he watched the butchering going on above him, his blank, empty stare said he knew nothing could save him from being next.

Without the slightest hesitation, I drew out the gun Adrian had given me and fired. The butcher went down, clutching his chest. I kept shooting as I advanced, part of me marveling at the quiet, cough-cough sounds the gun made. That silencer Adrian had screwed onto the end really worked as advertised.

I stopped shooting only when the butcher's body turned into ash. Adrian looked at the black ashes on the ice, at the slack-jawed minion who'd stopped mopping, and finally at me.

"Shit," he said simply.

CHAPTER TWENTY-ONE

MOPPING MINION OPENED his mouth. Before he could scream, Adrian's punch to the throat cut him off. Then Adrian gripped him in a brutal headlock that ended with a jerk, a snapping sound, and the minion dissolving into a pile of ashes on the floor.

"Move, Ivy," Adrian ordered. "We don't have long until someone finds them."

With the same eerie calm I'd felt when I shot the butcher, I put my gun away and knelt next to the naked boy.

"Give me your knife," I said to Adrian.

He frowned but passed it to me, and I cut through the plastic that bound the boy's hands. He blinked once, but said nothing, even when I took off my parka and wrapped him in it.

"Ivy," Adrian said in a warning tone.

"We're taking him with us," I replied, kicking off my boots.

Pity creased Adrian's expression. "I wish we could, but—"

"We're taking him *with us*," I repeated, almost spitting out the last two words. "I don't care if it's more dangerous. I don't care if he'll slow us down. He's coming or I'm not."

"You'd risk your sister's life to save him?" Adrian asked harshly.

I shoved my boots onto the little boy's feet. He couldn't have been more than twelve, so they were too big. Tightening the laces would have to do.

"I can't save Jasmine right now," I said, my voice calm from the absolute certainty I felt that this was the right thing to do. "But I can save him. Don't pretend you don't understand. Costa and Tomas are proof that you do."

Adrian muttered something in Demonish, but picked the boy up, throwing a hard glance at my now-bare feet.

"Put the boots back on. I'll carry him."

"He's freezing and I can manage," I argued.

"We do it your way, all of us die," Adrian said flatly. "Put the boots back on, then shut up and do what I say."

I bristled, but our survival outweighed pride, so I took the boots off the boy and put them back on. He still didn't say anything. Maybe he was in a state of catatonic shock.

"Now, activate your power and search the castle from right here," Adrian ordered.

I tried to clear my mind enough to concentrate. It didn't work, probably because I was in a small icebox with two piles of minion ash on the floor and a chopped-up body less than five feet away.

"I need to get out of this room," I said.

Adrian's sapphire gaze seemed to burn into mine. "Not an option, and we're running out of time."

I tried again, closing my eyes, but I still couldn't concentrate on anything except the carnage around me. I was standing on layers of frozen blood, for crying out loud.

"Adrian," I started to say, but his sudden grip on my throat cut me off.

"Maybe you don't understand," he said, fingers

slowly tightening. "You need to search this castle *right now,* and you're not moving from this spot to do it."

I grabbed his wrist, digging my nails into his skin. His hand only tightened more, until my throat burned from the pressure. He didn't even need to shift his grip on the boy to throttle me, and the child watched us with dull, empty eyes. Panic filled me as I couldn't get in more than a few thin, insufficient breaths. My chest started to heave in urgency, trying to force in air that Adrian wasn't allowing me to have.

Stop! I thought, unable to say anything. My nails ripped into Adrian's wrist, yet that ironlike grip didn't lessen.

"Still can't utilize your power?" he asked, staring into my eyes with pitiless determination. "Then I'm going to choke you unconscious and leave this kid behind while I carry you out instead. You can't look for the weapon anyway, or can you?"

My gasp of horror caught in my throat. He wouldn't do that…would he? Had I been wrong about him? Was he every bit the monster he'd warned me about?

"The only way you'll stop me is to access your power and search this place," he went on. "And, Ivy? I can feel it when you do, so don't bother trying to fake it."

I'll never forgive you! my gaze swore, but then his grip loosened and air rushed into my lungs, claiming all my attention. My second deep breath was ambrosia, quelling the frantic clenching in my chest. The third took away my panic, and the fourth had me closing my eyes as I sagged with relief—

An invisible flare ripped out of me, like I'd fired off a sonar ping that somehow made no sound. With it, I *felt* the castle and nearby grounds as though I'd managed to scour them in an instant. At the end of it, I knew, with a certainty as strong as my decision to take the boy, that the weapon wasn't here. Nothing hallowed was. This was a frozen wasteland of evil.

With a measured look, Adrian let me go. Red drops blended into the ruby-colored floor as blood dripped from his wrist where my nails had ripped into it.

"I'm sorry," he said stonily. "We couldn't take the boy into the castle without getting caught, so I had to do something extreme to make you access your power from here."

"How's this…for extreme?" I rasped, then slapped him as hard as I could, anger tapping into strength I normally didn't have. Adrian's head rocked sideways, and when he turned to face me, a red handprint was already swelling along his cheek.

"I deserved that," he said, still in that flinty voice. "Now, let's get out of here."

I was furious at him for choking me into near-unconsciousness and threatening to leave the boy, but I filed that away under a rapidly growing list titled Paybacks To Come. I did shake his hand off when he led me toward the exit, and my glare warned him not to touch me again as I followed him down the pink-floored hallway.

Before we reached the door, Adrian took my gun out of my parka, replaced the empty clip with a full one, and then handed it back to me.

"We might have to shoot our way out," he said, mouth curling with the dark anticipation he always showed before a fight. "But this time, don't fire unless I do."

I bit back my caustic reply because talking made my throat hurt more. Besides, we might not live through this. If we did, though… Paybacks.

"Don't fall behind," Adrian warned, and then exited

the castle, running at a crouch in the opposite direction from where we'd come in.

I followed, keeping low like he did. As soon as I was outside, glacial air seemed to pummel my upper body, my thin sweater no protection against the realm's frigid temperatures. At once, my teeth began to chatter, the wind making it worse as I ran as fast as I could to keep up with Adrian's form-blurring sprint. Even as I shook, I comforted myself by thinking of how warm the boy would be in my parka. It was made to withstand sub-zero temperatures, and right now, that was what it felt like outside.

No guards chased us, which was a happy surprise. Maybe it was because we'd run right into the wall of darkness that bordered the rear of the castle. Nothing and no one seemed to be out this way, and as I abruptly fell on the hard, slick surface, I realized why. Adrian had led us out onto the island's frozen coastline.

I scrambled to my feet, ignoring the jabs of pain from whatever I'd bruised. At least I hadn't lost the gun or shot myself from the impact. I couldn't see in front of me, but the glittering castle behind me was all the motivation I needed to keep running toward where I'd last spotted Adrian. Despite my best efforts, I fell again, cutting my elbows and forearms on the uneven ice. Grudgingly, I had to acknowledge that Adrian had been right. I wouldn't have been able to run ten feet on this without boots. My feet would've been cut to ribbons.

Something large and dark rushed out of the blackness toward me. I lifted the gun, only to hear a familiar voice growl, "I *told* you not to fall behind!" before Adrian grasped my arm.

This time, I welcomed his grip as he propelled us farther onto the ice. If the town was close enough for me to use its light to see, then we were close enough for the guards to spot us. Adrian didn't have my visual handicap, of course. He drew me next to him while he moved with his usual breakneck speed, keeping us well inside the blackness while we ran parallel to the coast. By the time he slowed to a stop, I was gasping so hard that I was almost hyperventilating, and icy trails had frozen on my cheeks from wind-induced tears.

"Be very quiet," he ordered. "We have to go back on the island to reach the gateway."

I tried to squelch my noisy breaths by sucking in air through my nose instead of my mouth. It only made me sound like a winded horse instead of a winded human. Adrian rolled his eyes, keeping low as he ran across the ice to the mainland. Deciding that meant speed was more important than silence, I followed him.

Light from nearby igloos meant I could see the figure that strode toward Adrian when he reached land, the guard holding out his hand in the universal gesture for "stop."

"Hondal—" the minion began, but didn't finish the word. Two short coughing sounds later, the guard dropped like a stone. When I caught up to him, I glimpsed a gaping hole in his forehead before his body dissolved into ashes. In an attempt to cover the evidence of what had happened, I kicked at the ashes, hoping they'd blow away before someone found them.

"Ivy!" Adrian hissed, waving his gun impatiently at me.

I dashed toward him, my thighs burning from running while trying to stay low. A few minutes later, Adrian stopped. I didn't see anything, but I braced myself when he clasped me to him and then threw the three of us backward.

We tumbled through the gateway into our world, coming out at the base of the split tree trunk. My relief at the embrace of warm temperatures was cut short when I saw how dark it was.

"What?" I rasped. It still hurt to talk, damn him. "We've only been in the realm two hours, and we entered it at noon!"

Adrian pulled me to my feet after adjusting his grip on the boy. "Time moves differently there," he said, leading me through the woods. "Sometimes faster, sometimes a lot slower. Costa told me he and Tomas waited two days in the desert for us in Mexico."

Two days? That seemed impossible, but then again, so did everything associated with the realms—myself included. I'd shot someone in cold blood, and I didn't feel the slightest bit bad about it. In fact, it was the only memory I wanted to keep about the glittering, icy realm.

"Something's not right," Adrian muttered, his pace quickening. "That was easy. Only one guard stopped us, and I expected to kill at least half a dozen minions on our way out."

We were lucky, I almost said, and then I paused. We were *never* that lucky. I looked behind us, seeing nothing except trees and darkness, but that didn't mean we were alone.

"What's the plan?" I whispered.

"Get more guns," he replied grimly. "Now."

We ran past the now-closed Visitor's Center to the parking lot. Adrian's car was still in the back, and Costa stood next to it, an overhead streetlight revealing the automatic weapon he'd set on its roof. That wasn't what made Adrian stop, yanking me to a halt with him. It was the woman next to Costa, her arm almost casually draped over his shoulder, head cocked in apparent curiosity as she looked us over.

I recognized her at once. Those long, ebony-copper locks were unforgettable, not to mention that dazzlingly perfect face and the pale skin she was showing off in her low-cut dress. Full red lips drew back into a chilling smile as topaz eyes flicked over me, Adrian and the boy he held.

"So," the gorgeous demon from Mayhemium's realm said, her voice as sensual as her appearance. "Which of you three is the Davidian in disguise?"

CHAPTER TWENTY-TWO

"I AM," ADRIAN STATED.

My gaze swung to him in disbelief. Adrian flashed the demon a hard little grin as he let the boy slide from his grip, stepping away from him once he slumped on the ground.

"No, he's not," I snapped hoarsely. I was going to tear Adrian a new one later for choking me, but no way was he sacrificing himself now. "*I'm* the Davidian!"

The demon's gaze gleamed as she looked between Adrian and me, seeing nothing except an old man and an unfamiliar young one due to our Archon glamour.

"Who's a noble liar, and who's the would-be savior?" she mused aloud.

"I'm not a liar," Adrian ground out as if offended.

"You lie your ass off all the time!" I countered, words coming easier due to my anger. "Here's a sure-fire 'Who's the girl?' test—give him to the count of three to name a brand of tampons."

Adrian shot me a furious, if disbelieving, look. The demon laughed throatily, her features softening into something that resembled affection when she looked at Adrian. Then they turned flinty as she looked at me.

"Ivy, isn't it?"

Her accent held the harshly musical cadence that denoted her first language as Demonish. I hated hearing that accent from anyone except Adrian, and I put all my revulsion toward her kind into my gaze as I stared back at her.

"Ivy," I repeated, wondering if I could shoot her before she hurt Costa. "So unpleasant to meet you."

Bloodred nails dug into Costa's shoulder. He let out a yelp, which only caused the demon to jab them in deeper.

"Don't, Obsidiana," Adrian said quietly.

I was wondering where I'd heard that name when the demon inclined her head. "Give me what I want, and I'll release him."

"You know I can't," Adrian said, still in that low, resonant voice.

Obsidiana managed to make an evil chuckle sound sexy. "Oh, but you can, my love."

My love? I almost got whiplash from how fast I looked at Adrian. "You *didn't* tap a demon," I gasped out.

The way his expression closed off said that he had, and a lot. *Now* I remembered where I'd heard her name! Demetrius had said that Obsidiana missed him when he'd urged Adrian to come back home. From the way Adrian had stopped dead when we ran into her in Mayhemium's realm, part of him had missed her, too.

I could guess which part, and it was all I could do not to kick it. "*Me* you keep pushing away, but a demoness is good enough for you?" My glare was withering. "Nice."

"With how plain Demetrius said you were beneath that disguise, I'm not surprised" was Obsidiana's smug response.

Hey, I'd been hot as a glamoured blonde! Besides... "Beauty fades, but Evil Bitch is forever," I snapped.

Obsidiana flung Costa to the ground. Adrian grabbed her before she reached me, his arm like a vise around her neck.

She stilled at once, her topaz gaze sliding up to look at him. "You would harm me? Over her?"

She actually sounded surprised, and I'd heard people refer to feces with more respect than the way she said "her." I told myself it wasn't jealousy or spite that made me hope he ripped her head off. She was evil.

"I can't let you hurt her," Adrian said grimly.

Obsidiana seemed to sag in his arms. "When I heard someone had killed two of my people, I knew you'd come to my realm. That's why I came alone to see you." Her voice deepened with apparent distress. "It wasn't even to capture the Davidian! I thought if you would finally speak to me, you'd let go of your anger. Does nothing matter to you except this fruitless quest for revenge? Don't you love me at all anymore, *benhoven?*"

"Does this answer your question?" Adrian's arm whipped back, snapping her neck with an audible sound. If she were a minion, she'd start turning into ashes, but all she did was go limp. I glanced away when he ripped something pulpy out of her throat. I hated Obsidiana, but my gross quota had already been exceeded today.

"Why do you do that?" I asked, busying myself by helping the boy up.

"Keeps them out longer," he replied, dumping Obsidiana's limp form in the grass. "Demon physiology is different. Their version of a heart is in their neck."

The vindictive glow I felt was *not* because he'd metaphorically ripped Obsidiana's heart out, I assured myself. It was because now we had more time to get away.

"Costa, are you okay?" Adrian asked, striding over to him.

A groan was his response. Adrian lifted him up, depositing Costa in the passenger seat. Then he cranked the driver's seat forward so I could climb in behind it.

"Is he okay?" I asked, half lifting the boy to the car.

"Just a concussion. A little manna, and he'll be fine," Adrian said. It didn't escape me that he sounded pissed, as if he had a right to be. When we were all loaded into the car and driving away, he started in on me.

"Why did you bait Obsidiana?" Adrian demanded. "Were you *trying* to give her more reasons to kill you?"

What was I going to say? That I'd been so insulted over the bitch's comments and learning about their past relationship that I'd almost forgotten my life was in danger? Ah, noooo. That was too stupid. And humiliating.

"I did it *to* bait her," I said, widening my eyes for increased innocent effect. "I was trying to get her to charge me so she'd let Costa go!"

Adrian's stare said he wasn't buying it. Time for another tactic. I tossed my hair, letting out a scornful laugh. "You really think I care that you used to get it on with her, or anything else I said? *Please.*"

Costa muttered something in Greek as he pressed a handful of manna to the gash on the back of his head. Whatever it was, Adrian let out a snort of agreement. When he looked at me, his expression was less stern, but no less intense.

"Unlike me, you're a terrible liar, but since we didn't have a better plan, I'm glad what you did worked."

Did that mean he believed I'd been faking jealousy? Or did it mean he knew I was lying now? Asking would only show how much I cared, so I focused on the boy. He was slumped in his seat, most of his body tucked into the parka except his feet. He still wasn't reacting to anything going on around him. Was it shock, or did he have something physically wrong that we couldn't see?

"We should take him to a hospital," I stated.

"That'll do more harm than good," Adrian said, with

a sardonic glance back at me. "Remember being told you were crazy your whole life? What do you think they'll tell him, once he starts talking about demons, minions and different worlds?"

I winced. "True, but he needs the kind of help we can't give him while we're looking for the weapon. Besides, he might have family that's worried sick about him."

"Next time we see Zach, I'll ask him," Adrian said, his tone roughening. "He always knows about kids' families."

I tried not to let that statement affect me, but it did. *Your real mother didn't leave you because she was running from the police,* Zach's voice whispered across my mind as if he were here. *She did it to save you, just like your dream revealed....*

I forced those thoughts back. One monumental crisis at a time, thank you. Until I found this weapon, it didn't matter why my birth mother had left me beside that freeway. If I was the last Davidian, then whatever her reasons, she was dead. Gone forever, just like my adoptive parents I hadn't even been able to say goodbye to because that detective tried to kill me before I could give them a proper burial....

"Ivy." Adrian's tone was urgent. "What's wrong?"

I swiped under my eyes, only now realizing that I'd started to cry. "Nothing."

"Bullshit," he said emphatically.

"Just a little post-traumatic stress." I forced a shaky laugh. "I'm still not used to narrowly escaping death, okay?"

His gaze repeated the same thing—bullshit. Okay, so maybe I *was* a terrible liar. I pretended not to notice him staring at me as much as he could without wrecking, and busied myself by tucking the boy's feet under my legs so they'd be warm.

Then an idea struck me, exciting me so much that I reached over the seats to grab Adrian's shoulder.

"Drive to Bennington! We snuck the boy out with our disguises, so we can use them to get Jasmine out, too!"

Costa gave me a pitying glance, and I felt as well as heard Adrian's sigh.

"Remember I told you that your sister will be the best-treated human in all the realms? She'll also be the most guarded. Bennington might not be Demetrius's main realm, but he'll expect you to try that. I guarantee he's given an order that if anyone unfamiliar shows up, they're to be detained."

My brief hope crashed. Adrian was right. The demons had no intention of making this easy on me, so either I went in with the ability to kill them all, or I died.

Or both. No one had said that, but no one needed to. Having the weapon didn't mean I'd suddenly be bulletproof, so finding it didn't guarantee victory. It only gave me a chance at it.

"You're going to be okay," I told the boy, giving him the assurance I so badly wished someone could give to me.

A slow blink was his only response. Either he still wasn't processing what was going on, or he didn't believe me. I patted his leg, wishing I could tell him I knew how it felt to be surrounded by people and yet still be on your own.

I couldn't fix that for myself, but I could fix it for him. Then I'd keep trying to save Jasmine while trying not to get killed by demons, and maybe somewhere along the line, reclaim my own life, too.

Dreams were beautiful things to have, weren't they?

CHAPTER TWENTY-THREE

WE LEFT NORTH CAROLINA and drove to a Catholic seminary in Washington, D.C. Adrian knew two of the priests who met us around the back of the large church complex, which was Surprise One. Surprise Two was him telling them that the boy had been rescued from a demon realm. The priests didn't accuse Adrian of being crazy, either. Instead, one of them hurried to take the boy back into what they called the "house" section.

"Are demon realms an open secret to priests?" I whispered to Costa while Adrian continued to talk to the other priest.

Costa grunted. "No. These two know about them because Adrian saved them from a demon kidnapping a few years ago."

I don't know why that surprised me. It was how we'd met, and Adrian had said he'd been "retrieving" people for Zach for a while. Guess I never expected to meet anyone he'd rescued, let alone find out that they were priests.

I was too tired to swap rescue experiences with the two Fathers, which was why I was relieved when Adrian came back to tell us that the seminary had rooms for us tonight, too. Even more wonderful than that, it had leftover pizza and a microwave. I devoured several pieces, then showered and flopped onto the narrow bed in a room that reminded me a lot of my college dorm. Just with a lot more crosses and pictures of saints and popes.

I was almost asleep when my door opened. No locks meant relying on the honor system, but since Adrian hadn't knocked, he must not be in an honorable mood. Situation normal, then.

"What are you doing here?" I demanded wearily.

He'd showered, too, the dampness making his hair look darker than its usual honeyed shades of blond. I refused to notice how that same dampness caused his shirt to cling to him. I was still too mad.

He shut the door behind him. "I'm sorry for hurting you," he said, actually managing to sound as though he meant it.

Which time? I thought, but touched my throat as if the bruises there were the only damage he'd inflicted on me today.

"Did you know choking me would work to activate my abilities?" I asked, my tone grating. "Or was it a lucky guess?"

His stare reminded me of ancient sailors' legends of sea serpents. On the surface, all I saw was roiling blue, but every so often, glimpses of the monster appeared beneath.

"Demetrius wanted me to be the strongest Judian ever, so he did whatever was necessary to hone my abilities. Like throwing me into the gladiator rings at thirteen. Lesser demons fought there, too, and if a ruler wanted to show off, he or she jumped into the fight. Demetrius didn't let anyone kill me, but he let them beat me within an inch of my life enough times that I learned what he wanted me to know—the fastest, most efficient way to use my abilities. So, no, I wasn't guessing. I was counting on you being just like me in that regard.

I hated hurting you, but it was the only way you could search the castle without getting caught with the boy."

Since the minions' ashes must've been discovered right away for Obsidiana to beat us back to our realm, he was right. We would've gotten caught taking the boy with us to search the castle. If I'd known him throttling me would make my powers flare that way, I would've demanded that he do it. I'd take bruises any day over abandoning a child to a demon realm.

"And Obsidiana?" I hated that I couldn't stop myself from asking, so I tried to hide my motivation behind a fake laugh. "Now I know why you stopped in your tracks when you saw her in Mayhemium's realm. Must've been weird to run into your old girlfriend, but you should've told me who she was. It's not fair to keep finding out from other demons where they used to rank in your life."

His jaw clenched, and I thought he'd leave as he'd done so many times before. Instead, he began to pace.

"I stopped in my tracks that day because I was worried that Obsidiana would sense who I was through my disguise. Demetrius always can, and if she had, she would've realized who you were, too. As for why I didn't tell you about her, it's because she means nothing to me. The whole time we were together, she lied to me just like the rest of them did."

"About what?" *Your supposed destiny?* I thought but didn't say out loud.

He gave me a measured look. "Tomas told you what it was like for me in the realms before I walked out."

"Girls, gold, power, adulation..." I forced another insincere laugh. "Your basic hedonistic fantasy."

"He didn't tell you why I hated Archons back then.

My earliest memory was of them trying to kill my mother and me."

"What?" I gasped.

His mouth twisted. "Judas's descendants are a threat to Archons, so eliminating the line means eliminating the threat. Throughout history, demons have tried to do the same to David's descendants. They nearly succeeded several times, most recently with the Holocaust."

"I'm Jewish?" That should've occurred to me before....

"Possibly. David's line started out that way, but over thousands of years, beliefs changed, even if genealogy didn't."

"Back to Archons trying to kill you," I said, filing the other away under Future Musings.

Those beautiful features hardened. "All my life, I've had nightmares about my mother and me being chased through the tunnels. My mom said I was remembering when I was five and Demetrius saved us from Archons trying to eliminate the Judian line. I was brought up believing we were only safe in their realms. Since the demons gave us everything we wanted, it took a long time before I even asked to see the world we'd come from."

"But when you did, how could you go back?" I said, voicing the question that had been eating at me. "You would've seen how evil the demon realms were by comparison."

His jaw tightened. "They thought of that, so they hid the uglier aspects from me for as long as they could. After I discovered them, they took me to places in the human world that looked the same. Like Darfur, where hundreds of thousands of people have been slaughtered while the world gives a collective shrug. Or African diamond mines, where laborers are regularly worked to death, or all the countries with unchecked human trafficking, and of course, the countless sweatshops around the world." His sigh was bitter. "Seeing those things made it easier to believe what the demons taught me—that the only difference between them and humanity was more opportunity."

"Bullshit," I said at once. "Yes, atrocities exist here, too, but so do people who try to fight them. For every horrible example you gave, you can find a thousand more of people helping other people, even from several continents away."

Adrian's expression softened. "I know. When I started sneaking out to explore on my own, I saw that, too. The first time I encountered children at a playground, I watched for hours." Brief smile. "Someone called the cops, but that made an impression, too. Strangers came to protect the young of other strangers. I'd never seen that before, and for the first time, I understood what I'd become. A monster."

"Is that when you left?" I asked softly.

He threw me a jaded look. "That's when my drug addiction began. I couldn't leave because I was afraid the demons would retaliate against my mother, and she said she'd never leave while Archons were after us. So instead, I escaped through every mind-altering substance I could find. Of course, I couldn't snort enough, shoot up enough or smoke enough to forget all I'd done. I thought my bloodline kept me from overdosing, but after what Demetrius said the other week, it might've been him. I wanted to die, though. That's why I kept sneaking out of the realms, hoping Archons would find me. One night, I got my wish."

"What happened?"

His smile was jagged. "I was puking in an alley behind a bar when light suddenly exploded all around me. You've seen what Zach looks like when he shows his true nature, so I knew what he was. He said, 'If you're ready, come with me.' I thought he meant ready for death, so I did. He didn't kill me, though. He took me to the old Shanghai tunnels in Portland."

"Why?"

His expression became haunted. "My dream was always the same—Mom and I were running through the tunnels, trying to get away from the monsters. She was screaming at them to leave me alone, and I was so tired, but I kept going because she was terrified. We were almost at the end when a black cloud swallowed her. At the same time, the exit got really bright and a voice told me to keep running. Then my mom came out of the cloud, picked me up…and that's when I'd wake up."

He paused, his mouth curling down. "That night, in the same tunnels, Zach showed me what really happened."

After I'd seen what Demetrius could do, I'd already guessed, but it still made me ache to hear Adrian say it.

"What came out of the darkness that day was Demetrius, not my mom. He'd killed her, but he used her appearance to trick me into staying in the realms while he molded me into someone who hated Archons as much as demons did. I didn't think to question why I never saw my mom and Demetrius in the same room, and everyone played along, pretending he was my mother when they knew she was dead. All so when I met the last Davidian, I wouldn't hesitate to fulfill my destiny and betray him." He met my eyes. "Or her, as it turns out."

My throat felt tight, both from unshed tears at the merciless manipulations Adrian had been put through back then, and the pain he still carried now. No wonder he'd reacted with such horror when Zach told him who I was. I was the destiny he'd been groomed for, and then rebelled against by turning his back on the creatures that raised him.

Well, I didn't believe in destiny. Fate couldn't override free will, and just because Adrian's ancestors were betrayers didn't mean he was doomed to be. He'd already had several opportunities to hand me over to the demons, yet instead, he'd fought them with all the power they'd assumed would be to their benefit. No matter what anyone thought, his choices determined his destiny, not the other way around.

Now to convince Adrian of that.

"If your fate was already sealed, Demetrius wouldn't have worked so hard to mold you into a monster." My voice was raspy from all the emotion I held back. "He must know your destiny is still up to you. Same with Zach. He helped you back then, and he keeps looking out for you now—"

Adrian's laugh stopped me. For a moment, it sounded so ugly, it could've come from a demon.

"Zach showed me *everything* that happened in the tunnel that day." Something sharper than pain edged his tone. "He was the light I saw at the exit. Ever since, I've wondered if Zach could've stopped Demetrius from taking me if he'd wanted to. That night at the Mexican sanctuary, when Zach decimated Demetrius's shadows in seconds, I finally got my answer."

Shock made me stammer. "But that…that's…"

"Indifferent at best, cruel at worst?" Adrian supplied with another ragged laugh. "I know, but Zach'll say he was only following orders, so that means his boss doesn't want me to beat my fate. No, I'm supposed to play my part like a good little Judas, but screw them.

Once Demetrius is dead, I'm gone, both from your life and theirs. It's the only way I can pay them back for what they allowed Demetrius to do to me."

I didn't know what to say. Everything he'd been through was made more awful by the knowledge that it had all been preventable. Zach should've stopped Demetrius, with or without "orders." He also should be supporting Adrian now, not telling him to resign himself to a fate he clearly didn't want. Couldn't they see how hard Adrian was trying? Didn't they even care?

If they didn't, I did. I might not be able to do anything about their former betrayals, but I wasn't helpless. I got out of bed and took Adrian's hand, tightening my grip when he tried to pull away.

"You're right," I said huskily. "We'll find the weapon, use it to save Jasmine *and* kill Demetrius, then we'll walk away from each other. Both sides can choke on their expectations of your fate. They don't know how strong you are, but I do, and I trust you, Adrian."

He jerked his hand away. "Ivy, don't—"

"I trust you," I repeated, gripping his shirt so he either had to stand still or risk me ripping it off. "There's no danger of you betraying me while we're working to get this weapon. I can always trust your hatred of demons, remember?"

Some of the tension eased from his shoulders as I used his own argument to make my point. "Yeah, but you still don't understand your full part in this—"

"I do," I interrupted grimly. "Tomas and Costa said that only a Davidian or a demon from Goliath's line can bring out the weapon's true power, which means I have to be the one to use the slingshot, and I'm not even that good with a gun."

He stared at me, emotions flickering across his face

too rapidly for me to translate. Then his jaw flexed, and his expression hardened into one I recognized well.

Pure, unadulterated determination.

"I'll teach you how to use a slingshot," he said, his voice rougher. "With practice, you can do anything."

"Then we have a plan," I agreed, smiling because I had another plan. One that involved showing Adrian he didn't have to walk away from me when this was all over, but for now, I'd keep that to myself.

Demetrius had said the bond between us would grow every moment that we spent together. Demons were liars, but my heart knew *that* much was true. Already, I cared about Adrian more than I'd cared about any other guy, and he'd admitted that he was powerfully drawn to me, too. By the time we'd found the weapon, killed Demetrius and rescued Jasmine, I intended to convince Adrian that he wasn't doomed to betray me. Everyone else might have given up on him, but I hadn't, and I'd use every bit of our supernatural bond to show him he shouldn't give up, either.

Now to break down the wall he'd erected around himself, one stubborn brick at a time.

CHAPTER TWENTY-FOUR

ADRIAN WAS RIGHT. Zach didn't even need to look at the boy before he told us that his name was Hoyt, and his family was dead. I was a little skeptical, but Adrian believed Zach. When I asked him why, he reminded me that Zach had told Adrian the exact time and place that minions would attempt to kidnap me. How Zach knew these things, I still didn't know, but according to Adrian, the Archon had never been wrong.

It was all I could do not to ask if Zach had taken the day off when my sister was kidnapped. I didn't because I'd bet Zach's response would contain the word "orders," and I didn't trust my reaction to that. Until I had the weapon, I needed Zach, plus punching him in the face might be the last mistake I ever made. In this case, ignorance wasn't bliss. It was necessity.

Costa was taking Hoyt to Tomas's family in Phoenix. They'd agreed to shelter the boy, and the long drive would give Costa a chance to share his own realm experience. Hoyt still wasn't speaking, but I held out hope that, with time, he'd be able to recover mentally, physically and emotionally.

I had to believe that, for Hoyt's sake, and for Jasmine's.

This time, Zach glamoured me into looking like a young guy with shiny, cloud-rolling eyes. Having both Adrian and I pose as minions came from our being zero for two on finding the weapon, and two for two on getting caught. Not an auspicious start, but if at first you don't succeed and demons haven't killed you…well, trying again was a given.

Collinsville, Illinois, was the proud owner of the world's largest ketchup bottle. It was also home to over a hundred man-made earthen mounds. Such quaint distinctions should've meant the city wasn't a hotbed of demonic activity, but guess again. Tourists visiting the Cahokia Mounds only saw lots of little green hills and one big one amidst a tranquil park, but I saw a bustling populace in a dark, glacial world where the little mounds were a lot bigger, and the big one was a gargantuan pyramid.

"I gotta ask," I said, following Adrian to the realm gateway, "what's with demons and pyramids?"

"Ego," he replied succinctly. At my raised brow, he elaborated. "The first demons were Archons who rebelled against their boss because they wanted to be masters instead of servants. After they were sent to the dark realms as punishment, they built their kingdoms there, using force to get the worship they craved. Pyramids, castles, towers…they're the demonic version of bling, so whoever has the biggest and best wins."

"And they realm-snatch from each other to get more." I nodded as if it made perfect sense.

The look Adrian gave me made me wonder if I'd missed something important. "Not just from each other. Every chance they get, they absorb more of our world into theirs."

"You never mentioned how," I reminded him.

A shrug. "If you believe in M theory, they do it by manipulating gravity to force contact between two dimensional layers, creating a new interdimensional bubble."

He sounded like a physicist. "Laymen's terms, please."

"When a vacuum gets switched on, it sucks whatever's closest into a lint bag, right? When they get enough power, demons use gravity like a vacuum's on switch to activate an area's natural geographic instability, crashing one multiverse into its reflective duplicate. Once the gravitational layer restabilizes—in essence, the vacuum getting turned off—everything in the new lint-bag realm is trapped."

"So gateways are like the hose that runs from the sweeper to the lint bag," I mused, adding, "Why do you always grab me when we go through them? Couldn't I make it through myself?"

A smile ghosted across his lips. "Try it," he said, gesturing to an empty space to his right.

I gave it a doubtful look. "Nothing's there. All the other realm gateways had markers."

"All the others?" He snorted. "You've only seen two. More than half the gateways aren't marked, Ivy. That's why they're so hard to find unless you can feel them."

I didn't feel anything, and all I saw next to Adrian was air and grass. "You're sure it's there?"

Another snort. "Even if I hadn't been through this one before, I'd still be sure. Think you could *not* notice jamming your finger into a light socket? That's what gateways feel like to me."

Wow, my abilities must be weak. I had to concentrate like a fiend to sense a hint of something hallowed, and Adrian felt dark objects like they were electric shocks. Then again, he'd had years to hone his abilities. I'd just found out about mine less than a month ago.

I squared my shoulders. Time to exercise some supernatural muscle! I focused on the space Adrian indicated, and then flung myself forward like I was diving into a pool.

Face-plant. Ow, ow, ow!

Adrian's chuckle penetrated the part of me that wasn't seeing cartoon birdies fly over me in circles. My body vibrated from the impact, and I now knew that dry grass tasted like uncooked spaghetti with dirt sauce.

"Not funny," I groaned.

He knelt next to me, still chuckling as he offered me a hand up. "If you saw the air you caught before you hit the ground, you'd disagree."

I flipped over, glaring as I swatted his hand away. "Payback's a bitch. Remember that."

"I'm trembling."

He pulled me to my feet. Even as I swore revenge, part of me savored his unfettered amusement. Adrian rarely laughed unless it was in derision, bitterness or challenge. Seeing him do it with only mischief tingeing his features was like seeing a diamond in the sunlight versus glimpsing it in shadows.

I shouldn't, but I stared anyway. No wonder Obsidiana had wanted him back enough to risk coming after him alone. I hated the hell-bitch, but I couldn't fault her for her taste.

Adrian's laughter died away, and he glanced at our hands, as if just realizing that he still held mine. Our eyes locked, and his words from before replayed in my mind.

I've wanted you since the first time you touched me…. Nothing but dark magic had ever felt so powerful, and when I touch you, it's a thousand times worse….

My grip started to tighten, but he pulled away, a familiar hardness turning his expression into an impenetrable mask. His gaze flared, though, and his hands clenched into fists as he drew in a harsh breath. His expression might be statue-like, but in those seething sapphire eyes, I caught a glimpse of the wildness he held back, and it made me shiver.

If Adrian ever freed the part of him that wanted me, would I be able to stand it? Or would I love every second of being overcome? Only concern for my sister kept me from testing both of us by throwing myself into his arms and forcing him to feel what he kept telling himself he couldn't have.

His muscles bunched, as if on a primal level he sensed the reckless passion growing in me. Maybe he did. Maybe it was more than our bond that made me throb in places he'd never touched, as though demanding to feel his hands, his mouth, on me there.

Adrian spun around, his coat unable to hide how his whole body had suddenly tensed, as if he'd been zapped with the electric shock he'd alluded to before.

"Let's go," he said hoarsely. "Places to be, minions to kill."

My hands trembled as I drew on my thick winter parka and gloves. I already had on the insulated pants and boots.

"First, tell me why I can't get through the gateways on my own," I asked, stalling so I'd get a second to compose myself.

He half turned to show a smile like uncut crystal— beautiful, yet jagged around the edges. "Same reason as everything else— bloodlines. You need minion, demon or Judian blood to cross through the barriers that lead to the dark worlds. You don't have that, so by wrapping myself around you, I'm essentially covering you with my blood to get you through."

That explained so much. No wonder demons didn't

bother to station guards at every gateway. Even if the humans they captured managed to navigate the pitch-blackness to find them, they couldn't cross through them to get back to their world. Once in a realm, they were hopelessly trapped.

My jaw tightened. Not Jasmine. As soon as I found that weapon, I was coming for her, and with Adrian's help, she *would* see the sun again.

"I'm ready," I said, my tone now only slightly breathy.

He didn't look at me when he pulled me to him and then dropped us into the gateway I hadn't been able to see, let alone penetrate. As soon as we finished tumbling through the invisible membrane linking our realms, he let me go. I blinked, my eyes adjusting to the darkness that seemed to seep inside my soul, chasing away my desire while hardening me with purpose. If the weapon was here, Jasmine's awful captivity would be over. All I had to do was stay strong, focus and find it.

Light from the town reflected off the icy ground, adding an eerie, faint luminescence that kept me from being totally blind. Still, it was dark enough that I couldn't see Adrian's face. Only the bulk of his large body next to me. The tall silhouettes around us must have been trees, frozen into place from the cold. I couldn't see more than the widest part of their out-lines; their branches, if they had any, were invisible against the darkness that hovered above us like a ma-levolent spirit.

Adrian leaned down, his warm breath in stark con-trast to our frozen surroundings as he spoke near my ear.

"Anyone stops us, let me do the talking."

Since I didn't speak Demonish, I'd already planned on that. I was about to tell him the same when his whole body froze with such suddenness, it was as if he'd been transformed into stone.

"Ivy, don't move," he whispered in a low, vehement voice.

I tried to will every part of me to similar stillness, but I couldn't stop my eyes from darting around or my chest from rising as my heart sped up and my lungs responded with a demand for more oxygen. What was out here that was so dangerous, Adrian was playing statue instead of reaching for his gun?

My answer was a hissing sort of growl that raised every hair on the back of my neck. It sounded like a feral wolf that had just found a meal, and somewhere to my left, an answering, howling hiss shattered the dark in answer.

"Adrian," I whispered, terror skittering through me.

Fast as lightning, he was behind me, his arms like twin bands around me. "Close your eyes," he ordered, his voice barely audible. "It can't hurt you if you don't move."

I slammed my eyes shut. I'd seen people butchered plus demons transform into deadly clouds and crows, but if Adrian didn't think I could handle whatever this was, I'd believe him. The growls came closer, and with a sudden vibration in the ground, I felt something big land right in front of me. Reeking breath came in pants that hit my face like light slaps. I fought a fresh surge of panic as I realized I was standing, yet the creature was still eye level with me. What *was* it?

Its hiss turned guttural before I felt something slimy and wet flick across my face with the quickness of a snake's tongue. Fear-driven revulsion would've made me immediately swipe at the spot if not for Adrian's warning.

It can't hurt you if you don't move.

I didn't know how that could be true. The thing had licked me; it *knew* I was here! Not a muscle on Adrian twitched, though, and after that disgusting lick, the creature didn't do anything except wheeze in that weird, hissing way. I mimicked Adrian's stillness, keeping my eyes shut and willing my breaths to be soft and shallow. Then a new, ominous vibration shook the ground. Another creature had landed right behind us.

More reeking breath filled the air with the stench of old garbage and rotted fish. A hissing snarl blasted out, loud as a trumpet and so terrifying, my knees felt like they turned to Jell-O. Only Adrian's grip kept me standing perfectly still as something massive bumped my body, like a shark testing its prey. I squeezed my lids tighter, fighting a near-overwhelming urge to go for my gun. I felt beyond helpless, beyond vulnerable. If Adrian's arms hadn't been wrapped around me, a tangible reminder that I wasn't facing this alone, I might have started shaking.

Then a roar blasted in front of my face, so loud it seemed to reverberate inside me. My heart pounded as something sharp grazed the top of my head, parting my hair with multiple hard points. I didn't need to open my eyes to know what it was. The creature's gigantic fangs. My guts twisted with terror and resignation. One snap of those jaws, and it would all be over.

It can't hurt you if you don't move!

I couldn't tell how long I frantically repeated Adrian's promise, but the fangs on my head eventually vanished. Then, with two sets of vibrating thumps, the space around us felt less oppressive and I knew the huge, hulking beasts had gone. I still didn't move or open my eyes, though. Not until Adrian lifted me up, ran, and I felt us tumbling through the gateway back into the light and warmth of Collinsville, Illinois.

Grass hit me in the face from our hard landing, but I didn't care. Instead of standing up, I started to swipe at my cheek hard enough to bruise, and still it felt like the slime from the creature's tongue remained. I wanted to wash my skin with scalding water, but I couldn't. All I could do was keep rubbing my face with my gloved hands.

"What were those things?" I whispered, still too traumatized to speak in a normal tone.

Adrian knelt and grasped my wrists, forcing me to stop my rough grooming. His face had shiny trails on it, too, showing I hadn't been the only one the creatures had licked.

"Hounds," he said evenly, "which means we have a problem."

I started to laugh. Not the exhilarated, yay-I'm-alive kind, like when I'd survived Demetrius's first attack, but wild cackles that hovered between derangement and despair.

"A problem? You *don't* say," I gasped out. "I thought huge demonic dogs would only be a minor nuisance."

Adrian smoothed the hair out of my face, his hand lingering to cup my chin.

"'Hound' is a nickname. They're not dogs. They're ancient reptiles the demons selectively bred until they made the most vicious thing on four legs. Can't see, taste or smell for shit, though, which is why you're safe if you don't move. If you do, they're trained to tear you to pieces."

I stopped laughing, but that didn't mean I felt more stable. "I vote we skip this realm and only search ones without demonic, man-eating reptiles."

"It's not that simple," he said, still in that infuriatingly calm tone. "They weren't supposed to be there, so the demons must be amping up their security. They know you've searched two realms for the weapon, Ivy. Looks like they're trying to stop you from searching a third."

The suck never seemed to end. "But now that we know they're there, can't we just bring bigger weapons and kill them?"

"Hounds are almost as difficult to kill as demons," Adrian responded, a hint of grimness making me wonder if he spoke from experience. "Plus, they're cold-blooded, so they have to keep returning to their handlers to warm up, which means it wouldn't take long for one of them to be missed."

Crawling into the world's largest ketchup bottle and not coming out was starting to sound like a great idea. "Now what?"

He gave me a level look. "Now we talk to Zach."

CHAPTER TWENTY-FIVE

WE USED MOST of our remaining Archon-glamoured sticky notes for gas money to return to Costa's house in Miami. Once there, we waited. And waited.

By the fourth day, Zach was still a no-show despite Adrian repeatedly trying to reach him. I tried, too, mostly by folding my hands, glaring upward and thinking multiple variations of *Where are you, Zach? I know you can hear us!*

Costa wasn't around, either. At least he'd called, saying he was staying a few more days with Hoyt at Tomas's family's house. With no one actively trying to kill me and our realm-searching put on hold, I had nothing to do except brood. I couldn't even enjoy the sunny warmth of South Florida. If I wasn't feeling guilty over Jasmine languishing in her captivity, I was being tormented in another way.

For the past three nights, I'd fallen asleep listening to Adrian pace. He spent his days in the outdoor carport, claiming that he needed to work on his car. Bullshit. The Challenger was in mint condition, and he could only wax and detail it so many times before it was obvious that he was just avoiding me.

Tonight, I was finding out why.

I got out of bed, hearing his pacing come to an abrupt halt when I opened my door. Too bad. I was done playing the avoidance game. He wasn't, though. By the time

I came downstairs, he was nowhere to be seen and his bedroom door was shut.

Quietly, I went to his door and tried the knob. Locked. My mouth curled. He was the one who'd taught me not to give up that easily when something needed to be done.

I grabbed the car keys he'd left on the counter and went out the front door. I'd barely slid them into the Challenger's ignition when Adrian came flying out of the house after me.

"Where do you think you're going?" he demanded, yanking open the passenger door after he tried mine and couldn't get in. I waited until he'd shut it, then I hit the lock button.

The sound was like a gun going off in the sudden quiet. Adrian stared at me, knowing better than anyone that he was now trapped. He was the one who'd rigged the Challenger so that the only exit was through the driver's side when the doors were locked.

"I'm not going anywhere," I said evenly, "and neither are you until we have a little talk."

"What are you doing, Ivy?" he asked, his voice very low.

"Ending our stalemate," I responded, leaning back into the leather seat. "For the first few days, I thought you were avoiding me because I'd done something wrong. Then I realized it wasn't my fault, so now I want to know why."

He looked away. "I haven't been avoiding—"

"Ooh, lies, looks like we'll be here awhile," I mocked. "Seriously, Adrian, Costa's house is on hallowed ground and it doesn't contain a single mirror, so I'm totally safe. Yet aside from getting groceries the first day, you haven't left once. If you can't stand to be in the same room with me, why is it that you can't stand to leave me alone here, either?"

His hands slowly closed into fists. "Let me out, Ivy. Now."

"Not until you give me a straight answer," I countered.

He looked at me, anger sharpening the gorgeous lines and hollows of his face. "I'm warning you, don't push me."

"Or what?" I flared. "You have nothing to threaten me with! The only reason I can stand to keep going is because I don't have anything to lose, so pushing you doesn't scare me—"

I didn't see his hands flash out, but suddenly, they were in my hair as he yanked me to him, his mouth scorching mine. I gasped in shock, and his tongue slid past my lips, claiming mine with a passionate desperation that sent heat rocketing through me.

My shock vanished. So did my questions. Desire hijacked my emotions, leaving nothing except a surge of blistering need. I kissed Adrian back, opening my mouth in a silent demand for more. Hints of alcohol flavored his kiss, but beneath that was his taste, infinitely more intoxicating, and I responded as if it was my drug of choice. I moaned as my head tilted back from the force of his kiss. Then he pulled me across the seats until I was on top of him, his strong grip molding me against every muscled inch of his body.

"This is why I stayed away," he growled against my mouth as his hands started to rove over me with knowing, ruthless passion. "Can't be near you without wanting you. Can't stop myself anymore—"

His words cut off as his kiss deepened, until I could hardly breathe from the erotic thrusts and delves of his tongue. I'd been kissed before, but never like this. He wasn't exploring my mouth. He was claiming it.

And I couldn't get enough. All the feelings I'd had to fake with other boyfriends came roaring through my senses, shocking me with their intensity. My heart pounded while my body felt hypersensitive, making each brush of his skin, lips and tongue dangerously erotic. I needed more of his kiss despite barely being able to breathe. More of his hands moving over me with sensual urgency, and more of the hard, muscled body I could feel but not touch because of how tightly Adrian held me against him.

I moaned when his lips slid down to a spot on my neck that made every nerve ending jump with exquisite anticipation. They jumped again when he pushed up the back of my pajama top, his hands now roaming over flesh instead of fabric. Everywhere he touched seemed to burn with a need so intense, it left me aching, and when he sucked on my neck, a blast of pleasure reverberated straight down to the throb between my legs.

"All I think about is you. Every day, every minute… you," he muttered hotly.

I was so lost in sensation, the words barely penetrated, especially when his mouth slanted over mine with carnal hunger. Before, my hands had been trapped against his chest, but I forced them free, gripping his head while I kissed him back. His mouth was addictive, and the sinuous flicks of his tongue had me arching against him in wordless, primal need. Desperate to feel him the way I'd secretly fantasized, my hands left his head to slide down his body. Our cramped space limited my exploration to his shoulders, arms and sides, but I wanted to touch him so badly, I didn't care. Muscles bunched and flexed as he reacted to the feel of my hands on him. His body was so hard, but his skin was sleek and smooth, as if someone had stretched heavy silk over stone. Touching him while he kissed me made my mind reel from desire, and when my hand grazed his taut, flat stomach, a tremor went through his whole body.

He broke our kiss to pull my pajama top over my head, groaning as he flung it aside.

"You're so beautiful, Ivy."

His hands on my bare breasts ripped a cry from me. My skin felt too tight, too sensitive, and when his mouth closed over a nipple, the pleasure was so intense, it was almost painful. I gripped his head without thinking, my gasps turning into groans that caused him to hold me tighter. His mouth was a brand that seared those unbelievable sensations all through me, making my whole body feel fevered. Every part of me ached for him, but when his hand slipped inside my pajama pants, I couldn't stop myself from tensing even as I cried out at the jolt of pleasure.

His mouth immediately left my breast and his large hand slid up to thread through my hair instead.

"What's wrong?"

Adrian's eyes were darker with passion, making their silver rims more startling, but it was the barely leashed wildness they contained that caused the words to stick in my throat.

"I, ahem… Before we… Ah, I need to tell you something."

I could actually see the moment he guessed what I was having trouble articulating. His eyes widened, and his hands ceased the sensual way they'd been running through my hair.

"You've never had sex before."

A statement, not a question. I still had on my pajama pants, but suddenly, I'd never felt more exposed. My arms crossed over my chest, and for the first time, I was glad I didn't have D-cups because they covered everything.

"Yeah," I mumbled. "Sorry."

"Don't." Adrian's sigh was ragged. "Don't ever apologize for being who you are. You're perfect, and I'm the one who's sorry. Touching you made me forget all the reasons why I have to stay away from you."

That was the last thing I wanted to hear. Frustration rose, covering my previous embarrassment. Was I supposed to go back to pretending that he didn't consume my thoughts as much as I apparently consumed his? Damn my momentary hesitancy that had ruined this!

"I don't want you to stay away," I said. To prove it, I dropped my arms.

His eyes closed while he shuddered as though absorbing a punishing blow.

"Don't," he said roughly. "After you find and use that weapon, I *have* to walk away from you, and I can't do that if we're lovers. I can barely do it now, and I need to, Ivy. It's the only way I can protect you from my fate."

Before I could say anything else, he flipped us until he was on top of me. Then he punched the window so hard that it shattered. His body shielded mine from the instant rainfall of glass, then he opened his door from the outside and left.

For a few dazed moments, I stayed in the passenger seat, clutching the top Adrian had handed me right before he walked away. He loved this car like it was his baby, yet he'd smashed his own window to get away before he lost control and finished what he'd started.

I didn't know whether it was the most romantic thing he'd ever done, or the most insulting.

CHAPTER TWENTY-SIX

THE NEXT DAY, Zach showed up with his usual style of no warning. I looked up from my book to see him seated in the chair opposite mine, a book in his hands as if he'd been reading, too.

"Adrian!" I called out, not bothering to say hello. "Zach's finally here!"

"Why do you seem angry with me?" Zach asked, to the accompanying sound of the front door slamming.

"I shouldn't be upset that you took your time getting back to us when we're not able to search for the only weapon that can save my sister?"

Frustration over more than that scalded my tone. Zach didn't get a chance to respond before Adrian came into the room. No surprise, he'd been outside all day. At least he'd given himself a reason to work on his car instead of just pretending to. As for me, I'd been pretending to read so it wasn't obvious that I hadn't been able to stop thinking about what we'd almost done in that shiny black Challenger.

"What the fuck, man?" Adrian asked, summing up his feelings more succinctly than I had.

Zach stood. "I am not a man," he stated crisply. "Nor am I yours to command or to reprimand."

Adrian replied with a burst of the exquisite form of Demonish, the sound caressing my ears like a symphony. Instead of being mollified, Zach was more upset.

"How dare you use the tongue of my brethren, mortal!"

"That's angel-speak?" I asked in surprise.

Adrian threw me a brief glance. "Yes, and I know it because it's what demons originally derived their language from." To Zach, he said, "We didn't have a week to waste waiting for you. You of all people know we're on a countdown."

"What countdown?" I piped up, but both men ignored me.

"I needed time to procure your solution," Zach said, his dark gaze blazing with pinpoints of light. "Did your impatience prevent that from occurring to you, *endante?*"

At the foreign word, Adrian looked more pissed than Zach.

"How about texting a cloud version of 'brb' then?" Acidly.

I got up, the anger between them starting to concern me. We were dead in the water without Zach, so I had to shove my own feelings aside—again—to smooth this over.

"Zach, you've been around forever, but we *are* mortal. Five days might be nothing to you, but with no word and only unbeatable obstacles to dwell on, it's been tough on us."

The Archon glanced my way, his gaze stating that I hadn't smoothed anything over. Okay, time for rough honesty, then.

"For starters, I barely sleep because I keep wondering if this is all for nothing." My voice caught. "No matter what Adrian said about the demons not wanting to lose their leverage, Jasmine might already be dead. Sometimes, I even wish she was. Then she wouldn't be suffering, and I wouldn't have to enter another realm. Then I hate myself for thinking that, so guilt torments me."

I paused to draw in a shuddering breath. "Worse, after last night, I know that I want Adrian so bad, I don't care what happens afterward. Another night alone together and I won't be able to stop myself from going to him, and no matter how much he thinks he has to, I know he won't have the strength to turn me away again."

I made sure to keep staring at Zach as I spoke. If I so much as glanced at Adrian, I wouldn't have been able to admit such raw, personal truths. Guilt over my sister wore me down on a daily basis, so last night with Adrian had used up the last of my willpower. Since he'd resorted to damaging his beloved Challenger rather than wait for me to open the driver's side door, his willpower was on empty, too. Another night alone and it would all be over.

A large part of me wished the Archon would have waited one more day to show up.

Zach stared back at me, his expression turning thoughtful. I still didn't look at Adrian, but I could feel his gaze moving over me, flaring everything it touched. I'd never been so hyperaware of anyone before, and when he let out a low, harsh sigh, I found myself inhaling so I could absorb his breath inside me.

Zach's hand on my head whipped my attention back to him. The Archon closed his eyes as if concentrating, and this time, I actually felt a tingle run through me. Or maybe it was still my body responding to Adrian's unrelenting stare.

After a moment, Zach removed his hand. "This new

disguise will see you past the demon's Hounds," he stated.

"How?" Adrian and I asked in unison, but then a car pulled up in the driveway. Adrian let out a sigh of relief this time.

"Costa's back."

Costa parked behind the Challenger. When he got out, I waved at him through the window—and then was slammed to the floor, Adrian's large frame almost crushing me from the impact.

"Don't shoot," I heard Zach say over Adrian's urgent, "Are you okay? Did he hit you?"

I couldn't answer because I couldn't breathe. My hands smacking at his shoulders must've conveyed that, because Adrian leaped off me with the same speed, though he remained crouched in front of me. I took in a deep breath, wincing as my ribs and the back of my head throbbed with pain.

"Why'd you…squish me?" I managed.

Over his shoulder, I saw Costa burst into the room, his gun drawn and his tanned face pale. "Is it dead?" he snarled.

Adrian had Costa against the wall, the gun knocked out of his hand, before I could grunt out a confused "Huh?"

"Why the fuck did you shoot at Ivy?" Adrian demanded.

Costa threw a horrified look my way. "That's *Ivy*?"

"I can explain," Zach said in an unruffled tone. "In order to get past the beasts, I glamoured Ivy to resemble one."

Adrian let Costa go, his gaze sliding to me with disbelief. "She looks like a Hound?"

"Biggest, ugliest one I ever saw," Costa croaked.

"That's rude," I muttered, trying to reconcile the fact that I now looked like one of the demons' guard reptiles.

Costa's mouth curled down. "Make it—*her*—stop hissing."

"I'm not hissing!" was my immediate protest, but Costa winced and backed away a step. "Oh, crap, all he hears is hissing, right?" I asked resignedly.

A strangled sound came from Adrian's throat. I looked sharply at him, realizing he was fighting back a laugh.

"Ivy, stop hissing at Costa," he said with mock seriousness.

So it was all fun and games now that he realized I hadn't gotten shot? I'd never get used to Adrian's mercurial moods.

"You're sure this will get me past the Hounds?" I asked Zach.

He inclined his head. "They've been trained not to attack their own. Glamouring you to look exactly like another Hound is what took me additional time, as first I had to catch one."

"How?" I blurted, watching Adrian's eyes narrow, as well. "You said Archons can't go into demon realms."

"The sounds she makes are seriously disturbing," Costa muttered, but at least he put his gun away.

"We can't, but the demons are stationing Hounds in every realm as a precaution," Zach stated. "Waiting at vortexes for them to appear as they were transported from one realm to another is how I procured the Hound you now resemble."

Zach had spent the past five days Hound-hunting to help us, and we'd both bitched at him as soon as we saw him. No wonder he'd gotten mad. If I were him, I might've left without giving me my new disguise, too.

"Thank you," I said sincerely, "and I'm sorry."

Once again, he inclined his head. "Apology accepted."

Adrian's mouth thinned, but he didn't ante up an apology. From Zach's expression, that wasn't a surprise. Then again, after what Adrian had told me about that day in the tunnels, the person who really owed the other an apology was Zach.

I cleared my throat, knowing that wasn't going to happen, either. "Okay, now that we've got a way past the guard reptiles, let's head to the nearest realm and search it."

Adrian nodded at me and then gave Costa a measured look. "You up for going with us?"

"I am, but Ivy's the problem," Costa said bluntly. "You can't take her out in public. She looks like what would happen if a werewolf humped a Komodo dragon."

I bared my teeth at him, intending it as a joke, but he visibly flinched. All right, so I was horrifying. I'd say I was sorry, but it would only sound like threatening hisses to him.

"And her clothes!" Costa went on. "You can't expect a fully dressed Hound to go unnoticed in the realms."

"You can see my clothes?" I asked stupidly, then waved an impatient hand and said, "Adrian, translate."

"I don't need to," he said, giving me an appraising look. "Your disguises have only ever been skin-deep, so right now, Costa's looking at a Hound in shorts and a tank top."

"And flip-flops," Costa added, shuddering.

I turned to Zach. "Well, *that* needs fixing."

The Archon raised a single brow. "The answer is obvious."

I waited for him to put his hand on my head again,

but he didn't. Realization dawned and, with it, incredulity.

"You expect me to enter the realms stark naked? Not only would I freeze, I'd be *naked!*"

Logic failed in the face of the appalling thought. Zach looked unconcerned by my dismay, but Adrian raked his gaze over me in a way that was both foreboding and anticipatory.

"Hounds wear leather straps for easier handling. If we placed some strategically on you, they would cover the necessary parts without drawing undue attention, and as I said, Hounds return frequently to the town to get warm."

I closed my eyes. Either I let my sister rot, or I had to run around freezing demon realms wearing the equivalent of a leather bikini. How had this become my life?

"Let's get the bondage lizard party started, then," I finally said, opening my eyes.

Like it or not, this *was* my life, so I had to make the best of it.

CHAPTER TWENTY-SEVEN

WE DIDN'T GO back to the gateway in Collinsville, Illinois. Instead, the three of us drove to Boone, North Carolina so we could access something we'd been avoiding for weeks. A vortex.

Since Hounds were being transported through vortexes, and I now looked like a Hound, Adrian said it was time to chance one. According to him, vortexes were like revolving doors, hitting several realms back-to-back. The bigger the vortex, the more realms it could access. Adrian said if Demetrius hadn't stopped us in Oregon, and minions hadn't chased us through the vortex in Mexico, we could've covered all the realms in North and South America through just those two entranceways.

By contrast, the Boone vortex was much smaller, hitting only about a dozen realms. Still, it would take two weeks to reach each of those realms separately, and with my new disguise, limiting travel time was mandatory.

Something I hadn't thought of when I learned that I looked like a huge, prehistoric dog-lizard to everyone except Zach and Adrian: public restrooms were out of the question. I had to use the bushes along the interstate. If that wasn't humiliating enough, Adrian and Costa had to walk me to and from them so their bodies blocked Ivy-monster from passing motorists' view. When all of us were in the car, Costa would complain that parts of my beastly frame hung over his seat even though my arms and legs stayed completely in the back. And in gas stations or drive-throughs, I needed to have a blanket thrown over me so no one freaked out over seeing a monster in the backseat.

Yeah, I was sick of this disguise already, and the worst of it was about to start now.

We waited until after dark to enter the vortex marked by a tourist site called Mystery Hill. As with other vortexes, people knew there was something off about the spot due to its gravitational anomalies, but little did they know it contained a revolving door to demon realms. I wished I didn't know, either, but that didn't stop Adrian from pulling me through the gateway, which was situated on a concrete slab called the Mystery Platform.

When we tumbled into the shadowy, cold version of the Mystery Hill site, the concrete platform was gone. So were the tourist buildings and the nearby highway. The scent of wood smoke remained, surprising me until I realized there were trees around us. Frozen ones, of course, but if some remained, it made sense that they'd be burned as a heat source.

As expected, we'd been spit out onto the outskirts of the realm's epicenter, so we were alone on the icy hill. For now.

"Okay," Adrian stated. "Stick to the plan, and remember, don't show any fear, either to the Hounds or the handlers."

It was too dark for me to see his expression, but with his enhanced vision, he could see mine as I unzipped my ankle-length parka and let it drop to the ground. Beneath it, I wore only boots, a leather strap across my breasts, and the most uncomfortable leather G-string ever invented.

The blast of cold on my bare skin felt like a full-body punch, knocking out my awkwardness at standing in front of Adrian with almost nothing on. My teeth began to chatter like a windup toy's, and when I kicked my boots off, the ice made it feel as though I was standing on knives. I thought I'd mentally prepared myself, but "mind over matter" didn't exist when you were all but naked in freezing temperatures.

"C-can't do th-this," I stuttered.

Adrian pulled me to him, his arms chasing away the cold on my back and his body warming up my front. Without thinking, I stood on the tops of his boots, easing the stabbing pain in my feet. The last time I'd been mostly naked in his arms, he'd overwhelmed me with passion. This time, tenderness seemed to pour from his embrace, soothing parts of my emotions I hadn't even realized were bruised or broken.

"You *can* do this," he said, his words low but resonant. "The otherworldly abilities of legendary warriors, kings and queens run through your veins. With it, you are capable of so much more than I ever will be, but even if you didn't have that bloodline—" his voice deepened "—I'd still believe in you, Ivy."

I let out a laugh that was half gasp, half choked sob. How could he say that? I'd screwed up every challenge thrown at me, and that was *with* his help. Without it, I'd be dead several times over by now.

A growling hiss jerked my head to the right. To our left, another sounded, and another right in front of us.

Ready or not, the Hounds were here.

"You can do this," Adrian repeated, going absolutely still. I disengaged myself from his arms, seeing him keep them in their half circle as though still cradling me. Amidst the smash of cold, my fear at those ominous growls, and the sole-splitting pain in my feet, I also felt a tinge of wonder.

In our time together, Adrian had yanked me up, knocked me down, hurtled me through realms, trapped me against a wall and kissed me until I burned with need, but this was different. When he'd held me, I realized there was more between us than legacies and lust. He was what I'd been missing my whole life, and if he felt the same way, I'd be damned if either of us was going to die before we could do something about it.

I turned around, shaking and all, to confront the lizard monsters who crowded around us.

"Back off!" I yelled, hoping to them it sounded like the meanest, most badass hiss ever.

Then I stared, my mind taking a few moments to process what I was looking at. When I could think again, Costa's description was right. They *did* look like what you'd get if a werewolf and a Komodo dragon had a monster baby. No wonder he'd opened fire at the sight of me disguised as one.

Even on four legs, the Hounds stood almost as tall as me. Their snouts were elongated like a bull terrier, only with lots more teeth, as I saw when their mouths opened impossibly wide. Their front legs were small, but their back ones were massive with muscle, and they were balanced by a thick tail that narrowed into a point at the end. Claws as long as my fingers stabbed through the frozen ground, and though their skin had the leathery look of a reptile, it was also covered by a thin layer of dark hair.

I could see all these things because light radiated from the spots on their backs, giving off an eerie glow, as if the Hounds needed any enhancement to their menace. Forked, thin tongues flicked out of their mouths, and when the biggest of the three came close enough to give me what I hoped was a friendly lick, I forced myself to stand still and not scream.

If we made it through this, I was drinking an entire bottle of Adrian's superstrong bourbon. Count on it.

"B-back off," I said again, making my voice authoritative and firm, which wasn't easy with chattering teeth. One of the Hounds cocked its head, as if trying to translate the sounds from my rapidly clicking jaw. Then it came forward, leaving a trail of slime over my arm as it gave me a lick, too.

"Gross," I muttered, but it was better than them ripping me to shreds. Zach's glamour was fooling them. I knew it worked on demons, minions and humans, but I hadn't been sure about beasts. Oh, me of little faith.

"Okay, guys, let's go into town and get warm," I announced, starting to run toward where Adrian had told me the town was.

One followed me, but the other two stayed back, as if sensing Adrian's presence even though he hadn't moved a muscle.

"Come *on*!" I said, circling back and nudging both beasts, then running toward the town again. Hey, that's what my dog used to do when I was a kid, and he wanted me to follow him. Here's hoping the Hounds lived up to their nickname and understood.

After a few more nudges and circles, during which I was pretty sure the nerve endings in my feet had become frostbitten, all three Hounds finally went with me. I let them lead since I couldn't see in the stygian woods, but I was so eager to get this over with—I was *cold!*—that I had to force myself to slow down to keep from outrunning them. Finally, we reached the realm's epicenter: a mountain-turned-mini-city, from all the lights, terraces, pathways and courtyards dug into the rock.

The Hounds seemed to know exactly where they were going, taking me up a smooth stone bridge that led inside the metropolitan mountain. If I didn't know that forced human labor had built it, I would've been impressed by the stone city. As with other demons' headquarters, it had electricity, heat and beautiful architectural touches. I also saw jewels artistically embedded into parts of the rock, which reminded me of Adrian's ego comment. Whoever ruled this realm wanted to show off their wealth, and studding jewels in the wall of your mountain castle was certainly one way to do that.

Looking like a Hound meant that I ran past the guards without once being stopped. We streaked through the courtyard with everyone stepping aside to get out of our way, and as the Hounds led me down a stone hallway past that, the air grew noticeably warmer. When we arrived at the end of the hallway, it was almost humid. Once inside the dimly lit room, I understood.

The Hounds jumped into a large, steaming pool cut into the rock, immersing themselves up to their eyes. The water smelled atrocious, but I jumped in, too, telling myself I was just doing it to avoid suspicion.

It was a lie. That steam sold me. It could've been hot mud, and I would've still dived right in. After a few painful minutes where my feet and hands felt like they were on fire as circulation returned, I stopped shaking and my teeth quit chattering. Another few minutes, and I felt focused enough to concentrate. Here was as good a place as any to search the castle with my hallowed-radar.

I'd just begun to do that when rolling noises echoed through the nearby hallway. I tensed, but the Hounds next to me began to wiggle in what could only be called joyous expectation.

Moments later, two minions bearing lightning-like marks in their skin pushed wheelbarrows into the room. The Hounds leaped from the water, jostling each other for position as the contents were dumped into a corner. Then they fell on the pile like hungry pigs at feeding time, and what they'd been given to eat was as revolting as it was expected in a demon realm.

I looked away, rage scalding me with such intensity that it flared my abilities. They pulsed outward, covering the castle with the same sonar-like efficiency as before, and my supernatural ping returned with nothing at the end of it.

The weapon wasn't here.

I got out of the water, still looking away from the Hounds. My anger made my near nudity irrelevant as a minion looked my way, not that he'd see a girl in a belt bikini anyway. He seemed surprised that I wasn't joining the feeding frenzy, but then came toward me while holding out a large blanket.

I stood still as he dried me, speaking in Demonish the whole time. He even used exaggerated vowels and the singsong voice people affected when talking to babies or favored pets. When he was done, he scratched my head and patted my ass as if I'd been a good little Hound.

"I *wish* I was one of them right now," I told him, knowing all he heard were hissing noises. "I'd bite your head off."

He replied with the Demonish version of what was probably "Whoooo's a grumpy guuurl?" and patted me again. This time, I bared my teeth at him.

"Touch my ass one more time and I'm clubbing you with the nearest femur from that pile."

Not that I could, because using a bone like a club was un-Houndlike enough to get the other minion's attention. Also, I needed to seize my chance. With my search complete and the other Hounds occupied, now was the perfect time to return to Adrian.

I ran out of the Hound-spa, glad there weren't many turns to remember to get out of the castle. Once again, no one attempted to stop me, and when I was dashing down the hill on my way to where I last left Adrian, something else occurred to me.

I could see where I was going. Not great, as the several times I tripped proved, but I wasn't blinded by the darkness, and I was far enough away from the lights of the mountain castle that I should've been. My abilities were growing at an incredible rate. Was it because I was finally using them, or was it the virulent seesaw of emotions that kept kicking them into hyperdrive? Between my feelings for Adrian, my guilt over Jasmine, and the rage that demon realm atrocities brought out in me, I wouldn't know a moment of calm if it bit me in the ass.

"Ivy, over here!"

I adjusted my course at Adrian's directive, now noticing him next to the cluster of dead trees. He'd remained so still that he'd blended in at first glance. Once I reached him, I almost hurtled myself into the ankle-length parka he held out and yanked my boots on fast enough to leave skid marks.

"It's not here, let's go," I panted.

We ran the short distance to the gateway, but before he dropped us through it, he paused.

"Are you up for doing another realm now?"

My body felt like a Popsicle and I never wanted to

see another Hound feeding trough again, but I didn't hesitate.

"Yes."

I'd find this weapon, and not only would I save my sister, I'd kill every damn demon and minion in the realm she'd been trapped in.

CHAPTER TWENTY-EIGHT

I MADE IT through seven realms the first day, and finished the other five two days later. A stint with hypothermia was responsible for the delay, but it wasn't just manna combined with Adrian and Costa treating it that got me past it so quickly. I was changing. I could feel it in the muscles I'd never had before, and in the hallowed-hunting sensor that was easier and easier to utilize. I'd searched the last realm without even entering the main building, and despite keeping that to myself, Adrian had sensed the changes, too.

That's why he said it was time for me to learn how to use a slingshot.

Because of my hideous disguise, we went into the Pisgah National Forest to practice. Costa came with us in case we needed an extra trigger finger, if minions happened upon us, though I doubted it. We were out in the middle of beautiful nowhere, with tall trees, waterfalls and bubbling creeks as far as the eye could see. Compared to demon realms, the forties temperature was also downright balmy, but it seemed to keep park visitors at bay. Good thing, too. Forget innocent hikers—if Bigfoot were real, he'd crap himself at the sight of me.

After Adrian set up a target, Costa sat on a fallen tree stump to watch. I stood next to Adrian, frowning when I saw the long, braided rope he pulled out of his duffel bag. Was *that* a duplicate of the infamous weapon? In my head, David's slingshot looked like a Y-shaped branch with stretchy material wound around the opposing ends. Not what resembled a skinnier version of a child's jump rope.

"What am I supposed to do with that? Hang the demons with it?" I wondered.

Adrian grinned, taking a stone from the bag and placing it in the small section of rope that split into two pieces. Then he began to spin the rope in a lasso-like circle, increasing the speed until it made a low, whirring sound. That turned into a crack as he snapped it forward. I didn't see the stone release, but one of the glass bottles he'd set up thirty feet away suddenly exploded, spewing beer over the branch he'd set it on.

"Wow," I said, impressed. "You nailed that like you were using a sniper rifle. How long have you been practicing?"

His grin vanished. "When I met Zach and learned about my mother's death, I researched the slingshot David would've used, then made sure I knew how to use it. Zach didn't bother telling me until recently that only a Davidian or a demon from Goliath's line can utilize the slingshot's true power."

Somehow, I wasn't surprised. It could be that Zach hadn't cared enough to relay the information before, but I thought the Archon might've had another motivation.

If Adrian had known he couldn't use David's slingshot to kill demons, he wouldn't have learned how to use the ancient weapon. Because he had, now he was teaching me. Was that Zach's plan? To keep Adrian near me at every opportunity so he'd be unable to avoid his fate?

If so, I intended that plan to backfire, and I knew how to do it because Adrian had told me himself that touching me was his weakness. So I deliberately brushed against him when he showed me which finger the loop went on and how to hold the rope. His lips tightened, but he acted as if he didn't notice. Then he took my wrist, moving it to mimic the far faster manner I'd need to perfect to get the stone to fly out.

"First you spin the rope to build up momentum," Adrian said. "Then you aim and snap it when you let go. Try it."

I did, and the stone dropped near my feet instead of slinging toward the target. Legendary bloodline or not, clearly I wasn't a natural.

"That happens to everyone the first time," Adrian said evenly. "Try again."

I did three more times, and got the same results. My spirits sank. No wonder Demetrius had said he wasn't afraid of me. I couldn't hit the broad side of a barn, let alone him or any other demons guarding Jasmine.

"Here." Adrian pulled me to him, his body so close that I could feel his heart beating. Then his hand covered mine, though he spread his fingers so he didn't impede the rope. "We'll do it together. Move when I do, Ivy."

We began to spin the rope, first in slower circles, then fast enough to hear that whirring noise. My sense of despair diminished because it was easy to move with Adrian. So easy. His arm shadowed mine while his chest was a muscled wall that teased my back. Every time I adjusted my stance, his thighs brushed the backs of mine, making my breath catch. He was so big, so powerful, yet his breathing roughened when I leaned into him, and brought my body tighter against his. I'd started the taunting touches to chip away at his self-control, but I might end up being the one who came undone.

"On the count of three," Adrian ordered, voice much hoarser than before. "One…"

I leaned forward and aimed. His body curved, following the movement, and feeling his hips line up with mine almost made me drop the rope.

"Two…"

His breath seared the back of my neck, making gooseflesh spring up. When his jaw brushed my cheek as he adjusted to look at the target, I almost rubbed against him like a cat. The feel of him was more than exciting. It was the stuff obsessions were made of.

"Three!"

I let go when I felt his fingers lift, and the slingshot snapped forward with a crack. The rock didn't hit the beer bottle, but it hit the branch it was on, bouncing off after leaving a gash in the wood.

"Yes!" I shouted, so happy I spun around and hugged Adrian.

His arms tightened until it was hard to breathe, but all at once, I didn't care about breathing. I hadn't hugged him with ulterior motives, yet my whole body seemed to come alive in his embrace. I reared back, suddenly desperate to see him. The ridges and hollows that made up his high cheekbones, full mouth, dark gold brows and straight nose were arresting enough, but it was his eyes that had me transfixed. Molten silver gripped sapphire in the same unbreakable hold Adrian had me in, and the blatant need displayed there made things low in my body clench.

"You can't keep teasing me this way." His voice was so guttural, it was almost animalistic. "I'm not the good guy, Ivy. I'm the bad one who'll take everything and then leave."

My mouth felt dry, but that wasn't why I licked my lips.

"You're wrong," I breathed. "Maybe you were once, but you're not anymore. Otherwise, you'd have already done it."

"Do you two mind?" a disgusted voice muttered behind us. "I know that's Ivy, but I'm still going to have nightmares about you dry-humping a Hound, Adrian."

The mental image caught me off guard, and I burst out laughing. We'd hardly been doing that, though the mere sight of Adrian hugging a Hound would be highly disturbing.

Adrian released me, but his smoldering gaze promised that this wasn't over. I couldn't agree more, though for different reasons. Now wasn't the time, however. We had an audience, and we'd already traumatized Costa enough.

Adrian must've thought so, too. He strode over to Costa, twisting the top off one of the beer bottles he'd brought for target practice.

"This'll help wash away the memory."

Costa took it, muttering something in Greek that had Adrian snorting as if in agreement. I turned my attention back to the target, taking out another stone from the duffel bag.

Now that I knew I *could* operate the slingshot, I just had to learn how to do it better.

CHAPTER TWENTY-NINE

SEVERAL HOURS LATER, I flopped back against the couch, letting the remote control slide from my fingers. The cabin we'd been staying in boasted a wood-burning fireplace, but the cable channel lineup sucked.

For the fifth time in the past thirty minutes, I glanced at Costa's suitcase. Tonight was our last night in this cozy, remote hideout, and Costa, ever prepared, had already packed. He even had his suitcase by the door, leaving out just the items he'd need to get ready in the morning.

I hadn't meant to spy on him while he packed. I'd been flipping through channels, and his room happened to be to the left of the TV set. His door also happened to be cracked, and it just so *happened* that I saw what he slipped into his suitcase before he hauled it to the door and left with Adrian to get dinner. See? Total accident.

Besides, I reminded myself as I gave into temptation and slinked over to Costa's suitcase, he hadn't told me I wasn't allowed to use his laptop. He just hadn't mentioned it, much like I intended not to mention taking advantage of the cabin's Wi-Fi connection. Okay, if I got caught, the guys wouldn't be happy, but yesterday, Costa had eaten my bag of Fritos without asking permission and I didn't flip out. Why? Because friends shared. Everyone knew that.

I unzipped his suitcase and felt around through the

pile of clothes until I came across something hard and flat. Then I slid the laptop out as gingerly as if it were booby-trapped with alarms. Once it was free, I almost ran to the desk where the cabin owners had the Wi-Fi information. As I turned the computer on, I found myself holding my breath. When the screen lit up and I saw that I didn't need a password, I let out a whoop. No security? It was like Costa *wanted* me to use it!

I did follow Adrian's warning not to log in to any of my accounts or contact any of my friends. I desperately wished I could message my roommate to tell her I was okay, but minions could still be scoping out Delia or my other friends. Instead, I Googled "Beth and Thomas Jenkins" to see if my parents' funeral had still taken place, even though I hadn't been there to attend. Not being able to officially say goodbye to them had been tearing at my heart for weeks, but I hoped they'd had a proper burial, at least—

I froze over a headline that had my name along with three words I'd never expected to see: Wanted For Murder. With trembling fingers, I clicked the article beneath.

"... Ivy Jenkins, daughter of recently deceased Beth and Thomas Jenkins, has still not been found. Jenkins fled the town of Bennington after murdering Lionel Kroger, the detective assigned to her sister's case. Jenkins has a history of abnormal psychosis and should be considered armed and dangerous...."

I heard a car pull up, but I couldn't stop reading. The article went on to detail how I was also a "person of interest" in Jasmine's disappearance. Worse, it implied that the brakes on my parents' car might have been tampered with, and noted that I was the only other person with access to their vehicle.

In short, it accused me of being a mass murderer.

"What are you doing?"

Under other circumstances, Adrian's harsh tone would've made me flinch. Right now, I was too numb from shock.

"Finding out that I'm a wanted criminal," I said with as much calmness as I could manage. Then I swung around to face him. "But you already knew that, didn't you?"

Adrian set down the bag he'd been holding, and I ignored the delicious aromas coming from it. Costa shut the cabin door and went straight for the food. He couldn't understand what I'd asked Adrian anyway. *Thanks again, Hound disguise.*

"I knew," Adrian said, giving me a measuring look. "What did you think the police were going to say? That you went into hiding with the last descendant of Judas because the detective assigned to your sister's case tried to deliver you to his demon master? They had to explain Kroger's death somehow."

I waved an impatient hand. "Fine, but why claim that I murdered him? Or make me a suspect in Jasmine's disappearance, let alone my parents' deaths? Aren't the demons begging for unwanted attention with this?"

Adrian sighed. "Bennington isn't the first police force they've infiltrated. They're everywhere, and with their connections, they made sure your picture was plastered all over the news and internet, turning everyone who sees you into a potential informant for them."

"But they know I'm disguised!" I protested.

"And now they've made sure you have to stay that way or they'll catch you," was his inexorable response. "Same as me."

I opened my mouth—and nothing came out except a

short, sharp sound, like a last gasp before dying. Adrian stared at me, his expression filled with a hard sort of empathy.

"I told you before, Ivy, we don't win this war. Archons or demons do, but either way, there is no going back for us."

I looked away, staring at the online article that had shattered the last of my hopeful illusions. This whole time, I'd kept telling myself that if I found the weapon and saved Jasmine, I could go back to some semblance of my old life. I might not have had the greatest one, what with pretending more than actually living, but it had been *my* life to screw up or improve. Sure, once I was back, I'd have to avoid mirrors and move Jasmine and me from the WMU dorms to hallowed ground, but I could handle that. Eventually, I'd make new friends, maybe finish college online, get a decent job, and—

And what? Go back to pretending that the dark, icy places I'd glimpsed were figments of my imagination? Hope that every new person I met wasn't a minion in disguise? Even if demons hadn't been behind the warrants for my arrest, what did I *really* think was going to happen if I saved Jasmine by decimating one of their realms? That the demons would call a truce and let my sister and me live in peace? No. We'd have to hide for the rest of our lives, and to do that, we'd have to leave everything and everyone we'd ever known behind.

My head dropped into my hands. Adrian was right. Even if I won, I didn't really win. The Archons did, but Jasmine and I were still screwed.

"Is that what you really look like?"

I picked my head up to see Costa staring at my computer, a half-eaten burger still in his hand. I glanced back at the article. My Facebook user pic was next to the part that talked about my abnormal psychosis.

Was I still the smiling girl staring back at me? Right now, I felt decades older, but that wasn't what Costa meant. I nodded, which needed no translation despite my Hound disguise.

Costa let out a wry snort as he glanced at Adrian. "No wonder you've been having such a hard time, bro."

Was that a compliment? I looked at my picture again, trying to see it through the viewpoint of the handsome Greek. Okay, so I probably wasn't as hot as I'd been with my blonde disguise, but my brown hair was thick enough not to need mousse, my eyes were a nice hazel shade and my mouth had a pouty kind of fullness. A guy I'd briefly dated had even called it lush.

Then I caught a glimpse of my reflection in the screen. My hair looked like it had been styled by drunk witches, raccoons would be jealous of the dark circles under my eyes, and if my skin was any oilier, the shine would light up the room. I needed a hairbrush, concealer and lots of pressed powder, stat!

Of course, that wasn't possible. Even if it was, Costa would only laugh at the image of a Hound trying to primp. As for Adrian...the best makeover in the world couldn't fix our issues. Only a broken destiny could, and while I still believed that was possible, Adrian didn't. Not now and maybe not ever.

"I need to see my sister."

Costa didn't react to my statement, but Adrian froze in the middle of picking up a burger.

"Ivy," he began.

"I so don't want to hear it." The words came out as a sigh despite my screaming on the inside. "You want me to embrace the suck? Fine, but I'm also finished with guessing if I'm weapon-hunting for Jasmine, or for you."

He dropped the burger and stalked over. "What do you mean?"

I met his gaze without flinching. "You don't want me entering the Bennington realm without the weapon, but is that because you're worried about extra demon security? Or because you're afraid that if I find out my sister's already dead, I'll stop looking for it and you'll lose your chance at killing Demetrius?"

Anger suffused his face, flushing his cheeks and turning his eyes into burning gems. "Is that what you think?"

Costa glanced between us. "You two fighting?"

"What's the only thing you told me I could trust about you, Adrian?" My voice was flat from the weight of my desolate future bearing down on me. "Your hatred of demons. So I'm supposed to believe you *wouldn't* string me along about my sister's survival to keep me looking for the one weapon that can kill them?"

Adrian's hands closed into fists while he stared at me. The last time he'd done that, he'd grabbed me and kissed me, but something darker than passion seethed in him now.

"Get your stuff," he said in a voice that vibrated from barely controlled rage. "We're leaving for Bennington tonight."

CHAPTER THIRTY

"THIS IS A BAD IDEA," Costa said for the eleventh time.

Adrian and I responded the same way we had to his other ten warnings—with stony silence. We were too busy playing our high-stakes version of "chicken" to let Costa deter us. Adrian was counting on me changing my mind about entering the world's most dangerous demon realm, and I was betting he'd refuse to pull me through the gateway when the time came.

We'd see who swerved first.

"Obsidiana's seen your ride, so you can't drive this into town without every minion knowing who you are," Costa went on, not giving up his attempt to talk sense into us. "This is a mint-condition, '68 Challenger, so it's gonna draw some eyes."

"We'll leave it outside Bennington," Adrian replied, the tightness in his tone saying he was still steaming mad.

"And do what with the hulking demon lizard in the backseat?" Costa shot back, adding, "Sorry, Ivy," as an afterthought.

Adrian didn't even glance my way. "We'll hide her in something else."

Costa cast a dubious look over his shoulder. "It'll need to be something big."

My lips tightened. "Enough with the fat-lizard cracks," I snapped, hoping the hiss Costa heard sounded as pissy as I felt.

"This is a bad idea," Costa muttered once again. Apparently he was going for an even dozen.

"The gateway's inside the B and B, but your sister won't be there anymore," Adrian stated, not glancing away from the road even though he was now talking to me. "The spot where it's located was swallowed recently, after Demetrius took over the realm. She'll be in old Bennington. That and parts of New York got swallowed a long time ago, so that's where his palace is."

"I don't remember glimpsing a palace when I went through Bennington." Then again, I'd been focused on showing Jasmine's picture to hotel and motel employees, not on paying attention to what I thought were hallucinations.

Adrian grunted. "It's there."

Every realm I'd entered had had a grand structure, and Adrian hadn't been wrong about his realm blueprints yet, but something about his tone made his surety sound more...personal.

"You lived there before, didn't you?" I guessed.

His eyes briefly met mine before he returned his militant attention to the road. "For a long time, I ruled it."

Anger shot through me. Of course, he'd failed to mention *that* before.

"You're only a few years older than me, so it couldn't have been that long, Adrian. Unless you were a toddler king."

"If I'm guessing right about where this conversation's going, it's time she knew anyway," Costa muttered, giving Adrian a sympathetic look.

"Knew what?" I asked curtly.

Adrian's hands tightened on the steering wheel. "I told you time moves differently in the realms. Once I was old enough to fight, Demetrius made sure I lived in realms where time almost froze to a stop so he'd have plenty of it to perfect my training. I might only look a few years older than you, Ivy, but I was born in 1873."

My mind froze while doing the math. Adrian couldn't—just could *not!*—be over a hundred and forty.

"No," I croaked.

Costa reached around to pat my head. "I know it's hard to take in. When Adrian got me out and I realized fifty years had passed over here, I had trouble adjusting—"

"How old are *you?*" I burst out before remembering he couldn't understand me.

"Costa's seventy-three, or seventy-four, I guess." Adrian gave his friend a humorless smile. "Forgot your birthday."

Denial still had me in a fierce grip. "But Tomas's family is still alive! We sent Hoyt to them so he could recover!"

"Those were his grandkids, Ivy," Adrian said, sparing another glance my way. "Didn't you notice the old clothing his parents wore in the photographs in Tomas's room?"

I had, but I'd thought his family had just liked to wear more, um, quaint apparel.

"You're really a hundred and forty?" Call me slow, but I needed to hear him confirm it one more time.

"Yes."

I angled my head so I could see him more fully, as if he'd look different now that I knew his true age. He didn't, of course. Same piercing sapphire eyes, curving brows, high cheekbones, sensually full mouth and strong jaw, all making up a face that left gorgeous behind in the dust. Considering that face was on top of a body so built that it could make a superhero jealous, Adrian's looks were unforgettable.

So was this revelation. He hadn't just spent his childhood and teen years living with demons. He'd spent nearly a century and a half with them. No wonder Demetrius had referred to Adrian's working for Zach as a "little rebellion." It barely registered next to the staggering length of time he'd lived in the realms as the demons' prophesied savior.

I understood then, more than I ever had before, the absolute assurance that Demetrius, Zach and even Adrian had that he couldn't avoid his destiny. How could a few weeks of being attracted to me compare with thirteen decades of being groomed to betray the last Davidian? It's not like Adrian was trying to kick a recent bad habit—he'd literally spent a couple of lifetimes training so he could bring about my doom!

And I'd pretty much done everything I could to help him, I realized with a scald of self-recrimination. Even now, I was insisting that Adrian take me to a realm where his demonic foster father and a few hundred of his closest evil friends waited. A realm Adrian had admitted he'd once ruled over, and where he could now return as the conquering betrayer.

All I needed to do was slap a bow on my ass to make myself the perfect, too-stupid-to-live sacrifice.

"Having second thoughts, Ivy?"

Adrian's voice broke through my crushing musings. His accent was as darkly alluring as ever, but it was a *demon* accent. When I met his gaze, those gemstone-colored eyes held their usual mixture of brooding danger, but who was his veiled violence aimed at? The girl he was destined to destroy, or the demons he'd told me he intended to take down?

After all, they wanted the weapon, too. I'd bet Demetrius and the rest of them would consider the minions

Adrian had killed as acceptable losses if he delivered the slingshot—and me—to them in the end. What if all the times Adrian had saved me were just so I'd willingly lead him to the powerful weapon that his demonic brethren needed? What if all his claims to care about me were only so I'd run headlong into my own betrayal? In short—what if the only time Adrian had been telling me the truth was when he told me *not* to trust him?

"Yes, I'm having second thoughts," I said hoarsely.

"Tell me she said yes," Costa muttered. "Because this—"

"Is a bad idea," I finished, though only Adrian understood me. "Costa's right. Let's stop off somewhere. I, ah, don't feel so hot all of a sudden."

Adrian shot a suspicious look my way, but my stomach gurgled as if in agreement. Either he heard it or decided not to push me, because he turned off the highway at the next exit.

I drew in a deep breath, trying to force back the clenching in my gut that came from fear, anger, and a very real sense of betrayal. Despite all his warnings, I *had* trusted him. Hell, I'd done more than that. The rest of my ancestors might have been drawn to Judians out of compassion or the belief that darkness could be overcome by light, but I'd allowed myself to fall for Adrian, making me the stupidest Davidian to ever walk the earth.

My teeth ground together. Fine. I might have been the most gullible person in my ancient, illustrious ancestry, but that ended right now. I'd make sure my sister was alive and if so, I *would* find that weapon. I'd just do it without Adrian.

But first, I had to find a way to get away from him.

CHAPTER THIRTY-ONE

ADRIAN RENTED ONLY one room at the Motel 6. We had enough money and Archon-blessed oil for more, so I guessed he intended us to just grab a few hours' sleep before we hit the road again.

The single room worked for me, but for different reasons. I'd come up with a plan. Not a great one, but I couldn't think of anything else in the short time I had. Adrian parked around the back of the hotel to hide my monstrous disguise from other guests, and once I'd been hustled inside the room, he followed his usual protocol. That meant drawing the drapes and then sprinkling the interior with holy oil to render the room temporarily hallowed.

I waited until Adrian took his turn in the bathroom before I wrote on the little pad of paper every hotel room seemed to have. Then I handed it to Costa, hoping my Hound disguise didn't somehow screw up the words he saw on the page.

Need to talk to Adrian alone. Give us a couple of hours?

Relief washed over me when Costa nodded, then crumpled up the page, tossing it into the trash.

"Gonna go clear my head, bro," Costa called out, grabbing some money from the duffel bag. "I'll be at the bar next door."

He left before Adrian could argue. Or maybe he

wouldn't have. When Adrian emerged from the bath-room, his expression was serious and water clung to his hairline, as though he'd splashed some on his face while he was in there.

I sat on one of the double beds, suddenly finding it hard to look him in the eye. Knowing what I had to do didn't make doing it any easier.

"I know you're not really sick," Adrian stated, his gaze searching mine as he came nearer. "Just upset. Is it from finding out my real age, or because I used to rule the Bennington realm?"

"Both," I admitted. A surge of anger made me able to look at him fully. "After the new section was swallowed, was it your idea to restore the bed-and-breakfast on this side so minions could use it like a Venus flytrap?"

That must have been how Jasmine had been taken. None of the other Bennington hotel employees had rec-ognized her picture. How simple it would've been for Mrs. Paulson to make all records of Jasmine's stay at the B and B disappear. Add in more minions on the police force to take care of any snooping family, and it was the perfect setup for funneling humans into the demon realm.

"No, that was Demetrius's idea," Adrian replied, sitting on the bed opposite mine. "But he's not alone. Demons have rackets like that all over the world. Ho-tels, guided tours, boat rentals, chauffeur services…any business that gets people alone and vulnerable, there's a chance a minion's planted in it."

"And nobody cares." My snort was bitter. "People like Jasmine disappear every day, and the world shrugs because she's not their sister." Pain sharpened my voice as I added, "Or daughter. Minions killed my parents, too, didn't they?"

Adrian sighed before running his hand through his hair. "Probably. They'd be considered too old to be decent slaves, and if they were making waves over her disappearance, their having an 'accident' would be the simplest solution."

I stared at him, silently daring him to look away. "Then I showed up making more waves, but I'm young, so they tried to make me a slave instead."

"Yes," he said, his gaze boring into mine while varying emotions flitted across his features. Disgust, anger and the most telling of all. Guilt.

"You did that to people, too." My accusation filled the space between us, creating an invisible barrier that seemed to grow with every second.

"Yes, I did." Something too bitter to be a smile twisted his mouth. "I told you, for a while, the demons had convinced me that humans were no better than they were. Just more hypocritical, because on this side, human slavers, murderers and oppressors were called dictators, kings and presidents, if they did it to enough people. Only the humans who did it to just a few were called criminals."

"Our race has issues," I acknowledged, still holding his stare. "Doesn't excuse what you or the rest of them did."

"No, Ivy, it doesn't," he replied, his voice very soft. "And I see the faces of everyone I harmed whenever I close my eyes. That's why I started working for Zach. Every person I save feels like washing a drop of blood from my hands, but deep down, I know I'll never even the score. Some things can't be atoned for, and all the lives I've saved will never restore the ones I've taken or ruined."

I wanted to believe the regret resonating in his tone.

Wanted to trust the pain etched on his features, or the look in his eyes that seemed to urge me to revile him for all the things he reviled himself for. But Jasmine's life—and mine—hung in the balance, so I couldn't trust him. He'd told me that enough times, and this time, I'd believe him.

I looked away and forced out a shaky laugh. "I don't know about you, but I could really use a beer. Aren't there still some that didn't get used for target practice in the trunk?"

He didn't say anything. I sneaked a glance at him. Adrian still sat exactly as he had been, his elbows braced on his legs while he leaned forward. The only thing new was his frown.

"After everything I just said, your response is to start drinking?"

More than a hint of disbelief tinged his tone. I scrambled for a convincing reply and found myself answering with the truth. Part of it, anyway.

"You might want to keep stewing over all the horrible things in your past, but I want to move forward. Right now, that involves getting a drink."

A slight snort escaped him. "Guess there are worse ways to move on with our lives."

He went to the door, but as he opened it, I couldn't stop from asking a question that had nagged at me. This was the last chance I'd get, even if his answer was just another lie.

"Forget our roles, fates, whatever for a minute. When it's all said and done, who do you think is going to win this war? Archons or demons?"

He half turned. Though his face was only in profile, I could see that his expression matched the absolute certainty in his tone when he spoke.

"Archons."

I let out a short laugh. "Is it me, or do they seem outnumbered? I've seen several demons, but only one of them."

"You're right, they're outnumbered." Something else lurked in his voice now. A pained sort of wistfulness. "When it's light versus dark, that doesn't matter. One shadow in a brightly lit room goes unnoticed, but shine a ray of light into even the darkest corner…and everything changes."

Then he left, splitting my emotions right down the middle. If he believed Archons would win, how could he betray me to the losing side? Was he that brainwashed by what he'd been told was his fate, or was he just saying that to play me?

Jasmine's face flashed in my mind, reminding me that I didn't have time for second-guessing. I ran over to Adrian's duffel bag, quickly rifling through it. Once I had what I needed, I dragged a chair over to the hotel room door and stood on it. Despite my preparations, two sides of myself remained locked in battle.

Believe him! my hopeful half screamed. *Just because he thinks his awful past has doomed him doesn't mean it has!*

It's too late! my cynical half roared. *You can't trust him, he's already admitted that he's too far gone!*

Somewhere in the parking lot, a trunk slammed closed, then footsteps approached the door. I sucked in a breath, my vision blurring as I raised my hands. I didn't want to do this. I didn't.

But I had to.

The door opened—and I slammed the same large rock we kept to smash mirrors down onto Adrian's head before he even cleared the threshold. His fist shot out with his lightning-fast reflexes, but in the instant before it landed, his eyes met mine. His sapphire ones widened, then his hand buried into the wall instead of my face.

"Ivy?" he asked, as though confused.

Tears streamed from my eyes as I whacked him in the head again. This time, Adrian fell to the floor, and the thump his body made seemed to reverberate all through me. I dropped the rock, sickened at how it was now stained with blood.

"I'm sorry," I choked out.

He didn't reply. In fact, Adrian was so still, I wasn't even sure if he was breathing. I knelt, my whole body rigid from fear as I checked his pulse.

It throbbed beneath my fingers, sending an instant wave of relief through me. He was alive! Even if he'd always meant to betray me, I never would have forgiven myself if I'd killed him. I didn't think I'd be able to forgive myself for doing this, and I wasn't done yet.

I grabbed the slingshot from his bag, tying his hands and feet together with it. Then I put duct tape over his mouth, deciding to add a few more layers to his wrists and ankles, too. When he woke up, he'd be pissed, and that was only if he were innocent. If he *had* intended to deliver me to Demetrius after I found the weapon… Well, maybe I should use all the tape.

When Adrian's wrists, arms, ankles and mouth were covered by the thick gray tape, I paused. There was one more thing I had to do, and I dreaded it even more than I'd dreaded knocking him out.

With shaking hands, I went back to his duffel bag and pulled out his knife.

CHAPTER THIRTY-TWO

I TRIED TO ignore the screech of brakes from the car next to me, but I couldn't ignore it suddenly swerving into my lane. I veered left, avoiding that crash, yet swiping the front of the Challenger against another vehicle in the process.

Forget everything else I'd done. Adrian was going to kill me for damaging his precious ride.

The driver I'd sideswiped blasted his horn and slowed down, but when he drew even with me, his expression changed from anger to pure terror. I hunched down and drew the bedspread over my head until I could barely see. Too late. Another screech of brakes and he was driving off the road, coming to a stop in the grassy shoulder along the highway.

It was dark out, and I used the hotel bedspread like a veil, but one look at my face destroyed the notion that I was just your average commuter. Seeing a hulking demon lizard behind the wheel was too much for my fellow drivers. At least it was well past rush hour, so while I'd caused a few individual spinouts, I hadn't been responsible for a real accident yet.

If I wanted to keep it that way, I had to get off the road. Sooner or later, some cop would finish a hysterical motorist's sobriety test and decide to check out their story of a monster driving a vintage Challenger. Add in the fact that some of the Bennington cops were minions and I'd *really* be screwed.

Still, I had to get as close to Bennington as I could. Ditching the car to run around in the open raised my chances of being seen. Not driving also meant it would take longer to get where I needed to be. I'd left Adrian back at the motel over two hours ago, so at any minute, Costa would return to the room and find him.

Adrian. I forced back the guilt that made me feel like I'd swallowed a bellyful of acid. He'd *told* me he'd betray me if we continued to spend time together! Demetrius and Zach had thought so, too, and with Adrian's admittedly bloody history, many people would agree he deserved what I'd done.

So why was I the one who felt like a betrayer?

To keep myself from brooding over that, I turned off at the next exit. According to the map on Adrian's phone—yes, I'd swiped that, too—the Green Mountain National Forest bordered the part of Bennington where the B and B was located. I vaguely remembered the woods from my visit to the B and B, so if I kept to the trees, I'd be able to stay hidden until I reached it. The realm gateway was in there, Adrian had said. Too bad he hadn't specified *where* in the B and B, but I had a plan for that, too.

I ditched the Challenger in the woods behind a gas station, but only after I wrapped some supplies in my blanket. Then I hoisted it over my shoulder like a sack, held Adrian's phone out in front of me so I could see the map, and started running.

Once, I would have found the dark expanse of woods creepy, but not now. Maybe it was because no animal in its right mind would attack me with my Hound disguise. Same went for people, and though the air was distinctly chilly, the cold didn't affect me like it once would have. Must be my growing abilities. After all, it couldn't be coincidence that I barely needed the light from Adrian's cell phone to see.

You can do everything I can do…. It's in your blood. Adrian's words stole through my mind, encouraging me and slamming me with guilt at the same time. Dammit, I needed to stop thinking about him! I'd made the only choice I could by not trusting him, same thing he'd urged me to do over and over again. Jasmine was the person I should feel guilty about. If Adrian had been lying and she was dead, then I'd failed my only remaining family. Worse, I'd lost my best friend.

Memories began to assail me. *Jasmine screaming with excitement because she'd been accepted to the same college as me. Her countless pranks, like adding BENGAY to my suntan lotion or replacing my shampoo with bubble bath. How she'd hugged me after my disastrous prom night, and how she'd never told any of my friends—or hers—why I really went to the doctors so frequently. Jasmine as a little girl, sitting with me in a psychologist's waiting room, her blue eyes somber as she whispered, "If you say you see stuff, Ivy, I believe you…."*

The cell phone vibrated, startling me so much I almost dropped it. *Incoming call,* read the screen. *Unknown.*

I slowed, torn between curiosity and caution. If I answered and heard Demetrius's voice on the other line, it would confirm all my suspicions. But what if it was Zach? I could really use the Archon's help, and for all I knew, Zach contacted Adrian by phone; not to mention *unknown* would be a damn good description of where *his* calls were routed from.

I hit Accept but didn't say anything, hoping whoever was on the other line would speak first.

My gamble paid off.

"Ivy." Adrian's voice was hoarse from anger or urgency. "Don't go in there alone. Don't—"

I hit the end button so hard, it cracked the screen. Then I threw the phone down, as if that would further sever the connection between us. Still, the forest seemed to fill with Adrian's presence, until I could swear that the breeze ruffling through the trees was whispering his name.

"Leave me alone!" I yelled, sinking to the ground next to his phone. "You were going to betray me, so I had to do it."

Saying it didn't make me feel any better. Believing it hurt almost as much as hoping I was wrong. If I was, I'd ruined any chance between us by doing the one thing Adrian had managed *not* to do, despite heaven and hell telling him he had no choice. He wouldn't forgive me for that. No one would, myself included.

With a hard swipe at the tears filling my eyes, I grabbed the phone, got up and started to run again. Right or wrong, I'd made my choice. Whether Adrian intended to stop me or betray me, he knew where I was headed, so I didn't have much time.

LAST TIME I'D seen the Paulson bed-and-breakfast, autumn leaves had been swirling around the lovely white house. Now, all the trees were bare and a dark, decrepit shell hung over the B and B, like the negative of a double-exposed photo. It didn't vanish after a couple blinks, either. It stayed, mute testament to how much my abilities had grown.

That's also why I could now see words carved into

the side of the house, like "LEAVE!" "HELP!" and "DEMONS." Of course, no one else could see the warnings from people trapped in the other realm. Tourists who pulled up would only see a sign that said "Welcome, Friends!" on the portico over the front door.

I lurked at the far end of the yard, concealed by the trees that butted up against the foothills of the green mountains. Lights were on inside, giving off a warm amber glow, and two cars were in the gravel section where I'd parked the first time I came here. The B and B had guests.

And I was going to crash the party.

I started taking off my clothes, not stopping until I was down to only boots and the itchy leather bikini that doubled as Hound straps. I put the clothes in the blanket with my other supplies and hefted it over my shoulder again. Then I ran toward the house. When I reached the front door, I tried the knob. Just like before, it was unlocked. Silently, I entered the house, trying to focus on the *here* instead of the dark, double image that showed a place far different than this one.

No one was in the parlor where I'd first encountered Mrs. Paulson, but laughter came from farther down the hallway. I followed it, ending at the dining room. Two youngish-looking couples sat at the table, and for a frozen second as their heads swung toward me, no one moved.

Then screams coincided with the sound of chairs and other items crashing as they knocked things over in their panic to leave. I bared my teeth, hissing and waving my arms, hoping to scare them right into their cars. They needed to get out of here for more reasons than what Mrs. Paulson had probably been planning for them.

Not that the guests were grateful for my saving them. I had to dodge several plates one of the guys threw at me before he ran down the hallway. Finally, the woman I'd been waiting for appeared, looking flustered as she entered the dining room.

"What is going on—" Mrs. Paulson began, only to stop dead at the sight of me.

"Dyate," she whispered.

CHAPTER THIRTY-THREE

MY GRIN MUST'VE looked savage, because I felt every inch the fearsome creature she thought I was as I came toward her. The innkeeper looked like the same salt-and-ginger-haired old lady I'd first met. She even still had on an apron, as if I'd interrupted her while she was baking dessert, but out of the two of us, she was the real monster.

This bitch had delivered my sister to demons. She'd also sent Detective Kroger after me, and for all I knew, might've been the person who'd messed with the brakes on my parents' car. I wanted her dead so badly, it burned. But first...

I dropped my sack when I was a few feet away. She still didn't move, following protocol on how to avoid being mauled by a Hound, but her gaze flicked to the sack in surprise. Guess she hadn't noticed it before, what with not expecting a hulking demon lizard to show up in her dining room. Then I pulled out the note I'd written earlier, shoving it in front of her.

Take me to the gateway.

Her face puckered into a frown as she stared at it. I knew she could read what I'd written; my note to Costa had proven that. My hope was that she'd think I was a stray who'd gotten separated from its handler, but that had a note telling whichever minion that found me to send me back home. As for the sack, well, dogs carried stuff sometimes. Maybe I should've held the sack in my teeth to look more Hound-like.

When her frown cleared and she looked at me with palpable hatred, I knew my plan had backfired.

"Davidian," she hissed, yanking something out of her apron.

I lunged to the left when I caught sight of a barrel. Her first shot missed me by inches and her second one went over my head as I ducked. Then I charged, steam-rolling into her, fueled by hatred and strength from a legacy I still didn't understand. She went down, the back of her head smacking against the tile floor. But she still didn't let go of the gun.

I yanked its barrel to the side just in time, sending the shot she fired into the wall instead of my stomach. Despite her aged appearance, she had a grip like a bear. Teeth like one, too. She tore into my shoulder, making me yelp with pained surprise. I couldn't get the gun free, yet I didn't dare let go of it to pull her mouth off me.

As if Adrian were whispering instructions into my ear, I suddenly knew what he would do. So I did it.

I threw myself forward, my momentum causing Mrs. Paulson's head to smack against the tile again. Her scream reverberated against my aching shoulder, yet she didn't let go of the gun or stop biting me. I flung forward several more times, ignoring how it drove her teeth deeper into my flesh. Finally, her grip on the gun loosened and I was able to yank it away. My shoulder throbbed—I'd need a tetanus shot now, dammit!—but my grip didn't waver when I pointed the gun in her face.

"Where's the gateway?" I snapped, forgetting for a second that she couldn't understand me.

Mrs. Paulson spat at me, landing a disgusting glop

on my cheek. I wiped it off with my other hand before
grabbing the note that had fluttered to the floor near us.

"Where?" I said, shaking it at her.

She responded with a torrent of Demonish, some
of which I recognized as more curse words. My jaw
clenched. Adrian was on his way, and I didn't know
whose side he was on, so I had to be gone before he arrived. That meant I couldn't waste any more time asking Mrs. Paulson nicely.

I lowered the gun and shot her in the arm. At this
range, it blew a large chunk off, coating me in an instant spatter of red. She howled, her agonized writhing
almost dislodging me, but I held on and shoved the note
in front of her again.

"Where?" I yelled, putting the barrel to her leg next.

She didn't need to understand my words to translate the threat. "In my office!" she gasped. "Please,
no more!"

She deserved more. So, so much more, but I didn't
have the time or the stomach to give it to her. I hauled
her up, planting the barrel of the gun into her side. She
sagged, leaning against me so heavily, she almost toppled us over.

"Show me," I said, jerking my head at the hallway.

Once again, she got the gist and began staggering
down the hallway. From the quiet around us, we were
now alone in the inn. Guess if a massive demon lizard
hadn't been enough to scare the guests off, hearing several gunshots had done the trick.

"Here," she said, leaning against the doorway to an
office.

I couldn't see through to the dark realm here, but
then again, I hadn't with any of the other gateways, either. Still, I wasn't going to take her word for it. I jabbed

her harder in the side with the gun and shook the note for emphasis.

"Where?" I said, shoving her into the room.

Blood had turned her graying hair crimson, and more dripped from what was left of her upper arm, but she still managed to catch herself instead of falling. Again I was reminded that minions might look human, but they weren't, so while Mrs. Paulson was acting weak and defeated, the bitch still had lots of fight left in her.

"There," she said, pointing at the corner. Then she braced herself against her desk, as if she didn't have the strength to hold herself up on her own.

Sure she didn't. I kept the gun aimed at her as I went inside. The corner had a bookshelf on one side and an oil painting on the other. Certainly nothing that screamed "Demon door!" but when had any of them been helpfully marked? I stretched out my hand toward the center of the corner—and gasped when the blood coating it suddenly pulsed with an almost painful energy.

Adrian was right. It *did* feel like an electric shock, but only for the parts of me that Mrs. Paulson had bled on. That's why I'd done the most awful, unforgivable thing to him before I left him tied up and alone in that room.

I'd bled him.

Adrian told me I needed minion, demon or Judian blood to cross through a gateway. I hadn't been sure if Mrs. Paulson would be here tonight, so I'd taken precautions to ensure that I could get through the gateway anyway, and by precautions, I mean about two beer bottles' worth of Adrian's blood.

Maybe now, I wouldn't need it. The last thing I wanted to do was paint my skin with the proof of my awful deed. I could barely look at the bottles without feeling guilty enough to cry, so hopefully Mrs. Paulson had bled on me enough to—

An ominous click had me throwing myself to the side, and not a moment too soon. White hot pain grazed my arm, but my otherworldly speed had saved my life. While I'd let thoughts of Adrian distract me, Mrs. Paulson had gotten another gun from somewhere.

I fired back, not even getting a chance to really aim because I was too busy running out of the room. Just as quickly, I ran back in, cursing myself the whole time. *Don't leave a minion alone with a demon realm gateway, dumb ass!*

Mrs. Paulson was on the floor, one hand stretched toward the gateway as if she were trying to claw her way inside. She wouldn't be going anywhere, though. A single smoking hole dotted her forehead and the back of her head was gone. Then the rest of her disappeared as her body disintegrated into ashes.

I didn't have time to marvel at my shot, celebrate this small revenge for Jasmine, or be worried about how little it bothered me to kill someone. Again. Instead, I went back to the dining room to grab my sack and rub more of Mrs. Paulson's blood on me. Then, bracing myself, I went back to her office and ran straight for the corner.

Every other time I'd entered a realm, I'd tumbled out of the gateway into a barren landscape of frozen darkness. This time, I landed in a decrepit version of the same bed-and-breakfast, with lights glowing from the nearby hallway.

Mrs. Paulson's office looked a lot different on this side. It didn't have a stick of furniture and the only decorations on the walls were holes. Aside from some ratty-looking blankets, it was also empty. When I crept out into the hallway, however, I found out that the rest of the B and B wasn't.

"Hound!" a brown-haired guy who looked about my age yelled. Then he froze, giving me a chance to take in his ragged clothes, unkempt hair and wiry build. If I'd seen him in the real world, I'd have expected him to be holding up a sign asking for money. For a human in a demon realm, he looked great. His clothes were dirty and torn, but they were *real* clothes. Not disgusting human hides, and though he was lean, he didn't look half-starved.

Was the Bennington realm slightly less appalling than the other ones? The thought gave me hope that my sister was still alive. I wished I could ask the guy about Jasmine, but all he'd hear were hisses, and I'd left my notepad back on the other side.

Adrian had told me that Jasmine wouldn't be in the B and B, yet I checked it anyway. All the people stood like statues in whatever posture they'd been in when they heard the "Hound" warning, making them look like exhibits in a wax museum. They were in their teens or twenties and looked as disheveled as the first guy I'd seen. Still, no one looked abused, and the kitchen had real food in it. From the makeshift beds in almost every room, these people seemed to live here, yet I hadn't come across a minion yet.

I also didn't see Jasmine, but she'd been here. One of the girls had on a sweater that I recognized as hers. Again, I ached to ask, but I didn't have time to find a way to communicate, not to mention that minions could show up here any minute.

So could Adrian. I let that thought spur me as I left the B and B, dropping my sack by a nearby tree stump so I could grab it on my way back. Then I ran toward the lights in the distance. The temperatures made my teeth chatter, but being here filled me with a desperate sort of hope.

Soon, I'd know for myself if Jasmine was really still alive. If she was, I'd keep up my search for the weapon, even if I'd be doing it without Adrian. Zach would help me, if only because he didn't want the demons to get it. After I found the slingshot, I'd use it to free Jasmine. Then we'd hide out from the demons and I'd help her get over her captivity while helping myself get over my feelings for Adrian.

Bleakness threaded through me. Guess I should focus on one impossible task at a time.

Growling sounds made me skid to a stop midway up the hill. Lots of trees remained in this realm, standing like tall, petrified monuments to the world they'd been snatched from. That made it hard to see, even with my abilities working at full capacity. Had to be Hounds patrolling the woods.

Those odd snarls came nearer, echoing in ways that almost sounded like they were coming from above. I looked around, expecting a demon lizard to pounce out from behind a tree, but none did. Since I wasn't supposed to act afraid, I continued back up the hill, though going at a walk instead of a run.

Crashing noises above were my only warning. Then I had to run to avoid being flattened by a pile of frozen tree branches. Even at top speed, I still got struck, but I forgot about the pain when I saw what had caused them to come down around me.

Gray, leathery wings snapped back from their protective circle, revealing a creature that had to be nine feet tall. It crouched in almost apelike style, with its straight, massive arms resting between its bent legs. Shoulder and chest muscles bulged as it raised its head, showing red, glowing eyes and a face that was wider than a Hound's, but no less animalistic.

If Hounds looked like what would happen if a werewolf mated with a Komodo dragon, then this thing looked like the love child of a Komodo-werewolf-pterodactyl threesome. Worse, the way it stared at me said that moving or standing still made no difference. It could see me either way.

Gargoyle ran through my mind with a morbid sort of fascination. The Bennington realm had a gargoyle.

CHAPTER THIRTY-FOUR

I DID THE only thing I could think of when confronted by a much-larger creature who thought I was a dog-lizard: I rolled on my back and showed it my belly, hoping the "Don't kill me, I'm friendly!" gesture was as universal among animals here as it was in my realm.

The gargoyle cocked its head, staring at me as if I was the strangest thing it had ever seen. It didn't start tearing into me with those knifelike claws or teeth, though, so I considered my move a win. Cautiously, I rolled over, twitching so much from nervousness that my Archon-glamoured tail probably looked like it was wagging. I wasn't just in over my head with this situation—I was a thousand feet underwater.

The gargoyle chuffed at me. That's the closest way I could describe it, but at least it didn't start speaking Demonish. Hey, gargoyles could talk in cartoons; how the hell did I know if they could talk in real life, too?

"Hiya," I said back, hoping what it heard was a similar-sounding chuff.

It chuffed again, beating its wings for emphasis. Clearly I was supposed to do something. Damned if I knew what.

"Uh, follow you?" I guessed, taking a hesitant step back up the hill.

It rose with an explosion of air from those powerful wings, which I took as a yes. Then I had to scramble to avoid another shower of frozen branches as it blasted through the tops of the trees. Triumph and terror mingled inside me. I'd met a real-life gargoyle and survived. Now *there* was a Facebook update for a later time, not that anyone would believe me. Besides, what if gargoyles weren't the only unexpected creatures in this realm?

For the space of a few heartbeats, I wasn't sure what to do. Run toward the demon town over the hill? Or go back to the gateway inside the B and B? Adrian hadn't been kidding when he said the demons in this realm would beef up their security. No wonder there hadn't been any minions at the B and B. They didn't need them to keep the humans in line. Not when death flew from above.

And prowled along the ground, I realized as familiar hissing noises heralded the approach of three Hounds.

"You're late," I told them dryly, letting the beasts smear me with disgusting, slimy licks as they said their versions of hello. Between meeting a gargoyle and getting a Hound tongue-bath, I'd have nightmares forever from this realm alone.

Decision made, I followed the Hounds back up the hill. Since I was already scarred for life, I wasn't leaving until I'd seen for myself that Jasmine was still alive.

When we reached the top of the hill and I caught my first look at the city, I paused. *Beautiful,* I thought grudgingly.

A lot more time had passed since this section of the realm had been swallowed. Most of the forest had been cut down, leaving smooth, flat ground. Frozen rivers snaked through the valley in zigzags, ice reflecting the lights from the castle. The effect made the castle look like it sat on silver necklaces, and the significance of its blue stone walls wasn't lost on me.

Silver and sapphire, the same color as Adrian's eyes. I was staring at his former home, and it was barbarically magnificent.

I felt like I was leaving pieces of my heart behind as I followed the Hounds down the hill to the huge castle. Of course Adrian must have been playing me. No one raised by demons would have the fortitude to give all this up. People *not* raised by demons would struggle with saying no to all the power, money and supernatural bling that was Adrian's for the taking.

Like his castle. It could double as an icy version of Hogwarts with its massive size. Add in stone gates with elaborate frozen carvings glittering along their tops like cake frosting, and it was breathtaking. The minions who guarded it had shadow markings in their skin, showing they belonged to Demetrius, but their silvery breastplates all had an elaborately scripted *A* stenciled into the metal. So did the frescos in the outer courtyards, as if I needed more proof that I was in Adrian's former realm.

And all of this would be his again, if only he turned me over to the demons like everyone expected him to.

One of the Hounds nudged me, almost knocking me over. Okay, so I'd stopped running to stare at Adrian's once and future kingdom. It had all the extravagance of the other realms, but with one notable difference. Where were the slaves? I hadn't passed any ramshackle villages on the way, and most of the people milling around the courtyards were minions. Had—?

Something at the top of one of the towers caught my eye. This tower was lit up more than the others—that I'd noticed from the top of the hill—and it also had more open spaces, allowing for easier viewing inside.

That's why I could see the girl in the cage. Amber light surrounded her, coating her hair and body in varying shades of gold. The cage hung by a thick chain from the tower's roof, and the girl was sitting in it, her back resting against a corner. She wasn't wearing much more than I was, making me wonder how she hadn't frozen to death, until the humming noises coming from the tower clicked with the golden lights bathing her.

She was surrounded by portable heating devices. When she glanced down at the Hounds, who'd started to bay in annoyance because I'd stopped moving again, I glimpsed her face. Even though she was more than forty feet above me, my heart started to pound while my soul felt like it sucked in a breath.

Jasmine. My sister was alive and in that cage!

An avalanche of emotions rolled over me, making my eyes blur with a surge of tears. All these weeks, I'd been risking my life to save her, but an ugly, hidden part of me had thought she was already dead. Everyone else I cared for had been snatched away from me, so why should she be any different? That's why, for the space of several stunned seconds, I couldn't stop staring at Jasmine. That hopeless, jaded part of me was convinced that if I blinked or looked away, she'd disappear.

She didn't, despite my finally being brave enough to close my eyes. When I opened them and saw that she was still there, a noise tore from my throat that was part sob, part laugh. She was alive! Really, truly alive, and unhurt, from what I could see of her. If I hadn't been surrounded by minions who'd kill me the second they realized who I was, I might have giggled from the maelstrom of relief that flooded me, joining all the other feelings that seemed to compete with each other for maximum intensity.

Then something unexpected happened. My hallowed-hunting abilities kicked into gear. Maybe my sudden overload of emotions had activated them. I hadn't tried using them because the weapon couldn't be here. It was in a weak ruler's realm, and Demetrius ruled this one in Adrian's absence.

Yet the instant flare that thrummed through me wasn't relief at discovering that Jasmine was alive, though I was beyond relieved at that. It wasn't even anger over how she was displayed like a taunting trophy, and that made me damned angry. It was something completely different.

The only other time I'd felt anything similar was when I'd found hallowed ground for Adrian and me to flee to. If that had been a blip on my internal radar, this was a *boom!* that shook me from the inside out. Even feeling Mrs. Paulson's blood react to the demon gateway paled by comparison, and that meant one thing: something hallowed was here. Something *so* hallowed my entire body felt like it had multiple alarms blaring inside me, all pointing toward a single location as if it were a tracking transmitter and I was the antennae.

Shock turned into wild, inconceivable hope. Not only was Jasmine alive, she was in the same realm as the weapon that could save her.

CHAPTER THIRTY-FIVE

I FOLLOWED THE Hounds inside the castle, but instead of turning down the low hallway that must've led to their version of a spa mud bath, I veered off into a corner. A baying hiss was probably one of them cursing me for not keeping up again, yet the lure of getting warm kept them from coming after me.

Good. One Hound roaming though the castle would already garner suspicion. A pack of them? I might as well write my name on my chest so everybody would know who I was.

Then again, maybe it didn't matter. I could *feel* the weapon yanking on my abilities, urging me to free it from its hidden location. Once I did, I wouldn't need to be afraid anymore. Instead, the demons and minions would fear.

The thought emboldened me. I left the corner, ignoring the startled looks I got as I ran through the inner courtyards. At least these food vendors sold cow, pig and poultry instead of human meat, which meant I didn't have the urge to vomit as I wove through them. Then I was past the vendor area and running for the first stone staircase I saw. The weapon was several floors above me, according to what I could feel, and its power pulsed through my emotions like a beacon.

I passed some humans on the way, so this realm did have more. In fact, they seemed to live in the castle, judging from the instant slamming of doors as they caught sight of me and hid. The ones I came across on the staircase froze in midstep, only their eyes moving as I dashed past them. Just as I'd thought, Hounds must have certain designated areas, and the main castle interior wasn't one of them.

A voice shouted in Demonish behind me. Had someone sent the Hound handlers after me? I ignored the shout, running faster, a fearful exhilaration rising up to almost strangle me. I couldn't let someone stop me when I was so close to my goal. I just couldn't.

I left the staircase at the fourth-floor landing, the slingshot pulling me toward it like I was a fish being reeled in on a line. Following that inner pull, I dashed down the hallway to an ornate, wood-paneled room that looked like a library, of all things. Either word of a Hound on the loose had preceded me or this room wasn't used a lot, because no one was in it.

That didn't mean it was empty. My body pulsed from the weapon's nearness, drawing me toward the center of the room. A huge, four-sided fireplace rose up through the floor, the stone chimney disappearing into the soaring ceiling. Shields adorned the side facing me, with wicked-looking battle-axes on the opposing sides. The hearth was almost as tall as I was, and warmth radiated from the crackling flames, but that wasn't why I stood next to it, reaching as high as I could to touch the stones above the mantel.

There. The slingshot was right up *there,* and I was too short to reach it!

I spun around, grabbing the nearest chair and hauling it over to the fireplace. Then I paused, eyeing the polished stone chimney. I couldn't punch through it without breaking every bone in my hand, and then I wouldn't be able to use the slingshot.

Seized with inspiration, I stood on the chair and yanked one of the battle-axes off. It felt heavy and solid like a real weapon. Time to see if it worked like one.

Stone shards pelted me with my first swing, their sharp edges stinging. Okay, so the ax worked! I swung it again, harder, and a bigger chunk of stone split off. The chair tilted from my momentum, reminding me to watch my balance. I used my legs to counter my force as I swung the ax again and again, until I was whacking at the chimney like a lumberjack trying to chop down a tree.

My heart pounded when enough stone crumbled away to reveal a smooth wall beneath, like a hidden panel. Something brown and twisted clumped at the bottom of it, and I threw the ax away. No way would I risk severing the slingshot by chopping my way to it. Instead, I used my hands to pry the rest of the stones away before reaching down into the panel.

Power sizzled up my arm, the sensation so sudden and strong, it was painful. Instinctively, I snatched my hand back, then grinned, bracing myself as I reached down again. This time, I pulled up a long, braided rope that was identical to Adrian's slingshot—except this one was stained brown from age.

"Hondalte!" someone shouted behind me.

I turned, seeing two armor-wearing minions and a third minion with so much mud covering him, he had to be a Hound handler. Muddy Minion had a harness in one hand and what looked like raw pot roast meat in the other. My enticement to come quietly, I supposed.

I jumped off the chair, which made all of them flinch. Guess they hadn't expected to see a Hound standing on the furniture. They also didn't expect one to use a slingshot, and as I slid my finger through the loop on the weapon, I smiled.

This was it. Jasmine's freedom and our ticket out of here, all courtesy of the raggedy-looking weapon that vibrated with so much power, my arm throbbed just from touching it. I picked up one of the rounder pieces of stone that had chipped off the chimney, and placed it in the thicker section of the sling. Adrian might have intended to betray me, but he'd taught me how to use this, and I didn't hesitate as I began to spin the rope, walking toward the minions while savage anticipation flooded me.

The minions began to back away, either in incredulity at seeing a Hound wield a slingshot, or in realization of what was really going on. I spun the rope faster, determined not to let them or any of the other awful creatures in this realm get away. Then I aimed, sending the stone hurtling toward them with a snapping sound that was music to my ears.

Take that, bastards!

The stone hit the blond minion in the chest, denting his armor right in the middle of its elaborately embroidered "A." Then it dropped to the floor, which was what I expected the blond minion to do. In fact, I expected *all* of them to drop dead on the spot, but the blond minion only stared at me. Then he stared at the stone and his friends, his expression changing from fear to bewilderment.

"That's it?" he asked in English.

My exultation turned to ashes, which was what the minions should have done. Yet they stood there, a dent in Blond Minion's armor the only sign that I'd hit him with the famed, long-sought-after weapon.

I grabbed another chunk of stone, desperation making my fingers tremble as I slid it into the slight pouch. *This has to work, it has to!* my mind roared. No way was this the wrong weapon. Not only had it been hidden in a wall within a demon realm, its power made my arm ache. So why wasn't it killing everyone like it was *supposed* to?

I whipped the stone toward them without really aiming this time. It hit Muddy Minion, and he let out a yelp that gave me a wild flash of hope before I realized I'd only pissed him off.

Then the three minions lunged toward me, all their former wariness gone, and I did the only thing I could do.

I ran.

CHAPTER THIRTY-SIX

TRYING TO HIDE while looking like a half-ton demon lizard would be impossible. That's why I ran straight to the tunnel in the lower courtyard where I'd seen the other Hounds disappear to. As expected, it led to the mud room and I submerged myself into the warm, stinky water along with the rest of them. I even took off my leather bikini since I'd noticed that none of these Hounds wore straps, but I kept the slingshot. I intended to choke Zach with it as soon as I saw him—if I managed to live through this.

All for nothing! I kept inwardly howling. I'd risked my life repeatedly based on the promise that if I found the slingshot, I'd be able to save my sister. Now I had the stupid, ancient weapon, and it couldn't even help me save myself.

After about ten minutes, the Hounds decided they were warm enough to patrol again. I got out with them, intending to run straight for the B and B as soon as I cleared the castle grounds. When we rounded a corner in the stone hallway, however, a barricade of minions blocked our path, lined so deep that I couldn't count them all.

The other Hounds turned, deciding this must mean they got more time in the mud bath. I followed them, hoping like crazy that there was another way out except the one that was blocked. Just in case, as soon as we were back in the small room, I slipped the slingshot under a pile of animal bones in the corner. Much as I wanted to throttle Zach with the useless weapon, I didn't want to get caught because I was the only Hound that appeared to be carrying its own leash.

It took just a few seconds to realize there was no exit down here. Out of options, I got into the water with the other Hounds, feeling as naked and helpless as I was. *Why'd you run to the only place that didn't have another way out?* I silently lashed myself. So much for my plan to blend in.

My situation went from bad to worse when Demetrius strode into the underground room. The demon's shadows filled the small space, brushing across my head and shoulders like tiny, icy fingers. I sank farther beneath the water, suddenly glad to be covered by the smelly, muddy liquid.

Three more people filed in after him. With sinking spirits, I recognized Blond Minion, Muddy Minion and their friend, whom I now dubbed as Scowling Minion for obvious reasons.

Demetrius said something to them in Demonish. Muddy Minion came up to the edge of the water and barked out one word. The Hounds sprang forward like he'd yelled "Lunch!" I did, too, standing at attention as they seemed to be doing.

Demetrius walked along the length of us. Whatever word the Hound handler had used, it kept all of them in perfect formation like dutiful lizard soldiers. So much for my hope that they'd charge anyone moving and I could slip out in the ensuing melee. No, I had to stand in line with them, all the while feeling like I had a neon sign over my head that flashed "Davidian." Terror slithered through me, making me almost oblivious to the fact that I was stark naked in front of Demetrius and a few other men. If Demetrius could tell I wasn't a Hound, I was dead.

Or worse.

Demetrius spoke sharply to Muddy Minion, who looked at the other Hounds and me with such obvious confusion that I almost whooped in relief. He couldn't tell us apart! Okay, I wasn't going to strangle Zach if I got out of this. I'd only punch him in the face. His Hound disguise was so good, not even their handler could tell me apart from the others—

"Ivy."

Willpower alone kept my head from snapping up at the sound of my name. Demetrius wasn't getting me to out myself that easily. My fortitude must've surprised him because he went to the nearest Hound, petting it in apparent bemusement.

"I know you're here," Demetrius went on, flashing his cruel smile as he fondled the beast. "No Hound would use an ax to smash through a chimney, so it's obvious you came to this realm looking for the weapon. Very clever of the Archons to disguise you as one of our pets. We're so used to having Hounds run about, we don't even notice when we have an extra one."

I said nothing, of course. Didn't even breathe loudly. My continued pretense was just staving off the inevitable, but what was I supposed to do? Serve myself up with a smile?

"Clever also of you to soak yourself in here," Demetrius continued, leaning in to smell the next Hound in line. "That mud bath reeks so much, I can't pick up anything that might give you away, like the lingering trace of perfume."

Haven't worn any lately, I thought to distract myself from the fear that made me want to start shaking.

Being on the run with Adrian hadn't allowed for many shopping trips to the mall.

"But I will discover which one you are," Demetrius all but purred as he reached me. I forced myself not to recoil when his hand slid over me, brushing my breast on its way to my back. His touch was somehow burning cold, like holding an icicle for too long. Still, I tried to school my features into the bland, compliant mask the other Hounds wore. My situation might be hopeless, but if Demetrius wanted to kill me, he had to figure out on his own which one I was.

His hand slipped down my arm and he leaned in, taking a deep breath. *Please, let me stink as badly as the rest of them!* I silently prayed. What if he could smell the shampoo I'd used when I washed my hair this morning? Or the deodorant I'd put on because it hadn't occurred to me that I'd be demon-sniff-tested tonight?

It was all I could do not to sag in relief when Demetrius moved on to the Hound after me. *How I love you, filthy reeking mud bath!* I inwardly crowed. *If I get out of this, I'll take a mud bath every night in your honor—*

Two more minions came into the room, freezing my thoughts in midvow. Not because the minions were the largest men I'd ever seen, but because they didn't come alone.

They thrust Jasmine out from between them, causing her to stumble for a few feet before Demetrius caught her. My sister looked at the demon with all the horror I felt, and when he ran a hand over her dirt-matted blond hair, a tremor of pure rage shook me. *Don't touch her!* I silently seethed. *I'll kill you, I'll kill you!*

But I couldn't. The weapon was across the room under a pile of animal bones, and even if I *could* reach it, the damn thing didn't work. Despair threaded into my rage, forming a toxic mixture that ran like poison through my veins. Everything I'd risked, all the pain I'd endured, everything Jasmine had been through…it had all been for nothing.

"With you here, Ivy, I don't need her anymore," Demetrius said, his tone filled with the surety of victory. "So you have a choice—reveal yourself, or watch your sister die."

"Ivy?" my sister asked, looking around. "Where?"

I drew in a breath that was probably going to be my last. I didn't want to give the demon the satisfaction of making me reveal myself, but no matter what he'd do to me, I couldn't watch my sister die.

"Don't bother."

Adrian's voice filled the room, chilling and thrilling me as my traitorous emotions responded in wildly conflicting ways. Then my heart nearly stopped at his next words, which were delivered in a flatly emotionless tone.

"I can see which one she is."

Adrian pushed past the huge minions like they were nothing more than toy soldiers. Then his gaze landed on me, and the coldness I saw devastated me. For a split second, I actually *wanted* to die. My worst fears were confirmed in those merciless sapphire depths, and the curl to his mouth seemed to mock me for ever believing the lies he'd told me.

And I *had* believed them. Even when I'd knocked him out and tied him up, part of me had hoped I was making a terrible mistake. Yeah, I had, but not by doing that. By not listening to him the first time he'd told me not to trust him.

Demetrius's dark gaze flared as Adrian walked toward him. "My son," he said almost reverently. "I never doubted that this moment would come."

I suppressed a bitter snort. A demon with unwavering faith, how ironic. And his faith would soon be rewarded, how unfair.

Adrian smiled as he embraced his foster father, practically shoving Jasmine out of the way to get to him. I don't know why I didn't run to my sister in the last few seconds I had left. Maybe shock froze me in place, keeping me from doing anything except staring at the man who'd proven to be every bit as traitorous as his infamous ancestor. *Everyone* had warned me about Adrian, yet just like my gullible or well-intentioned family members, I hadn't listened.

Now, just like my ancestors, I'd also die after being betrayed by a Judian.

"I kept everything in this realm the way you left it," Demetrius murmured, pulling away. "Even your ridiculously burdensome means of feeding and housing your slaves."

Adrian chuckled like Demetrius had told a joke. "Makes them work harder to avoid being sent to one of your realms... Father."

The word was the final nail into my heart, but Demetrius smiled with such joy, it transformed his face, making him appear as he must have once looked however many aeons ago.

Angelic.

"Let us finish this," he said, kissing Adrian's forehead. Then he turned toward the other Hounds and me, his arm still around Adrian's shoulders as though he couldn't bear to let him go. "Which one is she?"

Adrian met my gaze—and strode over to the Hound next to me, shoving it toward Demetrius with such force that he actually managed to make the huge creature stumble.

"Here she is," he said clearly.

CHAPTER THIRTY-SEVEN

I LOOKED AT the Hound, then at Adrian, emotion after emotion crushing me as though I were being hit by multiple tidal waves. He hadn't come here to betray me. Once again, against all odds and destinies, he was trying to save me.

I wanted to throw my arms around him and sob out an apology for ever doubting him, let alone all the other terrible things I'd done. Then I wanted to kiss him until neither of us could breathe. But I couldn't do either of those things. If I so much as moved, I'd undo the ruse he was trying to pull off.

"That thing isn't Ivy."

My sister's confused whisper cut through my inner battle, but the surge had already activated my abilities, and they zeroed in on Adrian. Granted, my hallowed-sensor should've picked up on what was in his pocket before, but in my defense, I'd been a little preoccupied thinking I was about to die.

"Her appearance is disguised," Adrian responded, flashing a nasty smile at the Hound. "Not that it does any good with me."

The Hound looked mildly irritated at being shoved around, but it didn't attack. Talk about well-trained. Demetrius pulled a knife out of the sheath on his belt, and I braced in pity for the creature. Here's hoping the demon would make it quick—

Faster than I could blink, he had Jasmine in his grip,
the knife against my sister's throat. The Hound barely
spared them a glance, but I lunged forward with an an-
guished cry.

"No!"

Adrian caught me before I reached the demon, and
for a split second, his eyes met mine. So many feelings
spilled from his gaze that I could barely believe he was
the same person who'd looked at me so coldly moments
before. Then four incensed words brought our attention
back to Demetrius.

"You lied to me."

Adrian took off his long coat, putting it around me.
The whole time, his gaze never left Demetrius's, even
when I felt him furtively remove something from the
coat's pocket.

"You wanted me to be a betrayer." Adrian's voice
was thick with sarcasm. "Be careful what you wish
for, *Father*."

"If you won't rule with me, then you can die with
your whore," Demetrius hissed, digging the knife
deeper into Jasmine's throat. "But not before she tells
me where the weapon is. I know you found it, Davidian. Where did you put it?"

Adrian's gaze swung to me. "It was *here*?"

I nodded, too horrified by the line of blood trailing down Jasmine's throat to answer audibly. Another
ounce of pressure, and her jugular would be severed.

Adrian let out a short laugh. "Right under your nose
this whole time. Must've been hidden here before you
stole this realm from Ciscero."

"Give it to me, Davidian, or watch her die," Demetrius ordered, ignoring that.

I tightened the coat around me, then went over to the

pile of bones and pulled the slingshot out from under it. Damned thing didn't work anyway, but maybe it would provide enough distraction for Adrian to use whatever he'd brought with him.

"Ivy, don't," Adrian said, grasping my arm.

I glanced at his hand and then back at him, trying to tell him with my eyes to get ready.

"If he has this, he doesn't need us anymore," I said, knowing the demon would try to kill us anyway, but hoping Demetrius believed *I* was that naïve.

The two minions who'd brought Jasmine began to circle around us. Blondie, Muddy Minion and Scowling Minion moved to block the tunnel entrance, as if the dozens more behind them weren't enough to prevent our escape. Demetrius didn't seem to notice the extra activity. He stared at the braided rope dangling from my hand with something akin to rapture.

"So let us all go," I continued, "and it's yours."

Adrian translated my words to the demon. He dropped my arm, too, his hooded sapphire gaze flicking between me and Demetrius.

I hoped that meant he understood and was on board. Demetrius was. He lowered the knife, revealing a small, still-bleeding cut on Jasmine's neck. Then he shoved my sister toward me. She caught herself before she reached me, staring at me with horrified confusion. Right, I still looked like a Hound. How could I keep forgetting that?

"A deal's a deal," I said, tossing the slingshot toward the demon.

He reached out to catch it—and Adrian hurled the small object he'd concealed in his coat. Dazzling white exploded in the underground room, throwing Demetrius backward while briefly blinding me. The demon's agonized scream seared my ears as Adrian yanked me into his arms, and I felt rather than saw him haul my sister against him next.

When my vision cleared, the five minions were dissolving into ashes from the Archon grenade and the Hounds were dead, but Demetrius was still alive. And mad as hell.

"You failed," the demon spat, hauling himself over to block the exit to the tunnel. "You may have killed these men, but you will not escape!"

Adrian's response was to whistle, loud and long. Demetrius cocked his head, confusion replacing the pain on his pale features. Then his eyes widened as screams erupted from farther down the tunnel. He sprang aside right as a huge gray form hurtled into the room. Dark gray wings unfolded, revealing the monstrous, massive gargoyle I'd encountered earlier.

"Thanks for keeping everything just the way I left it," Adrian told Demetrius before throwing Jasmine at the gargoyle. "Especially for keeping my most loyal pet, Brutus."

Jasmine screamed as the gargoyle caught her against its chest with one leathery, muscled arm. Then it was my turn to yelp as Adrian shoved me at the creature. The gargoyle pressed me next to Jasmine, its arm an unbreakable band across our stomachs. Adrian ran across the room, snatched up the slingshot and then threw himself at the gargoyle right as it began to beat its massive wings. The gargoyle caught Adrian and shot forward, the powerful expulsion of air propelling us down the tunnel.

The gargoyle was so strong that it could hold us without difficulty, but the weight of our three bodies proved too heavy for it to fly. We smashed into some of the minions lining the tunnel, resulting in a brief, fierce fight before another rush of the gargoyle's wings cleared us over them in a sort of hop. Then we plowed back down again.

Demetrius's enraged scream filled the tunnel behind us. "Kill them, kill them!"

Countless hands seemed to pull at us, weighing the gargoyle down even more. Adrian punched and kicked while the creature rallied valiantly, another burst of power clearing us over the seething mass in this section of the tunnel. Before we could reach the end, though, we dropped back down again. Only fifty yards away, a wall of minions rushed toward us, urged on by Demetrius's furious commands in English and Demonish.

Adrian looked at me, then barked out a few words that made the gargoyle halt and, unbelievably, let him go.

"What are you doing?" I gasped.

He took my head, his silvery-sapphire gaze almost burning into mine.

"He can't fly with all of us, and I'm the heaviest. Brutus'll take you to the B and B, then you need to cross through the gateway." A dark, quick smile. "You already know how."

I was appalled. "Adrian, you can't—"

He pulled my head down, his mouth searing mine in a kiss that matched the blazing intensity in his eyes. Desperation, desire and despair seemed to pour from him into me, but when he broke the kiss and pulled away, he was smiling.

"I love you, Ivy. I love you, and I didn't betray you. For the first time in my life, I feel like I can do anything."

Then he stuffed the slingshot in my coat pocket,

smacked the gargoyle on the side and yelled, *"Tarate!"*
Those mighty wings began to beat at once.

"No!" I screamed, struggling to get free.

The gargoyle rose up, no longer encumbered by too
much weight. The last thing I saw before we cleared the
tunnel and the realm's eternally dark skyline enveloped
us was Adrian turning toward the horde of minions that
was almost upon him.

CHAPTER THIRTY-EIGHT

JASMINE SCREAMED IN terror the whole way to the B and B. I screamed, too. In anguish. Adrian was strong, but he couldn't beat dozens of minions when they were armed and he wasn't. He was going to die, and he knew it, but he'd willingly doomed himself to save me.

I love you, Ivy.

I thought my heart had been wounded before. Now, I could feel it ripping wide-open, scalding my insides with the kind of pain that would never heal. There had to be a way to save him.

As soon as the gargoyle released us at the entrance to the B and B, I started yelling the same word Adrian had used to make it leave him.

"*Tarate, tarate!* Go back and get Adrian!"

The creature only stared at me. Jasmine backed away a few feet, rubbing her arms against the chill I barely noticed in my desperation.

"If you're really Ivy, do something to prove it."

Do something? Like what, start miming out the letters to my name? Couldn't she see that I was trying to get the winged monstrosity to save Adrian, yet the stupid thing just kept *looking* at me!

In complete frustration, I flipped Jasmine off. She blinked in disbelief, then threw herself at me.

"Ivy!"

She started crying in the loud, hiccupping way she

used to do when she was a child. I held her with one arm, flapping the other at the gargoyle in a last-ditch attempt to get it to understand that it had to *fly*. Now.

The creature chuffed at me in obvious annoyance. Then its wing whipped out so fast, for a second, wild hope filled me. I shoved Jasmine back, screaming "That's it!" while flapping both my arms. Then I noticed something rolling on the ground toward me. What was—?

Jasmine shrieked and I recoiled. It was a head, and as it dissolved into a small pile of ashes, I noticed the form to the right of the gargoyle just before it, too, dissipated into ashes.

The gargoyle angled its wings flat like two massive, leathery blades. Then it took one step toward me, and a burst of motion behind me made me spin around.

The minion who'd been sneaking up on us turned around and started hightailing it into the woods. The gargoyle chuffed loudly, as if saying, "Yeah, you'd better run!" before folding its wings into two compact piles on its back.

I wanted to thank it and rail at it at the same time. Yes, it had just saved my life, but it should be saving *Adrian's*. Not standing here like a dinosaur version of a knight in shining armor. Since I couldn't seem to communicate that, I ran to the tree stump where I'd left my supplies. Where there were two minions, there'd soon be more, so I had to get Jasmine out of here while I still could. Besides, maybe Costa and a lot of weapons were waiting on the other side of this realm. If I couldn't make the gargoyle rescue Adrian, maybe I could find a way to do it myself.

Once I had my sack, I took Jasmine's hand and led her into the B and B. Unbelievably, the gargoyle followed us, though it stayed bent down because it was

taller than the ceiling. The human residents of the B
and B stood stock-still in terror at the sight of a Hound
and the winged creature in the house, and I had no way
of telling them that neither one of us were dangerous.

Well, the gargoyle probably wasn't dangerous.

I drew Jasmine into Mrs. Paulson's office, pain knif-
ing my heart again when I pulled out one of the two beer
bottles filled with Adrian's blood. *I'm coming back for
you,* I silently promised, hating myself for what I'd done.
Then, because I had no choice, I smeared my hands with
Adrian's blood and started running them over Jasmine.

She let out a noise that was half whimper, half fearful sob. "Wh-what are you doing, Ivy?"

I wasn't about to waste Adrian's blood by using it
to write out an explanation, so I held my finger to my
lips in the universal gesture for silence. Once I esti-
mated that she was covered enough, I used the rest of
his blood on myself. *Betrayer!* those red smears seemed
to scream at me.

My eyes blurred with tears. Yes, I was a betrayer and
Adrian wasn't. Now, to make sure he lived so I could
apologize to him for the rest of my life.

I put the second bottle in the opposite corner of the
office, then grabbed Jasmine around the waist and
hurtled us both toward the gateway. That push-pull-
stretch-puke sensation as we crossed through the realms
seemed worse, but we tumbled out into the non-demon
version of Mrs. Paulson's office.

Unfortunately, we weren't alone.

"What the *hell?*" the young, sandy-haired cop sputtered.

Right, the guests would've called the police after I'd
scared them out of here with my rampaging monster act.
I let go of Jasmine, but put myself in front of her. If the

cop went for his gun, I had a better chance at stopping
him since I was faster than Jaz.

Then something knocked me over from behind. I
didn't have time to register what had caused me to suddenly face-plant before the cop's head was on the floor
in front of me. The rest of him was still up where I
couldn't see.

I rolled over, stunned to see the gargoyle looming
like a dark shadow over me and Jasmine. His one wing
was still extended in that chopping formation, and a
thump nearby had to be the guard's body falling next
to his severed head.

"Why'd you do that?" I snapped, only to feel a small
"poof" by my face. When I looked again, the head had
turned into ashes.

The cop was a minion. Of course. Detective Kroger
wasn't the only one at the Bennington Police De-
partment, and who else would investigate stories of
a monster at the same inn that doubled as a demonic
Brimstone and Breakfast?

"Uh, good boy," I told the gargoyle awkwardly.

"What is *that* doing here?" a familiar voice asked,
his tone heavy with disapproval.

Zach! I bolted up, so excited to see the Archon in
the doorway that I knocked Jasmine over in my haste
to get to him.

"Get me out of this disguise, I need to talk to the
gargoyle!" I said in a rush. It hadn't understood me
as a Hound, but maybe Adrian had taught it to speak
English.

Zach touched the top of my head. I knew the instant
my disguise disappeared because Jasmine choked, "Oh,
Ivy!" and threw her arms around me again.

I wanted to hug her back. A big part of me even

needed to after everything we'd been through, but I was too terrified for Adrian to do anything except gently shove her aside.

"Brutus, you have to go back and save Adrian," I told the gargoyle, grabbing the edge of its wing in my urgency. "Please, go back now!"

The gargoyle cocked its head, the wing beneath my hand quivering. From his expression, he seemed to *want* to do what I asked, yet he made no move toward the gateway.

"Go, now!" I repeated, trying to shove him in the right direction, but the gargoyle was way too heavy for me.

"He doesn't understand you," Zach said, sounding bemused this time. "This must be Adrian's pet. Why did he follow you here?"

"Adrian said something to him and he hasn't left my side since, but that doesn't matter." I let go of the gargoyle's wing to grasp the Archon's trademark sweater. "Adrian's fighting for his life, so I need all the weapons you have, now!"

"I don't have any weapons," Zach said, as if the idea was preposterous.

"Then glamour some up," I all but snarled. "Didn't you hear me? Adrian's going to *die!*"

"I can't. Glamour is illusion—it's not creating something out of nothing." Zach's dark gaze narrowed as he looked at my pocket. "But you already have a weapon, don't you?"

I don't know why, but I backed away, my hand flying to cover my pocket. "It doesn't work," I said breathily.

Zach snorted with something like contempt. "Without faith, it wouldn't." Then his expression became deadly serious. "Give me the slingshot, Ivy."

I edged away farther, glancing at the invisible gateway. "Why? You can't cross into a dark realm, so you're not going to use it to save Adrian."

"Demetrius won't allow him to be killed," Zach replied, sounding almost careless now. "He may take out his anger on him, but Adrian should survive that."

"And that's okay with you?" I snapped, fury boiling over. "Wait, of course it is. This wouldn't be the first time you left him at the mercy of demons, would it?"

Zach's features hardened, and he held out his hand in silent, imperious command. *Give me the weapon,* his stare warned.

He really would just take the slingshot, give it to his boss and call it a day, regardless if it meant Adrian's torture or death. *We can only depend on each other. To Archons and demons, we're just pawns that they move around for their own purposes,* Adrian had said. From the unyielding expression on Zach's face, he'd been right.

And I'd betrayed him just as awfully as Zach had all those years ago. I'd believed the worst of Adrian's words when his actions should've shown me that he would never hand me over to Demetrius. In the end, it was our actions that defined us. Not words.

I glanced at Jasmine, who was looking out the window as if she couldn't believe she was back in the real world. She was and so was I, all because of Adrian's sacrifice. Now, it was my turn. *I love you, Jaz,* I thought, choking back a sob. *But you're not the only one I love.*

Then I looked at Zach. "You might be willing to abandon Adrian again. I'm not."

His shout was cut off as I ran into the gateway, leaving him, my sister and the rest of my world behind.

CHAPTER THIRTY-NINE

I LANDED IN the icy, decrepit version of the B and B on top of a dark-haired boy, who shoved me aside with a yelp.

"What the—?" he began, only to stop talking so fast, I whirled, expecting to see a minion or a demon behind me.

Nothing. I spun back around to see the boy staring at my chest with widened eyes. I looked down—and then yanked the coat together. It had flown open during my tumble, and I no longer had my Hound disguise, so not only had I landed on a kid who looked about ten, I'd done so while mostly naked.

And being a prepubescent boy, he'd fixated on that even while trapped inside a demon realm. My hand went to my coat pocket, anxiously checking for the slingshot. Still there.

"Sorry," I said, then stopped when I saw what the boy had in his hand. He must've found the beer bottle of blood that I'd left here.

"Rub some of that on your arms and legs," I said quickly. "Then run at the corner I just came through. You'll come out in the real world, promise."

"Are you a minion?" the boy asked suspiciously.

I let out a snort. "No. In fact, I'm here to kill them and all the demons."

"You're crazy," the boy scoffed.

I didn't believe that I could do it either, but that was the problem. *It doesn't work*, I'd told Zach. *Without faith, it wouldn't*, he'd replied. And Costa had said, *thousands of years ago, a shepherd boy killed a giant with nothing more than a slingshot and blind faith*. All right, I had the weapon. Now, I had to find the blind faith. Fast.

"Rub that stuff on you, and you can get out of here," I repeated. "Tell the others."

"You're gonna die, crazy naked lady," he muttered.

The scary truth was, he was probably right. After Zach's cold dismissal of Adrian's situation, I had less faith now than I'd had the last time I'd tried to use the weapon. Let's face it: it was too hard to believe in a benevolent, cosmic "boss" when His employees were made of so much suck!

Fear urged me to turn around and run back through the gateway. A far stronger emotion had me pulling out the slingshot and running out of the B and B as fast as I could. Yes, I was probably crazy, and yes, I'd probably die, but if there was even a chance that I could save Adrian, I had to try. Besides, if the Archons' boss didn't want the equivalent of a nuclear bomb in His enemies' hands, then He *had* to show up—

The braided rope pulsed with a sudden flare of power. I was so surprised, I almost stumbled during my mad dash up the hill. What had caused that? I hadn't been thinking anything pious. I'd been thinking that only an idiot would fail to realize the weapon would either work for me, or I'd be delivering it right into the demons' hands—

The slingshot pulsed again, stronger this time, until my right arm almost felt numb. The reason why hit me then, and I began to laugh with wild, ragged whoops.

I didn't need to have pious faith. I didn't even need to have complimentary faith. No, this weapon's batteries ran on the same juices that had kept Adrian going when no one else had believed in him. *You can trust my hatred of demons,* he'd always told me. That had been his faith. Mine, apparently, was believing that the Archons' boss didn't want the slingshot to end up in demon hands. I didn't trust the Great Being with much, but it seemed that I trusted Him not to be stupid.

Power sizzled up my arm and light infused the rope, making it glow against the darkness. At the same time, shouts sounded about a hundred yards ahead of me, with more close behind those. With the Hounds dead and the gargoyle gone, minions must be on patrol, and I didn't have a disguise anymore.

I stopped running to grab a stone for the slingshot. Since nothing was around except frozen ground, all I managed to get was a ragged piece of ice. I put it in the glowing, pulsating rope, starting to spin it as soon as I reached the top of the hill where the trees abruptly ended.

The valley spread out below, faint, iridescent lights from the castle showing three minions dashing up the hill toward me. Worse, it looked like a larger group of them weren't far behind. Demetrius must've been hoping I'd come back.

Well, here I was, armed with nothing except cynical faith and a weapon that hadn't worked in thousands of years. I spun the rope faster, my emotions feelings like they were whirling in circles alongside the ancient weapon. I was scared beyond belief, yet I also felt the strangest sort of exultation. I was about to die or about to kick some serious ass, but either way, I'd be doing it for Adrian. Prophecies, destinies...they weren't why I was here. He was, and in life or in death, I wasn't going to fail him again.

Raising the weapon, I ran down the hill to meet my enemies.

The three closest minions leaped forward with such ferocity, they were briefly airborne. At the same time, an incredible surge of power caused pain to rocket through my whole body. Then light shot out from the weapon. As soon it touched the minions, they stopped moving so abruptly, it looked like they'd hit a wall in midair. Another agonizing surge caused those thin streams of light to hit the group of minions behind them. They froze, too, some with weapons still pointed in my direction.

I staggered, trying not to fall over from the searing sensations that made my insides feel like they were boiling. The beams of light coming from the slingshot kept the minions frozen into place, but the overwhelming pain made me want to fling the weapon aside. My body must have been the power conduit, and if this was what two supernatural blasts felt like, would I survive more?

Sirens came from farther down the hill. Someone must've seen the strange lights and sounded the alarm. I clenched my jaw, trying to keep from screaming as I spun the rope into a tighter, faster circle. This hurt so much, my bones actually ached. Who knew they could do that?

Then I walked past the first group of minions. If I only had one shot, I needed it for saving Adrian. The lights coming from the slingshot stayed on them, though, until the weapon had glowing strings both behind it and ahead. By the time I reached the bottom of the hill, the castle was in full defense mode.

Gunfire sounded, making me duck while holding

the weapon aloft enough to keep the rope spinning. Another blast of power emanated from the slingshot, the subsequent pain almost driving me to my knees. As soon as that light touched them, the bullets stopped with the same suddenness as on that day in the desert when Zach had intervened. Hope clawed through my agony. The slingshot held the same power as an Archon. It really could do everything it was supposed to, as long as I could stand to wield it.

I forced myself to keep walking toward the castle. This time, I didn't duck as a barrage of gunfire came my way. I braced, a cry ripping out of me at the sizzling pain of dozens of bullets being supernaturally frozen in midair. Then more light shot from the weapon, landing on the guards like laser sights on a rifle. The new surge of power had me shaking in torment. I wasn't sure I could walk, let along keep the rope spinning. The slingshot felt like a thousand pounds of molten agony being funneled from my arm into the rest of my body.

A new wave of minions began to flood the lower section of the castle. The weapon reacted, beaming light onto every one of them and freezing them in place. I screamed, tears almost blinding me as I used both hands to keep the rope spinning. *Adrian, Adrian,* I repeated feverishly, forcing my feet to keep moving even though shudders racked me so fiercely, I staggered. He was trapped in the tunnel, but if I could get close enough, the weapon would incapacitate his attackers. No minion or demon could stop me, as long as I kept walking. The weapon took them out as soon as its light touched them.

Problem was, the weapon might also take me out.

Somehow, I made it past the gates and into the outer courtyards of the castle. By that time, I couldn't stop my screams at the merciless blasts of pain. Each new minion the light landed on sent agony shooting through me, until everything else faded beneath the constant, brutal onslaught. After a few minutes, I couldn't be sure if I was still holding the weapon anymore. A few minutes after that, I couldn't remember where I was or why I'd come here. Only the pain was real, and it was excruciating. I couldn't take it, and the pressure building inside me warned me that I wouldn't have to for much longer. Something was about to happen. Something big.

I fell to my knees from the next surge of power, which felt like a thousand knives ripping into me at once. *This is it,* I thought dazedly. *I'm dying.* Instead of being afraid, the thought filled me with profound relief. Anything to escape the pain.

Release the stone.

The whisper somehow made it past the torturous insanity strafing my mind. That's right, the stone. Until it was free, this wasn't over. With my last reserves of strength, I stood up and snapped the slingshot, releasing the ice rock into the nothingness that was coming for me.

My whole body convulsed as the light marking every minion suddenly exploded with sunlike brightness, until I couldn't see anything except burning, dazzling white. Just as swiftly, my agony disappeared, leaving me almost paralyzed with weakness. Unable to move or see, I fell onto the ground, feeling countless brushes of something light across me.

Slowly, that blinding whiteness faded, though at first, I thought the swirls around me were snowflakes. Then, as my vision returned even more, they changed color, turning from white to gray to charcoal. *Ashes,* I realized, shock giving me enough strength to sit up. Ashes were blowing everywhere, yet I didn't see a single minion or demon. I *did* see several humans venturing into the courtyard, their expressions mirroring the same sort of hopeful disbelief I felt, now that I could think again.

The slingshot seemed to have done the impossible, killing all the demons and minions without harming any of the humans. I'd kiss the weapon, if I knew where it was. My hand only had smudges from ashes in it at the moment.

Then a horrible thought crept into my mind, demolishing my happiness with one brutal question.

What if the slingshot had killed Adrian, too?

Fear got me to my feet, though I swayed so much, I expected to fall when I took my first step. Adrian was human, but his lineage had so much dark power, he could cross into demon realms. Did that same power cause the weapon to mark him for death as it had the minions and demons? Had he survived the attack Demetrius ordered against him, only to have me kill him?

God, please, no! I half ran, half staggered toward the Hound tunnel where I'd last seen him. The low, enclosed space kept the wind out, so the thick layer of ashes lining the floor weren't swirling around. They were ominously, deathly still.

"Adrian!" I cried out, sloshing through the grayish-black mess. "Adrian, please, answer me!"

I heard nothing but my own voice echoing hollowly back at me. I'd almost made it to the end of the tunnel when my legs gave out. Then I sank into the ashes, despair filling me as the pile I knelt in came nearly to my waist. From all the minion remains, the fighting must've been thickest here, so this was probably where Adrian had died. I plunged my hands into the embers, tears making everything blur as the particles either fell from my fingers or curled into wisps and floated away.

Gone, just like Adrian was now gone. More tears fell, making pale trails through the stains on my hands. I wanted to scream the way I had before, but though this pain was just as intense, it tore at my soul instead of my body, so there was no outlet for it. I hadn't been able to tell Adrian how sorry I was for what I'd done. Or tell him that I'd come back for him, or tell him the most important thing of all.

"I love you, too," I whispered to the ashes.

I'd never said that to a man before. Now, with Adrian gone, I'd never say it again. I didn't need the gift of prophecy to know that I wouldn't feel this way about anyone else. Ever.

"Are you okay?" a hesitant voice asked.

My head jerked up, and through the tears, I saw the outline of a woman at the entrance to the tunnel.

"I saw you go down here," she went on. "You won't find anyone in here, though. This was where they kept the Hounds."

"I know." My voice was thick from anguish.

She took a few steps toward me. "Are you...her?"

"Her who?" I asked wearily.

"The one who killed them," she replied in an awed whisper.

Her words were a fresh blow to my heart. Yes, I'd killed them. All of them.

I didn't say that. As I heaved myself to my feet, I said the only thing I could think of to make her go away. I needed a few minutes to pull myself together. Or a few lifetimes.

"Go to the B and B. The dark-haired boy knows how to get through the gateway, if he hasn't left already."

She turned around and left. Moments later, I heard her excitedly telling someone that she knew a way out.

I dragged a hand through my hair, feeling physically and emotionally beaten beyond my ability to cope. I didn't want to move from this spot, but the single bottle of blood at the B and B wouldn't be enough. More minion blood would be needed to bring everyone through the gateway. Fast, too, before other demons showed up to commandeer this realm. The slingshot only worked once, so even if I knew where it was, it was useless to prevent other demons from re-enslaving the people here.

That meant I'd have to leave this realm to find a minion, capture it and bleed the hell out of it. Tonight. The realization had me shuffling toward the exit to the tunnel. My body ached like I'd been pummeled from the inside out, but I forced myself to keep moving. If I didn't, I'd stay here and cry my eyes out, which wouldn't help the people trapped in this realm. Besides, my tears were already starting to mess with my vision. For a second, I'd thought the ash pile next to me had shifted.

I had gone about ten feet when a distinct rustling sound made me freeze. That wasn't a figment of my imagination. Something was in the tunnel with me.

Very slowly, I turned around. It looked like a dark pillar had appeared at the entrance to the Hound spa. Then the pillar doubled in height as the person beneath the embers stood up, revealing the form of a tall, broad-shouldered man. When he wiped his face, a layer of blood showed beneath the soot, and the hair he brushed back was stained black from the ashes swirling around him, but I didn't care. Right now, they were the most beautiful things I'd ever seen.

"Adrian," I whispered, my tears starting to flow faster.

His head snapped up—and then he moved with his incredible speed, gripping me in those powerful arms.

Tilting my head back and covering my mouth in a bruising kiss that made joy rip through me with all the intensity of the pain I'd felt before. When he finally broke away several minutes later, I could hardly breathe, but I still managed to speak.

"I love you," I choked out. "I love you, I love you, I love you—"

His kiss cut me off again, and this time, I wasn't crying when I kissed him back. I was smiling.

EPILOGUE

WE DIDN'T NEED to leave to catch a minion for its blood. Adrian pulled through the remaining people in the realm, taking them in groups of twos and threes. It still took the rest of the night, but I wasn't afraid of demons stopping us. Not when Zach stayed at the B and B, which rapidly filled to overflowing from all the survivors of the Bennington realm. I might still be mad at him, but no demon would take on one Archon, let alone three of them.

One moment, Jasmine and I were passing out blankets to the people who'd spilled out onto the lawn; the next, I was staring at two people whom I knew were not human despite their normal appearance. The brunette girl had freckles and the guy had blond dreadlocks, of all things, but for an instant, both of them radiated light like Zach had the first time we met.

"Uh...hi," I said, so surprised I stumbled over my words.

Screams erupted from the people outside. I whirled, groaning when I saw the gargoyle coming toward us. Adrian had *told* Brutus to stay hidden in the trees. Dreadlocks gave it a single glare. "Tell your creature to stay back."

"Admanta!" I yelled, using the word Adrian had taught me. The gargoyle chuffed warningly at the Ar-

chons but turned around and disappeared into the trees again.

"Sorry," I muttered, glad that Freckles was calming the people down.

"He's not hers," Jasmine offered, staring at the stranger curiously. "He, uh, belongs to Adrian."

"Not anymore," Dreadlocks said, with another grunt of disapproval. "Adrian bound him to your sister as her protector before he sent the two of you out of the realm."

"What?" Jasmine gasped.

I stared at the Archon, too stunned to speak. Thoughts, accusations and questions bombarded my mind, and after a moment, he began to answer them.

"No, Zacchaeus did not lie to you. Archons cannot lie, as he told you. We also cannot enter the dark realms, as he told you, but we can see into them. You never asked him that."

"Sonofa—" I began furiously, only to have his warning look stop me. "You mean Zach knew my sister was alive this whole time and never *bothered* to tell me?"

Jasmine wiped her eyes. This was too much, too soon for her. The Archon merely shrugged. "Those weren't his orders."

Orders. A slew of curses ran through my mind. The Archon gave me another glare, but I snapped, "Oh, please! I didn't *say* any of them, so give me a break!"

"Mortals," he muttered. "So obsessed with technicalities."

"Jaz," I said, controlling my anger with great difficulty. "Can you see if Adrian's back, please?"

I didn't want him to stop transporting humans, but I wanted to get my sister out of here for a few minutes. She was running on shock and adrenaline, so at any moment, she could snap.

She disappeared into the house without arguing, another indicator that she wasn't herself. Moments later, Adrian came out onto the lawn, eyeing the two Archons with guarded optimism.

"I hope you came to help. We'll need several buses to get all these people out of here."

"We will not," Freckles replied. With those words, she and everyone else vanished, leaving me, Adrian and Dreadlocks alone on the lawn. From the sudden silence in the house, that had been cleared out, too.

"What. Just. Happened?" I managed. Even Adrian appeared startled.

The blond Archon wasn't. If anything, I'd say he looked bored. "These people needed to be taken to safety. Sarai has done that."

"But they're just *gone*," I stressed, as if I was the only one who'd noticed that.

A shrug. "Archons aren't limited by your laws of physics."

After everything I'd seen, why did that surprise me? "Is Jasmine still here?" I asked in sudden anxiousness.

"Yes. We will provide care for the others, but she is yours to look out for."

Good. I didn't want it any other way.

Adrian drew me next to him, his arm a welcome weight across my shoulders. Aside from those few, blissful minutes in the tunnel, we hadn't had a moment together since I found him alive. He'd been ferrying people through the gateway and I'd tried to do what I could for the traumatized survivors. I hadn't even had time to wash my hands. Calling dibs on the bathroom when so many of these people hadn't had a hot shower in years would've been selfish in the extreme, so I was still covered in ashes. So was Adrian. We looked like coal miners after a cave-in.

Zach came out onto the lawn. He exchanged a glance with the blond Archon that had Adrian tensing into stonelike stillness.

"Don't," he said low.

"It is too late," Zach replied, his voice equally soft. "The second trial has already begun."

"What trial?" I asked, stiffening, as well.

Zach's dark brown gaze rested on me. "Adrian no longer needs to transport the survivors. They are crossing through to this realm on their own."

I was incredulous. "How?"

"The gateways are opening," Zach said simply.

Adrian's arm dropped from my shoulders as he ran both hands through his hair. They were still covered in blood beneath the soot from all his injuries. Without Zach healing him the first time he'd crossed over to this side, I didn't think Adrian would even be conscious now. Zach's statement back-burnered my concern for Adrian, however.

"The gateways are opening," I repeated. "From your tone and Adrian's reaction, that's bad, but why? If trapped people can now get out of the realms without the aid of a demon, Judian or minion, isn't that a good thing?"

"The gateways are opening because the walls between our worlds have started to crumble," Zach said. "The gateways are affected first, since they connect the realms."

Now I understood, and horror filled me. "But if the walls crumble until nothing separates the demon realms from ours, it'll be hell on earth in no time at all."

"Exactly," the blond Archon stated in a mild tone.

His nonchalance made me want to slap him. "Well, someone's got to *do* something!"

A pained sound came out of Adrian right as Zach said, "That someone is you, Ivy."

"Me?" I sputtered. "What can I do? I lost the slingshot, not that it matters since I already used it—"

"It's not lost," the blond Archon interrupted. "It's been forever embedded in your flesh."

I gaped at him, then shoved my coat sleeve up. I couldn't see anything beneath the grime, so I ran to the hose people had been drinking from and splashed water onto my arm.

As the soot cleared away, I began to tremble. The outline of a brown, braided rope ran from the loop on my finger all the way up to my elbow, the length of the slingshot curling around my arm several times. It looked like an extremely detailed tattoo, only this wasn't ink. It was like a supernatural brand.

Large hands gripped my shoulders and I turned in Adrian's arms. He was shaking, I realized with shock, and when his cheek brushed against mine, it was wet.

"Whatever happens next," he whispered. "Remember I love you. I didn't lie about that, Ivy."

Whoa. I pushed him away, a foreboding chill sweeping through me at his stricken expression, not to mention his words.

"What don't I know?" I asked, starting to tremble.

"Your destiny, Davidian, was not merely to find the slingshot," the blond Archon stated. "You must acquire the remaining two hallowed weapons before the demons get them, or the world you know will cease to exist."

"Wait, *what* other weapons?" I blurted before memory seared me with pitiless clarity.

To take down demons, you need one of three weap-

ons, Adrian had said the day we met, *and the second and third ones will probably kill you.* Then when he'd taken me into the first realm, he'd said, *That's why I still hide things from you, Ivy. If you can't accept the way the board's set up, you're not nearly ready to learn the endgame yet....*

"You knew," I breathed, staring into his tormented jeweled gaze. "You knew *all along* that finding the slingshot was only the beginning, but you let me believe that if I did, this would all be over. You lied to me, Adrian!"

He flinched as if my words had struck him like a physical blow. Amidst my anger, disbelief and blistering hurt, I also felt a fresh wave of exhaustion. I'd thought if I got the slingshot and saved Jasmine, I'd be done with demons and their horrible realms. I didn't have it in me to take on one more fight against them, let alone two. Right now, I didn't even know if I had it in me to keep standing.

Zach came over to me, his brown eyes filled with a knowing sort of pity.

"Judas was guilty of three betrayals. The first was trust when he robbed the money set aside for the poor. The second was greed when he accepted thirty pieces of silver, and the third—"

"Was death," I finished, my heart breaking all over again. "You did betray me, Adrian, just like everyone said you would. You just haven't killed me yet."

"Ivy, I'm sorry," he said, catching my hands and holding on when I tried to yank away. "I didn't believe I could beat my fate before, but I do now. *You* made me believe, and—"

My laughter cut him off. It was dark, ugly and filled with all the anguish of love lost, found and lost again.

"How ironic. Now you believe, and I don't." He opened his mouth, and I let out a harsh scoff. It was that or I'd start to cry, and it was taking all the fading strength I had not to do that already. "Just leave. I can't listen to you right now. It hurts too much to even look at you."

He released my hands but gripped my shoulders, his sapphire gaze blazing into mine. "I'll leave, but not for long. I'll make you believe again, Ivy, if it's the last thing I do."

Then he was gone, using his blinding speed to disappear into the trees. I waited until I was sure he wasn't coming back before I finally allowed myself to sink to my knees, tears leaking past my clenched eyelids. Everyone had warned me, but not only had I trusted Adrian, I'd fallen in love with him. Worse, even after all this, I still loved him. Was that because I had the world's worst case of stupidity? Or was it another example of the curse of my fate?

"What's this second weapon and what's it supposed to do?" I asked, not really wanting to know but needing something to distract me from my urge to call out for Adrian.

Zach knelt until he was eye level with me. "The staff of Moses. It parted the Red Sea, sent ten plagues upon Egypt and caused water to pour from rocks in the desert. In short, it controls nature, so it can repair the walls between the realms."

My head dropped into my hands while a gasping laugh escaped me. "No wonder the thing's supposed to kill me if I use it."

"It might," Zach said steadily. "But the slingshot didn't, and it could have, too. You're strong, Ivy. Now you need to be stronger, so you can stave off the destruction of your world."

Another gasping laugh. "Oh, is that all?" We were all doomed. *Doomed.*

"If you succeed, you will save Adrian, too," the blond Archon said almost casually.

My head snapped up. "How? He's destined to betray me, remember?"

"And so he has," Zach said in a mild tone. "Yet now there is a chance that he won't do it again. Adrian's hatred of demons was the first thing that made him struggle against his fate, but hate was never going to be enough for him to overcome it. Only light can defeat darkness. Loving you is his light, Ivy. Without it, he was doomed to fail, but with it, his fate is truly in his own hands."

I stared at him, thunderstruck, as different details started falling into place.

If Zach hadn't abandoned him all those years ago, Adrian wouldn't have learned how to be the insanely strong fighter that he was. He also wouldn't have hated demons for their countless deceptions, giving him a reason to fight them in the first place. Then later, his hate ensured that he went with me when I was looking for the only weapon that could kill them. As I'd accused Adrian before, he wouldn't have gone with me otherwise, no matter how Zach tried to persuade him…

Hope began to spiral through my wildly swinging emotions. That's right, Zach had *wanted* Adrian to go with me, so maybe the Archon was using the supernatural tie between us to help Adrian, not to doom him. After all, if Adrian hadn't gone with me to search for the slingshot, we wouldn't have fallen in love. Yes, Adrian had horribly betrayed my trust, but I'd betrayed his, too, and he'd forgiven me. Could I really refuse to forgive him, if there might be a future for us after all?

I drew in a deep breath. I wasn't ready to throw myself back in his arms, but what if the Archons were right? What if love was the wild card that gave us a chance to beat the demons, save the walls between the realms from crumbling *and* save ourselves from our fates? It was a long shot, true, but I now had a three-thousand-year-old weapon tattooed into my arm, so anything was possible.

I rose, giving the two Archons a nervous yet determined look.

"All right, when do we start?"

* * * * *

Turn the page for a sneak peek at
THE SWEETEST BURN,
the breathtaking second novel in
New York Times *bestselling author*
Jeaniene Frost's BROKEN DESTINY *series,*
which finds Ivy and Adrian rekindling their
alliance—and passion—as the struggle for
the fate of the world begins...

"*ET TU,* BRUTE?" I muttered as I walked along the beach, pulling my cardigan a little tighter against the salt-scented breeze. It would be hot soon, as per usual in Miami, but at this predawn hour, the spring air was a little cool for the knee-length dress I'd thrown on to look for my missing pet.

"Brutus!" I called out, loudly this time. "Where are you?"

I'd been calling him for over fifteen minutes with no response, and I was getting worried. He had never been away from home this close to dawn before. I might not have wanted Brutus when he'd been dumped on me, and he definitely wasn't anyone's idea of a normal pet, but over the past couple months, I'd really come to care for him.

Every night for the past two months, he left the house at dusk and was back by 5:00 a.m. at the latest. Before me, Brutus had spent his entire life in darkness, so he didn't just hate sun; he was afraid of it. That was why, when he hadn't shown up by five thirty this morning, I'd gone looking for him. North Shore Open Space Park in Miami was one of his favorite places, and at this hour, the stretch of beach I walked along was deserted.

I scowled at the slowly lightening horizon, my worry increasing. "Brutus!" I yelled again. He'd better not be avoiding me because he'd broken the rules and eaten someone.

Even if he'd done nothing wrong, if I didn't find him soon, he'd probably break into someone's house to avoid the sunlight. If that happened, God help the homeowner if they noticed him and tried to shoo him outside. Talk about an incident that would make the evening news.

"Did you lose something?" an unfamiliar male voice asked from right behind me.

I stiffened. No one else had been on the beach moments ago. Even with the sounds of the surf, my recently upgraded senses should have picked up on someone running straight at me, and he would've had to run to cover that much distance in mere seconds.

There was another explanation for how the man behind me had so suddenly and soundlessly appeared, but if that was the case, then one of us wouldn't be leaving this beach alive.

I couldn't let on that I knew something might be wrong. I turned around and fixed a false smile on my face.

"You startled me!" I said, hoping I sounded more surprised than scared.

A lock of black hair fell over the stranger's face as he smiled back at me. "Sorry. I heard you yelling, so I came over to see if you needed any help."

He looked a few years older than me, putting him in his early- to mid-twenties. Though he was on the skinny side, he was also cute in a boyish sort of way. If I'd have met him when I was back at college last semester, I would've thought the shadows that appeared and disappeared beneath his skin were figments of my imagination. After all, I'd been diagnosed with hallucinations by more than a few doctors. Problem was, now I knew I wasn't crazy, although some days I wished I was.

Then I saw his eyes shine like an animal's that had caught the light, evidence of the supernatural equivalent of *tapetum lucidum*. My suspicions had been correct. The guy in front of me might look human to anyone who didn't have my abilities—which was over 99 percent of the world—but he wasn't. He was a demon minion.

"I do need a little help," I said, still smiling although my heart had started to race. "I'm looking for my, ah, dog."

"Sure," he said, casually taking my arm. "I think I saw a dog over this way."

Both of us were lying. Brutus was no dog, and there hadn't been one anywhere around here. Still, I let him lead me toward the brush that grew along the seawall. As I walked, I hitched my dress up on the side that he couldn't see. I'd learned a few things in the past several months since I'd discovered that minions and demons existed. The most important lesson? Never leave your house unarmed.

Even as I reached for the knife strapped to my thigh, I glanced at the sky. Brutus was over nine feet tall, as wide as two gorillas and had leathery wings that could double as swords, so now would be a *really* good time for him to show up.

He didn't, though, and I drew in a deep breath for courage. Okay, so I was alone on a dark, deserted beach with a minion who'd been endowed with superhuman strength from whatever demon he served. Not good, but hysterics wouldn't help. I knew that from experience.

"You seem nervous," the minion remarked.

He sounded amused by the prospect, and that was like a shot of adrenaline to my body. Minions and demons had ruined countless lives, not to mention killed my parents, kidnapped my sister and almost killed me more times than I could count. This jerk thought that I was just another human slave to bring back to his demon master's realm. Well, I had a surprise for him.

I whirled, balancing my weight on my right leg while kicking out with my left. At the same time, I pulled the knife out, smashing it into his face with more force than any human should be able to muster. That, combined with the minion's downward momentum from suddenly getting his feet kicked out from under him, caused him to drop like a stone. My roommate, Costa, had been training me in hand-to-hand combat, and it had paid off. For the barest second, the minion's shocked gaze met mine, and I felt a savage thrill at the disbelief in his gaze.

Who's afraid now? I thought fiercely.

I shouldn't have taken that brief moment to celebrate. Even with a knife sticking out of his face, he was still deadly. His hands closed over my ankles, yanking hard. I lost my balance and fell backward, twisting away to avoid his immediate tackle. He landed on sand instead of me, but then his fists smashed into my lower body. I doubled over, feeling like I'd been hit by a truck. He held on and started to crawl up my body, his grin visible through the streams of blood coming from where the knife stuck out of his face.

I couldn't break his grip, so I didn't try. When he made it up to my thigh, my knee smashed into his face with all the extrahuman strength I had in me. Pain reverberated up my leg, but this time I didn't spare a single second before attacking again. I grabbed his head and yanked it to the side as hard as I could. A *crack* sounded and the minion's whole body went limp.

I managed to roll away, my knees and ribs throbbing so much that vomiting felt like a good way to celebrate. Still, I was exultant. Looked like those fighting lessons had really paid off! In fact, Costa had trained me so well, my actions had felt more like muscle memory instead of a conscious decision to kill someone. I *had* killed the minion, though, and he wasn't the first one, although he was the first one that I'd taken on by myself with only a normal weapon.

Being a killer hadn't been anywhere on my list of life goals six months ago, when I'd been a junior at WMU. Since then, I'd had to learn how to do that, as well as a lot of other strange, unpleasant things. *Thank you, unexpected supernatural lineage. You are the gift that keeps on giving.*

With a suddenness that still startled me, the minion's body dissolved until nothing but ashes remained. They began to blow away in the same ocean breeze that whipped my hair around like dozens of dark brown scarves. The way minions and demons turned to ash after death was the only considerate thing they did.

Even though everything hurt, I heaved myself up from the sand. Bruised and battered or not, I still had to find Brutus.

I was in the process of brushing the sand off me when my surroundings changed in an instant. The sand turned to sheets of ice, the light became pitch darkness and the sounds from the surf ceased with such abruptness that the new silence was ominous. The worst part was the cold. My teeth began to chatter, and the frigid air felt like it scattered razors across my skin.

Just as quickly, the dark, frozen world disappeared, leaving me back on the beach with a warm, salt-scented breeze and mauve-colored shades of dawn starting to paint the horizon. Still, I felt stiff from more than the cold that seemed to linger on the air. That hazy, alternate version of this area wasn't a full-on sensory hallucination, although all of my former doctors would've sworn otherwise. Instead, it was a glimpse of a realm that hovered right over this one.

Physicists call it M theory—the idea that different dimensional layers existed next to each other. I called it a shitload of trouble, because that sunless, icy world was a demon realm. My lineage gave me the ability to catch glimpses of these deadly realms, but for some reason, I hadn't spotted this one before. If I'd known that a demon realm existed right on top of this place, I would've never walked this beach at all, let alone by myself before the sun was fully up.

Before I could turn around to leave, a large slash suddenly appeared in the air and three people stepped out of it. At once, the supernatural tattoo on my right arm began to burn. I gripped it without looking away, and the part of my brain that wasn't freaking out figured out what was going on.

The minion I'd killed hadn't sneaked up on me using his supernatural stealth and speed. He'd simply crossed from a demon realm into this one through a gateway that I hadn't known was there.

I didn't have time to wonder if the realm was new, or if it had always been there and was now accessible to this world through an ominous crack. The three new minions seemed startled to see me, but then their gazes roved from the blood on my dress and cardigan to the very incriminating pile of minion ashes near my feet. When the palest one stretched out hands that turned into living, writhing snakes, it was all I could do not to scream.

Not three minions. Two minions and an unkillable, shape-shifting *demon*.

Standing and fighting would be suicide, so I snatched my knife from the pile of minion ashes and began to run. The demon barked out an order in a language I recognized all too well, and then the minions gave chase. They were *fast*. If I had been a normal human, they would have had me in five seconds flat, but I wasn't normal, and right now I was glad about that.

I was also glad I had a mental map of the closest hallowed ground near the North Shore Park. In fact, I'd memorized every plot of hallowed ground near my house just in case something like this happened. St. Joseph's Catholic Church was about seven streets away. If I made it, the demon couldn't touch me because demons couldn't cross hallowed ground. Minions could, but I'd already killed one today. Why not go for more?

Since sand was harder to run on, I headed toward the sidewalk along the park, needing the flat ground to increase my speed. Behind me, I could hear the minions cursing. They hadn't expected me to make them work for this. That gave me grim satisfaction as I darted around benches and tables in the deserted picnic area. My knees and ribs still throbbed from my earlier fight, but nothing was as great a painkiller as survival instinct. As I ran, I counted down the wooden street markers in the park for encouragement. Eighty-Third Street. Eighty-Fourth. The church was just after Eighty-Seventh Street. I was going to make it.

Then, even though he was much farther away, I heard the demon yell, "She's the Davidian!" in a rage-filled roar, and I knew all bets were off. My speed might have been preventing the minions from capturing me, but it also outed me as number one on the demon's most-wanted list.

The demon was no longer content to send his minions ahead of him like a bunch of hunting dogs. Several quick glances over my shoulder showed him now tearing after me himself, and he made the minions look as if they'd been moving in slow motion. Benches, tables and other large objects were hurled my way; he didn't just chase me, but actively tried to kill me.

I ducked and weaved around as many as I could, but some still found their mark. I cursed when something heavy smacked me in the back, and while it made me stumble, I forced myself not to fall. Instead, I put all of my energy into running, staying within the limits of the park despite its greater dangers of projectiles. Taking the main road, A1A, would give me a straight shot to the church, but even at this hour, cars were on it. I couldn't risk someone else getting hurt, and demons loved nothing more than collateral damage.

I'd just rounded a corner that brought me briefly back onto the beach when something slammed into my legs, knocking me over. I rolled, making sure not to stab myself in the process, and was back up when a loud, trumpeting snarl sounded overhead.

Brutus, my pet gargoyle, flew toward me, the dawn's rays highlighting his large, beastly form in different shades of pink. I would've been relieved to see him, but I was too shocked by the man gripped in Brutus's talons.

The minions and demon saw them, too, and at their confused expressions, I remembered that they didn't see a large man being suspended by the claws of a hulking, grayish-blue gargoyle. Due to Archon glamour, all they saw was an angrily squawking seagull somehow carrying his muscular male passenger, and from the way they cocked their heads, they didn't know what to make of the sight.

"Ivy, duck!" the man yelled.

I hit the sand even as I reeled with shock. Only one person in the world could treat the deadly gargoyle like a winged pony, and that was the same person who'd broken my heart months ago, and then disappeared.

Adrian.

The saga continues in back-to-back releases from Jeaniene Frost and HQN Books! Don't miss a single book in the BROKEN DESTINY series:
THE SWEETEST BURN, available July 2017
THE BRIGHTEST EMBERS, available August 2017

ACKNOWLEDGMENTS

BEFORE ANYONE ELSE, I have to thank God for continuing to give me the ability and the opportunity to live out my dreams. Ten years ago, I first started trying to get published. Twelve novels, five novellas and two short stories later, part of me still can't believe that my dream has become my reality.

Sincerest thanks also go to my husband, Matthew, whose love and support is the stuff romance novels are made of. Further gratitude goes to my agent, Nancy Yost, who's been riding this roller coaster with me almost from the beginning. This book also wouldn't be possible without the wonderful people at Harlequin, who've championed *The Beautiful Ashes* as though they wrote it themselves. There are too many of you to list, so in the interest of space, I'm only highlighting Shara Alexander from Publicity and Reka Rubin from Subrights. "Thanks" doesn't even begin to cover everything you and the rest of the Harlequin HQN team have done.

Finally, a huge thank-you to readers, book sellers, librarians, reviewers and bloggers. Without your enthusiasm for reading and spreading the word about books, authors like me would have no one to share our stories with, and that would be very sad indeed.

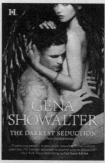

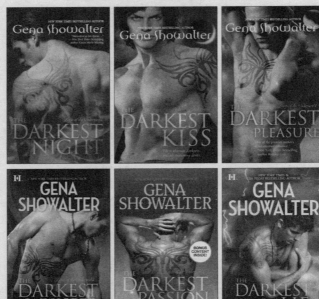

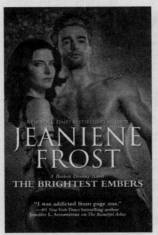

Get 2 Free Books,
<u>Plus</u> 2 Free Gifts –

just for
trying the
**Reader
Service!**

STRS17

Turn your love of reading into
rewards you'll love with

Harlequin My Rewards

Join for FREE today at
www.HarlequinMyRewards.com

Earn **FREE BOOKS** of your choice.

Experience **EXCLUSIVE OFFERS** and contests.

Enjoy **BOOK RECOMMENDATIONS**
selected just for you.

PLUS! Sign up now
and get **500** points
right away!

Earn
FREE
REWARDS
HarlequinMyRewards.com
Join
Today!

MYR16R